It took some small but measurable time before the fact sank home: they weren't where they were supposed to be. Janille started to reach for a weapon that wasn't there, then fell into unarmed fighting stance. Corin snatched out his link and rapped, "This is Commodore Marshak! Come in, anyone . . ." Then, as no enemy appeared and the link proved inoperative, the trio lapsed into silent staring at their surroundings.

They were in an enclosed space that seemed too large to be enclosed, although there was nothing familiar to give a sense of scale. A smooth stone floor stretched away in all directions, until it met the curving, rough-textured rock wall that curved upward to form a dome. They could not discern what lay beyond.

Janille, combat-trained, did not panic. "Where are we?" she asked in a small but steady voice.

"I don't know. My link is dead. We're still on Neustria—at least the gravity feels the same."

"Or *in* it." She looked around again.

"You're probably right—although if this is a cavern it's a damned big one. The question is, how did we get *out* of here?"

"Actually, the 'malfunction' to which you refer was an accident for which I am responsible."

Almost instantly, they realized that the accentless, asexual voice wasn't really a voice at all, for they hadn't *heard* it. Then the dim movements in the shadows beyond the archway resolved themselves into the figure that now emerged into the cavern, its not-really-crocodilian head reaching not much more than three times Corin's height, its sinuous body with coppery-gold scales, its folded wings which at full extension would have spanned the full width of the chamber. . . .

BAEN BOOKS by STEVE WHITE

Also in this series:
Prince of Sunset

The Disinherited
Legacy
Debt of Ages

with David Weber:
Insurrection
Crusade
In Death Ground

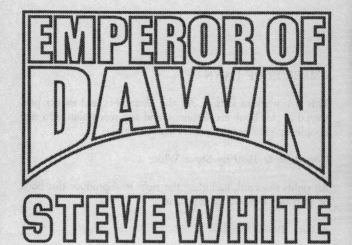

EMPEROR OF DAWN

STEVE WHITE

This is a work of fiction. All the characters and events portrayed in this book are fictional, and any resemblance to real people or incidents is purely coincidental.

Copyright © 1998 by Steve White

All rights reserved, including the right to reproduce this book or portions thereof in any form.

A Baen Books Original

Baen Publishing Enterprises
P.O. Box 1403
Riverdale, NY 10471

ISBN: 0-671-57797-4

Cover art by Larry Elmore

First printing, May 1998

Distributed by Simon & Schuster
1230 Avenue of the Americas
New York, NY 10020

Printed in the United States of America

EMPEROR OF DAWN

This is a work of fiction. All the characters and events portrayed in this book are fictional, and any resemblance to real people or incidents is purely coincidental.

A Baen Books Original

Baen Publishing Enterprises
P.O. Box 1403
Riverdale, NY 10471

ISBN: 0-671-57797-2

Cover art by Larry Elmore

First printing, May 1999

Distributed by Simon & Schuster
1230 Avenue of the Americas
New York, NY 10020

Printed in the United States of America

To Sandy, as always.
And to Tu Kuang-t'ing, who had it coming.

TIMELINE OF THE EMPIRE
(In standard years of the Common Era of Old Earth)

1939-1945	World War II, culminating with the formation of the United Nations and the first use of nuclear weapons. Beginning of two centuries of rapid technological advancement accompanied by social disintegration.
2152-2185	The General War (actually a series of interrelated conflicts).
2187	U.N. restructured into a global federation committed to halting technological and social change in the name of stability.
2190	First STL interstellar colony ship launched, beginning a century of out-migration.
2588	Sigma Draconis colony establishes a new libertarian constitution, in defiance of the U.N.
2607	Sigma Draconis launches first experimental FTL vehicle, via time-distortion drive. The resultant closer contact with the U.N. leads to deteriorating relations, culminating in war.
2683	Sigma Draconis dissolves the U.N. and founds the Solarian Federation, with its ceremonial capital at Earth but its working capital (especially for military purposes) at Prometheus, Sigma Draconis II. Subsequently, elements opposed to the Federation use time distortion drive to leave it; this is the origin of the "Beyonders," including the Sword Clans.

2939	Attempted coup, utilizing Beyonder mercenaries, subjects Prometheus to nuclear bombardment. The following year, the Federation relocates to Earth for all purposes, turning Sigma Draconis over to a governor-general charged with preventing further incursions. Over the next fifty years, the Federation declines into a respected but powerless institution, with military and political power in the hands of multisystem extrasolar states fighting limited but endemic wars.
3032	Republic of Zeta Tocanae becomes the first of the "Protectors of the Federation."
3257	Breakup of the last Protector-state (the Greater Eridanus Combine), leaving a power vacuum.
3306	Federation ratifies the partition of the Greater Eridanus Combine. Tachyon beam array invented. The Unification Wars begin.
3360-3372	Totalitarian reorganization of the Government-General of Sigma Draconis.
3454	Draconis forces occupy Earth, officially dissolve Federation five years later.
3489	Unification Wars end with the establishment of the Draconis Empire.
3504	Fall of the Draconis Empire, followed by four years of civil war.
3508	Solarian Empire founded.
3718	Usurpation by Delmore Rajasthara, an Imperial minister who rules for fifteen years.
3733	Restoration of the legitimate dynasty by a member of a collateral branch. (The direct line is believed to have been exterminated.)
3894	Open rebellion by the "New Human" collectivist movement.
3906	Admiral Yoshi Medina becomes the Empire's *de facto* dictator.
3909	New Humans finally crushed by Medina and his protégé Basil Castellan.

3910	Castellan breaks with Medina, seeking to restore the dynasty, of whose direct line he is the last survivor.
3930	Death of Medina. His son officially assumes the Imperial title; Castellan and Admiral Lavrenti Kang each do the same, ending even the legal fiction of Imperial unity.
3931	Castellan defeated and believed killed in the course of a campaign against Kang.
3975	Medina dynasty deposed by the Marvell family, which reconquers the Empire over the next fifteen years. With the death of Basil Castellan's son, the old dynasty is thought to become extinct.
4014	Zyungen break into the Empire, which is exhausted by eighty years of civil war.
4021	Sol falls to the Zyungen. Five years later, Sigma Draconis also falls, and the Solarian Empire (still calling itself that) relocates to the Bootes/Serpens region and holds out there, leaving the old Imperial core area to squalid, ephemeral regimes ruled by the Zyungen or by the Beyonder groups that followed them into the power vacuum.
4096	Return of the Sword Clans. Proclaiming themselves the saviors of Earth and the human race, they begin wiping out the Zyungen and Beyonder fiefdoms and announce the Empire of Man.
4149	Empire of Man secures the last of the former Imperial holdings outside the Bootes/Serpens region (but fails to conquer the rump Solarian Empire there).
4244-4287	Succession struggles in the Empire of Man.
4291	Armand Duschane seizes power in the momentarily reunified Empire of Man.
4299	Duschane conquers the rump Solarian Empire, proclaims the Solarian Empire of Man.

CHAPTER ONE
Santaclara (Iota Pegasi A IV), 4325 C.E.

The primary sun was breaking over the rim of the world below, flooding the observation bubble with light that banished the distant red-dwarf companion star. Corin Marshak stood silhouetted against that blaze as the steward cleared his throat.

"We've established orbit, sir. We can begin transposing passengers down shortly, and you have top priority."

"Thank you." Slowly, as though reluctant to take leave of the view, Corin turned around to face the steward. He stepped forward with the limp that had grown less pronounced in the course of the voyage. Away from the star-glare beyond the transparent armorplast, details emerged: a tall, slender, youngish man, dark of hair and complexion, prominent of nose. He wore his maroon civilian jumpsuit like a uniform.

"Thank you," he repeated a little less abstractedly. "I'll be ready shortly. Tell them not to delay anyone else's departure on my account."

"Very good, sir." The steward gave a small bow and departed. Corin looked around. People were drifting away, leaving only a few in the observation bubble. He turned back to the spectacle outside. They were approaching the terminator, and Santaclara's day side

1

stood revealed. A hot young F5v star such as this had no business possessing a blue cloud-swirling life-bearing planet. . . .

"Think we'll see a Luon?"

He started at the voice and turned to look at its owner. He'd noticed the auburn-haired woman before, but had never been presented with an opportunity for self-introduction that met his rather exacting standards in such things. Now she herself had finally made the move, and was giving him a gaze of frank appraisal with clear blue eyes that suited a complexion fair enough to be potentially inconvenient under this sun. And, to his annoyance, he found himself struck most by the way she'd paralleled his own thoughts, which had been leading him by a natural chain of association to the ancient terraformers, now dying out, who had bequeathed worlds like Santaclara to their human successors.

"Probably not," he replied. "I've heard that some people here claim to have seen one, still alive in the mountains. But stories like that are usually just imagination and alcohol. Nobody sees the Luonli unless they want to be seen."

"You mean . . . the stories about them being mind-controllers?" Like a cloud shadow on a windy day, an uneasy frown crossed her face. Those features were too strongly marked for conventional prettiness, and too expressive to mask her feelings. Once seen, they lingered in the memory.

"That's probably a little strong. As I understand it, *influencing* the mind is about the extent of their tele-pathic capacity. And they've never shown any inclination to use it except to preserve their privacy as they quietly dwindle toward extinction." Corin decided he was waxing altogether too serious, and that self-introduction was in order. "By the way, I'm Commander Corin Marshak. I had to use civilian transportation for the last leg of my trip to this system because—"

"—the Fleet is swamped at this end of the Empire as a result of the preparations for the Emperor's visit to the Cassiopeia frontier," she finished for him. "Yes, I know. I'm Major Janille Dornay . . . sir."

Corin extended his hand. The Marine major returned his handshake with a grip whose strength didn't surprise him. It went with her lithe leanness. Still, civilian clothes looked better on her than on him. . . .

"So, Major, you must be in the same position I am."

"Yes . . . except that I haven't come nearly as far." She hesitated, unable to think of a graceful way to refer to his limp. "I've heard talk that you saw action against the Ch'axanthu—that you're only just back from there." She paused, inviting reminiscences.

"Yes." He realized the monosyllable had come out more curtly than he'd intended, and sought to perform conversational salvage. "Actually, I wasn't thinking of the Luonli just now," he lied, indicating the planetary panorama unfolding below. "I was thinking of all the history this world holds."

"History?" Her brow crinkled with puzzlement, then cleared. "Oh, yes. I remember now. Many centuries ago, the Iota Pegasi system was part of the New Human rebels' state, whatever it was called."

"The 'People's Democratic Union,'" Corin supplied. "And it was four and a half standard centuries ago, to be exact. But I was thinking of what happened after that. This was where Basil Castellan declared himself Emperor."

Her eyes widened. "You mean . . . *the* Basil Castellan? And his friends Sonja Rady and Torval Bogdan?" Her eyes strayed to the planetscape of Santaclara. "Right here?"

He could understand her incredulous astonishment. The New Human rebellion against the old Solarian Empire was a matter of dry history, but the trio she had named belonged to the realm of legend, beyond any tedious fixity of time and place. He might as well have told her that Old King Cole had held court on the planet beneath them, or that the Argonauts had sailed its seas.

"Right here," he affirmed. "They really did live, you know—even though they've been so mythologized by now that it's hard to separate the facts from the fables. After he broke with Yoshi Medina, Castellan established himself in former rebel space, where the people saw him as the hero who'd freed them from the New Humans. He only reigned a little while, before he was defeated by treachery."

"Is it true," Janille asked, eyes still on the planet that had suddenly taken on a whole new aspect for her, "that he and Rady disappeared afterwards? That their bodies were never found?"

"That's right. On the backwater worlds of these sectors, they still say that he never died, that he's in cryogenic suspension somewhere, and will return when the people need him."

She laughed nervously. "Cryo suspension for four hundred years? I don't think so. Besides, it's for damned sure he didn't come back to save the Empire from the Zyungen, or from the rabble of Beyonders who followed them." She couldn't quite sustain her scornful tone to the end of her last sentence. "I wonder," she resumed after a moment, as much to herself as to him, "what it was like to live in those days?"

"You mean Castellan's lifetime and the generation or so after it? The age of romantic high adventure?" Corin gave a short sound that held too little humor to be called a laugh. " 'Adventure' has been defined as somebody *else* having a horrible time hundreds of years ago or dozens of light-years away. It was an age of nonstop civil war and murderous intrigue—just the kind of age that makes for great historical fiction." He gazed moodily through the transparent armorplast. "The real question is, what would Castellan think of *our* age?"

Somehow, he could feel her stiffen from across the few feet that separated them. "What do you mean? There's only one way he could see it. Why, within our lifetimes, the Empire has finally been reunified. The dream he gave his life for has come true!"

An idealist, Corin thought sadly. *Like me, you grew up on the news stories of Armand Duschane's reconquest . . . no, more like 'triumphal march' after he'd established the only real power base in Imperial space. And, like me, you went into the military to join the grand and glorious parade of the Renewed Empire.*

And, unlike me, you haven't just returned from the Ch'axanthu war. . . .

His mind flashed back to his Academy days, and the words of wisdom Tristan LoBhutto, the class lady-killer, had condescendingly dispensed to his envious fellow cadets. "The object of a conversation with a woman is neither to enlighten nor to persuade. Nor is it to score debating points. It is to get laid." Of course, Corin had outgrown that sort of thing by now. Of course. Or perhaps he had simply reached the end of his ability to hold his bitterness inside.

"Yes, the Empire has been reunified. But it isn't the first time that's been done since Castellan's death. Medina's old military henchmen of the Marvell family did it when they kicked out his grandson and founded their own dynasty."

"But that dynasty's reunification was just a false start. It only lasted . . . how many years?"

"Less than forty. But it remains to be seen whether we'll do as well."

Her eyes flashed blue fire, but then they strayed involuntarily in the direction of Corin's left leg. And when she spoke she sounded almost contrite, remembering where he'd been. "Yes, I know—not as well as you, of course—that the Ch'axanthu have handed us a setback—"

"The third in as many standard years," Corin interrupted drily.

"—but they show no inclination or ability to follow up on it," she finished doggedly. "They can't bring us down like the Zyungen did the Marvell dynasty."

"You're right about that. I don't think aliens like the Ch'axanthu or Beyonders like the Tarakans are going to do us in. Actually, we're doing such a good job of it ourselves that it would be superfluous."

This time her stiffening was visible. Her blue eyes met his brown-black ones and silently asked the question she couldn't put to a superior officer: *If you feel that way, then—*

"What am I doing in the Fleet?" he finished aloud for her. "Maybe I'm an idealist too, Major. Or, more likely, maybe I prefer anything to passivity—even futility."

"But . . . Look, I know there's a lot of unrest and resentment around, but—"

"I doubt if you know just how much." Corin thought of the Ursa Major frontier region from which he'd come, and which—as was always the case with the worlds nearest the seat of an interstellar war—had borne a disproportionate share of the burden. His convalescence had kept him out of the "police actions" as minor rebellions had flickered through those sectors. But some of the things he'd heard . . . "Or how justified they are."

A moment's silence passed as she visibly clamped control down on her features. "Excuse me, sir, but I need to prepare for departure." She turned on her heel and marched from the observation bubble.

Corin turned back to the transparency, but this time he was looking at his own reflection in the armorplast. *Ass*, he thought dispassionately in its direction. Then he departed from the now-deserted dome.

❖   ❖   ❖

"Well, Commander, your record speaks for itself." Vice Admiral Julius Tanzler-Yataghan looked up from the hardcopy and gazed across his desk at the newly arrived officer. "Yes, very impressive indeed. And you've certainly come quite a distance."

"I have that, sir," Corin replied. The Ursa Major frontier was on the far side of the Empire. It had been a journey of almost two months. "At least it gave me time to adjust to my new leg."

"Ah, yes. I would hardly have realized it was regrown if your record didn't describe the circumstances under which you lost it." The admiral indicated the citation which contained the description. Fleet uniform regulations prescribed that decorations be worn only with full dress. Corin was wearing the gray tunic and trousers of planetside service dress. So his chest was bare of the medal the citation had accompanied. "It must have been an appalling experience, Commander. You're certainly due for reassignment to a quiet sector like this one. Of course," he added with a little too much emphasis, "we here also do our part. We're not far from the Cassiopeia and Perseus regions, where the threat of a Tarakan incursion can never be ignored. Indeed, you might say we were standing guard against different aspects of the same threat. As His Imperial Majesty has explained, it is necessary to prevent the Ch'axanthu from joining forces with the Tarakans and presenting us with a . . . yes, a second front."

"Yes, sir." There wasn't much else Corin could say, for the admiral was reciting the official line. But his mind leaped across a light-century and contemplated the beings he'd fought: compact bipeds little more than half human-average height, with huge dark eyes. In addition to high intelligence, they had astonishingly dexterous hands with two mutually-opposable "thumbs" almost as long as the five "fingers," and it was unsurprising that they were master technologists.

They had colonized several systems before humankind had left its homeworld. But those colonists had traveled at the slower-than-light rates permitted by ordinary physical laws, for by some fluke the Ch'axanthu had never discovered the time-distortion drive on their own. And, having acquired it from some Beyonders or other, they'd shown no interest in using it to expand their sphere much beyond its long-established limits. They'd merely consolidated their already-colonized systems—systems of which they'd made far more intensive use than humans would have.

And that was why three invasions by the incomparably larger Empire had failed so dismally.

Long before the first interstellar probe had departed from Earth, it had been recognized that Homo sapiens' muscles, bones and immune system would not allow indefinite relinquishment of weight. Until the advent of artificially generated gravity fields, long-range space voyaging had required dodges like spinning a portion of the ship to produce angular acceleration. But not even that had permitted realization of the old dreams of colonizing asteroids and deep-space habitats . . . for the colonists had lost interest in reproducing.

Humans, it seemed, had a psychological need for Earth or a planet like it—a need unsuspected by the early space-colonization enthusiasts. At a minimum, they needed such a planet floating huge and blue in their sky. They mined and garrisoned flying mountains, and had for millennia, but they never called them home.

The Ch'axanthu were different. They'd evolved on a planet more or less similar to Earth, but their bodies and minds could adapt to microgravity environments. And by now the great majority of them lived in a myriad such environments, spread throughout the systems they had made their own.

And that, Corin reflected (not for the first time), was the problem: their lack of vulnerability.

Humanity had learned what vulnerability was in the early fourth millennium, as the gentlemanly limited warfare of the Age of the Protectors had given way to the Unification Wars. When total, high-intensity war was waged with interstellar-level technology, the populations of Earthlike planets survived only by grace of their economic value to potential conquerors. And the few Ch'axanthu-inhabited planets were no more survivable in the face of antimatter warheads—and the far cheaper relativistic rocks—than human ones.

But the Ch'axanthu could afford the loss of those sitting-duck worlds. The habitats where most of them lived were too numerous, too scattered and too mobile for convenient destruction. And they could wage a kind of spaceborne guerrilla war that had never been possible for humans. It had taken three disastrous campaigns for the Empire to learn the lesson—still publicly unacknowledged—that the Ch'axanthu were, as a practical matter, unconquerable.

Equally belated, and equally unadmitted, was the realization that they'd never posed a threat in the first place. . . .

Taking refuge from the thought, Corin let his eyes stray to the virtual window behind the admiral's desk. This office was deep within the sector headquarters. Tanzler-Yataghan preferred a more picturesque view than a simple transparency would have afforded, and the holo image showed the suburbs of the city outside the base, as though seen from a tall building. It was spring in Santaclara's northern hemisphere, as— by sheerest coincidence—it also was on Old Earth, whose standard year was the ordinary measure of time, however ill-fitting it might be in terms of local seasons. Hills, cloaked in subtropical vegetation whose species had originated on Earth or the unknown Luonli homeworld, stretched away toward distant smoky-blue mountains. Among that bright-flowering greenery nestled villas in this world's traditional style, with red-tiled roofs and fountained courtyards. The classical Old Earth cultures the early interstellar colonizers had sought to preserve had been diluted beyond those colonizers' recognition by centuries of population movements—both the spectacular forced variety and the ongoing process of individuals "voting with their feet"—but they had left a legacy of distinctive planetary and regional styles. The element of Old Earth's heritage that the histories characterized as "Hispanic" hadn't totally failed to leave its imprint on Iota Pegasi and the other sectors of the old "People's Democratic Union." There had been so many such cultural forms and textures on the planet of humankind's birth. Too bad, what the Zyungen had done to it . . .

Corin dismissed the always-depressing thought and turned his attention back to his new commanding officer. His name advertised his descent from the Sword Clans—partial descent at any rate, for there were few unmixed ones left by now, almost two and a half centuries after their return from their doomed world. That ancestry doubtless hadn't hurt his Fleet career. But he certainly didn't fit the lean, hard-faced stereotype of the military aristocracy the Sword Clans had bred by intermarriage with the old Imperial elite. His expensively tailored uniform couldn't conceal his pudginess, and self-indulgence had left its marks on his face. Corin had heard rumors about the ways he'd augmented his personal fortune during his tenure as Sector Admiral of Iota Pegasi.

"Yes," the admiral was continuing, "this sector may seem out-of-the-way. But don't be deceived." He manipulated controls, and a multicolored display floated in midair between two holo plates set into the floor and the ceiling. Corin instantly recognized the very rough spheroid as a representation of the Empire, its sectors in bright translucent colors. As per convention, it was oriented in terms of Old Earth's ecliptic plane, just as regions were still described by the names of the mythological persons and beasts that some ancient Greek—doubtless after ingesting too much *retsina*—had thought to see among the stars.

Tanzler-Yataghan touched more controls, and two vaguely outlined expanses of sinister slate-gray appeared outside the bounds of the gaudy spheroid, like obscene growths. The smaller and less vague of them clung to the outer edge of the turquoise Xi Ursae Majoris Sector, beyond the bright beacon of Denebola, on the right of the display as viewed from where Corin sat and about a fourth of the way "north" from its equator. The larger and less sharply delineated one seemed to slouch against the crimson and yellow expanses of the Beta Cassiopeiae and Theta Persei Sectors, about forty percent of the way around the spheroid and considerably higher. Still further around to the left, but at the same "latitude" as the smaller gray blotch from which it was diametrically opposite, a blinking light indicated the position of Iota Pegasi, in the azure of the sector that bore its name.

"As you can see," the admiral intoned, pointing to a purple shape that lay between the azure and the crimson, "only the 85 Pegasi Sector separates us from the sectors directly threatened by the Tarakans." He glowered at the ill-defined gray smudge polluting his side of the display. "Naturally, that represents only the Inner Domain. We don't know enough about the Outer Domain's extent to accurately depict it. Anyway, it's the Inner Domain that's the immediate threat."

Corin wondered what the Tarakans themselves called the two Domains, each ruled by its own Araharl, into which they'd schismed shortly after the great Zhangula had unified them and made them masters of an unprecedentedly large expanse of extra-Imperial space. Almost certainly not the Empire-centered terms "Inner" and "Outer." But, he reflected, that had always been the problem. To its inhabitants, the Empire was by definition the sole source of civilization and political legitimacy in the human universe, the lawful trustee of Old Earth's legacy. The humans who occupied an unknown percentage of the galaxy outside its frontiers were simply "Beyonders"—dwellers in outer darkness, sometimes dangerous, sometimes to be employed as mercenaries, but never to be taken seriously. Curiously enough, this attitude had survived the Empire's reunification by descendants of the Sword Clans—technically Beyonders themselves—because by then those descendants had become more Imperial than the Imperials. For the *really* curious thing was that the Beyonders themselves mostly accepted the Empire's self-estimate, and sought to buy into the assumption of superiority it entailed.

But the attitude also carried a penalty: chronically wretched intelligence concerning the Beyonders. In normal times, this could be lived with. The innumerable Beyonder states, few of which comprised more than a single planetary system, seldom posed more than a localized threat. And whenever a larger political unity arose among them, it could be overawed by Imperial prestige, bought off by Imperial money and, eventually, broken up by Imperial diplomacy.

Only . . . the first, at least, didn't work with the Tarakans. Zhangula must have been more than a mere military genius. He'd been that far rarer thing, a lawgiver—the creator of a nation. No one knew from what scraps of human history or legend he had rummaged up his ideology. (Or was it a religion? And did the distinction mean anything?) The point was that the Tarakans, in their own minds, ruled their clutch of subject peoples by a right which was *not* conferred by the Solarian Emperor.

Shrewd old Armand Duschane had recognized that his reunified Empire faced something new under the suns. He'd made it his business to play the two

Domains against each other. His instinct hadn't always been infallible; on at least one memorable occasion he'd outsmarted himself in a fashion that had necessitated an embarrassingly abrupt change of sides. But, like so many of Armand's initiatives, it had worked out well enough to leave his successor in an advantageous position.

Too bad that, in this as in so much else, Oleg Duschane had been congenitally unable to leave well enough alone. . . .

"No doubt the Emperor will set the Cassiopeia/Perseus frontier to rights when he arrives there," Corin said aloud.

"Of course. The expedition he's leading there has been in preparation for months." *Preparations the Empire could ill afford after last year's expensive failure against the Ch'axanthu,* Corin reflected. But Tanzler-Yataghan was hitting his sycophantic stride. "Still, no amount of tonnage and firepower can be as impressive as the Imperial presence itself—the fact that His Imperial Majesty himself is condescending to take personal command! It will be like his previous visit to those sectors, before . . . ahem!" The admiral hastily faked a cough to cover his narrow avoidance of a faux pas. Six or seven years before, Oleg had conducted a kind of Imperial progress through Cassiopeia and Perseus, a showing of the flag to a neighbor rendered complaisant if not precisely friendly by his father's patient maneuverings. Now he was coming to shore up a threatened frontier. But one couldn't very well verbalize that fact without opening the door to unsayable conclusions concerning the reasons for the change.

"Well, Commander," the admiral hastily changed the subject, "that's enough talk for now. I'm sure you're tired—always fatiguing to adjust to a new planet, isn't it? Take the rest of the day to settle into your quarters. Tomorrow will be soon enough to report to Captain Yuan, my chief of staff."

"Thank you, sir." Corin rose from his chair, came to attention, and turned on his heel to leave. He was halfway to the door when the admiral stopped him with a throat-clearing noise.

"Ah, Commander Marshak, I believe you weren't the only officer who arrived here aboard *Canopus Argosy*. A Marine officer was also en route here."

"Why, yes, Admiral. A Major Dornay."

"Indeed. She's already reported to Brigadier General Toda. But, as per routine procedure, I've seen her records. Including her picture." The tip of the admiral's tongue briefly appeared to lick his lips. "Since you and she were fellow passengers, I couldn't help wondering if you had . . . well, if you can give me any insights concerning her."

Corin knew precisely what sort of insights Tanzler-Yataghan had in mind. He kept his voice bland. "Sorry, sir. I only met her at the very end of the voyage. So it was a very brief and superficial acquaintance. My chief impression is that she's very strong-willed."

It was hard to tell from the admiral's expression if he'd taken the hint, or if he was merely disappointed that he wouldn't be getting any specific pointers as to technique. "Ah, well. I suppose it can't be helped. Dismissed, Commander."

"Sir." Corin departed. Outside, under the dazzling light of Iota Pegasi A, he took a deep breath of fresh air.

CHAPTER TWO
The Beta Cassiopeiae Sector, 4325 C.E.

DM +63 137—a dim K7v orange star—wasn't much like Iota Pegasi. And the rust-red planet it was peeking over wasn't at all similar to Santaclara. But Roderick Brady-Schiavona was gazing through the transparency at it in a way that made him resemble Corin Marshak to a remarkable degree, given that they didn't look in the least alike.

In fact, he wasn't looking at the local astronomical scenery, but at the ships that reflected the dawning sunlight as they orbited in company with the titanic orbital fortress from which he gazed—the sector military headquarters, and therefore the natural location for the ceremony that was about to commence. He turned from the transparency and looked around him. He stood on a mezzanine that overlooked the fortress's vast docking bay where a Marine honor guard, like the row of dignitaries at right angles to it, faced a dais. That dais filled the space which would have accommodated an arriving shuttle, and it was unoccupied—for now.

Roderick moved to the railing and looked down, watching for a moment as Marine noncoms dressed the honor guard's lines to an even higher degree of exactitude. Then he glanced to right and left along the railing, at others who, like him, were of rank insufficiently exalted to be with the reception committee below.

"Why, Roderick!" The familiar voice was in bantering mode. "I expected you to be down below with the rest of the social elite."

Roderick turned around, and his moody expression dissolved into a grin that wasn't quite as dazzling as its wont—he'd been away from the light of any sun long enough for his face to lose the accustomed ruddy tan that went well with his chestnut-brown hair and provided contrast for his white teeth and blue-gray eyes. He greeted the civilian-clothed figure the way a man who is leaving youth behind greets his mentor.

"You must be joking! A mere captain? You have to be flag rank, or a damned highly placed civilian, to get anywhere close to that receiving line down there."

"A captain, true . . . but hardly a 'mere' one," Jason Aerenthal demurred. "After all, as the Sector Admiral's son—"

"Now I *know* you're joking."

"Of course I am. Anything smacking even remotely of favoritism would be anathema to your father. He is unique in my experience: a man with an *accurate* public image of probity and rectitude. Besides . . ." Aerenthal didn't need to complete the thought. In the four and a half centuries since the First Empire had begun to unravel, familial ties had waxed in significance as societal ones had waned. The urge to advance one's own blood had assumed an importance it hadn't seen since Old Earth's unimaginably ancient preindustrial days. Even if Admiral Ivar Brady-Schiavona had harbored any dynastic ambitions, he would have been well advised to keep them concealed in the presence of his master the Emperor—holder of the Empire's sole *officially* hereditary office.

Roderick needed no coaching on the subject of forbidden topics—he'd spent part of his youth at the

Imperial court on Prometheus. Nevertheless, he couldn't resist asking the question that had been uppermost in his mind since he'd seen Aerenthal. "But why aren't *you* down there? Surely you ought to be."

"Hardly. As you know, I prefer to avoid the limelight." Roderick did know it. He reflected that every one of the officers around them knew about the results of Aerenthal's exploits, but only a few of them knew the name of the man responsible—and of those, not one recognized the civilian sharing the railing with them as that man. The celebrity secret agent of popular fiction exists there alone.

"Yes, I know you've raised inconspicuousness to a fine art. You cultivate it like a banker cultivates conservative respectability—and for much the same reasons. But still . . ."

"There's more to it than that, at the moment."

Roderick's face clouded. "It's totally unfair! You were just carrying out a policy—"

"—with which I disagreed. Softly, please." Aerenthal smiled in a way for which the term "world-weary" would have had to be invented had it not already existed. "But, you see, if I'm not to blame, then who is?" He let the question hang suspended in silence for a heartbeat, then nodded. "So the point is, it's necessary to have someone to blame who *can* be blamed. And I'm the logical choice."

Roderick leaned forward, suddenly alarmed. "See here, how seriously out of favor with the Emperor are you, really?"

"Oh, don't concern yourself. I hardly think the scapegoating process will be carried to its ultimate conclusion. And if things do get hazardous . . . well, I still have a lot of friends and associates in both Domains. My well-established cover persona can become actuality."

"You're lucky I know you too well to take that seriously."

"True." Aerenthal's contrite look might have fooled some people. "With you, I can indulge my abiding vice of flippancy. But look down there. I believe things are about to happen."

An anticipatory hush was falling, only to be shattered as the loudspeaker system filled the vast space with the opening notes of Kolodin's *Imperial Anthem*. A split second later, a series of bellowed commands brought the honor guard to attention. Without any noise at all, a figure appeared on the dais, dressed in a Fleet officer's uniform which bore a golden dragon in place of rank insignia because its wearer transcended rank.

A more stately, impressive ceremony could probably have been built around the arrival of a grav shuttle and the Emperor's descent down its ramp. But this was typical of Oleg, second of the Duschane dynasty. The Emperor who had installed transposer networks on all the newly restored Empire's principal worlds would hardly pass up an opportunity to make dramatic use of the technology. Roderick knew him only slightly—they were distant relatives—but he knew that much. He mentally reviewed what else he knew as Oleg stepped forward to receive the homage of the sector's military and civilian leadership.

The dynastic name was not that of a Sword Clans family, but Oleg had about as much of their blood as Roderick himself did. Old Armand Duschane, an official of the Sword Clans' "Empire of Man," had married a Moran-Tulwar and arranged for his daughter to marry the Emperor he'd served. Dynastic chance had left Armand regent for his infant grandson. There was still some controversy as to how Armand had parleyed his regency into the Imperial title; there was none at all about the ruthlessness with which he'd purged all possible rival claimants. But none of that mattered. What mattered was that, for the first time, a man of genuine ability and ambition had been at

the helm of the Empire of Man at a moment when
the rump Solarian Empire which had taken refuge in
the Serpens/Boötes region, and which the Sword Clans
had never succeeded in conquering, had lain helpless
in the aftermath of its latest factional struggle. Armand
had his detractors, but not even they denied that he'd
had an eye for the main chance. He'd recognized his
unique historical opportunity, and taken it. And, for
the first time in more than two and a half centuries
(more than three and a half, not counting Marvell's
ephemeral reunification), the Empire had found itself
one.

Armand had been a prudent, canny ruler, cautiously
husbanding his resources—which, thanks to the ease
of his reconquest, hadn't been decimated by protracted
warfare. The only real blunder of which he could be
accused was that he hadn't availed himself of the
Emperors' traditional prerogative of choosing their
successors from among their blood relatives. He surely
could have found somebody besides his son and heir
apparent, Oleg. . . .

No, Roderick told himself, *that isn't fair*. This wasn't
the stereotypical case of a dynasty brought to premature grief by its founder's lounge-lizard son—like the
second and last Emperor of the Draconis Empire, or
Basil Castellan's son. Oleg wasn't that sort. Far from
it. True, his appetite for ostentatious grandeur was
notorious, as witness his pet project of restoring Old
Earth as a secondary capital world, an alternative to
frightfully earnest Prometheus. But that was just one
among many outsized appetites—most notably, for
planning and executing grandiose projects of all kinds.
Many of those projects were even farsighted. His
crusade to abolish distance on the planetary scale by
use of transposer technology—an artificial duplication
of the very rare and limited psionic teleportation
effect, introduced by the Sword Clans and heretofore
used only for military purposes and as a toy of the

super-rich—would surely yield economic fruits in the long run. He certainly wasn't stupid. He just lacked a sense of proportion, a recognition of limits.

Maybe I'd lack them too, in his position, Roderick thought ruefully as he watched the Emperor acknowledge a stately salute from his father, to whom almost everyone deferred. But the fact was that Oleg had tried to do too much too fast. Not even antimatter power and nanotechnology could repeal the fundamental economic law of scarcity. His internal projects would have laid the Empire's peoples under a crushing load of taxation even if they hadn't simultaneously had to support his ambitions beyond the frontiers.

Overreaching, Roderick thought bleakly. *You'd think that's the one lesson our history would have taught us.* He thought back to the Founder, but like most people he shied away from even mentally pronouncing the name of the first Emperor of the Draconis Empire. Eight centuries had been powerless to dispel the memory of that totalitarianism which, however inherently horrible, had been but a means to an even more horrible end: a vast processor into which *Homo sapiens* was to be fed, emerging as specialized subtypes serving a master race from Sigma Draconis, an interstellar ant colony blending with its own machines in an obscene fusion of flesh, metal and plastic. And yet the decade-and-a-half nightmare of the Draconis Empire had merely capped the two-century nightmare of the Unification Wars. Humanity had finally awakened, with certain phobias so strong that they might as well have been encoded in its genes. Sovereignty must be universal and undivided, and centered in the person of a single individual so as to reinforce its universality by reducing the basis of social organization to its original common denominator. But that sovereign must be limited to the most inarguable governmental functions, presiding over individuals and societies which were allowed to be themselves.

Very belatedly, the totalitarian temptation had been burned out of the race's collective soul—and so it had remained, despite the brief New Human relapse.

Oleg could not be compared with the Founder. But he'd lost sight of the fact that the Emperor's legitimate functions were almost entirely negative ones, at least as far as internal matters went. And even in external ones, he'd never known when to stop. Instead of learning from the failure of his first Ch'axanthu campaign, he'd dragooned the Ursa Major frontier sectors into a war effort that had grown all out of proportion to the objective, creating a logistics infrastructure to support a second invasion and then a third, on a steadily increasing scale of grandiosity. The uprisings in those sectors against the ever-increasing exactions, and the repression that had followed, had left a legacy of bitterness that would, Roderick was certain, do the Empire a kind of long-term harm that military defeats could not.

And as his last invasion had ebbed back like a spent wave, Oleg had managed to create a new enemy for his bankrupted Empire, on its opposite side. . . .

"It's really too bad," Aerenthal interrupted his thoughts even as he mirrored them. "All he had to do was do nothing."

"He doesn't have it in him to do nothing," Roderick said absently, not taking his eyes off the Imperial figure below.

"Too true. But the settlement I'd engineered was holding together so well . . ." Aerenthal's tone was that of an artist who'd watched his masterpiece being "improved" by a bumptious amateur—and, in fact, been forced to do the desecration himself, under that amateur's direction.

It had all started back in the previous reign. Armand had barely ascended the throne before he'd begun intriguing to neutralize the Tarakans, inciting the Outer Domain to attack the Inner Domain which had been bullying it. But he'd been too clever by half; for his orchestrated war had turned into a rout of the Inner Domain. Not even Armand's hasty switching of sides had stopped the Outer Domain's grim Araharl. By 4295—before completing his reunification of the Empire—Armand had found himself facing a unified Tarakan state such as hadn't existed since Zhangula's corpse had grown cold.

Fortunately, the Outer Domain's need to digest its new acquisitions had given Armand time to reorganize—which sounded better than "purge"—the section of the Inspectorate that concerned itself with the Tarakan Domains. The situation had been grave enough for him to override bureaucratic precedence and place matters squarely in the hands of his principal on-scene agent, a man with an established persona as a businessman from the Empire dealing through interlocking partnerships in the Inner Domain. (Any interstellar boundary is, of necessity, a porous one.) That man now stood beside Roderick and mused wistfully concerning squandered opportunities.

"Yes, it worked out rather well, if I do say so myself . . . and before Armand was dead." Roderick had been in his first year at the Academy in 4313, when a rebellion had ousted the Outer Domain's Araharl and established friendly regimes in both of the again-sundered Domains. He still wasn't altogether clear on how Aerenthal had engineered that, for all the older man's reminiscences. They'd met on Prometheus a few years after that, when one of Aerenthal's periodic returns to the capital had coincided with Roderick's stint at court, and the agent was always willing to avail himself of an appreciative audience; but there were too many things he couldn't talk about. By then, Oleg had inherited the throne—and a Tarakan situation which couldn't have been better. Unfortunately, he'd also inherited a congenital need to meddle.

"To a certain extent, I'm to blame," Aerenthal was

saying, paralleling Roderick's thoughts in his always-startling way. (He was, Roderick knew, a telepath. It was useful enough, despite the ubiquity of psi-damping technology, to allow intelligence agents a conditional exemption from the general strictures against psionics. But he didn't have the kind of powerful abilities whose possessors were generally unfit for anything else; he was limited to accessing active surface thoughts like those formed in the process of preparing to speak. And he would, Roderick was certain, never use it on a friend without knowledge and consent.) "I should have resisted—even to the point of threatening to resign—when Oleg ordered me to destabilize the Outer Domain five years ago."

"Popular legend has it that resignation is discouraged in your line of work," Roderick said playfully.

"There's something to that—and it may possibly have influenced my decision not to make the threat. Still, I should have expressed my feelings more emphatically. The possible benefits—replacing a compliant regime with an even more compliant one—never justified the risks. There's always an element of uncertainty in these things, you know."

"And, in the end, the faction you were ordered to support turned out to be hostile to us. Yes, I know. But at least having them in power is only a limited inconvenience to us. After all, given the Outer Domain's remoteness . . ." Roderick's voice trained miserably to a halt. *Open mouth, insert foot,* he recited to himself.

Aerenthal smiled. "Finish the thought. The Inner Domain *isn't* remote. It's the immediate danger. So I had even less excuse for not digging my heels in two years later when Oleg was taken in again—by Tarakan malcontents offering to break up the Inner Domain. I warned him that they were all talk."

"But why did Oleg even *want* the Inner Domain balkanized? The Outer Domain would have gobbled up the fragments, leaving the Tarakans united under a hostile regime."

"Unfortunately, my efforts to tactfully point that out merely reminded him of the reason for the Outer Domain's new hostility—which didn't exactly enhance my credibility. At any rate, I again followed orders under protest. And, as I'd expected, my efforts had no result except to irritate a basically friendly regime and turn it into an enemy."

"The enemy he's here now to overawe," Roderick finished for him. He heard a fresh set of orders being bawled at the honor guard below, and looked down over the railing. "Things are breaking up down there. And I *am* invited to the reception. Are you coming?"

"Oh, yes. I can't avoid that. Hopefully it won't be too unpleasant." Aerenthal stood up from the rail and straightened the cravat that fashion decreed for semi-formal attire. He had always been good-looking in a saturnine way, and he was wealthy enough from his business dealings in the Inner Domain—which were legitimate, as far as they went—to afford anagathics, to which he took unusually well. Nevertheless, he was some years past the blood-chilling moment when a man accustomed to being described as handsome first hears the dread words "distinguished-looking."

"Maybe the hors d'oeuvres will be better than usual, considering who's the guest of honor," Roderick speculated hopefully as they set out through the dispersing crowd.

The reception room was at the "top" of the orbital station, as defined by artificial gravity: a vast circular chamber whose wall curved upward to join the ceiling in a seamless ellipse. Vertical transparencies all around the room's circumference admitted the light of DM +63 137 and a billion more distant stars, as well as the reflected light glinting off the flanks of the ships matching the station's orbit.

The throng that filled the room was less dazzling than might have been expected, given its social composition. Current civilian styles were on the sober side; and the Sword Clans, with their centuries-long heritage of bitter struggle, had established an enduring tradition of utilitarian plainness in military uniforms. Even the full-dress versions on display for this occasion were austere by the peacocklike standards of the old Solarian Empire.

Both sorts of dress were in evidence in an especially select knot of people near the room's center, a group set apart as though by an invisible wall. The man who was the focus of that group turned to his host with an easy smile.

"Admiral, we were given to understand that your younger son would be present. We were looking forward to renewing our acquaintance with him."

"Yes, Your Imperial Majesty. He should be here any time." Admiral Ivar Brady-Schiavona was a big man— not fat, but large-framed, with a massive square-set solidity. He didn't look like one given to fidgeting, and as a general rule he wasn't. But he cast an anxious look around and ran a hand over his broad, gleaming scalp. In an age when baldness was correctable, its presence was widely regarded as a sign of a man above vanity. Some men had their hair-growth artificially suppressed for that very reason. The admiral was not one of them.

"Good. We haven't seen him since his time at the capital, you know—and that was several years back."

"Before his *meteoric* rise," one of the Emperor's civilian flunkies simpered. Then his eyes met the admiral's—and froze.

Ivar Brady-Schiavona's uncharacteristic jitters had departed, burned away by anger, and under his rock-steady gaze the flunky wilted rapidly. It was a sore point, and a matter for mixed emotions, to have a son who was a captain at the unheard-of age of twenty-nine standard years. The admiral was death on any hint of nepotism and determined to lead by example. But he could hardly tell the boy to underachieve.

Oleg's eyes twinkled as he observed the byplay— he had no use for stupid courtiers, and enjoyed watching them squirm in the coils they created for themselves. He was about to say something when he noticed two approaching figures. "Ah, here he is now."

"Your Imperial Majesty." Roderick came to attention as was proper for a serving officer in uniform, below decks and uncovered. His civilian companion bowed from the waist.

"Ah, Captain Brady-Schiavona! Please be at ease. We were just discussing the splendid course your career has taken since your time at court as a junior officer." Oleg glanced sideways at Aerenthal and his mouth drooped at the corners. "Inspector," he greeted coolly. It was the correct form of address for all officers of the Inspectorate, originally a watchdog agency over the bureaucracy, which over the centuries had grown to encompass all Imperial security functions, including external espionage. But Oleg said it in the tone one uses when unavoidably referring to an unfortunate social disability.

"Your Imperial Majesty," Aerenthal acknowledged. His bland expression excluded the courtiers' snickering and whispered remarks from notice. Roderick, determined to match the older man's urbanity, ignored the flunkies and studied the Emperor.

Oleg was very tall, and his build—wide in the hips and narrow in the shoulders—gave him the look of an attenuated rectangle, which his face mirrored. Now in his fifties, he had the indeterminate early-middle-aged look of those who'd been on anagathics from the earliest age—the late twenties—at which they could be usefully applied. The staggeringly expensive annual regimen slowed the aging process by a factor which was almost three in some individuals and averaged a little less than two—except for the six percent or so of humanity for whom they had no effect whatsoever. . . . Roderick thrust the thought down below the level of consciousness in a way which, in less than a year and a half, had not yet attained the automatism of habit. He concentrated on his father's voice.

"Roderick will be in command of the screening force we're providing, sir." The admiral's "sir" was as acceptable as Roderick's coming to attention had been, for he too was a Fleet officer and these were field conditions despite the background music—something semiclassical from Old Earth's unthinkably ancient past—and the waiters who circulated with trays of wine glasses and canapes.

"Excellent. Not that we expect to need one. After all we're merely reinforcing this frontier against *potential* dangers." Oleg gave Aerenthal another sidelong glance. "A potentiality which wouldn't exist had our agents in the field executed our directives properly."

Sheer outrage at the injustice took Roderick's breath away, preventing him from saying the unsayable. The courtiers, recognizing their cue, resumed their tittering. One of them—a Fleet captain named Vladimir Liang, who was chief of the Emperor's personal military staff, spoke up with a sneer in Aerenthal's direction. "Yes, it's a pity that His Imperial Majesty himself has to come here, applying his own incomparable gifts to a problem that his agents should have been able to deal with, given the ordinary competence he has a right to expect of them."

Oleg beamed, and Roderick began to understand how Liang—whose dress tunic was innocent of combat-related decorations—had attained his post. He started to open his mouth, but caught his father's warning glance out of the corner of his eye. *Well*, he told himself, *if Jason can continue to disregard this shit, so can I.*

"Still, sir," the admiral said in his formidable bass, as though the byplay had never taken place, "it can't hurt to have a screen out as per tactical doctrine. Standard procedures should be observed at all times."

"Spoken like a line officer of the old school, Admiral! And of course we couldn't ask for a finer officer to command it." He favored Roderick with a smile. "And now, we need to speak to the Sector Governor, if you and Captain Brady-Schiavona will excuse us." Pointedly ignoring Aerenthal, Oleg moved away, the flunkies following in a sycophantic swarm.

"Be careful what you say," the admiral rumbled in Roderick's ear. "He's . . . unpredictable. He can sometimes be very tolerant. But he can also be vindictive—especially with slime like Liang around to goad him in that direction."

"True," Aerenthal agreed. "The secret of success as a courtier is to play to the ruler's mood of the moment, thus amplifying it and translating into actions what are, for most of us, mere passing impulses. Small wonder that monarchs have always been noted for extreme behavior." Abruptly, the bantering tone dropped from his voice. "By the same token, the lickspittles who surround him are likely to confirm him in his disinclination to take the dangers out here seriously. This would be . . . unfortunate."

The admiral looked up sharply. His feelings about Aerenthal were ambivalent. The military class to which he belonged had always despised intelligence work, which doubtless helped account for the Empire's traditional weakness in that area. But he also valued expertise in any workman, and he knew full well that Aerenthal's work—however unappetizing he himself found it—had given the Empire a decades-long respite on this frontier. So he'd never been inclined to disapprove of Roderick's association with the agent. "What do you mean?" he asked quietly.

"In spite of everything I've managed to maintain contact with most of my sources of information in the Inner Domain. And my impression is that . . . well, the individual personalities involved would mean nothing to you. Suffice it to say that the Inner Domain's attitude goes beyond the mere annoyance that has to be expected in light of the pathetic intrigues to which I was required to lend the Empire's support. I believe something major is in the offing."

The admiral's gaze grew even sharper, and his voice harshened. "If you have reason to believe there's a serious danger to the Imperial person, why didn't you speak up?"

"To repeat, it's only an impression—albeit an impression backed by not inconsiderable experience out here. I have no real proof. And how much weight do you suppose my opinion would carry with the Emperor just now?"

"Some truth in that," the admiral admitted gruffly.

"Just so. And now that I've put in my obligatory appearance, I must be going. Thank you for your hospitality, Admiral. Good luck, Roderick." And Aerenthal was gone, leaving father and son in thoughtful silence.

"I've never quite known what to make of him," the admiral finally said. "But if he's worried, I'm worried. And I know better than to waste my time trying to persuade the Emperor to change his plans." His massive head turned slowly toward Roderick, and his voice grew even deeper than its wont as he spoke with obvious effort. "I know I don't have to remind you of your duty. But this goes beyond ordinary duty. The reunification is still young, and fragile. His life"—he jerked his chin in the direction of Oleg, across the room—"is the knot holding everything together. He may not be everything we could have wished for in an Emperor, but he's what we've got. He *has* to be kept alive. You're not old enough to remember what it was like before Armand's reconquest, but I am."

"I understand, sir. We can't afford a succession struggle. I'll bear that in mind at all times." Roderick spoke formally. He'd always found it difficult to speak to his father in any other way. It wasn't that Ivar was frightening or unapproachable. He wasn't even humorless—not totally. He simply had no lightness in him. His way of speaking suggested that his words were being chiseled into marble above a Classical colonnade. Roderick forced himself to try and bring the conversation down to a more human level. "By the way, I'm sorry I didn't have a chance to pay a personal call before the ceremony, but I'd only just arrived here. How is everyone?"

"Well." The admiral's expression softened as much as it ever did. "At least Maura *was* well the last time I heard from her." Roderick's younger sister was off in Ursa Major, executive officer of a cruiser which, like her, had survived the latest Ch'axanthu war. Since then, she'd been involved in the police actions among the restive Imperial worlds near that frontier—a topic Roderick and his father avoided in conversation. "Ted is as always. In fact, he'd hoped to be here by now, but was delayed by business."

Why am I not surprised? Roderick didn't voice the thought. There was something special about a firstborn son, something that tended to banish objectivity. Something that outweighed Ivar's mild disappointment that Teodor had left the Fleet after satisfying the minimal demands of family tradition by serving a single hitch. And it didn't help that his serene blond handsomeness recalled the admiral's long-dead wife. So Roderick contented himself with a neutral response. "Too bad. But maybe it's for the best. If Jason is right, this sector may not be any place for a civilian to be visiting for a while."

"No." The admiral was preoccupied, and his eyes focused on something far beyond the confines of the station. Then he shook his head as though irritated with himself and turned his thin but genuine smile on Roderick. "Just remember what I said earlier. I

didn't put you in command of the Emperor's screen
to hand you a plum assignment—whatever some
people may think. I did it because you're the best
choice for the job . . . the most important job in the
Fleet at this moment."

"Yes, sir. I won't forget."

In fact, Roderick was recalling the conversation
weeks later as he lay in his bunk, staring at the overhead.

They had proceeded along a string of closely spaced
K-type stars which formed the terminus of the Beta
Cassiopeiae Sector, leaving one element after another
of the Emperor's convoy behind. Now they had
departed the sector and entered a starless gulf beyond
which lay Theta Persei, capital system of the sector
of the same name. Roderick's dozen cruisers had taken
their accustomed position—about a light-month to
starboard of the convoy, which placed them between
it and the volume of space occupied by the Inner
Domain. Now that the deployment was complete,
Roderick had turned matters over to Commander
Tatsumo, skipper of HIMS *Cataphract*—the "flag
captain," since Roderick had been gazetted to commodore for this command—and retired to his cabin
for a moment of relaxation.

The Imperial procession had been uneventful, and
Aerenthal's apprehensions were beginning to look like
the kind of compulsive worrying that often overtook
people above a certain age. *About time, at almost a
standard century—in spite of anagathics . . .* Roderick
winced away from the thought, which as usual he
hadn't forestalled before it could blossom into hurtful life. With time, the knack would doubtless come.

Justice, I suppose, he brooded, picking compulsively
at the emotional scab. *I've spent most of my life being
told I'm exceptional. So why should I expect to be like
ninety-four percent of humanity in this one thing?*

His father had, characteristically, never uttered a word suggesting disappointment. Just as characteristically, he'd been unable to relax his stiffness and cry out to his son that it didn't matter.

And it shouldn't matter, Roderick's thought flared. *Should I whine because I'll have to settle for the lifespan that my ancestors were content with, and that most humans—those who're neither rich nor socially valuable by Imperial definition—still have to accept? Not even that; I've always had access to the best conventional medical technology money can buy, so I ought to outdo the Biblical threescore-and-ten.*

But . . . Does Father overlook every fault of Ted's because, at the back of his mind, he's thinking that at least he has one son who can be expected to outlive him?

And do I try so hard because I know my time is limited?

He began to drift off as the thoughts pursued their endless loop, and was spiraling down into sleep when the general-quarters klaxon began to whoop.

He came sailing up out of the bunk, jabbing for the intercom button with the disoriented clumsiness of the rudely awakened. Before he could find it, Tatsumo's voice rasped from the grille as the flag captain spoke on the emergency link that needed no acceptance.

"Commodore, we've received an Ultimate Priority distress call from His Imperial Majesty's flagship. They've detected a hostile force on intercept course. The energy signatures indicate Tarakan ship classes."

"But—" Roderick savagely shook the last tatters of drowsiness from his head. "But how could we have not detected them?" It was the whole *raison d'etre* of the screen. Its function wasn't to fight off a serious attack—not with ships of cruiser size and below— but to provide early warning by deploying sensors between the Emperor and that region of space from which danger might come. Roderick wouldn't be able to send instantaneous warning, of course—cruisers could receive instantaneous tachyon messages from the mammoth communications ship that accompanied the Emperor, but they couldn't begin to carry the vast transmitter arrays required to send such messages across interstellar distances. But he could dispatch a frigate with the tidings his near-realtime sensors would have provided.

"They're coming from *inside* Imperial space, sir. We've got their vector plotted—"

"I'm on my way. Get us moving immediately." Roderick cut the connection without waiting for an acknowledgment and strode from the cabin. He proceeded toward the bridge, oblivious to the running figures and the raucous klaxon. His thoughts were raging.

From inside *Imperial space—the far side of the convoy from us! Somebody must have sold the Inner Domain his complete itinerary. So they slipped a force into this gap between sectors, where it's been lying undetectable in space, waiting to pounce from the direction nobody expected. Meanwhile, we of the screen are out here in the middle of nowhere, playing with ourselves. . . .*

He shook off the useless self-reproach as he entered the bridge, automatically muttering "As you were" and waving people back to their seats. A *Cuirassier*-class cruiser leader like *Cataphract* had no separate flag bridge, just a command chair beside the captain's. Roderick flung himself into it and ran his eyes over the readouts and displays that lent color to the dimly lit space.

"We're continuing to receive messages from the convoy, sir, and displaying the data as quickly as it can be downloaded," Tatsumo reported. "By now, we've got a fairly comprehensive force composition as well as the vector."

"So I see," Roderick murmured, studying the display and feeling ill. It was an even more powerful force than he'd feared. The Emperor's convoy was just that, not a fighting fleet. At its original strength, it could have held off the fleet bearing down on it. But now, after having left various components behind to reinforce the systems it had visited . . .

The good news was that the hostiles hadn't just sprung into detectability right on top of their prey—they were coming from a respectable distance, and thus had been discovered at the maximum range of the sensors that Admiral Rahmani, commander of the Emperor's escort, had at least had the sense to have out in all directions. Instead of trying to evade, Rahmani was proceeding at his best speed—that of his slowest ship, hence none too good—toward Theta Persei, hoping to reach the shelter of its defenses. The computer's extrapolation of the enemy's intercept course foretold that he wasn't quite going to make it. Nor was Roderick's command going to be able to rendezvous with the convoy until after the latter had come under attack—and had probably surrendered, given the identity of the passenger for whose life Rahmani was responsible, assuming that the Tarakans offered quarter.

Not that it would matter if we could, Roderick thought as he studied the breakdown of enemy classes and numbers. His light vessels would be little more than a feather in this balance of forces. But he never even considered ordering a change in Tatsumo's course. His ships continued to arrow toward the rendezvous they wouldn't make at a speed flatly forbidden by the laws of physics—at least as far as the outside universe, and their personnel's own time-sense, were concerned.

It never occurred to any of those personnel, from Roderick on down, to marvel at what they were doing. Seventeen centuries had passed since mankind had

learned how to fool the gods into thinking their laws
were being obeyed, in the words of Chen Hsieh, a
leading member of the team that had produced the
prototype time-distortion drive . . . which wasn't really
a "drive" at all, for it didn't actually move the ship.
Rather, it surrounded it with a field within which the
passage of time was enormously accelerated. Within
that bubble in the continuum, the ship disobeyed no
cosmic speed limits. But to outside observers, the
acceleration its impellers imparted sent it hurtling past
the velocity allowed by the semi-mythical Einstein.
Meanwhile, a second, inner field around its crewed
spaces slowed time down by the same factor, lest the
trip seem to the crew to take the centuries it would
have taken without the drive. So Roderick was able
to watch the stars stream impossibly past in the
viewscreen as he tried to will the drive to even greater
compression of time.

But of course it couldn't be done. All military ships
mounted drives that speeded the time-flow by the
same factor: the highest permitted by existing technology. Had they not, they would have been helpless
in combat against ships that did, given the drive's
amplifying effect on the power of energy weapons and
corresponding defensive value against directed energy
from outside. So speed differentials between ship
classes were strictly a function of old-fashioned thrust-
to-mass ratios. On that showing, Roderick's ships were
fast—faster than either of the other two forces in play,
which included massive battleships and transports. But
there were no tricks by which they could be made
even faster.

And, he asked himself, *just what are we going to
do when we get there, besides die?*

Time crawled by at a protracted rate which had
nothing to do with the inner field. Food was brought
to the bridge, and neither Roderick nor Tatsumo left
save to answer calls of nature. No one on the bridge

felt inclined to interrupt the commodore's intense
brooding.

At last there came a time when Tatsumo reported
quietly. "The Emperor's convoy has come under attack, sir." She indicated the holo tank, where the
string-lights of the opposing fleets' courses had crawled
together.

Roderick nodded. He didn't need to be told that
it meant the comm ship, like every other ship in the
convoy, would have killed its inner field, thus maxi-
mizing its crew's time to react to outside events that
seemingly moved at a crawl.

"Disengage our inner field," he ordered Tatsumo.
It was necessary, for they could only continue to
receive transmissions from the convoy if they and it
were existing at the same time-rate. Besides, they'd
need all the subjective time they could get to prepare
themselves. The flag captain obeyed, and the stars
abruptly became motionless in the screen, even though
Cataphract was still moving through the outer universe at the same speed.

Soon, Tatsumo had another report. "Sir, the convoy is continuing to fight back."

*So Rahmani isn't going to surrender after all. Or
maybe he wasn't given the option.*

With startling abruptness, Roderick sprang up from
the chair in which he'd been sitting motionless, and
began pacing. Then he stopped and turned to Tatsumo.
"Aline, the Emperor is going to be *killed.* I refuse to
believe there's nothing we can do."

"I concur, sir. But . . . Well, we haven't been able
to set up any meaningful tactical models to work out,
not knowing exactly what situation we're going to be
facing when we—"

"We can't accomplish anything by fighting. We both
know that. The numbers and tonnage and firepower
just aren't there. Besides, that battle's probably going
to be over by the time we arrive." Roderick resumed

pacing, then halted in front of the holo tank. "We're going to be within sensor range of the battle soon. And presumably the Tarakans will have some sensors out, as a routine precaution. I want our stealth systems set for sensor confusion—make them think we're stronger than we are."

"Yes, sir," Tatsumo nodded, unsurprised. She'd thought of it herself; it was virtually their only option. The systems collectively and anachronistically known as "stealth" couldn't render a vehicle massive enough to carry them invisible to sensors, except temporarily. But they could induce distorted returns. "We can make our cruisers appear to be battlecruisers. But I must point out that the Tarakans *know* we can, and will therefore view the returns with caution. And given our small numbers, they won't find us very alarming even if they *do* think they're dealing with battlecruisers."

"I know, I know," Roderick muttered. He watched his force crawl along in the tank, nearing the Tarakans' sensor range. It wasn't easy to keep the implications of that range in mind. The sensors were active ones, using treated antineutrinos which could be given superluminal acceleration but which lacked the virtual instantaneity of tachyon communications. It took a finite interval for the antineutrino stream to go out to its extreme range and back again. So some little time would pass before the Tarakans would realize they were there. . . .

Then it burst on Roderick with a force that left him physically immobile, staring into the holo tank and thinking in a fury of concentration.

After a while, Tatsumo spoke hesitantly. "Uh, Commodore . . . ?"

Roderick whirled around and faced her. "Commander, listen very carefully, because it is essential that my orders be carried out to the letter and without a second's hesitation. Clear?"

"Y-y-yes, sir," Tatsumo stammered, caught flat-footed

by Roderick's sudden formality and rocked back by what she saw in his eyes.

"Good. Now, on my command, just before we enter the Tarakans' sensor range, we will implement sensor confusion, with a view to spoofing their sensors into seeing our ships as battlecruisers, as per our earlier discussion. Then, after waiting thirty seconds to assure that we'll register on their sensors, we will shift our stealth suites to invisibility mode—"

"But, sir—"

"Don't interrupt, Commander! Immediately thereafter we will disengage our drives, turn around, and get out of their sensor range."

"What?" Tatsumo's shock wiped the commodore's ban on interruption from her mind. "Run away? Damn it, sir—"

"Commander, you will implement my orders, or I will relieve you and bring you up on charges." Roderick thrust his face to within inches of Tatsumo's and spoke too low for the bridge crew to hear. "Shut up and listen, Aline! I'm going to try something a little different—it's our only chance." He rapped out his plan in a few swift sentences, overriding her occasional protests. When he was done, her lower jaw was hanging agape.

"But, but," she finally sputtered, "you can't! I mean, nobody's ever . . ." All at once, her face cleared, leaving room for a roguish smile. *"Yes!"*

For a second his blue-gray eyes and her dark almond-shaped ones held each other, alike in the gleam they held. Then he straightened up and spoke in a normal volume. "Stand by to execute orders, Commander."

"Aye aye, sir. But may I suggest that you communicate directly with the other ship captains first, so they'll know what to expect?"

"Not a bad idea. Have comm connect me with them—quickly, because we haven't much time."

It was as Roderick commanded when they crossed the invisible line beyond which they could be detected. When Tatsumo ordered the withdrawal, faces turned toward her from all around the bridge with expressions ranging from incredulity to mutiny—until their owners met her quelling glare. Then the little formation turned around and swung out of the Tarakans' sensor range in the kind of near reversal of course the drive permitted.

Then Tatsumo turned briefly to Roderick, and they exchanged a brief, knowing look before she gave her next orders: to disengage the drive again, go back to sensor confusion, and swerve back into enemy sensor range . . . *while the first signals were still on their way back to the Tarakan ships.*

One by one, the bridge crew's expressions changed as understanding dawned.

They completed the maneuver . . . and tidings of *another* dozen battlecruisers sped toward the Tarakans.

Again, they performed the maneuver. And again. And again.

By the time the returns began to register on the Tarakans' scopes, a phantom armada was sweeping down on them.

Of course, those incoming squadrons of battlecruisers were going to concealment mode immediately—which was curious, for given the notoriously short-lived nature of the invisibility it conferred, most commanders preferred to withhold it until battle was almost joined. Or at least it *would* have seemed curious had the Tarakans possessed the leisure to calmly consider the matter. . . .

"That must be one flustered admiral they've got," Tatsumo murmured to Roderick, barely able to sustain the frowns she periodically directed at the bridge crew as she sought to forestall an incipient manic glee that escaped in occasional splutters and chortles.

"I imagine so," was Roderick's measured reply. For the swarms of apparent Imperial battlecruisers were coming in from frontierward—the one direction from which the Tarakans had *known* no reinforcements could reach their prey. "In fact, I imagine—"

"Skipper! Commodore!" The yelp came from the young lieutenant j.g. at the comm station. "They're starting to—"

"We see it, Lieutenant," Roderick said quietly as he settled back in his chair and watched the holo tank where the scarlet icons of the Tarakan units were swinging away from the battered convoy, breaking off the engagement and fleeing in the direction from which they'd come. *It worked, it actually worked!* The words seemed to sing in his head . . . but only for a moment, before being drowned out by the storm of cheers and applause that Tatsumo, with all the centuries of Fleet discipline behind her, could no longer contain.

It is given to only a few people to be present at moments that give birth to legends—and to even fewer to realize it at the time. But every member of the bridge crew knew that HIMS *Cataphract* had just sailed through the gauzy curtain that separates fact from myth. And they crowded around their impossibly young commodore who'd just sent an entire Tarakan battle fleet scurrying with just a dozen scout cruisers, and saved an Emperor.

Tatsumo yelled into Roderick's ear to make herself heard. "They know this story will be good for free drinks for the rest of their lives!"

The afternoon light of Theta Persei A was streaming through the conference room's tall windows as the Emperor entered, with Captain Liang following like an eager poodle. They all rose to their feet: Roderick, wearing the insignia of the commodore's rank the Emperor had made permanent; Admiral Rahmani, who still hadn't stopped looking at Roderick with incredulous awe; Roderick's father, who'd arrived with a powerful task force lest the Tarakans come back, boiling with rage at the way they'd been snookered; and all the rest of the officers around the long, gleaming-topped table.

"As you were, as you were," the Emperor said, a little too heartily. He took his seat at the head of the table, with Liang hovering behind him. "We have called you together to make two important announcements. First, we are placing Admiral Brady-Schiavona in overall command of this frontier, with responsibility for this sector as well as Beta Cassiopeiae. In light of the Inner Domain's manifest hostility, a unified command structure is essential to deal with the further incursions that are bound to come." Oleg paused and looked around the table in an oddly furtive way, the precise nature of which Roderick found himself unable to define. "It is in light of these inevitable future hostilities that we have reached our second decision.

"After taking counsel with our advisors, we have come to accept the view that the Imperial person cannot be hazarded in what must realistically be regarded as a war zone. Indeed, even Sigma Draconis must be considered too close to this frontier. We have therefore decided, despite our private inclinations, to relocate the Imperial court to the secondary capital at Lambda Serpenti."

Maybe, Roderick thought, it was something about the room's acoustics that caused Oleg's last words to seem to echo for a few seconds as they dropped into a well of stunned silence. That silence stretched until Roderick feared it would snap like an overdrawn wire. He waited, too junior in this company to speak first, hoping someone else would blurt out what had to be said. Finally, his father spoke. Ivar's bass had its usual calming effect. One had to know him well to recognize the near desperation in that voice.

"Sir, surely the defenses of Sigma Draconis are

strong enough to insure your security. And it *is* the traditional capital—as well as being in an advantageous location from which to direct the defense of this frontier."

"It is precisely this 'location' that is the problem, Admiral—as we have already intimated." Oleg's voice held an undertone of nervous irritation. His eyes flickered in Liang's direction as though in search of support. Roderick's puzzlement deepened.

"But sir," the admiral persisted, "even if Sigma Draconis is too exposed in the present circumstances, there are other alternatives besides the rather . . . drastic one you are contemplating. There are more practical choices for the Imperial seat. Old Earth, perhaps. Much has been done to restore it, and with its central location and its unique prestige as the homeworld—"

Liang broke in, which at any other time would have left everyone at the table thunderstruck. "Sol is still too close to the threatened frontier, Admiral—as must surely be clear to anyone with His Imperial Majesty's safety at heart."

The admiral's expression stayed rock-steady, but his eyes flashed a dangerous fire. Ordinarily, he would have squashed Liang like the insect he was. But he ignored the courtier-captain and addressed the Emperor. The desperation in his voice was now unmistakable, and so was a note of pleading Roderick had never thought to hear in that voice. "Sir . . . Your Imperial Majesty . . . I implore you to reconsider. Lambda Serpenti's remoteness is such that the command-and-control problems for this entire flank of the Empire could well become insuperable."

"This is why we have granted you extraordinary powers, Admiral. We have the fullest confidence in your ability to contain the Tarakans—aided by your son, Commodore Brady-Schiavona." Oleg smiled in nervous self-congratulation for this transparent attempt at mollification. "At any rate, Lambda Serpenti's location is the very reason we have chosen it, for security must be the paramount consideration."

Yeah, Roderick thought, *seventy-odd light-years ought to be far enough from here.* All at once, he realized that in trying to analyze the Emperor's odd behavior he'd fallen into the classic clever person's fallacy: searching for complexity where there was none. Oleg was, quite simply, a coward. It had never been apparent before, because he'd never been in physical danger in his life. But now he was, and his nerves were shattered. He could think of nothing but putting as much distance as possible between his body and the Tarakans. If that meant abandoning all the Empire outside the Serpens/Bootes region, so be it.

"At any rate, Admiral," he was concluding with forced briskness, "our mind is made up. And now, ladies and gentlemen, you are dismissed." He stood up with an abruptness that screamed his relief to have this over with. The officers around the table barely had time to scramble to their feet before he was gone, leaving them exchanging nervous glances and separating into muttering groups.

Admiral Brady-Schiavona caught his son's eyes and gestured with his chin toward a door. Once outside the conference room, Roderick could barely keep up as his father strode down the corridor.

"I doubt if many of them back there realize how bad this really is," the admiral rumbled in a low voice. "From Sigma Draconis, or even Sol, he could maintain order by his presence. But he's effectively abandoning us out here at the very moment that war is breaking out. And it hasn't been that long since we came out of warlordism—four centuries when rebels and local military commanders took matters into their own hands whenever danger threatened or advantage beckoned. That's why we need the Emperor as a symbol . . . and he's taking that symbol away."

"And don't forget where he's taking it to," Roderick said. "It's a disastrous choice, not just astrographically but also historically."

The admiral came to a halt and gave a low moan, as though from physical pain. "Yes, you're right. Lambda Serpenti, the last refuge of failing dynasties. It's where the Marvell Emperors fled when the Zyungen took Earth." he shook his massive head slowly. "He usually has some sense of symbolism."

"I don't think that's what's on his mind at the moment." Roderick took a deep breath. "Sir, what are we going to do now?"

"Do? We'll carry out our orders, of course. We're officers of His Imperial Majesty—nothing more and nothing less."

"Of course, sir. But . . . may I suggest that we get in touch with Jason Aerenthal and ask him to join us at our headquarters? I think his counsel may be useful."

The silence didn't last quite long enough to become awkward. Then the admiral spoke heavily. "Yes, I imagine you're right. See to it." Then he drew himself up and walked away, moving like a man looking for something he'd lost and feared he'd never see again.

CHAPTER THREE
Santaclara (Iota Pegasi A IV), 4326 C.E.

The air of the Iota Pegasi sector base stank with fear, resentment, and apprehension.

With the dawning of the new standard year had come word of the Emperor's decision to relocate to the Serpens/Bootes region. It meant he was effectively abandoning the rest of the Empire to its own devices. This was as universally recognized as it was scrupulously avoided in all public utterances, so hypocrisy was added to the psychic miasma's unhealthy mixture. Morale hovered in the lower regions of surliness, just above the threshold that portended mutiny.

Admiral Tanzler-Yataghan had maintained a sphinx-like silence on the subject of his own intentions, maintaining the facade of a loyal Imperial officer and reminding everyone that Admiral Brady-Schiavona—whose name was a byword for incorruptibility—was in charge on the Cassiopeia/Perseus frontier. People clung to that solitary floating fragment of good news as the foundation of their lives dissolved under their feet. But they also knew that there were limits to how much good it could do them, in the face of the Tarakan invasion everyone knew was coming. There could be no such thing as a solid "front" in interstellar war. Brady-Schiavona might stand like a rock, but invaders could bypass him—perhaps through the 85 Pegasi Sector, next door.

Whenever possible, Corin Marshak felt the need to get away into the city of Nambucco outside the base, where the atmosphere of despair was less oppressive because the civilians didn't know as much.

The definition of an optimist, he thought as he stepped off the transposer stage. *Someone who just doesn't understand the situation.* He was in civvies, because a uniform in Nambucco was sure to draw appeals for information and reassurance, and he had neither to give. He came here to escape from reality among these spacious tree-shaded streets with their picturesque old buildings and sidewalk cafes, basking in the sun like a dream that didn't know the sleeper was awakening.

He was looking around as he walked along the edge of a plaza when he thudded sideways into another form—smaller than his but lithely muscular. "Oh, excuse me!" he exclaimed, turning to look at the other pedestrian, who turned toward him with a swirl of auburn hair, unusual on this world. "Major Dornay! Please forgive my clumsiness."

The Marine, also in civilian clothes, blinked with puzzlement before recognition dawned. "Oh—Commander Marshak. Quite all right, sir. My fault entirely."

"It's been a long time," he ventured. In the standard year since they'd both arrived on Santaclara, their respective duties—his as the Sector Admiral's ops officer, hers with the 79th Ground Assault Regiment that was based here—had rarely brought them together. But on those few occasions he'd remembered her, and gotten the impression that she reciprocated. "Can I buy you a drink?"

Her features seemed to come to a rigid position of attention. "Thank you, sir, but I need to return to base."

"Look, I know we didn't exactly get off on the best

foot, a year ago. But could we try again?" He gestured at a cafe whose terrace overlooked the plaza. "It's the least I can do, after almost knocking you on your butt."

Her expression wavered, firmed up again, then relaxed with finality into a kind of fatalistic half-smile. "Oh, what the hell. Might just as well be drunk as the way I am."

They seated themselves on the terrace and ordered the full-bodied local red wine. As they waited for it, Janille studied the panorama of the plaza and Corin studied her. She was dressed in a dark-green outfit that complemented her red hair, and Iota Pegasi A had been less unkind to her complexion than he'd once have thought possible. But her eyes flitted to and fro nervously, and her expression wore a strained look that would have puzzled him had he not had a fairly good idea of its origins. He'd heard stories about the admiral's maneuverings to have her in close proximity to him, and his broad hints about the beneficial effect of a sexually cooperative attitude on her career prospects. . . .

The wine arrived. She took hers a little too hastily, and lifted the glass in a toast. "Well, congratulations! You were right, and I was an idiot."

"What do you mean?"

"Oh, come on! You must remember our first conversation, aboard the liner that brought us here." Without waiting for him to respond, she inhaled half her wine. "Well, you were right."

"About the Empire, you mean?"

"What else?" She took a slightly more cautious pull on her wine. "Must be nice to feel vindicated."

"Not particularly. That's the disadvantage of being a pessimist." He sipped rapidly so as not to fall too far behind. "The advantage is that you're never disappointed. Maybe that's why I've cultivated pessimism ever since the Ch'axanthu war. The experience left me tender."

She looked at him with an interest that drew her out of her bitterness. "Survivor's guilt?"

"Possibly. I lost some friends. But I *won't* fall into self-pity like some of the survivors I know. Looking back over my life, I can't honestly say I have any grounds for it. You might even say I've beaten the odds. Starting with when I was adopted—"

"Huh?" She leaned forward, her interest intensifying. "That's a coincidence. I was adopted too. On Accadie, 82 Eridani II."

"Really? Was that where your birth parents were from?"

"Couldn't say. I was adopted in early infancy, and my parents—my adoptive parents, that is—never knew anything about them. Neither did the agency they got me from. It was like I came out of nowhere." She finished off her wine and waved at the waiter. "Let's order a carafe."

Corin stared at her. "That really *is* a coincidence. It was the same with me, only on Prometheus. I never could find out anything about my background either."

"I guess we must have both been war orphans. The civil wars were just ending. I was born the year before Armand Duschane came to the throne of the Empire of Man, you know."

"This is too much! So was I." Then its habitual bleakness closed back over Corin's face. "We were born at a unique moment. Now that moment's ending."

Janille glanced around nervously. This kind of talk could lead to trouble. "You mean . . . you really think we're headed back into the civil wars?"

"Or even further back. We're going to be going through a breakup like what they experienced four centuries ago."

"You really *are* a pessimist!" She gave a nervous laugh. "Well, maybe it'll at least be exciting. Didn't you once tell me an era like that is good for historical fiction?"

"And hell to live through." Corin nodded, and his brooding eyes swept over the city around them. "Yes, the age of Basil Castellan—who, by the way, is no hero of mine. He pissed away the chance—the *last* chance—to put the old Empire back together, so it could have stood against the Zyungen. He was more interested in pursuing a personal vendetta against Lavrenti Kang, with whom he needed to make a short-term accommodation against Yoshi Medina's son. It may have been history's most disastrous act of self-indulgence." He shook his head and gave her one of his rare smiles, albeit one of self-mockery. "Sorry. I let my enthusiasm for history run away with me. And I'm probably full of shit, as usual. We'll carry on here, and hope everybody else does the same everywhere. Speaking of which, how's it going with the new Mark 32-A?"

"Well enough." She didn't seem as grateful as he'd hoped for the change of subject. In fact, her grimness settled back over her. He thought he knew why. *Maybe talking shop wasn't such a brilliant ploy after all*, he chided himself.

But she continued after a heartbeat's pause, as though needing to talk but hesitant to step over a line of whose precise location she was unsure. "I was making some real progress with it. I've had some special advanced training in design theory. And . . . well, I've always been good with powered armor, you know." Corin did know. He'd seen her service record. It went without saying that she had the aptitude for direct neural interfacing—all combat Marines had to. But she was better than most. She had to be, to have attained major's rank and a billet as adjutant to the C.O. of an assault battalion.

" 'Was' making real progress?" he queried.

"Before the 79th and everybody else left for Sancerre."

"Of course! I knew there was some reason I ought

to be surprised to see you here. Why aren't you out
on planet five with the rest of your unit for the
exercises?"

Another layer of shadow descended on her face.
She spoke in carefully neutral tones. "Admiral Tanzler-
Yataghan has asked Brigadier General Toda to assign
me to his personal staff as . . . oh, yes, as 'special
liaison' for something or other."

" 'Asked' in terms that amounted to an order, I
imagine," Corin replied, striving to match her expressionlessness. He had a very clear idea why the admiral
wanted her at his headquarters and outside of the
close-knit Marine community. That this was the first
he'd heard of it didn't surprise him. He doubted Captain Yuan knew about it either. He'd learned early on
that the admiral's "personal staff" was a matter outside the chief of staff's cognizance.

The silence stretched embarrassingly. "Uh, look,"
he finally attempted, "if . . . that is, just in case . . . well,
if you need any kind of help, let me know."

She gave a short, harsh sound that was part laugh
and part snort. "What, exactly, could you do?"

A damned good question, he thought miserably.

In the old Solarian Empire's military, absolute
gender equality had prevailed. But that hadn't lasted.
The Sword Clans' centuries-long twilight struggle
with the Zyungen in their home system had made
them relearn a basic truth their ancestors hadn't
needed to know since clawing their way upward
from Old Earth's precivilized ooze: with species
survival in the balance, men are expendable and
women aren't. The resultant attitudes and social
patterns had—as always—long outlived the circumstances that had called them into being; they had
carried over into the Empire of Man. Nowadays, all
legal restrictions were removed and many women
were in the combat branches—but their numbers
grew less and less as the rank structure grew more

rarefied. Corin recalled hearing the expression "armorplast ceiling."

Of course, the Fleet's lingering Sword Clan ethos had another side: a sternly chivalric ideal that generally prevented the potential for abuse from becoming actuality. But when a really high-ranking officer failed to live up to that ideal . . .

"I understand your bitterness—" Corin began.

"Do you?" For an instant her eyes held his with icy flame. Then she seemed to remember herself, and the armor of formality clashed into place. "Excuse me, sir. I've spoken out of turn. And now my duties require that I return to base." And, with awkward haste, she was gone.

Corin was gazing at the spot where she'd vanished into the crowd when the waiter brought the carafe.

Be a sin to let it go to waste, he told himself.

The communicator beside his bed brought Corin out of a deep sleep. He took two tries to mumble clearly enough for the room to understand and accept the call. Another moment passed before the face on the screen registered.

"Janille—er, Major Dornay! What . . . ?"

"Sir, I apologize for calling you at this hour." She was in uniform. He could only see her from the shoulders up, but she seemed to be standing at attention, her face expressionless. "I have no right to . . . well, sir, you said to let you know if . . . I mean . . ." All at once her face's tightly drawn rigidity cracked. "I don't know *what* I mean, Commander. Please forget I called." She reached for her communicator's controls.

"Wait! Don't disconnect!" Corin cudgeled his wits into functionality and looked more carefully at the screen. He couldn't recognize the background. "Where are you?"

"The 79th's maintenance shed, at—"

"I know where it is. I'm on my way. Wait right there. If it takes an order to make you stay where you are, consider that an order." He broke the connection before she could argue, and began fumbling for his clothes.

The sentries at the Marine compound gave no trouble to the admiral's ops officer. And the maintenance shed—it was too large a structure for the word to really fit—was unguarded save by automated security systems set to pass people on his level without even recording their entry. He entered and activated the lighting, at "dim" level. A row of powered combat armor suits stood like steel idols of war gods, in a silence that belied the intrinsic menace they held for anyone who knew what they could do. Corin knew, and he had to lick his lips before speaking in a low voice. "Janille?"

"Here." She stepped from the shadows between two of the Mark 32-A's. "Come with me."

She led the way into a windowless storeroom-*cum*-workshop, where she sank down into a swivel chair at a computer station in a way that suggested familiarity. Corin seated himself on a bench and waited for her to make the first conversational move.

"Thank you for coming, Commander. I didn't know who else to call. But I *shouldn't* have called you. I have no right to involve you in my personal problems—"

"Cut the crap, Janille." His tone was gentler than the words. "I know precisely who and what you're talking about. And call me Corin."

She blinked, but made a quick recovery. "All right . . . Corin. Earlier tonight, he made me work late, in private. I'd always thought I'd be able to deflect anything he did in an acceptable way. But . . . he'd been drinking, and he . . . well, he tried to force me. I'm afraid I lost my temper."

Corin wondered why he was so appalled—after all, he'd never had any particular illusions about Tanzler-Yataghan. But it wasn't moral outrage that had floored him. It was the admiral's sheer stupidity. *My God! Is it possible that a man who'd try to get physical with a trained Ground Assault Marine has been entrusted with the defense of an entire sector? No wonder the Empire is swirling around history's toilet bowl.* Aloud: "Uh, you didn't . . . ?"

"No!" She shook her auburn head vigorously. "I said I lost my temper—not that I went insane! He's alive. But I left him unconscious, after I'd . . . Well, I sort of kicked him in the balls."

Corin managed to smother his guffaw before more than a couple of splutters had escaped. "Sorry. Not funny. All right, so afterwards just going back to your quarters and turning in for the night didn't seem like a viable option. You came here instead."

"After taking care of a few things first. I didn't completely lose my head. But yes, I went to earth here. When he comes to, he's going to be bellowing for my head."

Bellowing in soprano. Corin firmly thrust the thought down. "Well, what can he do? I mean, given the circumstances, he can't exactly court-martial you."

"Of course he can. On any charges he wants to dream up—charges completely unconnected with these 'circumstances.' "

"But . . . Look here, there's such a thing as an appeal process, you know."

She stared at him. "And I thought you were such a case-hardened cynic! Do you seriously believe any appeal process beyond the sector admiral's level exists any more, in any real sense? Besides . . . what makes you think he'll even bother with a trial at all? Why should he?"

Corin started to open his mouth, then closed it and thought hard. His thoughts weren't welcome ones.

His comfortable affectation of pessimism had been a prophylactic, shielding him from the full enormity of what was happening now that the Emperor had abandoned two-thirds of his Empire. Whatever organization remained above the sector level must have more urgent things on its bureaucratic mind than an aggrieved Marine major. As a practical matter, Tanzler-Yataghan was no more answerable for his actions than some baron of Old Earth's Middle Ages.

So, Corin thought, to his own dawning astonishment, *I guess it's time for a knight-errant. And never mind that the damsel in distress wouldn't even need her powered combat armor to wax his ass.*

"All right. I concur. Your life is in danger here. We've got to get you off-planet. Do you have any money?"

"Why . . . yes." His sudden briskness, and his voice's deeper timbre, had taken her by surprise. "As I said, I took care of a few things before coming here. One of which was to clean out my account via computer. I'd saved a little, and now I've got it all in the form of a general bearer draft."

"Good. Nobody will be able to touch that—or trace it. You'll also need civilian clothes—oh, you have them? Go ahead and change into them. Forget any personal effects you don't have with you. We've got to get you off this base right now."

"But I can't take the transposer without it being recorded."

"We'll take my slider. The sentries would ID a civilian woman I was bringing *onto* the base—but not one leaving it. Then straight to the Nambucco spaceport. We'll get you onto commercial transport out of this system tonight."

"But—but—*tonight?*" Her shock was understandable. This was moving pretty fast. And Corin noted her eyes straying in the direction of the door, beyond which stood the row of Mark 32-A's. The powered armor with which she mind-linked wasn't really sentient. But neither was a beloved cat or dog. And it was more than that—the armor represented all she was losing. *Has she even let the word* deserter *form in her conscious mind yet?* he wondered.

"We've got to do it right now, Janille," he said softly. "When he comes to, he'll seal the base and it'll be too late. This is your only chance. Better get moving."

"Yes . . . yes, of course." Moving like a sleepwalker, she picked up a duffel bag from beside the computer table and walked toward the nearest head to change out of her uniform . . . for the last time.

As they drove through the night into Nambucco, she sat in the silence of shock. It gave Corin a chance to examine his hastily conceived plan for flaws. It seemed to hold up. Losing oneself in the general population was far easier today than it had been before humankind had left Old Earth. In those days there had been but one world, made ever smaller by technology and divided among states whose appetite for control had been as totalitarian as their rhetoric had been democratic. But now, with swarms of planetary societies under a *laissez-faire* Empire only recently emerged from a centuries-long interregnum, the last resort that Janille was about to take—vanishing into anonymity—was once again possible.

"I shouldn't have let you do this." Her low voice interrupted his thoughts as they approached the light-blazing spaceport. "You're bound to get into trouble. It'll be the end of your career."

"I doubt it. The sentries saw me leaving the base with a civilian woman and coming back alone. That's all. I won't enter the spaceport with you, so nobody there will see me."

"But there's always a chance—"

"Undeniably. That's another reason for me to not accompany you past the gate. Just in case I should get probed at some point, I won't know where you went."

He saw her turn and look at him, but couldn't make out her expression in the dark. "The question is," he went on, "wherever you go, what will you do when you get there?"

"I'll think of something."

He essayed an attempt at lightness. "If all else fails, there are lots of mercenary outfits that would be glad to have you."

The noise she made with her mouth was at least an improvement over moroseness. "I hope you're joking! There are worse things than starvation. If I wanted to be a whore, I could have stayed right here."

Her reaction was as per expectations. Free companies had proliferated during the wars of the last four centuries, and Armand Duschane hadn't attempted to eradicate them. Instead, he'd hired them for his campaigns and gradually brought them under certain restrictions, allowing them no major space-combat capabilities or planetary-bombardment weapons of mass destruction. So they'd tended to specialize in ground action. To say the Marines regarded this as a form of patent infringement was to give their feelings an altogether too dry and legalistic coloration. Armand hadn't been displeased—a degree of rivalry has its uses.

The slider rounded a final curve, and the great terminal building was ahead of them. Beyond it, a cargo shuttle drifted soundlessly up into the night on gravs and vectored impellers, occluding the stars with its rising constellation of running lights. Corin pulled up to a curbside and halted, then turned to face Janille.

"Well, this is as far as I go," he said lamely.

At first she made no move to get out of the slider. She looked at him with an expression he couldn't define and spoke hesitantly. "Look, I know thanks are inadequate . . . I mean, all kidding aside, we both know this could come back to haunt you, and . . . Well, I mean . . ." She took a sudden deep breath and blurted it out. "Why don't you come with me? The way things are unraveling now, what kind of future have you got working for a fat fool like Tanzler-Yataghan?"

Corin took a while to regain the power of speech, because it was the last thing he'd expected to hear from her. "No," he finally said. "I can't. As long as the Empire still exists, my oath to it still exists too. At least it exists inside me." Suddenly aware of what he must sound like, he forced his features into a cynical grin. "The *real* reason, of course, is that unlike you I haven't converted my savings into bearer form. I'd be broke."

Her features quivered into a smile. "You really *are* a fraud, aren't you?" With the speed of combat reflexes, she grabbed him in a quick, hard embrace and kissed him with savage intensity. Then she broke off, and he had just enough awareness left to wonder if the glitter he saw against her cheeks was the spaceport light reflected from tears. He blinked, and she was gone.

The yellow light of 85 Pegasi, so different from the actinic glare of Iota Pegasi A, was even yellower than usual as the late-afternoon rays slanted through the bar's windows. Janille didn't notice as she waved for the bartender's attention and ordered another Promethean whiskey.

This piss-hole planet, capital world of the sector next door to Iota Pegasi, had been the only destination she'd been able to afford if she was to have enough left over for luxuries like food as well as necessities like getting drunk. So here she was, stuck on this largely desert world of Ostwelt, 85 Pegasi II, habitable only by grace of Luonli terraforming, watching a duo of already drunken enlisted Marines navigate their way through the bar's entrance. *This* would *be a sector capital, complete with Fleet base,* she thought, to drown out her whimpering inner cry.

There was a lot of movement of military personnel

in this sector, close to Admiral Brady-Schiavona's frontier region, as the bewildered Imperial command structure sought to redeploy its resources to counter the inevitable Tarakan invasion. Only, except where Brady-Schiavona commanded, there was no real command structure at all. It was every sector for itself, or at best cooperating on an *ad hoc* basis with neighboring sectors, for no one had any confidence in the Empire's ability to provide defense against that which everyone knew was coming. *How long,* she asked herself, *before the sector admirals begin to go into outright rebellion? We thought that kind of thing was safely in the past, for us to read about—unlike Basil Castellan and Sonja Rady, who had to live through it.*

Sonja Rady, whose body was never found . . .

A burly form shoved up against her from the next bar stool. It was one of the two Marines who'd just entered. "Hey, bartender!" he bellowed. "Yeah, I'm talkin' to *you*, shithead! I heard the lady order another. Move your fuckin' ass—an' put it on my tab." He slipped an arm around Janille's shoulders and brought his face close to hers, favoring her with a smile and a high-octane breath. "You just gotta speak up, Red. Hey, after this round why don't you and me get a bottle and take it someplace?"

Janille emerged from shock. She stepped backwards off the stool and thrust his arm away. "Get your hands off me, Private! And put yourself on report for touching an—" *But I'm not an officer anymore,* came the realization, twisting in her guts like a knife blade and stopping her in mid-breath.

The Marine rose unsteadily to his feet, eyes red with the kind of abrupt mood swing characteristic of his condition. "Don't get high an' mighty with me, bitch!" He reeled forward, groping for her. She shifted aside to avoid his grasp, and with the same movement pivoted on one foot and brought her left fist into the pit of his stomach. He doubled over, gasping for breath and fighting not to vomit.

Two muscular arms grasped Janille from behind, immobilizing her. "I keep telling you it don't pay to be nice to whores, Jax," said the voice that went with the arms. She'd forgotten about the second Marine.

The bartender waddled importantly forward. "Hey, this is a respectable establishment!"

Jax surged upright, his expression ugly. He grabbed a glass, smashed it against the edge of the bar, and brandished the jagged stump at the bartender. "Back off, fat stuff!" The bartender retreated, and Jax swung the broken glass toward Janille. "And now, cunt, you an' me an' my buddy Tomo are gonna go have us a private party."

Janille abruptly went limp in her captor's arms. Jax smiled and stepped closer, misinterpreting the classic breakaway tactic. As Tomo's grasp loosened in response to the deflation of her stiffness, she suddenly crossed her forearms, then snapped them outward, breaking free. Simultaneously, she brought her right foot around in a sweeping side-kick that connected with Jax's hand and sent the glass flying. The move unbalanced her, but she quickly righted herself, skipped sideways, and turned to face her attackers in fighting stance.

Ordinarily the two Marines could, of course, have taken her. But they'd had a good deal more to drink than she had, and her resistance had stunned them. They rushed her clumsily, Tomo first. He'd grabbed a stool and brought it sweeping down toward her head. She made a blade of her left hand, chopping outward against his left wrist and deflecting the stool, and with her right gave him a short, jabbing punch to the solar plexus, followed by a left behind the ear. As he folded, Jax arrived, roaring. He'd evidently sobered up a bit, for he launched a textbook combination of kicks and hand chops at her. She let trained reflexes think for her, rotating away from his first kick and coming around just as he was recovering from the second. She brought the edge of her right hand down on the base of his neck, hard. All at once, she was the only one standing in the deathly quiet bar.

"Not bad."

Janille whirled to face the door, from whence had come the quiet voice. A Marine lieutenant colonel stood there in fatigues. Behind him, impact-armored figures were crowding in. He turned to one of them and indicated Jax and Tomo. "Sergeant, get them to the brig. I'll deal with them when they've come to and sobered up."

"Yes, *sir!*" the sergeant replied with feeling. "You men, get these two scumbags out of here."

Janille slumped into a chair and studied the officer. He had well-chiseled features in a face of the young/ old sort, aged beyond its years by care. "About time the Patrol got here," she groused.

"We're not the Patrol, ma'am. We're scouring all the bars and whorehouses for our people who're on liberty."

" 'We'?"

"The 34th Ground Assault Battalion. I'm Lieutenant Colonel Nicholas Vogel-Sabre, commanding. And you are . . . ?"

Groping for an alias, her mind flashed back to the thoughts Jax had interrupted. "Sonja," she blurted, then hastily changed the subject. "But you say you're rounding up your personnel?"

"Yes. You see, we've just been placed on alert."

The last dregs of intoxication drained out of her. "You mean . . . ?"

"Yes. The Tarakans. The early-warning sensors of one of this sector's outlying systems have picked them up. A task force at least. We just got the word via tachyon beam, so we have some warning—though their lighter advance elements could show up any time."

"So," she thought out loud, "they've decided to bypass Brady-Schiavona, who they know is going to be the hardest nut to crack. Damned unsettling, how good their intelligence on us is." Belatedly realizing that this kind of talk might be incautious, she shut up and stole a glance at Vogel-Sabre. He was studying her with sharp gray eyes, and as they met hers he gave a slight smile.

"I already knew you used to be a Marine, after watching you take out two of my men—for whose behavior I apologize, by the way. But now, I'd be willing to bet you were an officer as well."

"You can't prove—I mean, I was never a Marine!"

"Well, then," he drawled, elaborately casual, "I suppose you must have been a mercenary instead."

She jumped to her feet, eyes blazing. "Why, you—" As she caught herself, his smile widened.

"That *definitely* settles it."

She drew herself stiffly up. "I fail to see, Colonel, how my background is any business of yours."

"Oh, don't worry. You're absolutely right: the circumstances under which you left His Imperial Majesty's service are no concern of mine, and I won't inquire about them. It's just that . . . well . . ." Vogel-Sabre's smile died, and his fine face's premature aging showed in stark relief. "Look, Sonja, or whatever your real name is, I'm desperate. My battalion is badly understrength. I can use anybody with training and experience—no questions asked."

She goggled at him. "Colonel, even if I was an ex-Marine—which I'm not!—you can't just go recruiting on your own, putting anybody you want into powered combat armor!"

"That's absolutely true, in normal times. But, in case it's escaped your notice, the times have ceased to be normal. We're on our own here. Unless Admiral

Strauss-Gladius surrenders this system, which he won't, we're almost certainly going to be facing a surface assault in overwhelming strength. I can't worry about legalities. I can't worry about anything except this planet's civilian population—which is going to *die*, Sonja, if we don't hold out."

She swallowed hard. "Colonel, I'd like to help you. But I repeat: you're mistaken. I've never had Marine training."

He sighed, and managed another flicker of a smile. "Well, if you haven't, you haven't. There are still a few civilian ships leaving this system. If you hurry, you might be able to catch one. But just in case you change your mind . . ." He reached into a pocket and handed her a commcard. "This will get you directly through to me." He turned to go, then paused and gave her a small salute. "Good luck, Sonja." And then he was gone.

Don't be stupid, she told herself as she strode out onto the street and headed for the sleazy room she'd rented, to collect her meager belongings. *How do you know you can trust his promise not to investigate you? Besides, these poor schmucks are going to die here. You can't make a difference.*

A whine of protesting impellers brought her out of her self-lecturing. A Fleet air carrier dropped down to street level, loudspeaker blaring the news that martial law had been declared. "All children of ages twelve and below are to be evacuated to within the sector Fleet base's deflector screen," the announcement concluded. "To repeat—"

Janille looked through the carrier's windows. They'd already collected some civilian children on their rounds. They sat, all ages jumbled together, adult attendants trying to comfort the youngest.

It's not your fight. Not anymore.

A little girl—Janille had never been any good at estimating ages—looked out through a window with huge, bewildered eyes, clutching a stuffed animal.

You can't save the universe!

The little girl met Janille's eyes and smiled tremulously.

You can't even save this damned planet!

The little girl was hustled toward the back of the carrier to make room for more children, who were being herded aboard in a tide of uncomprehending terror that must have communicated itself to her, for her smile dissolved into a mask of panic and tears.

Oh, shit. Janille turned toward a public comm terminal, fumbling for Vogel-Sabre's card.

"You do understand, don't you, that I can't just turn you loose without checking you out on the Mark 32-A?"

"Naturally," Janille affirmed as they strode along the corridor. "And you do remember, don't you, that I'm only signing on under the condition that no questions be asked?"

"That's the deal," Vogel-Sabre sighed. "Although a last name would be helpful . . . Ah, here we are."

He placed his palm in front of a security sensor, and heavy doors slid aside to reveal a large, warehouselike chamber. In the center stood a Mark 32-A, clamshelled open for boarding. The walls, ceiling and floor held devices that Janille recognized as the business ends of tractor and pressor beams. It was like every training room she'd ever seen.

She studied the Mark 32-A from every angle. It was seemingly unexceptional, with no outward sign that it was a training model. She grasped the edge of its upright lower half and, with practiced ease, swung her legs up and slid them into those of the powered armor. She touched a key, and the torso components swung shut around her with a faint hum of servos. Her body, clad only in the regulation nanoplastic body stocking, was now encased in a three-quarter-ton anthropomorphic construct of molecularly aligned crystalline steel which, given a trained operator, could by itself have won any of Old Earth's pre-spaceflight battles.

It also had a curiously low-tech look for its own era. Modern technology was quite up to producing strength-amplifying suits that were skin-tight, their very fabric composed of molecule-sized nanomachinery. But such suits could never provide the kind of armor protection that an older-style powered exoskeleton like this one could carry, to say nothing of its integral weapons. So the Marines continued to use armor of a pattern essentially unchanged since the General War that had ravaged Old Earth two millennia before.

Of course, the current suits added some new wrinkles to that basic pattern. . . .

Janille lowered the suit's helmet down over her head. It had no faceplate or even eyeholes. She was in Stygian darkness for less than a second. Then the neural interfacing engaged and she was seeing with the suit's sensors, just as she would move with its myoelectric "muscles." She took a minute to feel out the individual idiosyncrasies of the molecutronic brain with which she was now linked. The linkage presented no special problems; this was a normal Mark 32-A, within standard parameters. And now it was effectively her own body.

She ran through a mental checklist, testing the suit's defenses and countermeasures. All appeared to be in order. Then she hefted the eighty-pound-plus plasma gun that was the Mark 32-A's standard carried weapon. She inserted its butt into the firing socket that enabled the suit's own microfusion unit to power it. A readout told her the connection was functioning.

At that instant, with no warning, the interior of the training chamber vanished from her "sight," replaced by a desolate battlefield. Vogel-Sabre was giving her no breaks.

She got moving. Of course she wasn't really going anywhere, any more than her weapons would really be firing. The tractors and pressors, slaved to the suit, would apply just the right resistance to keep it in place as it duplicated her movements. She ran through the virtual battlefield at a speed a galloping horse could achieve but not sustain, sensors out, defenses tight.

Munitions landed nearby, and she grinned. Psi-ordnance, intended to panic her by invoking the cultural phobias of centuries. It might work on nervous newbies, but Janille remembered that her neuro-helmet provided psionic shielding. This was the easy part.

Her heads-up display awoke with the icons of incoming aircraft, screaming in on impellers. Their weapons crashed around her, but missed a target whose camouflage circuitry made its liquid-crystal skin blend into its background, and whose infrared shielding masked its heat emissions. Flying debris caromed off her deflector screen, not even connecting with the physical armor it couldn't have dented. She concentrated on targeting the plasma gun. The sensors automatically damped the glare and thunder of the blinding energy bolts she fired. Blossoms of flame flowered in the sky where her targets had been.

She continued to advance into the increasingly deadly virtual combat environment, blasting one threat after another out of existence. A glancing hit from a hostile powered-armor suit smashed the plasma gun out of her hands, as the pressors staggered her backwards as though from concussion. She righted herself and went to integral weapons. She pointed her right hand, fist clenched, and the gauss weapon in that forearm fired a stream of superconducting mono-molecular wire segments, electromagnetically accelerated to hypersonic velocities. A deflector screen wasn't at its best against projectiles one molecule wide; they sleeted through the enemy armor, shorting out its systems and leaving it paralyzed.

Janille had a premonition of what was coming, and she thought a command to the suit. The integral laser weapon in her left forearm began to shape-shift; its nanoplastic casing flowed and writhed, allowing components to rearrange themselves into new forms.

It was none too soon, for the crescendo soon came. An enemy powered-armor suit popped into existence in front of her, a few yards away. It hadn't gotten there via transposer; the device had little utility in a combat environment so permeated with countermeasures as to preclude the sensor lock it required. No, this was old-fashioned psionic teleportation. Human jumpers were few—a tiny minority among the tiny minority that had any sort of psi talent at all. But a powered-armor suit with which such a teleporter was mind-linked could, at great expense, be webbed with psi-reactive circuitry that rendered it an extension of his own body for purposes of teleportation's mass constraints. It was a new development, and one for which many Marines were unprepared. Janille had studied it because the Tarakans were known to make extensive use of psi power. (It was even rumored that they used questionable means to increase their supply of teleporters.) So she'd expected an opponent to materialize inside the effective radius of her ranged weapons. But the test was realistic—the teleporter spent the inevitable moment of disorientation on his arrival. It was all Janille needed. She lunged forward, jabbing with the contact plasma weapon into which her left forearm had reconfigured. There was a flash that momentarily overloaded the sensors' damping capacity, and the hostile armor collapsed in a fuming heap.

At that instant, the vista of devastation vanished,

and Janille was back in the training chamber. Vogel-Sabre stepped forward and offered his hand—a thing you only did with a wearer of powered combat armor when you were absolutely certain of that wearer's ability to control the pressure of the grip to a nicety.

"Welcome to the 34th, Sonja."

CHAPTER FOUR
The 85 Pegasi Sector, 4326 C.E.

The Tarakans were already commencing their investment of Ostwelt, the second planet, when the Deathstriders Company arrived.

"We should never have taken this job," Lieutenant Colonel Mariko Eszenyi grumbled, her lean, dark, high-cheeked face growing even longer than was its wont.

"We needed the work," her boss—the Deathstriders' commanding officer and principal stockholder—replied absently. He was studying the readouts of sensor data that swirled around the astronomical icons in the holo display. Seemingly satisfied, he rotated his chair to face his second in command. "You'll feel better when you've seen the money."

"*If* we see the money," she corrected, falling with long-practiced ease into the role of counterweight to his congenital optimism. "Which we won't unless the Empire decides to honor the contract Strauss-Gladius made with us via tachyon beam. And not even then, unless there's an Empire left to honor it. And unless we're still alive, which I doubt."

They both wore the Deathstriders' space service uniform of form-fitting nanoplastic, black and red with gold piping. There the resemblance came to a screeching halt. Colonel Garth Krona—his rank was, as per the guidelines laid down by His Late Imperial Majesty Armand, the highest a mercenary officer could hold—was an obviously heavy-planet man, with his thick, broad muscularity. Just as obviously, his ancestral world—of which he never spoke—was a cold one, where size was an advantage, for he was well over six feet tall. The overall effect helped account for his affability; nobody *ever* argued with him. His dark-brown hair shaded to reddish in the beard he affected. His trademark grin squeezed his hazel-green eyes into slits.

"Aw, come on, Mariko. Strauss-Gladius agreed to send warships out to escort us into the orbital forts' defensive envelope. And *don't* give me that look! It's in his own interest. He needs us if he expects to hold this system."

"Maybe you're right." Eszenyi's face looked only slightly less lugubrious than before.

"Of course I'm right. And now," Garth said, bass voice firming up from the tones of banter to those of command, "it's time for us to suit up and leave Commander Ying alone to do her job." He turned to the command station. "See you dirtside, Commander."

"Aye aye, sir." Free companies were allowed to operate their own transport, and the crews of those ships had Fleet-style rank titles. They cultivated naval customs of millennial antiquity to go with them.

Garth and Eszenyi went aft and donned their powered combat armor—not as up-to-date as the Marines' Mark 32-A's, but about as good as was available on the open market. Then they entered their drop capsules and, along with the rest of the Deathstriders, waited.

Mercenaries weren't allowed armed ships, and few of them opted for fat, comfortable orbit-to-orbit transports—you could never be sure there'd be some obliging soul to transpose you down at the destination. They wanted atmospheric capability, but not the sort conferred by gravs, for they weren't interested in wafting up and down in a leisurely way. The Deathstriders' ships were typical: overpowered lifting bodies, capable of fast, hard insertions. There were six of them, each carrying a platoon of power-armored troops and their supporting elements. Standard tactical doctrine called for them to drop the troops from the lowest practicable altitude, to secure the landing zone for them. That wasn't supposed to be necessary this time. But Garth hadn't lived this long (not that he was all that old, at thirty-seven standard years) by blindly trusting in his clients' ability to keep their promises.

Time crawled by, and Garth kept abreast of things through his command suit's HUD. He watched the vast silvery parasol that orbited Ostwelt crumple up under repeated attacks. "They've taken out the system's tachyon beam array," he informed Eszenyi over their private line.

"Typical." Cutting a target system off from outside contact was standard Tarakan procedure. 85 Pegasi was now unable to broadcast to the rest of the Empire. Next they'd be seeking out and targeting every receiver in the system.

As the Deathstriders entered Ostwelt's Chen limit, the promised escort showed up, engaging the swarming Tarakan ships *en passant*. But certain of the pursuers clung grimly on—mostly smaller vessels, for the battleships were staying further out, carrying on a missile duel with the orbital fortresses. Sweat broke out on Garth's brow despite the armor's cooling system, as he waited for one of those tenacious ships to get a shot past the escorts, for he knew he'd feel any hit on his unarmed ships as though it was piercing his own guts. But the volume of fire they were taking was less than expected given the number and tonnages of their tormentors. Then came the readouts identifying those ships by class. *Assault transports*, he thought. And he knew his decision to treat this as a combat drop hadn't been overcautious.

He passed his conclusions on to Eszenyi, who communicated them to her subordinates. And then they were screaming into the outer reaches of Ostwelt's atmosphere, and the ride became bumpy. Teeth-rattlingly so. The Tarakans were still with them—in large part, he knew, because the fortresses' fields of fire had been limited by the need to avoid hitting his own ships. He activated another private line and spoke to Ying.

"Go for the agreed landing zone," he concluded. "And contact Strauss-Gladius, or whoever's running things on the operational level. Tell them we're going to have to fight for the LZ, and that we can use whatever support they can give us."

"Including ground support, sir?"

Marines, he thought bleakly. *They'll be insufferable if they really do pull our chestnuts out of the fire.* "Everything."

"Aye aye, sir."

The Tarakan warships began to peel off, roaring back up to orbital space. They weren't intended for atmospheric combat. But the assault transports—essentially similar to the Deathstriders' ships—stayed with them, waiting for the mercs to make the first move. They didn't have long to wait.

"Commencing insertion . . . *now.*" Ying switched to the private line. "Shall I download outboard visual sensor input, sir?"

"Affirmative." All at once, it was as though Garth was sitting on the outside of the ship, with the star-speckled blackness above shading through violet to the atmospheric blue below, looking down—there really was such a thing as "down" now—at the dry planetscape of Ostwelt. As he watched, the drop capsules began shooting outwards and curving toward the sere land in a pattern that would cover the prearranged landing zone. His other ships, he knew, would be deploying their own drop capsules. A computerized voice droned off numbers, giving each of the Deathstriders momentary warning of his or her own turn to be inserted.

Ying's voice, still on private line, overrode the robot. "Sir, would you like a three-count?"

"Negative. I know my number as well as everybody else." *My, how noble,* he gibed at himself. But it was one of the things that made the Deathstriders something special. Most of the time, RHIP held as true with this outfit as did the laws of the ancient sages Murphy and Parkinson, and all the other immutable rules that governed human organizations. But when the time came for a combat insertion, the C.O. dropped exactly like the lowliest private. And every Deathstrider knew it.

Nevertheless, Ying managed to give him a little extra warning by killing his shipboard sensor input. For an instant he was alone in darkness with his neurally-fed readouts and he braced himself against the impact that came when his number was called.

Drop capsules were nothing but rigid ablative sacks; fripperies like artificial gravity were out of the question. The G forces seemed worse than usual this time, even for a heavy-planet man. *Can't be old age,* Garth told himself, to help ward off the black wings that beat around the edges of his consciousness. *I'm young for this job.* Then his powered armor's visuals engaged just in time for him to see the last of the capsule burn away from atmospheric friction. Then it was gone, and he was falling naked (if one didn't count the powered armor that his neurally-linked brain perceived as his own body) through Ostwelt's lower atmosphere toward the tawny surface far below.

Of course, none of the other Deathstriders were close enough to be visible. Still less so were the Tarakans he knew had been fired off by the assault transports that had stuck to his ships like leeches on the approach. The commencement of the Deathstriders' insertion had been their own signal to begin their own, and the computer-projected destination of the mercenaries' drop capsules had given them their target. But it couldn't be helped. Garth couldn't have worried about it even if he hadn't been otherwise occupied righting himself in midair and getting ready to deploy his gravchute.

Full-blown grav units compact enough for personal armor were still only a theoretical possibility. But the unit on Garth's armored back counteracted Ostwelt's gravity sufficiently to greatly enhance the performance of a parawing of immemorially ancient design. As he descended, he took in the landing zone and its environs. To the west lay the capital city of Karnthnerton and its adjacent Fleet base, the latter under a shimmering dome of spatial distortion that was its deflector screen. Beyond that was one of this world's salty, landlocked seas. To the east, the terminator was creeping up; night would fall on the LZ soon. Whether that would be an advantage for him or the Tarakans depended on who made the best use of it.

The arid, starkly beautiful landscape was rushing up. *Won't have the leisure to appreciate sunset over the desert,* he thought as he detached the gravchute and landed on the downthrust of his suit's integral impeller. He couldn't see other Deathstriders descending—their camouflage circuits, like his, would be activated, preventing their skins from reflecting the setting sun. But his virtual "sight" displayed them as icons. And the Tarakans who were following them down also appeared whenever sensors could provide any meaningful data. Garth noted one such return, and activated telescopic visuals in that direction.

Yes! What was landing over there was impossible to conceal, so the Tarakans didn't try. It looked like a blunt, ugly aircraft, coming in on vectored impellers. Then it was on the ground, and it began to change. Stubby wings folded up and retracted, and the fuselage rose slowly as a pair of mechanical legs unlimbered from its underside. Two arms deployed, terminating in "hands" that had been the aircraft's pod-mounted weapons.

A *Shapeshifter Delta*, he thought, recognizing the identifying details from intelligence briefings.

The Empire had never gone in for powered armor larger than the form-fitting sort that Garth wore, even though direct neural interfacing made it workable. It had too many disadvantages, of which high target profile was only the most obvious. But the Tarakans had decided it had its uses as heavy-weapons support for combat insertions. Garth had heard arguments both pro and con, from a cost/benefit standpoint. He wasn't sure which was right. He *was* sure that none of those armchair theoreticians had ever stared across a battlefield at a Tarakan Shapeshifter in bipedal mode.

And his readout was indicating more of the things coming down, like sheep dogs among the flocks of ordinary Tarakan powered armor. And he began to see the large-scale tactical projections, constructed from Ying's sensors and downloaded to his armor and thence to him. And he began to worry.

He and Eszenyi had a quick colloquy while he watched the last members of his headquarters unit—a very small one, given that his suit handled most command-and-control functions—descend and form up around him. "Get everybody into formation as per operational plan C," he concluded, "and get to the city fast."

"Affirmative." The Deathstriders began to coalesce into a preplanned pattern. Garth had little to do at this stage other than give general operational direction. If he had, the Deathstriders would have been an outfit in trouble. Everyone knew the drill, and most of the detailed work of tactical coordination fell on Eszenyi—a fact which she was not above reminding him.

Civilians sometimes wondered how ground-combat forces could survive long enough to fight each other, under the eyes and weapons of orbiting spacecraft. To the professionals, the reasons were so obvious they could hardly even be put into words. The cataclysmic weapons of mass destruction were ruled out not just by tradition but by practicality; it was difficult for a conqueror to get much value out of an expanding cloud of glowing radioactive particles that used to be an Earthlike world. Precision kinetic-kill weapons were another matter. But the countermeasures that pervaded the surface battlefield seldom allowed the targeting of such weapons, even if the spaceborne forces didn't have other things on their minds—as, in the present instance, the Tarakans were trying to fight their way in past the Imperial orbital forts and the latter were trying to prevent it. No, as a general rule the only answer to powered combat armor was other powered combat armor, close enough to see it. . . .

As Garth now found himself close enough to see the Shapeshifter Delta that strode in through the twilight, spearheading one of the pincers that sought to cut his people off from Karnthnerton.

His mental command activated his suit's impeller, and he jumped in time to avoid a rapid-fire stream of plasma bolts. His suit couldn't really fly, but it could do a long leap. He prolonged that leap as much as possible, stabbing with an integral laser weapon at a joint of the giant arm that was bringing to bear a weapon that could have incinerated him in his armor. Something happened in that arm, and the plasma cannon ceased to track. *I'll let myself think about all this later, and have a good case of the shakes and then get good and drunk,* he told himself as he impacted with the ground near the enemy behemoth's feet. His deflector screen kept the fall from being fatal or even incapacitating, and he struggled to keep the laser targeted on what ought to be the leg's vulnerable points. But then Tarakan infantry in powered-armor suits not too dissimilar to his own began to loom in the dusk, coming up to kill him if the oncoming Shapeshifter didn't crush him underfoot first. . . .

With a sound which would have deafened him had his aural pickup not automatically damped it, the Shapeshifter's fuselage/torso took a hit that rocked the techno-titan back, swaying on its legs for a moment before toppling over. *Marine squad-support missile launcher*, Garth thought automatically as he clung to the ground against the shock wave. When he looked up, the Tarakan infantry were redeploying to face a skirmish line of Mark 32-A's. He staggered to his knees, adding his own fire to the Marines'. They didn't need it. They had carried plasma weapons, while the Tarakans, like Garth's people, had landed with nothing but their suits' integral weapons. After a short interval of hell, it was over.

A Mark 32-A strode toward Garth, ghostlike in its camouflage, and a female voice came over the pre-arranged frequency. "Get moving! Most of your people are through, but there are more to come and we can't waste time with you." The speaker cut her camouflage circuits, and he saw a warrant officer's insignia on the suit. He wasn't about to stand on seniority, especially given the Marines' well-known disinclination to recognize mercenaries' ranks. He moved.

Night had fallen, and they passed through more than one nightmarish firefight in the flame-shot dark before the last of the Deathstriders were inside a field deflector screen in the outskirts of Karnthnerton. Garth was out of his suit and listening to Eszenyi report that Ying had brought all the transports in, when he noticed the warrant officer's suit—he was sure it was the same one—clamshelling open, and an auburn-haired woman clambering out. He walked toward her and extended his hand.

"Gunner, I'm Colonel Krona, and I owe you one big one. Thanks for—"

Heedless of his rank and size, she struck his hand away. "Don't thank me, *Colonel.*" Her tone left no doubt as to what she thought of mercenary titles. "I was just carrying out orders—and losing some good people doing it. And it was by sticking to your ships like glue that the Tarakans were able to get past the fortresses and gain a foothold here on the surface. We'll see if you and your outfit are worth it . . . *Colonel.*" Then she turned on her heel and strode off, exchanging ribald greetings with various Marines as they emerged from their armor.

Garth heard Eszenyi's chuckle. "I didn't have time to warn you. On second thought, maybe I wouldn't have anyway."

"Who the hell is she?"

"Name's Sonja—that's all any of the Marines I've had a chance to talk to know about her. Obvious ex-Marine officer, but not talking about it. Vogel-Sabre, the local Marine CO, recruited her a while back, before the Tarakans arrived. He can't hand out commissions, not even these days, so he's made her a warrant officer."

"Why? I mean, are the two of them . . . ?"

"No. Everybody's certain that's not it. He just can't afford to waste her. As I said, it's pretty clear she used to be an officer. It's probably why she despises mercs so much—to her, we represent the sewer she's fallen into." Eszenyi shrugged. "Oh, well, that's her problem. Let's get some rest. It'll probably be the last we get in a while." She gestured in the direction of the landing zone, to the east beyond the deflector screen. Far above, a firefly-like winking of lights told of the ongoing battle in orbital space. And descending fire trails revealed that the Tarakans were taking advantage of it to get reinforcements down to their beachhead.

No, we won't be getting much rest any time soon, he thought.

But, although he knew it ought to be the last thing on his mind, he couldn't dismiss the image of the Marine with the temper as fiery as her hair.

The last of the system's tachyon receivers died under the relentless Tarakan hunt. 85 Pegasi was as isolated from the rest of the Empire as if it had been in another galaxy. And the storm that now broke on it reduced all it had endured before to mere prologue.

Strauss-Gladius soon withdrew what was left of his mobile space forces from the unequal battle to the relative security of the screened planetside base. 85 Pegasi had to retain a mobile force in being, lest the Tarakans feel able to simply bypass the system and continue on. He kept this reasoning largely to himself, knowing that Ostwelt's civilian population—and not a few of his own officers—would have welcomed such a bypassing. But he would fight a delaying action for as long as might be. It was not in him to do otherwise.

So the orbital fortresses stood unsupported under the relentless pounding that gradually reduced them to titanic junk sculptures. They held grimly on, plying what weapons remained to them, as the standard year 4327 dawned unnoticed. But the defenders were less and less able to hinder the Tarakans from reinforcing their enclave on Ostwelt's surface.

That surface was spared the ultimate horror of unrestricted nuclear bombardment. The Tarakans' own landing forces were, in a sense, hostages against that; and besides, the enemy was seeking conquest, not obliteration. But the beamed energies that raved against the base's screen, and the tactical nukes that both sides used whenever they could do so to advantage, soon reduced Karnthnerton to ruins. Strauss-Gladius' firefighting teams, darting to trouble spots with the mobility of gravitics, held the threat of firestorm at bay. But when the Tarakan ground offensive finally came, it swept over a ruined cityscape under soot-blackened skies riven by the occasional solid bars of fire that were orbit-to-surface kinetic-kill weapons descending whenever one side or the other was in a position to launch one and thought it could achieve a targeting solution in the electronic chaos below.

For Janille, that landscape out of hell had become all the universe there was, and her life had narrowed to the wielding of her weapons. Her Mark 32-A received and expelled her waste products, and was supposed to keep her at a comfortable temperature at all times; nevertheless, she stank.

"Gunner!" Corporal Kim's urgent voice penetrated her fatigue-deadened mind. "We've got three Shape-shifters approaching from the north-northwest, spearheading an unknown number of regular powered-armor troops." Janille thought a command, and the new hostiles appeared in scarlet on the little map that seemed to hover in midair on the fringes of her vision. She didn't even bother consulting with the Mark 32-A's brain; it didn't take the suit's tactical analysis program to tell her they were in danger of being cut off.

"Inform Lieutenant Maslov," she ordered Kim.

"Lieutenant Maslov just bought it, Gunner."

She stared at Kim, and the others who were within "sight" of the visual sensors linked to her brain. Their faces were as invisible to her as hers was to them. But she didn't need to see them.

"Get the word out to all elements of the platoon, Corporal," she said quietly. "We're pulling back to the fallback position." She didn't bother giving its alphanumeric designation. They all knew where they were due to take their next stand.

"Aye aye, sir," Kim acknowledged in a voice that breathed relief. She had a series of brief colloquies with the squad leaders, then addressed Janille. "They report that there may be some confusion. We're not the only unit withdrawing, and we may get some stragglers."

"Can't be helped. Now, move out!"

They conducted a fighting retreat through that battlefield of surreal devastation, pausing occasionally to shoot back at the Tarakans who dogged their heels. The Tarakans were all standard powered armor, and the troops began to hope that they'd get to the prepared fallback position before the Shapeshifters made contact. Janille knew better from the sensor readouts she periodically had Kim download to her suit, but she kept it to herself.

At least, she told herself, the position itself was all right. It was being threatened from another direction, but—she fought down her automatic reaction—the mercenaries were holding firm on that front.

They were nearly there, and Janille had begun to entertain hope for a miracle . . . when Kim's final download crushed that hope. "Heads up, everybody," Janille called out—just before the first Shapeshifter came crashing through what was left of a building at four o'clock. One of its plasma bolts caught Kim and overloaded her screen. Luckily the corporal's communicator went at once, cutting off her screaming almost before it began.

No camouflage circuitry in that thing's skin, Janille reflected in a calm sector of her mind. Trying to conceal something that size would have been pointless—and counterproductive as well, because the terror the sight of the things produced was one of the reasons for using them. *And it's working*, she admitted to herself as she snapped out commands and brought her plasma gun around.

Two figures in Mark 32-A's, unknown to her, rushed

up with one of the particle beamers that took two people in powered armor to carry. They slammed the monstrosity down on its squat tripod of a mount, in the path of the onrushing Shapeshifter. A bolt of coherent lightning almost overloaded the dimming capacity of Janille's visual feeds, and one of the Shapeshifter's arm-mounted plasma weapons sparked and crackled with electrical discharges from a hit, and that arm flopped uselessly as the driver deactivated it to halt the spread of disruption through electrical systems.

Janille, who'd been frantically trying to contact the weapons squad the two had come from, started to open her mouth—but her cheer died aborning as the maimed titan came on, smashing a multi-ton foot down on the support weapon and one of its operators. A blast from the remaining plasma weapon caught the other Marine a glancing blow, and he collapsed.

Then her neural interface was bringing the voice of the weapons squad's sergeant into her head. "We've got the bastard, Gunner. Wait just a—*there!* Heads up!"

Janille was already down when the missile impacted at the Shapeshifter's hip, bringing it toppling over and crashing down across the lower half of the Marine it had—Janille assured herself—surely killed already with its plasma weapon. A hatch opened in the fallen giant, and a Tarakan in light skin-tight nanoplastic armor staggered out. With emotions she knew would disturb her later when she had the leisure to examine them, she took him in the chest with her plasma gun. In this gloom there was no daylight to let through him, but the expression still came to mind.

Her troops were securing the immediate area against the Tarakans who'd come after the Shapeshifter—and who apparently had been shaken up by its fall. She moved forward to the Mark 32-A whose head and torso extended from under the Shapeshifter's body. "Sergeant," she said, "two of your troops with a particle beamer fell in with us. I'm going to recommend them for the—" She stopped, for she was looking down at the stenciled name that the Mark 32-A's dead camouflage circuits no longer concealed.

Jax. And she had a feeling that the other Marine, now an obscene mass of crushed flesh and bone inside his flattened armor, was Tomo. She recalled hearing that Vogel-Sabre had returned them to duty because he couldn't afford to have anybody pulling brig time.

"Yes, Gunner?" the weapons squad's sergeant prompted after a heartbeat or two of silence.

"I said I'm going to posthumously recommend them both for the Silver Nebula. And now, let's get where we're going."

They made it inside the perimeter without further incident. Vogel-Sabre was there. "It doesn't look good, Sonja," he said after taking her report. His voice held a haggardness that must mark the face she couldn't see. She had no idea how long it had been since he'd slept. "What little data we're still getting from orbit suggests that their big push hasn't even come yet. But it'll be any time now. Get your people positioned."

They didn't have long to wait. All that had gone before paled beside what broke on the perimeter with a drumroll of heavy ordnance. They didn't have to deal with orbital strikes; in response to Vogel-Sabre's entreaties, the admiral released his mobile space forces, and they kept the Tarakans occupied beyond the atmosphere. But what screamed in from the ground and from Shapeshifters in aircraft configuration was bad enough. Night had fallen, and the glare of the explosions would have dazzled unprotected eyes had any been present. Those glares revealed the approaching Tarakan armor, ghostly in its camouflage, and the looming Shapeshifters.

Time lost all meaning for Janille. A robot with her voice directed her platoon's desperate defense of its

sector as her innermost self crouched within some
storm center of the mind and contemplated the fact
that only her Mark 32-A separated her flesh from
forces no unarmored human organism could have
survived for an instant. It was a combat environment
that made the most lurid visualizations of hell seem
insipid.

She grew aware that Vogel-Sabre was nearby. "Sonja,
the mercs have things under control in their part of
the perimeter. Krona is launching a counterattack to
take some of the heat off us. It's our only—"

The two Tarakan jumpers appeared in the undra-
matic way of all teleportation phenomena: they were
simply there, where they hadn't been the previous
instant. Janille didn't have time to wonder how they
managed to get the kind of visual fix required for safe
psionic teleportation—probably some kind of imag-
ing sensor using passive IR, downloaded to their
brains via their suits' neural interfaces. She just
screamed a warning to Vogel-Sabre, behind whom
they'd materialized.

The colonel whirled to face the nearer jumper. This
one was good—better than jumpers usually were, for
teleporters were so rare they simply couldn't be held
to the usual standards of Marine recruitment. He
regained his equilibrium more quickly than Janille
would have thought humanly possible, and lunged for
Vogel-Sabre with a weapon which didn't register on
Janille at first, because there are levels of horror the
mind will not immediately accept.

Deflector screens were ineffective against slow-
moving solid objects. The macelike implement in the
jumper's hand pushed through the screen and came
into contact with Vogel-Sabre's physical armor. At that
instant it released a cloud of aerosol.

Dis, Janille thought with horror.

Vogel-Sabre recognized it too. He started screaming
even before the swarm of nanomachines had eaten

their way through his armor and reached his body, reducing both to an obscene gray goo, neither organic nor inorganic.

Janille dropped her unwieldy plasma gun and pointed her left hand. That forearm of the Mark 32-A was still in ranged-weapon configuration. But there was no need to worry about hitting Vogel-Sabre—at this point, a quick death would be a mercy. Ionized air crackled along the path of the laser that drilled through the Tarakan's helmet. He dropped.

The other jumper was laying about him, and conventional Tarakan troops were swarming the position. Moving through a region beyond despair, Janille advanced, spraying one Tarakan with monofilament segments from her right forearm as she stumbled toward the second jumper. Just then the violence reached a crescendo with a volley of plasma bolts, and the camouflage-shimmering shapes of the Deathstriders appeared through the murk. One of them rushed up to the jumper with one arm upraised, and brought it sweeping down on his shoulder. The blade, glowing with the intensity of its molecular-level vibration, sliced through the shoulder and diagonally down through the chest. Blood exploded outward from the rent.

Janille knelt beside that which had been Vogel-Sabre. She'd grown used to the screaming, as inhuman as the body which produced it. That body was now melded into its armor in a ghastly fusion as the disassembler nanoids deactivated and the gray residue hardened. She didn't pause for anything as melodramatic as a last salute. She just put her laser in contact with the thankfully featureless helmet and thought the firing command. The form convulsed and the screaming stopped.

After a while she became aware of a silence that seemed unnatural, and of the combat-armored figure that was standing over her, its vibro-weapon dripping gore.

"Good man?" asked Garth Krona.

"The best."

"He shouldn't have gone that way." The bass rumble was unsteady.

"Nobody should." Janille looked around her. "Is it . . . ?"

"Yes. It's over for now. Damned near thing, but we held."

"We won't next time." She stood up and started to leave. "I've got to check on my platoon."

He restrained her. "Everything's being taken care of, Gunner. Come on. You've got to get some rest."

"The name's Sonja," she muttered automatically as she obeyed.

They moved through a series of semisubterranean bunkers under what had been a large building of Karnthnerton's outskirts, past chambers where Marines and Deathstriders, with a fine lack of distinction, were emerging from their armor. Finally, by unspoken common consent, Garth and Janille came to an unoccupied area. They emerged as though from steel chrysalises, and Janille stretched like a cat.

Garth fumbled in a pocket of his nanoplastic body stocking. Small objects could be carried in powered combat armor. He handed her a flask. "Vodka. From Lambda Serpenti. Best there is, except maybe what was made on Old Earth, before . . . Well, the best you or I can afford, anyway."

She snatched the flask and gulped recklessly. It seemed strangely powerless to affect her. "Look . . . I'm sorry for what I said before about you and your people. You saved our asses tonight."

"Don't worry about it." He retrieved the flask and took a swig. "I think I know what you went through tonight, with Colonel Vogel-Sabre."

"Do you?" Unbidden, the demons she'd been holding at bay for who knew how many hours crowded in past the defenses she'd finally let slip, and she lashed out at him for no reason other than his availability. "Do you really? Just how the fuck do you know? How do you know *anything* of what I've gone through? You mother-fucking—" She shuddered to a halt as a lifetime's self-discipline reasserted itself. He waited stolidly for silence before speaking quietly.

"I think I have some idea. I lost my second in command, Mariko Eszenyi, tonight. It wasn't dis . . . but it was bad enough."

Janille's features dissolved. "Oh, Garth, I'm so sorry! I'm such an ass." She reached half-blindly for him. His massive hands found hers. Then, by no one's plan, they were embracing tightly. And, with just a few yards of earth separating them from the techno-death above, they moved by an instinct as old as time into the act that was the ultimate affirmation of life.

Afterwards, they lay side by side on their improvised bed and she told him more than she'd ever expected to reveal to anyone.

"So this Commander Marshak helped you get away from Iota Pegasi?"

Janille nodded. "Yeah. God knows what would have happened if he hadn't come through for me. I'll never forget him."

"I hate the son of a bitch," Garth stated earnestly.

She punched him in the ribs. "Look at it this way: if it hadn't been for him, you'd never have met me."

"All right—so maybe he's not all bad." He hitched himself up on his elbows and reached for the flask. He took a quick swig, shook it experimentally, then handed it to her. "Last swallow, Janille." She'd told him her name, too.

Instead of finishing the vodka, she looked at him slantwise. "You know, it suddenly occurs to me that I've spilled the entire story of my life to you, and you haven't told me shit."

"Well, you tell such a fascinating story that I hated

to interrupt—*oof*!" He guarded his ribs against another punch. "No, seriously, you don't want to hear about me. I've led a very dull life. Nothing's ever happened to me."

"Right," she said archly. "That must be why you avoid talking about your past."

"I don't avoid talking about it. I just didn't want to bore you—and this is the thanks I get!" He stretched hugely. Actually, hugely was the only way he could do anything. He'd been gentler with her than he'd needed to be, as though caution to avoid inadvertently hurting a bed partner had become second nature to him.

"Come on! I've practically put my life in your hands. You owe it to me to tell me *something* about yourself. If you don't want to talk about your past, then tell me about your ambitions."

"Oh, sure. I can talk about that by the hour. Only . . ." His tone grew serious. "It isn't really an ambition. It's stronger than that. It's a . . . destiny."

She paused with the flask halfway to her lips. "Destiny?"

"Yes. Don't ask me how I know. But I do."

"All right. I'll bite. Tell me about this 'destiny' of yours. But," she added, raising the flask again, "it sounds pretty heavy—I think I need to fortify myself."

"I'm going to be Emperor."

The vodka that was starting down her gullet sprayed outward as she choked.

"Hey! What a waste!" he said, aggrieved.

She attempted to speak a couple of times before managing a kind of wheezing audibility. "You're joking, of course. Aren't you?"

"No, think about it. The Empire's just been reunified in our lifetimes, and now it's falling apart again. People have gotten a taste of what it's like to have law and order and predictability in their lives. So they think an Empire that can enforce peace is a bargain at any price. The time is ripe for somebody to come along and halt the collapse—catch the Empire before it hits rock bottom and splatters. Why not me? I've got the 'Striders—a damned good outfit—to start with. Of course I need to get my hands on some space combat capability—Armand's rules are a dead letter now—and start out by allying myself with some breakaway admiral and making myself indispensable to him, then—"

Once again Janille found herself speechless, this time with gusts of manic, uncontrollable laughter. "You're fucking crazy!" she finally gasped.

"Maybe that's what it takes." He leaned forward, eyes alight, and his deep voice lent his words a vibrant intensity. "Maybe Armin the Great was crazy. But unlike the other rebel leaders, he realized that after they'd overthrown the Draconis Empire there was no going back to the good old days of divided sovereignties. That's why he was able to sweep aside all his rivals and found the Solarian Empire."

"So you're an historian, too?" Her intended sarcasm didn't quite come off, and a wistful smile awoke as she recalled Corin Marshak.

"Not likely! But I've read up on Armin. Born into another era, he might never have been anything more than a medium-high-ranking bureaucrat. Don't believe the bullshit in the official histories; he was no war leader, and every time he tried to take personal command he stepped on his dong. But he won anyway, because he recognized a unique opportunity and seized it with both hands. That's all it took—and that's all it'll take now!"

She looked at him wonderingly. He was crazy, of course . . . and yet his sheer vitality gave an undeniable force even to craziness. Still, she found herself lapsing back into laughter and gasping for breath. "You're never going to get off this damned planet, you fool!"

At that moment the alarm began to whoop.

For some small fraction of a second they made eye contact. Then, without a word, they were scrambling into their body stockings. Then they were out the door, pounding down the passageway through a maelstrom of other running figures.

Major Torrento, the senior surviving Marine, was in the command post, leaning over the improvised comm station with its exposed bundles of gang-plugged cables. "Has the next attack started, sir?" Janille asked.

"Negative, Gunner. Their ground forces are sitting tight. But something's going on in space. What's left of our orbital forts are downloading the data to us." Torrento indicated the rudimentary sensor display. Something was definitely going on in the Tarakan fleet. Like an agitated hive of bees, the icons swirled about as they ordered themselves into new patterns.

"Maybe they're getting ready to finish off the forts and land more ground troops," Garth speculated.

"Maybe. But it doesn't look much like the build-ups before any of their previous attacks. Look, they're moving in one direction now. It's almost as though . . . No, this can't be right. . . ."

As the pattern in the display jelled and the Tarakans' withdrawal became unmistakable, everyone was too stunned to cheer.

The Tarakans left a task-group-sized force behind to keep an eye on the system and protect their dirtside foothold on Ostwelt. But there was no further activity, and for the first few days after that inexplicable retreat the defenders were content to rest and recuperate. Then the pressure of suspense began to build, for 85 Pegasi's ignorance of what was happening in the outside universe proved almost as difficult to live with as the daily proximity of death had been. Their inability to take any action—the Tarakan covering force was several times a match for Strauss-Gladius' surviving warcraft—didn't help.

"Maybe they think we've been too badly hurt to threaten their rear, and have decided not to waste any more time with us," Janille speculated.

"But in that case, why leave their ground force, and a task group to guard it, behind?" Garth argued, as they followed the endless loop of speculation that occupied everyone on Ostwelt.

"The landing force is stuck here," Janille rejoined. "And they couldn't leave it without spaceborne support."

Garth grunted acknowledgment of the point. A surface landing was almost a do-or-die proposition, for it was very hard to land, recover the ground troops, and take off, all under the fire of still-active defenders. The Tarakans had seized the opportunity to put a landing force onto Ostwelt because they'd been certain of their ability to carry the operation through to a triumphant conclusion. The question of what had changed their minds remained unanswered, and the two of them knew their latest circuit of the speculative merry-go-round had brought them no closer to the answer.

Garth was opening his mouth to say something further when the intercom spoke, in a voice whose quaver had nothing to do with the speaker's age. "Attention! This is Admiral Strauss-Gladius speaking. I am informed that an Imperial task group has been contacted, approaching from the direction of Iota Pegasi—"

His eyes sought hers, for he knew it was from Iota Pegasi that the past she'd fled would come in pursuit of her. Her expression was unreadable.

"—and the major elements of the Tarakan holding force are accelerating outward on an intercept course."

They pelted for the command post, for they didn't want to miss this. They were none too soon, for by the time they'd arrived and shouldered their way

through the crowd around the sensor display the
Tarakans were nearing Ostwelt's Chen Limit, where
they could activate their drives. Then they reached
it, and the scarlet icons ceased to crawl—they sped
outward at a rate that seemed impossible. At the same
moment, the display shifted to systemwide scale. The
green icons of friendly units appeared at the outer
edge of the display, arrowing inward at about the same
apparent velocity as the red hostiles who sought them.
With soul-shaking rapidity, the two forces flashed
together.

The tension in the command post was as palpable
as the aroma of unwashed bodies, for everyone present
knew there'd be no observing the battle that was about
to take place. Not from outside those ships' drive
fields.

Janille visualized the scenes aboard the ships, inside
the inner fields that slowed time down by the same
factor that the drive fields speeded it up. The crews,
to whom the ships seemed to be proceeding at the
rate they *would* have been making without time-
distortion drives, would be going unhurriedly to general quarters and putting their weapons through dry
runs, while their officers studied the enemy formations the sensors revealed and pondered tactical
options—all in the few seconds the silent crowd in
the bunker watched the hurtling icons in the display.
Then those icons came together, interpenetrating in
a sudden, angry swirl of colored lights. Janille didn't
have time to try to calculate how long the battle was
lasting for its participants; before she could even
attempt the mental arithmetic, it was over, and the
result they'd had so little time to sweat out was
apparent. A few fugitive red icons were returning
systemward, pursued by small, swift green ones.
Behind came the main Imperial body, arrayed in
unshaken order.

A long-contained storm of cheers broke in the

confines of the command center. Janille felt her own throat adding to it as she hugged Garth, all apprehensions momentarily forgotten.

She and Garth were still arm-in-arm when the leading elements of the Imperial task group entered Ostwelt's Chen Limit and could be communicated with. Torrento ordered the planet's hail and any response piped over the intercom.

The response wasn't long in coming. "Ostwelt Control, this is Task Group 17.1, out of Iota Pegasi," a voice replied with the instantaneousness of tachyon communications. "Let me patch you through to Commodore Marshak."

Janille heard no more. Nor did she see the look on Garth's face as he narrowly eyed the expression on hers. Nor did she feel it as he slid his arm from around her.

The Tarakan ground commander, not being a madman, had surrendered the instant it had become clear that the Imperials were in uncontested control of Ostwelt's skies. Now Janille and her two companions stood at the railing of the spaceport terminal's observation deck and watched the prisoners being herded past.

The officers among them all had the broad, high-cheekboned, prominently hawk-nosed faces of the original Tarakan ethnic type. The enlisted troops showed almost every cast of features Homo sapiens came in. But all had the same coloring—light green skin, greenish-black hair—for it was part of their uniform. The only exceptions were the minority who belonged to the crews of captured spacecraft, in whom blue took the place of green. It was a simple matter to nanotechnically rewrite the genetic code in as elementary a matter as pigmentation, and the Tarakans did so more readily than the Empire, with its ingrained aversion to genetic tampering. They likewise lacked

the much stronger response—bordering on a phobia—
to the cybernetic enhancements humans had once
surgically implanted in their bodies, beginning in the
early space age and culminating in the Draconis
Empire's obscene melding of man and machine. They
didn't take it *that* far, of course—if they had, the
Empire's war with them would have become a jihad.
Still, Janille's flesh-crawling knowledge that some of
the shuffling prisoners below were almost certainly
cyborgs should have made it easy for her to see them
as inhuman, as she was already inclined to see people
who used dis on personnel. And yet . . .

"I can't hate them," she remarked.

"I know what you mean," Corin nodded. "It's far
from clear who's most at fault in this war. At a minimum, our meddling policies over the last few years
have given them provocation." He turned toward her,
and his grimace was a self-conscious ghost of his old
cynical smile. "Anyway, it's not necessary to hate them
now. They're no longer a danger—at least not for a
while."

Garth cleared his throat in his seismic way. "I've
been meaning to ask you about that, Commodore. I
gather Admiral Brady-Schiavona's victory broke the
back of their invasion and forced them to withdraw
from this system, among others."

"That's 'Captain,' " Corin smiled. "I'm just a tem-
porary commodore, while I'm in command of this task
group. But to answer your question, yes. Brady-
Schiavona smashed their main force just after the first
of this standard year. He directed the operation, but
the on-scene commander was his son, Commodore
Roderick Brady-Schiavona—the one who fooled the
Tarakans so beautifully year before last. The Tarakans'
outlying elements, like the one here, then found
themselves isolated. It was at that point that Admiral Tanzler-Yataghan, over at Iota Pegasi, decided it
was practical to relieve this system." His eyes and

Janille's made a sidelong contact at the mention of Tanzler-Yataghan's name, and he hastily pressed on. "I'd only been a captain a little while. But I was overdue for a command billet, given the policy of keeping people rotating between staff and line. So I got the job." His eyes met Janille's again, and he seemed about to say more, when his left hand twitched from a painless neural stimulus. Muttering an apology, he raised his wristcomp to his ear. It was a military model; an integral sonic screen kept the message inaudible to the other two. He listened a moment, acknowledged, then turned to them with an apologetic smile. "You'll have to excuse me. Seems a courier boat from Iota Pegasi has entered the outer system, and it's squirting a priority message for me. I'll be down in the comm center."

After he was gone, Janille and Garth passed an awkward moment. They'd been having quite a few of those lately, since Corin's landing on the planet and his thunderstruck recognition of her.

"Well," she finally broke the silence, "I suppose you'll be leaving soon."

"Yes. The Deathstriders' job here is done. And thanks to your friend, we're in pretty good shape." Corin had taken it upon himself to certify the mercenaries' contract with Admiral Strauss-Gladius as fulfilled. More importantly, he'd used his discretionary funds to pay them off. There'd been a time when currency in the traditional sense had seemed about to go the way of the dinosaurs, superseded by electronic credit transfers via the comm network that blanketed Old Earth's global village. But it had made a comeback in the form of bearer paper which circulated freely throughout the Empire's wide-flung, diverse civilizations. No computer could bleep the Deathstriders' payment out of existence. For all the ambivalence of his feelings about Corin, Garth was properly grateful. "So it's time for us to move on," he continued. "There ought to be work for us over toward—"

"Can I come with you?" Janille blurted.

He managed to speak in a steady voice. "Don't you want to stay with him?"

"I don't know *what* I want! All I know is that I've got to get out of here. Now that his forces have relieved this system, Tanzler-Yataghan will have a lot of clout here. And I've put myself on the records of the 34th."

"Under a false name."

"Yes—but with pictures, retinal pattern, genotype and all the rest. I have to get away, whatever my personal feelings—" She jarred to a halt, wilting with embarrassment under his level regard.

"Yes, I could tell what those 'feelings' were the instant his name came over the comm. And I won't deny a certain degree of embitterment. But" —he grinned in his beard like sunshine breaking through a rift in clouds— "you're welcome in any capacity you want. If I can't have you as a lover, I'll take you as a damned outstanding soldier."

"Thanks, Garth," she whispered, but her smile was troubled.

Another awkward silence threatened to develop. A cheerful baritone voice broke it. Janille had never heard Corin speak in the precise tone his voice held as he trotted up the stairs onto the observation deck. It was a tone of release. "Sorry I had to run. But the courier brought orders for me from Admiral Tanzler-Yataghan. Secret orders."

"Uh . . . maybe you shouldn't be talking to us about them, if they're so secret," Garth suggested.

"Oh, it's all right. You see, I have no intention of obeying them." Corin smiled at their stupefaction. "It seems Admiral Tanzler-Yataghan has assumed 'extraordinary emergency powers' in the Iota Pegasi Sector."

"He's gone into rebellion." There was no trace of a question in Janille's flat statement.

"Of course. Lot of that going around, these days. Anyway, he intends to 'impose special security measures' here in 85 Pegasi to 'assure the sector's loyalty to His Imperial Majesty.' I'm to implement these measures."

"And old Strauss-Gladius won't be able to do a thing about it, after having his Fleet component almost wiped out." She regarded him levelly. "So, have you decided what you're going to do?"

"Oh, I decided some time ago. I've been expecting this." Corin turned to Garth. "I've got a proposition for you, Mister Businessman. By shifting personnel around, I can get solidly reliable crews aboard my flagship and two cruisers. You could use some warships. How about it?"

The big mercenary recovered first. "You *have* been thinking about this for a while, haven't you? And quietly making preparations."

"Well, as I said, this development isn't entirely unexpected." Corin looked into Janille's still-thunderstruck face. "Remember that last night on Santaclara, and what I said about my oath to the Empire? Well, Tanzler-Yataghan no longer represents the Empire. And . . . I've had time to think this out." A note of hesitation, almost of awkwardness, entered his voice. "The Empire is going to be reunified, one way or another. The moment is right for somebody to step into the power vacuum. And that somebody will do a thorough housecleaning. Tanzler-Yataghan will be one of those to go. I'm not going to wait around and be purged with him."

Janille and Garth exchanged a quick glance. Corin knew nothing of the destiny the mercenary colonel believed to be his. But Corin had looked the same facts in the face and reached the same general conclusions.

"I'll be honest," Corin went on, addressing Garth. "My first choice would be to go to the Beta Cassiopeiae

Sector and take service under Brady-Schiavona. But I know he wouldn't touch a deserter with a barge pole."

"And I'm your second choice?"

"I haven't had a chance to get to know you well. But I know what Janille thinks of you. Coming from her, any praise of a mercenary is high praise indeed!" Corin looked straight into the other man's eyes—they were the same height, although Garth was twice as broad and twice as thick—and held them. "Do we have a deal?"

"You'll have to give up those." Garth indicated the commodore's insignia on Corin's planetside undress uniform. "There's only one top man in the Death-striders, and that's me. Acceptable?"

"Perfectly."

The mercenary's signature grin broke forth and he extended a hand. "I think we've got some details to work out, and some planning to do for a very abrupt and irregular departure from this system. But let's go to my quarters and settle our preliminary agreement over a drink. By the way, remember what you were saying about how somebody is going to take charge in this chaos and become the next real Emperor?"

"Yes."

"Well, I've got to tell you something. . . ."

CHAPTER FIVE
The Beta Cassiopeiae Sector, 4327 C.E.

The conference room was on the uppermost level of the great orbital station at DM +63 137, like the reception hall, and it had the same kind of upward-curving transparencies that admitted the unwinking light of a myriad stars into the dimly lit chamber. That light shone on a long oval shiny-topped table and chairs which were mostly vacant, for this was no staff meeting. The select few people present rose to their feet as Admiral Ivar Brady-Schiavona entered.

"As you were," the admiral rumbled. As he resumed his seat with the rest, Roderick took the opportunity to view the others with new eyes, for he had reason to believe this meeting would be the start of much that was new.

Both his siblings were there. His father had pulled strings to have Maura transferred from the Empire's far side, and Teodor had arrived shortly thereafter. Now they sat across the table from each other, both in uniform—Ivar had reactivated his older son's Fleet commission, and used the latitude traditionally granted sector admirals to give him a provisional field promotion to captain. It wasn't just a family gathering, however. Jason Aerenthal was there, and so was Vice Admiral Otto Huang, Ivar's second in command.

"I've asked you here," the big admiral said heavily, "to confirm what you've already heard. I have been ordered to relinquish my command to Admiral Huang and report to Lambda Serpenti to answer charges of treason."

Huang gave a slow headshake of numb denial at the confirmation of the unbelievable rumors. "But don't they know your victory earlier this year *saved* the damned Empire?"

"Nevertheless, His Imperial Majesty has become convinced that I've been intriguing with the Tarakans to detach these two provinces from the Empire and make them a client-state of the Inner Domain. The evidence that convinced him seems to have come from captured Tarakan agents."

Aerenthal spoke smoothly. "It's perfectly obvious what we're dealing with, sir. This is a classic exercise in disinformation. The Tarakans are deliberately feeding this 'evidence' to low-level operatives who sincerely believe it's genuine, then setting them up to be captured. If they can drive a wedge between the Emperor and his best admiral, the sacrifice of some of their own people will have been well worth it."

"How typical!" Teodor piped up. "What else can one expect of Tarakans?"

Aerenthal smiled. "Actually, Captain, the technique predates the Tarakans by a bit. A most lucid discussion of it can be found in Sun Tzu's notorious thirteenth chapter, written almost five thousand years ago."

"Your analysis is doubtless correct, Inspector," Ivar said heavily. "But I see no way to make this clear to His Imperial Majesty except by obeying orders and turning command over to Otto, and going to Lambda Serpenti to state my case in person."

"Which isn't an option," Huang growled. "You wouldn't last long enough to make a case—not in that snake pit at Lambda Serpenti." They'd all heard the stories of the Imperial court, where Oleg lost himself in a neurally fed virtual world of erotic fantasy while conspiracy and intrigue ran unchecked. "And besides, I'll resign my commission before I'll take over command from you."

Ivar's jaw muscles bunched. "I will not accept such a resignation, Admiral. You will do as you are ordered, and—"

"Don't you *see*, sir?" The fact that Huang had interrupted his commander was less shocking than the beseeching tone that had entered the hard-bitten old war dog's voice. "It's you—your personal prestige, your stature—that's held these two sectors together while things have fallen apart everywhere else. The Imperial administration at Sigma Draconis is trying to carry on, but you're the only one even trying to implement its directives . . . and everyone knows it. You *can't* go!"

Roderick took a deep breath, licked his lips, and spoke into the silence that had fallen. "Father, this only heightens the urgency of what I've said to you before."

"And which I've ordered you not to bring up again!"

"I'm sorry, sir, but that's an order I must now disobey." He pressed on hastily. "The Empire, outside the Serpens/Bootes region anyway, is like a ship whose captain has abandoned it—and you're the only loyal officer left on the bridge. Tanzler-Yataghan at Iota Pegasi is only the latest to jump ship. It's your duty to take command. And you can only do that from Sigma Draconis."

"We've been over all this before," said the admiral in a voice which held impatience but lacked fullbodied outrage.

"Yes, sir. But now you have no choice. Oleg—or whoever is running things in his name—has, in effect, outlawed you. If you obey this order, you'll accomplish nothing except your own death and that of the Empire."

A generalized sound of agreement arose from the small group.

Ivar studied his slowly clenching and unclenching hands. "But this frontier has to be defended! That's my duty. Otto, if you assume command you could at least continue to mount guard here, whatever happens to me."

Aerenthal cleared his throat. "As it happens, sir, I have reason to believe that consideration need not be controlling. As you know, I've retained contacts in the Inner Domain—contacts I can trust. I have reliable information to the effect that a truce can be arranged. The Tarakans are discouraged since your victory. The Araharl is ready to talk. But he'll only talk to *you*, or your personal representatives. It's the way they think, you see."

Ivar looked up from his hands. His eyes were those of a man staring out of a private hell of impossible choices. "Every one of you knows that I have never sought anything except to serve the Empire—and the house of Duschane—to the best of my ability."

"Of course, of *course*, Father," Teodor assured. "*Everyone* knows that you're—unngh!" He glared across the table into Maura's bland countenance. Roderick hadn't caught the motion that must have accompanied the shin kick under the table. And Ivar, in his agony, noticed none of the byplay, but continued without a break.

"I've never had any personal ambitions, and still don't. I want it clearly understood that I'm acting only because I've been forced to—the Imperial administration is in chaos and there's no other way to restore order. I'm prepared to publicly state what's become obvious: that Oleg . . . that Oleg . . ." Ivar took a deep breath and tried again. "That Oleg is unfit to rule. But my loyalty to the legitimate dynasty is unabated."

Aerenthal spoke in his diffident way. "That, too, need not be an insuperable obstacle, sir. One member of the Imperial family, Oleg's uncle Julian, is in residence at Sigma Draconis."

Ivar gave a sharp glance. "Julian Duschane? But his career has been exclusively academic. He's never had any involvement in politics."

"True, sir. Indeed, one might say he's as apolitical as you yourself are—which means that, like you, he would never be suspected of ambition. Still, I am reliably informed that he could be induced to accept the throne if you offered it. Thus dynastic legitimacy could be preserved. Perhaps a new title could be devised for Oleg. 'Retired Emperor,' say." Belatedly realizing he'd let himself lapse into flippancy, Aerenthal subsided under Ivar's glare.

"Very well," the admiral said heavily after a brief silence. "So be it. Proceed along the lines you suggested earlier regarding overtures to the Tarakans. And have your contacts at Sigma Draconis—whoever they are—continue sounding out Julian Duschane. I don't want to know the details of either." He turned to Huang. "Have the staff draw up plans to seize Sigma Draconis. The operation is to be as bloodless as possible—that is to be the prime consideration. As an integral part of the planning, I want the public relations people to prepare a statement for general broadcast as soon as we've secured the capital, explaining that my hand has been forced, and that we're acting only out of loyalty. Until then, I want a communications blackout—no civilian transmissions from this system, and only those military ones that I personally approve." With an abruptness alarmingly unlike his usual stately formality, he stood up and stalked out the door before they could even rise to attention.

They all looked at each other awkwardly, as though each was waiting for someone else to set an appropriate tone for their reaction. Huang was no help; he left immediately, looking as preoccupied as the admiral. Teodor gave Maura a dirty look and made his huffy departure. She followed, shaking her head and chuckling. Roderick and Aerenthal were left alone with the starlight.

"Not bad," the agent approved mildly.

"I didn't rehearse it!" The young commodore knew he'd snapped at the older man, and had a fair idea of the kind of cold hostility his face must be wearing. But he couldn't help it. He wasn't even interested in trying. "I meant every word of it! We all know that he has to—"

"My dear boy, of course you meant it! I, of all people, agree with you. You hardly need to convince me."

"I am *not* trying to convince you!"

"Who, then, *are* you trying to convince?" Roderick's mouth opened angrily, then snapped shut. Aerenthal smiled. "So you see, you've no grounds for resentment. After all, *you* came to *me* for help with the dilemma in which you found yourself. Your father was, by reason of background, training and temperament, incapable of taking the action he had to take. So you asked me to—"

"I never meant to . . . to manipulate him."

"Then what, precisely, *did* you think we were going to be doing?" Aerenthal's tone lost its banter. "He had to be forced to act as the times require—be put in a position where he had no other option. You agreed, and asked me to take the necessary steps through my contacts at court and in the Inner Domain. I did so. I arranged for the falsified evidence to be planted and brought to the attention of those with a vested interest in poisoning what's left of Oleg's mind against your father. All at your behest. So spare me your protestations of sullied innocence."

"I suppose I never thought it through. I never realized what it was going to be like to actually do it, as opposed to just talking about it."

"Well, perhaps you really have lost a kind of innocence after all. And I suppose this incident will provide the revisionist historians with raw material, when they finally set to work on your character. Not, of course, raw material as rich as—" With the abruptness of a man catching himself on the brink of indiscretion, Aerenthal clamped his mouth shut and froze his features into immobility. Roderick didn't notice in his surprise at the agent's words.

"What makes you think I'll be of interest to any historians of any school?"

"Now you're indulging in false modesty, which at least is an improvement on hypocrisy." Aerenthal gazed at the younger man with unwonted gentleness but absolutely no humor. "Oh, you'll be a subject of very great interest to historians, never fear. And academic careers will be built on debunking the conventional wisdom by blackguarding your name—not that it will matter to your reputation among the vast majority."

Roderick fought a sense of unreality. Was Aerenthal drunk? "Surely you're thinking of my father."

"No, Roderick, I'm not. You have the one very crucial thing your father lacks: the ability to see what needs to be done, and to do it—regardless of its personal cost, and however much you may agonize over it later."

"What are you saying? My father is a great man!"

"No. He's a very *good* man. It is a perplexing fact of the human condition that the two are not always the same . . . especially in times like these. Your father has to be maneuvered into doing as history requires when it goes against his personal code of conduct. You, on the other hand, can recognize a moral imperative even when it seems to defy conventional morality. And," Aerenthal concluded firmly, "I've said far too much. Please blame my garrulity on advancing age. We scarcely have time for it. After all, we have a coup to plan!"

And with that flourish of his old cynicism, he was gone, leaving Roderick to his slowly cooling anger and his puzzlement.

◆   ◆   ◆

Roderick had been born on Prometheus, but he'd been away for years. Now he gazed at a holo display to renew his acquaintance with the system whose place in history was second only to Sol's.

Sigma Draconis was a G9v star, less massive and less hot than Sol but a close stellar relative. Its planetary system likewise had possessed a homelike familiarity from the standpoint of its twenty-third century colonizers. Indeed, it had seemed too good to be true. The second planet was really a binary like Earth/Luna: Prometheus (a near twin of Earth, old enough to have given birth to life without the midwifery of ancient Luonli terraformers) and Atlas (commonly called a "moon" but really a small planet with nearly half Earth's gravity and a thin nitrogen atmosphere). Beyond, where the ancient formulation of Titius and Bode said a third planet should exist, the gravity of the gas giant beyond had prevented planetary accretion, leaving an asteroidal belt far denser and richer than Sol's.

The system's untold natural wealth had brought colonists out from Earth in their hideously inefficient slower-than-light arks at an earlier date than might have been expected, given the 18.2-light-year distance. They had been North Americans and others of related cultural backgrounds, seeking, like all that era's colonists, to preserve one of the cultures that the restructured post-General War United Nations had decreed must die that Earth might live. Specifically, they had carried with them a smoldering resentment of the U.N.'s suppression of technological innovation and free-market economics. That ember had remained dormant over three centuries, for like the other colonies Sigma Draconis had gone through the motions of pretending to take seriously the U.N.'s claim to universal sovereignty. But it had finally flared into life, and the results had included the time-distortion drive and the Solarian Federation.

For the Federation's first two and a half centuries, Prometheus had been its working capital. The attempted coup of 2939 had ended that. The Federation had departed for the imagined security of the ceremonial capital of Old Earth, leaving Sigma Draconis under an emergency government-general which had proven permanent. The new blood that regime had introduced had been less important—given the already-diverse racial quality of the local population—than the militaristic orientation it had superimposed on the libertarian tradition. The stage had been set for an ideology whose totalitarianism had merely been the means to an end unimagined by its Nazi and Stalinist forebears: the differentiation of humanity into an anthill-state of specialized subspecies. The first step had been the caste of supersoldiers who had brought the Unification Wars to a sudden end, crushing and grinding the contending interstellar states into the iron-gray sameness of the Draconis Empire.

Those supersoldiers, and all other products of the Draconis Empire's genetic engineering, had perished to the last individual in the rebellions following the Founder's death and the subsequent spasm of civil war. Prometheus had been badly scarred, and Atlas—which the Founder had transformed into a palace of planetary dimensions—rendered uninhabitable. But the system had recovered, and reasserted its place as the Solarian Empire's economic powerhouse and military nerve center—a position it had kept through all the chaos of the Empire's collapse and the invasions, in which the official capital of Old Earth had so nearly perished. And Armand Duschane had made it the capital of his new Solarian Empire of Man.

Roderick shook his head briskly. This historical woolgathering was getting him nowhere. He expanded the scale of the system display. The golden dot of Sigma Draconis and the concentric golden string-lights of its planets' orbits shrank to a little targetlike object in the center of the tank, which now displayed on its outskirts the moving green lights that were the proper foci of his attention. The bulk of them were hanging back a trifle: transport for ground troops and equipment, convoyed by warships under his father's personal command, including the big battleships that could carry drive-equipped missiles. Those were more for effect than anything else, for there was nothing at the capital capable of contesting this force in deep space—even if it was so inclined, which was the great imponderable. The need to move swiftly, before Ivar's disobedience of the summons to Lambda Serpenti grew impossible to ignore, had left no time for the kind of preparation Aerenthal had advocated: feeling out the capital's defense command, and winning over—or buying—its crucial members. And there was no predicting what Vice Admiral Aaron Teller-Claymore, the local c-in-c, would do. So two screening forces preceded the main body: his own to the right, as the holo tank was oriented, and to the left . . . Teodor's.

The thought brought a frown, as always. His older brother's reactivation and instant promotion had been a necessity. Given the importance blood ties had reassumed during the last four centuries' interregnum, the admiral's family must be seen to be united behind him. *A phalanx of Brady-Schiavonas*, Roderick thought sourly. But had it really been necessary to tap Teodor as a commodore when he was barely a captain? His subordinate officers had accepted it because he was his father's son. And at least he had an experienced flag captain to back him . . .

Maybe that's the real reason I'm out of sorts, he forced himself to consider. *I wanted Aline Tatsumo myself. But I couldn't argue the point that Ted needs a good flag captain more than I do.*

But it wasn't just irritation at not having Aline. *If we had to have a family member commanding the*

other advance force, why couldn't it have been Maura?
In fact, he'd made the suggestion—which, he'd heard,
had gotten back to Teodor. But she had been declared
too junior, even though she had incomparably more
Fleet experience than Ted, including the combat
experience he totally lacked. And, besides . . . well, of
course it was out of the question. *Wish we could
change that*, he mused. *It wasn't always that way.*

He came out of his brown study as the holo tank
automatically resumed system scale, for their space-
eating effective velocity had brought them close to the
orbit of Sigma Draconis' outermost planet. Their green
icons crossed that curving string-light—a symbolic
Rubicon—and Captain Kalidj McKenna cleared his
throat for Roderick's attention.

"Excuse me, sir, but your fa—Admiral Brady-
Schiavona has replied to the hails from the Capital
Defense Center. He insists on speaking to Vice
Admiral Teller-Claymore personally."

"Put them on," Roderick ordered, and turned to
the comm screen. He'd been expecting this. They'd
been receiving the hails for some time, broadcast to
them by Sigma Draconis' great interstellar-range
tachyon beam array. Now they'd entered the range at
which shipboard tachyon communicators could send
as well as receive. He waited for a moment while
comm accepted the download from the flagship and
made certain adjustments, such as splitting the screen
he was viewing into two halves. To the left, his father's
craggy features wore their sternest gaze. To the right,
Teller-Claymore was speaking in tones of flustered
outrage.

"—I repeat, Admiral, I have no authority to turn
the system's defenses over to you. The Capital Defense
Command is outside the jurisdiction of your—"

"I will also repeat myself, Admiral." Ivar's rumble
overrode the plaintive bleat like a rockslide burying
some small animal. "You have just received such

authorization ... from me. The dissolution of Imperial administration outside the Serpens/Bootes region—of which Admiral Tanzler-Yataghan's insurrection is only the latest manifestation—has made it necessary for me, as commander of the only viable large-scale Imperial presence remaining on this side of the Empire, to assure the capital's security."

"But ... but I've heard nothing of this from the Emperor! I require authentication of this order."

"That is not practical in the present circumstances, Admiral. There will be time later to secure Imperial ratification of the emergency action I am taking, once the ultimate source of Imperial authority is ... clarified. For now, though, I am proceeding on course, and I must insist that you cooperate with my officers when they arrive at your headquarters."

Teller-Claymore had shifty eyes, and they shifted away from the pickup. Roderick imagined he was looking at a readout of the forces he was facing. "Very well, Admiral," he said after a quick, nervous swallow. "I accept your order—although with grave, yes, grave reservations—"

"I encourage you to put your 'reservations' into proper form, and submit them to higher authority as soon as all issues concerning the nature of that authority have been resolved. If you wish, you can also have my own signed statement that all actions taken in this system are by my authority and are therefore my exclusive responsibility. Signing off, Admiral." The two faces vanished from Roderick's screen, as the comm channels filled with a stream of orders through Ivar's staff—or, more exactly, through its computers. Teodor's command was, he knew, getting the same orders, setting prearranged plans in motion. He spoke the necessary confirmations to McKenna, then turned to the holo tank.

It never occurred to Roderick to wonder at the facility with which the green icons altered course. Two millennia had passed since his civilization had abandoned the old reaction drives that left spacecraft committed to ballistic trajectories. Instead, he studied the positions of the system's bodies. His own command was to proceed to Prometheus itself and secure the orbital station from which Teller-Claymore had presumably been speaking. But that was at opposition, and they were approaching roughly in the system's ecliptic plane—his ships' impellers were putting them into a hyperbolic course that would take them past the primary. Teodor would reach his destination first: the gas giant Cronus, whose satellary system held the great Fleet bases that policy required be positioned safely away from the capital world.

Time passed, and even the effective velocities permitted by the drive seemed like a crawl to Roderick. He watched as Teodor's ships crossed Cronus' Chen Limit—a distant one, as behooved a gas giant of more than Jupiter-like mass—and instantly reverted to normal time-rate, which meant they became effectively stationary in the holo tank. His own command swept on, under drive. So did the main body, far behind.

The uneventfulness had a mesmeric effect on Roderick, so much so that he barely noticed the sudden rapid-fire exchange from the flag bridge's comm station. But then McKenna turned away from the comm officer, snapped an order, and the general quarters klaxon shattered the quiet.

"Commodore," the flag captain said as he hurried up to Roderick, "we've received a distress call from Cronus. Our elements there have come under attack. I took the liberty of sending the ship to general quarters."

"Quite right, Captain." Roderick commanded his voice to remain steady. "Alert all our other ships. Kill our drives until we get turned around, then shape a course for Cronus." He didn't order McKenna to notify the flagship. His father would have heard. He didn't let himself think about that as he studied the holo tank. He didn't even let himself waste time damning Teller-Claymore to hell—it was pointless, even assuming this was being done on the vice admiral's order, and not by some loose cannon of a local commander. Whoever it was, he'd seized a perfect opportunity. With the main fleet still lumbering up and his own vanguard speeding ahead, this was a moment of isolation for Teodor—a moment that might be fatal. *Yes, if they can lop him off now, we'll be that much weaker when we face whatever else they plan,* Roderick thought mechanically. He consciously excluded from his mind the thought that Aline Tatsumo was there at Cronus.

"Turnaround completed, sir," McKenna reported. Roderick nodded as he watched the green icons, which had come to a dead stop in the tank, begin to accelerate in the direction of the third planet, around which scarlet icons had begun to blossom into malevolent life, intermingling with his brother's green ones. *Hostiles*, he thought leadenly. *The computer must not have felt a thing as it flagged Fleet units with red.*

"The admiral is trying to raise Vice Admiral Teller-Claymore," McKenna continued. "So far, he's received no response."

"Well, if he does we won't be able to hear it. Kill the inner field."

"Yes, sir." McKenna relayed the order, and they began to exist at the same fantastically compressed time-scale as the ship. To them, the trip to Cronus would seem as long as it would have taken under impellers alone. So Roderick would have tens of thousands of times as long to think about what was happening to Teodor and Aline as it took to actually happen. But he needed all the time he could get to make plans and analyze information.

"I want to see whatever data we got on the enemy

force composition before we went to fast-time," he told McKenna.

"I'll have it downloaded to your personal readout, sir."

There were few surprises. The bases among Cronus' moons didn't have enough warships to mount a challenge to Teodor's command. But they had fighters . . . swarms and clouds of fighters.

The little single- or twin-seat craft were useless in deep-space combat; they were too small to hold drives, and therefore could neither harm ships that did have them nor resist for a millisecond the fire of such ships. But a planet's Chen Limit acted as a great equalizer. Within it, fighters' maneuverability and the difficulty of targeting them came to the fore against ships whose drives could not function. So small craft were ideal weapons for close-in planetary defense, limited only by the scarcity of pilots who belonged to the minority capable of being trained in direct neural interfacing with machines of such complexity. Within that limit, they were extravagantly employed for the defense of important worlds—and nowhere more extravagantly than here, in the capital system.

In fact . . . Roderick studied the readouts, comparing them with the data for this system's defenses, and saw that his brother was facing far fewer fighters than could theoretically be deployed against him. *Teller-Claymore, or whoever, must not be sure of a lot of his personnel,* he reflected. *That limits the numbers he can safely commit. Hopefully Teodor will see that, and not panic.*

"Let's have a look at what's going on there, Captain."

"Yes, sir. The time-rate differential has given us plenty of time to sort out the sensor data." McKenna spoke a command, and the holo tank went to the scale of the Cronus subsystem. Moons' orbits took the place of those of planets, and icons representing individual ships maneuvered in a confusing swarm, practically frozen in time. Some of them blinked off and on, to indicate incomplete or conjectural data. And of course it was out of the question to display individual fighters. Crescent-shaped icons, representing the computer's identification of organizational units, hung poised like scimitar blades.

Roderick scrutinized the slow-motion battle, looking for omens . . . and one snaillike movement caught his eye, simply because it was counter to the general trend: a green icon, reversing direction and moving away from the fray.

McKenna noticed it too. "Uh, Commodore, isn't that . . . ?" His voice trailed miserably off as he remembered himself.

"Commodore Teodor Brady-Schiavona's flagship," Roderick answered the uncompleted question woodenly. *Have to use full names around here*, he thought in an irreverent corner of his mind. "Captain, reactivate the inner field. We need to communicate with him."

"At once, sir." The flag captain turned to give the order. As soon as it was executed, the battle at Cronus exploded into relatively rapid-fire action. And the retrograde movement of Teodor's flagship, as reported by the virtually instantaneous sensors, suddenly ceased and began to reverse.

"What . . . ?" Roderick's question died aborning as a call rang out from the comm station. After a few words with the comm officer, McKenna turned to his commodore with an expression eloquent of relief.

"Sir, fleet flag informs us that—"

"I see it, Captain." Roderick's eyes stayed on the holo tank, where the red lights were disengaging and returning to their bases. His father's voice intruded on his preoccupation, speaking from the direction of the comm screen. That voice gradually imposed its authority on his consciousness.

"—the return of all units of the Capital Defense

Command to their bases. Rear Admiral Bojador, in acting command, informs me that Vice Admiral Teller-Claymore has suffered a fatal stroke." Ivar's renowned poker face did not waver. "We can, in Admiral Bojador's words, rest assured that there will be no recurrence of the communications breakdowns that caused the unintended attack on our forces at Cronus. All elements will proceed to—"

As the mood on the flag bridge lifted like a fog, McKenna turned to Roderick and essayed a smile. "All's well that ends well, sir."

"No doubt, Captain." McKenna had heard robots speak less mechanically. The commodore's eyes remained fixed on the tank, and on one green icon in particular.

The Empire of Man had planned the Imperial palace on Prometheus, and Armand Duschane had brought it to completion. Oleg hadn't used it all that much, as he'd pursued his architectural fancies on Old Earth and in the Lambda Serpenti system. But it still hung in the skies above the capital city of Dracopolis by grace of multiply redundant contragrav: a mile-wide dish crowned with a profusion of domes, spires, cupolas, turrets, and other constructs. By day, it shimmered silvery in the light of Sigma Draconis, a magical floating castle. By night, it was a constellation of lights occluding the relatively drab heavens.

Roderick's gaze wandered out the wide transparency of the lounge, high in a tower on the palace's outer perimeter. It was night, and below him the coastline was clearly visible: the dividing line between the glowing cityscape that spread endlessly southward and the ink-black ocean to the north, marked out by tall, deceptively slender buildings. Atlas had risen, banishing most stars, and its light glimmered on the sea. That light was shot with red, in a way suggestive of blood.

All too appropriately suggestive, Roderick thought with a shiver.

He dismissed the thought and turned back to the study's cozy interior. It had the kind of decor typical of this part of the palace, the residence of the Grand Admiral (to which office Julian had appointed Ivar as his first official act), with its real walnut paneling, its rich heavy furniture and its well-equipped sideboard. Teodor was at the latter, refilling his brandy snifter and offering to do the same for the others in the room: Ivar, Jason Aerenthal . . . and one other, who settled into a deep armchair with the relief of age and accepted Teodor's offer with a murmured thanks.

"So, Admiral Brady-Schiavona," the seated man addressed Ivar, "I gather that your staff has completed an assessment of the threats posed by the various rebels, and preliminary plans for dealing with them?" He had a long, sensitive face whose expressive deep-brown eyes held a world-weary serenity.

"Yes, Your Imperial Majesty." The coronation had been performed with a shade more haste than dignity allowed, but since then Ivar had been scrupulous about addressing Julian Duschane in the proper forms . . . and about requiring everyone else to do the same. A cynic might have supposed he was taking pains to legitimize his puppet. Roderick knew better. After weeks of day-to-day contact in private, he had yet to see the admiral betray the slightest lack of respect for Oleg's scholarly uncle. Besides, he knew his father. Ivar *had* to believe he was acting in the name of the legitimate Emperor. That was his anchor in a maelstrom of ethical chaos, and without it he would have been unable to function. "Perhaps Inspector Aerenthal would present a brief summation of the rebel regimes."

"Certainly, Grand Admiral." Aerenthal turned to the elderly gentleman whose coronation had been his handiwork, and for the briefest instant they exchanged what Roderick recognized as a secret smile, for he shared the secret. Julian had no illusions about his role in the piece of theater they were acting out (*not* farce, for Ivar Brady-Schiavona could not help but impart dignity to anything) and was content to play it. Roderick, too, understood what his father could not let himself understand, and his self-disgust deepened as he watched Aerenthal suavely tread the boards.

"Of the various local rebels, Your Imperial Majesty, there are three whom we consider the paramount threats, by virtue of either potential strength or strategic positioning." The agent extended his left hand and spoke a short command to his wristcomp. The little brain and its equally diminutive holo projector couldn't manage any sort of detailed display. But an irregular spheroid of multicolored lights, not quite a foot across, appeared over the outstretched hand. "First is the republican movement led by Lauren Romaine, in the Ursa Major frontier region." The comp heard, and a flashing light appeared on the far side of the Empire. "The Ch'axanthu campaigns, as we all know, placed a disproportionate burden on the systems in that region. This legacy of discontent has enabled Romaine to take control of a wide area—and of all the rebels, only she and her followers present a fundamental ideological challenge to the Empire. However, the remoteness of the region makes her, in our judgment, the least immediate threat as well as the least accessible.

"On the other hand, Admiral Tanzler-Yataghan at Iota Pegasi—who scarcely troubles to conceal his intentions any more—is both nearby and vulnerable. Our intelligence suggests that he intends to assert control over the other sectors of the old 'People's Democratic Union,' which has become a power vacuum. Fortunately, he's almost as incompetent as he is corrupt. He's gotten bogged down in difficulties trying to impose his authority on 85 Pegasi, which his forces relieved after the Tarakan withdrawal early this year. So he is going to be our first target."

"I seem to recall you mentioned *three* threats, Inspector."

"Yes, Your Imperial Majesty. The third has come into prominence in the old Imperial core area, at Epsilon Eridani, in the person of an adventurer named Garth Krona. He styles himself 'General,' though he got his start as commander of a free company. In fact, at the start of the year he was still under contract with Admiral Strauss-Gladius at 85 Pegasi. I gather he was instrumental in holding the system against the Tarakans."

"Yes, I recall now. We all thrilled to the story of that system's resistance. What a pity we must now regard this man as an outlaw."

"Unfortunately, he subsequently came into possession of some warships—thus placing himself in flagrant violation of the Emperor Armand's statutes governing mercenary companies."

"Ah, yes. My late brother was rather a stickler on that point, wasn't he? How did Krona acquire this illegal capability?"

"As we've pieced the story together, the officer who led the relief force to 85 Pegasi defected to him shortly after arriving there, in company with some of his ships—an eloquent comment on the kind of loyalty Tanzler-Yataghan inspires."

Ivar interrupted Aerenthal's narrative. "Did this defection occur before or after Tanzler-Yataghan went into rebellion?"

Aerenthal understood the question's import. "The sequence of events is unclear, Grand Admiral. So the motives of the officer in question must remain obscure. But, to continue, Krona and his new cohorts—who, we can infer from subsequent events, must include some quite capable officers—moved on to the old Imperial heart worlds, where they found ready employment among the various squabbling factions. By now,

Krona has established himself as the effective ruler of Epsilon Eridani. His forces still aren't large. But he may soon be able to expand his power base, given the fluid situation in that region—especially at Sol itself, where there is still much support for the Retired Emperor." The agent had managed to get his term for Oleg accepted despite Ivar's misgivings.

"Hmm . . . yes," the admiral muttered. "Krona has shown himself to be adept at fishing in troubled waters, hasn't he? Still, as you say, his forces haven't grown to major proportions. It's just the astrographic position he's maneuvered himself into that makes him a problem. From every standpoint, Tanzler-Yataghan is the logical first objective." He turned to the seated old man. "Your Imperial Majesty, my staff has already prepared a tentative plan for the operation. In the morning, I will submit it for your consideration."

Julian waved a hand vaguely and smiled. "Please don't trouble yourself, Admiral. I have the fullest confidence in you." He chuckled. "*We* have it, I meant to say. Still can't get used to that. At any rate, consider your plan approved in advance." He rose laboriously to his feet. Ivar came to attention, and they all followed suit. Then, half-turned to go, Julian paused and faced Ivar with an expression whose complexity taxed even his mobile features.

"Admiral, I am nearly a hundred standard years old. I was born a subject of the Empire of Man in the last stages of its decline. I was in my adolescence when it collapsed into a welter of civil war punctuated by squalid, short-lived reunifications. At that, we were no worse off than the decadent wraith of the Solarian Empire that pursued its endless factional struggles and intrigues in the region where my nephew—sorry, the Retired Emperor—now resides. I suppose what I'm trying to say is that I have a longer experience than yours of what things were like in an age of disunion. Besides, I've spent practically my whole life here on

Prometheus, where we're never without a reminder of disunion's final end product." Julian's eyes strayed to the window, where Atlas shone in the sky with a glow whose red-shot quality was not a work of nature.

There was silence, for the shiver that ran through the men in the room was below the level of sound. Even Teodor was affected.

The motley coalition of rebels who'd swept away the Draconis Empire had bombarded Atlas—where the feeble second Emperor and the courtiers who'd manipulated him had cowered in the Founder's legendary palace—from orbit. They'd bombarded it until no life existed, or could exist, on its surface. Then they'd bombarded it until its atmosphere was blasted into space. Then they'd bombarded it until its very crust had buckled and cracked under the intolerable energies of antimatter annihilation, exposing the magma below. Military logic had had nothing to do with it. The human soul, hurt and brutalized for two centuries, had needed something to rend and tear at.

"After they'd done that," Julian Duschane spoke into the silence, "they didn't let the final bout of civil war last long. They knew that unity was essential. But the Draconis Empire had taught them that unity could have too high a price. This was the starting point of all subsequent political thought. That government should be unitary but limited has been beyond debate for eight hundred years. Which, by the way, is why Romaine, though admirable in many ways, will fail. She wants a federal republic. But federalism represents a compromise that smacks of divided sovereignties. It inevitably wears away, for too many factions find the central government too useful a tool for advancing their agendas. And when it does, it leaves a body politic with no antibodies against coercive utopianism. Old Earth's history around the dawn of the space age provides melancholy illustrations." he smiled gently. "Sorry. Lecturing is an inveterate

academic habit, and digression a hallmark of age. My
point, Admiral, is this. You are the one man who can
complete my brother's work by reimposing the unity
we need. I'm confident you'll succeed. But that unity
must be one of reconciliation, under an Emperor with
a clear awareness of limits. My brother saw this. I
believe my nephew did too, at first, even though his
character flaws prevented him from sustaining the
necessary balance."

The admiral's brow furrowed with puzzlement.
"Why are you telling *me* this, Your Imperial Majesty?
I'm nothing more than a servant of the Empire, and
of the dynasty. It isn't for me to set policy."

"Of course, Admiral, of course." Julian smiled his
gentle smile. "I merely wish to anticipate all possible
contingencies. Some of which" —the brown eyes
momentarily hardened— "must inevitably arise, sooner
or later."

This time Ivar kept silent, for there was no acceptable way of alluding to Julian's fundamental dynastic
deficiency: he had no children, nor any realistic expec-
tation of producing any. The admiral had overlooked
this in his relief when Aerenthal had produced a
Duschane like a rabbit from a hat. Only afterwards
had he come belatedly to the realization that the
agent's "solution" merely postponed the problem.

Aerenthal, of course, had never lost sight of this
for a second. Neither had Julian, judging from the
flash of ironic eye contact between them that Roderick
once again recognized—for he shared their knowledge,
and knew he shared it, which fueled his sense of
betrayal.

"And now, I really must bid you gentlemen good
night." Julian departed, followed shortly by Aerenthal.
The admiral, thoughts obviously far distant, muttered
his good nights and was halfway to the door when
Teodor, after a fortifying gulp of brandy, stepped
forward.

"Father! Am I correct in believing that Rod is going to be in command of the offensive against Tanzler-Yataghan?"

Roderick's face felt as flushed as his brother's looked. "I'll be obliged, Ted, if you don't discuss me in the third person when I'm standing in the room."

"Ummm?" The admiral came out of his abstraction. "Oh, yes, Ted. That's the plan. The politics of it—first operation carried out in the name of the Emperor Julian, and all that—mandate that a family member be in operational command."

Teodor held his father's eyes, making it a conversation between the two of them and pointedly excluding Roderick. *He's always had a way of doing that*, Roderick thought, anger twisting his gut as it so often did when his older brother was present. "May I remind you, sir, that he isn't the only family member available?" Teodor prompted.

Ivar spoke in soothing tones before Roderick could erupt. "The operation may be a difficult one, Ted. Not that we expect much effective resistance from Tanzler-Yataghan. But we plan to proceed directly to secure the other sectors of the old People's Democratic Union. Rod was judged to be the logical choice, given his combat experience and the prestige he commands among—"

"Then, sir, may I ask when I can expect to be given responsibilities commensurate with my status as your firstborn son?" Teodor gave his brother a toxic look. "The firstborn . . . and the one who can realistically be expected to survive you."

Roderick's rage came to a boil and spilled over. "Why, you—"

"Boys, boys!" Ivar's voice rose, but it was too weary to be hold real force. "Calm down, Rod. And Ted, that was uncalled for." He took a deep breath. "You must remember, Ted, that your rank is newly acquired. Such rapid promotion wouldn't have been possible in more stable times. Even now, it doesn't carry automatic moral authority to command. That must be earned."

Teodor spoke carefully. "That's all I'm asking, sir: the chance to gain experience and the respect that goes with it." Tipsy shrewdness: "It would make me far more useful to you . . . and to His Imperial Majesty."

"Yes, yes. Something to be said for that," Ivar rumbled. "I'll keep it in mind. But for now, the plan is set. And I insist that there be no quarreling between the two of you. We must stand together—and be *seen* to stand together."

"Of course, Father," they mumbled in unison.

"Good. And now, I'm tired. Good night."

As the door closed, Teodor returned to the sideboard without a glance at his brother and proceeded to refill his snifter. Roderick spoke to his back. "Unlike the great wines of Old Earth, you don't improve with age. If anything, you've become even more of a back-stabbing shit."

"What did you expect me to do?" Teodor asked without turning around. "Who's going to look after my interests if I don't? After you've had all this time to suck up to him and entrench yourself as his pride and joy who followed him into a Fleet career—"

"Spare me your self-pity. You know damned well that you can do no wrong in his eyes, and never could. He'll overlook anything in his firstborn. Otherwise he never would have jumped you up to captain's rank. It would have made a laughingstock of anybody but him. Speaking of which . . . since you never *were* interested in a Fleet career, what are you doing back here now?"

"Oh, come on!" Teodor whirled around and glared. Even at this moment, to his intense annoyance, Roderick couldn't help but be struck by his brother's handsomeness, verging on beauty. The thick wavy hair, in which several shades of blond mingled; the classical features, whose echoes of their mother always brought warm afternoon-colored memories to spoil the pristine purity of Roderick's dislike; the pure-blue eyes . . . which now held a feverish glint that wasn't all alcohol. "I'm here for the same reason you are. You don't fool anybody, you know. You're just trying to position yourself for the succession."

"What are you talking about?"

"Don't give me that!" Teodor waved at the door through which Julian had departed, spilling brandy. "As soon as that pedantic, doddering old faggot dies—"

"Father wouldn't forgive that kind of talk even from you."

"Well, he's not going to hear about it . . . unless you go tale-bearing to him like you always did. Which would make you a hypocrite on top of everything else, because you and that damned spy knew precisely what you were doing when you arranged to set up His Imperial Queerness as reigning puppet. It was never anything but a move in your little game of making Father Emperor!"

Roderick stood speechless in the eye of a hurricane of conflicting emotions. Dimly, as though from a great distance, he heard Teodor's voice take on a mollifying tone. "Now, don't misunderstand me. I agree with you completely! These things have to be done in stages, and Julian is as good a transitional Emperor as any. And Father *ought* to be on the throne. He's the only one who can restore order. And remember, we're distantly related to the Duschanes . . . and even to the ruling house of the old Solarian Empire, if there's any truth to that old family legend. So you see, I'm on your side. And I do realize that I have no presumptive right to follow him on the throne; the Emperor has always had the right to choose his successor from among his blood relatives. All I ask is a fair chance to prove my worth to him. And besides . . . I apologize for what I said earlier, but we've got to face facts. Even if you outlive him, I *am* the logical choice if we want a lengthy second reign in which to build a solid foundation for the new dynasty. And even if he chooses you, I'll still have a good few years left after you die. So I'd be an obvious choice as *your* successor. So you see," he finished, with the smile that could sometimes dazzle even Roderick, "Father is absolutely right: we need to stick together."

"You haven't covered all the possibilities, you know. Aren't you forgetting Maura?"

Teodor waved a dismissive hand. "A new dynasty needs all the continuity and tradition it can get. Father won't want to introduce *unnecessary* innovations like . . . well, you know."

Roderick released a long breath. "Now I finally understand why you discovered a well-concealed enthusiasm to resume your Fleet service. And why you're begging Father to make a fool of himself by giving you commands for which you're totally unqualified."

The sky-blue eyes flashed again. "How do you know? What makes you so sure? I might surprise you if I could just—"

"Lack of experience alone would disqualify you— to say nothing of . . ." Roderick hesitated on the brink of things he hadn't intended to say.

Teodor misinterpreted the pause. "Of *what*? What do you know, or think you know, that would rule me out for higher command?"

Roderick's resolve to hold his knowledge in reserve vanished, and he spoke one quiet sentence. "I've talked to Aline Tatsumo."

Teodor's face froze.

It had been just after their arrival. Everyone had been euphoric over their reception. The fighting at Cronus had been the work of the late Admiral Teller-Claymore, everyone had assured them. Ivar Brady-Schiavona's home system had welcomed him with open arms, and the general enthusiasm had extended to the announcement that a new Emperor reigned on Prometheus. With all the hoopla, it had been a while before Roderick's former flag captain had managed to get a message through, asking in oddly secretive terms for a meeting. They'd rendezvoused in the most inconspicuous possible place: the crowded officers' club. She'd had to yell into his ear the tale she'd meant to whisper.

"So you're saying he wanted to turn tail at the first sign of hostility?" he had shouted back over the din.

She'd nodded and taken a pull on her drink. "He panicked—went completely to pieces. I thought he was going to wet himself. I argued with him as long as I could. He finally threatened to have me arrested. We only got a little way before they caved in. Nobody but you noticed. He was hoping nobody at all had. And . . . he threatened me. Said my career would be over if I ever said anything about it." She'd lifted her glass again. Ordinarily, she drank very little. "I had to take it seriously, sir, considering who he is—and who his father is."

"Of course you did," he'd replied. "I'm surprised you took the risk of telling me all this."

"Well, sir," she'd replied, a little embarrassed, "I'm sure it must seem a little odd, what with his being your brother. But I . . . well, I know you. I know you'd never—"

"You're right," he'd assured her firmly. "I appreciate your trust. And I guarantee that you'll never regret having extended it."

Now he held his brother's eyes and said, "Yes, I spoke to her. I know everything—including your threats against her. And I'm going to make it my business to assure that you will regret it if you make any attempt to carry through on those threats. In other words, Aline Tatsumo is now under my personal protection. Do I make myself clear?"

Those vividly blue eyes shifted to and fro with a fear different from that which must have filled them at Cronus. "Have you . . . ?"

"No." Roderick sighed. "What would be the point? Father would never believe it of his golden Ted. He'll have to see it for himself . . . and I hope not too many good people die in the course of the demonstration. But *I'll* know. I probably can't prevent him from putting you in some higher command position, if you keep wheedling for it. Just try not to disgrace the uniform you have no business wearing."

He turned on his heel and left without a backward glance at the face that so disturbingly resembled his mother's.

CHAPTER SIX
Neustria (Epsilon Eridani II), 4328 C.E.

"So Tanzler-Yataghan is dead?"

"Certifiably," Garth assured. "After Roderick Brady-Schiavona wiped out his fleet, his officers suddenly discovered where their true loyalties had lain all along."

"It's possible that you're being too cynical," Corin cautioned. "I know a lot of those people, and I imagine many of them really were looking for an opportunity to turn on Tanzler-Yataghan—because, you see, I also knew *him*."

"Maybe you're right. At any rate, I understand Brady-Schiavona wasn't entirely pleased. He would have preferred a prisoner to a corpse. His father's policy is to co-opt surrendered enemies—give them posts in his own forces and let them prove themselves. Still, he's now got the Iota Pegasi Sector wrapped up tight, and is already starting to occupy the rest of the old People's Democratic Union." Garth gazed shrewdly out from under heavy brows. "What's the matter, Corin? I just confirmed what you thought all along: that Tanzler-Yataghan was living on borrowed time. Why the long face?"

"That's right," Janille put in, doing her bit by refilling Corin's wine glass. "This vindicates your decision to put as much distance between him and yourself as possible."

"Does it? I suppose so." Corin took a sip. The local wines lived up to their reputation; they'd even made a believer out of Garth. But unwelcome emotions came between him and full enjoyment of either the wine or the news. His eyes kept straying to the sleeve of his uniform. Garth had agreed with him that the Deathstriders' new deep-space component needed a distinctive uniform to go with its distinctive rank titles. ("A separation of services is a sound idea," the big mercenary had remarked sagely. "Everybody needs somebody to look down on.") He'd done it by simply reversing colors; instead of red faced with black, Corin wore black faced with red. Either way, it couldn't conceivably be mistaken for the Imperial services' grays, with flashes of color to denote branches.

"Yes, I suppose so," Corin repeated, as much to himself as to his companions. "I did the sensible thing . . . like a rat leaving a sinking ship."

"Ha!" Janille's bark of laughter held no humor. "The only rat on *this* sinking ship was the captain! You worry too much." Her only visible response to the news of Tanzler-Yataghan's death had been one of profound satisfaction.

"She's right." Garth nodded emphatically. "Anybody can see you made the right move. We—the three of us—make a good team. Haven't we done well so far?" He underlined his rhetorical question with a wave that took in the elegantly appointed office and the view through the wide old-fashioned windows, which overlooked the planetary capital of Haulteclere.

It was certainly a prospect calculated to soothe anxieties. Only eleven light-years from Sol, Epsilon Eridani had been among the first destinations for slower-than-light interstellar colonizers. That early tide of colonization had tended to branch into streams of distinct ethnic character, laying the foundations of the multisystemic states that were to dominate the age after the Federation withered away to insignificance. The Eridanus region had drawn Western Europeans, who in turn had followed their various national affinities. The resulting planetary particularisms had, in the end, brought about the partition of the Greater Eridanus Combine—unfortunately at precisely the time when it had been the "Protector-State" of the moment, standing between the thirty-third century's delicate interstellar order and total war. But Neustria's settlers, mostly from an Old Earth country called "France," had left a mark on this world that still persisted even though the population was by now as mixed as it was everywhere else. That imprint was most visible in Haulteclere's Old City, surrounding the capitol building in whose upper storeys they sat. Beyond, the soaring ramparts of modern towers gleamed in the afternoon light of Epsilon Eridani. Still further out, the land rose toward the distant peaks of the Massif Dornier. The lower slopes were covered with mixed vegetation; higher up, the bluish-green of Luonli plants predominated, legacy of the ecology established by this planet's terraformers.

I've heard rumors that one or two Luonli are still alive, in the mountains. . . .

"Yes," Garth's basso interrupted Corin's reverie as the recently self-promoted general answered his own question. "We've got this system sewed up, and the feelers we've gotten from Chewning at Sol are promising. Pretty soon it'll be time for our next move."

"It had better be soon," Janille observed dourly. Like Garth, she wore the original Deathstrider uniform—in her case, with lieutenant colonel's insignia on the cuffs. "Brady-Schiavona is rapidly becoming the most powerful factor in the Empire. And when his son has finished consolidating the sectors beyond Iota Pegasi his power base will be in a different class than everybody else's."

Garth's face wore that look of serene unconcern which could be maddening to people not blessed with his kind of certitude. "Brady-Schiavona could make himself Emperor, all right—if that was his ambition. But he doesn't have the fire in his belly. Look at the way he's saddled himself with a puppet Emperor instead of acting on his own. Besides, this is going to be decided largely by who's best positioned; and that 'power base' of his is in the outer fringe areas."

"Not any more. He's seized the capital!"

"But not the secondary capital of Old Earth. In the end, the game will go to whoever holds both capital systems, Sigma Draconis and Sol. And when I'm in control of Sol I'll be able to—"

"Chewning might have something to say about that," Janille cautioned. "At last report, when he says 'Jump,' everybody at Sol asks 'How high?' on the way up."

"But he won't be able to keep control there—not without my help. The first time somebody mounts a serious attack against him, I'll be able to make myself indispensable to him, just like I did with old Delon, which was how I got my foot in the door here. You see, he's got the same problem Brady-Schiavona does. Chewning claims to be acting in Oleg's name, commanding the remaining loyalist forces around Sol and Alpha Centauri . . . some of whose officers actually take it seriously. This limits his freedom of action."

"Good thing for us you've got it all figured out." Janille finished off her wine and stood up, giving Garth a glance at which he had the good grace to look abashed. The three of them had evolved a relationship which Corin recognized as odd on the rare occasions when he stopped to think about it at all. He and Janille had become lovers almost as soon as the Deathstriders had departed 85 Pegasi with their new "escort." He was well aware of what had passed between Janille and Garth on the besieged planet of

Ostwelt, and had been somewhat apprehensive of the latter's reaction to the new configuration of things. But the mercenary leader and would-be Emperor had accepted matters with his usual equanimity. Corin had a pretty definite idea of what lay behind Garth's customary good nature: a concentration on his grand long-term ambition beside which all else, especially in the interpersonal realm, shrank into insignificance. Still, he couldn't help liking the big heavy-planet man.

He stood up, enjoying the ease of it—Neustria's gravity was less than seventy percent that of the Prometheus he remembered, or the Old Earth his genes remembered. "And now, it's time for us to be going."

"Right." Garth set his own glass down. "I'm not satisfied with Deong's last couple of reports on the new construction at Val d'Argent Base. A personal visit from *both* of you ought to shake her up." He activated his desk communicator. "Is everything in readiness to transpose Captain Marshak and Lieutenant Colonel Dornay?"

"Yes, sir," a voice affirmed, speaking from only a few miles away, on the other side of Haulteclere. "And the reception committee's waiting at their destination."

"Good." Garth signed off and smiled at the other two. "Nice that Oleg's done *something* right." Neustria's transposer network had come unscathed through the civil disturbances, and the provisional government was doing as good a job of running it as of conducting the rest of the system's domestic business. Corin and Janille walked to the far end of the office and stood on a slightly raised rectangle of floor. Corin, a suspenders-and-belt man by temperament, reached into a pocket and withdrew his link, a specialized two-way communicator that provided the sensor contact the transposer would have needed had it not been focused on the known, fixed coordinates of the dais. "Ready," he spoke into it.

"Very good, sir," a voice replied from the link. And Garth's office vanished.

For a split second, too brief to take in details, Corin glimpsed the stage on which they now stood, and the control panel behind which its operators sat. The transposer couldn't send objects directly from one remote location to another; the process had to be through the device itself, which had brought them from Garth's office and would now send them to the base they were to inspect, a continent away. So quickly that Corin might have missed it if he'd blinked, the transposer room was gone—

And Val d'Argent Base wasn't there.

It took some small but measurable time before the fact sank home: they weren't where they were supposed to be. Then they reacted simultaneously in their own ways, each with equal futility. Janille started to reach for a weapon that wasn't there, then fell into unarmed fighting stance. Corin snatched out his link and rapped, "This is Commodore Marshak! Come in, anyone . . ." Then, as no enemy appeared and the link proved inoperative, they lapsed into silent staring at their surroundings.

They were in an enclosed space that seemed too large to be enclosed, although there was nothing familiar to give a sense of scale. A smooth stone floor stretched away in all directions, until it met the rough-textured rock wall that curved upward to form a dome. Near the floor, depressions in the wall held some source of indirect lighting that was surprisingly effective, although the vastness was still fairly dim. There were no windows of any kind, but across the floor from them a great archway opened onto darkness. They could not discern what lay beyond.

Janille, combat-trained, did not panic. And Corin couldn't let himself do so in her presence, for reasons whose archaism was not lost on him. "Where are we?" she asked in a small but steady voice. The acoustics were better than might have been expected.

"I don't know. My link is dead. We're still on Neustria—at least the gravity feels the same."

"Or *in* it." She looked around again. "If this isn't subterranean, somebody's gone to a lot of work to make it seem that way."

"You're probably right—although if this is a cavern it's a damned big one. The question is, how did we get here?"

"Some transposer malfunction, I suppose. The *real* question is, how do we get *out* of here?"

"There seems to be only one way." Corin indicated the cavernous archway. Janille nodded, and they set out across the wide floor.

They were halfway to the opening, when the darkness beyond it seemed to move and shift.

"Actually, the 'malfunction' to which you refer was an accident for which I am responsible."

Almost instantly, they realized that the accentless, asexual voice wasn't really a voice at all, for they hadn't heard it—at least not in the usual sense. And they knew what it must truly be. But they didn't feel the shuddering horror they should have felt at unpermitted telepathic contact. Or perhaps they simply didn't notice such trivia as the traducing of a cultural taboo. For the dim movements in the shadows beyond the archway had resolved themselves into the figure that now emerged into the cavern, walking on its legs and its pair of limbs that could serve as either legs or arms, so that its not-really-crocodilian head reached not much more than three times Corin's height—half the total length of the sinuous body with its shimmering pattern of coppery-gold scales and its two pairs of arms and its pair of folded wings which at full extension would have spanned the full width of the chamber. . . .

Shock held Corin in a grip of icy steel, as his sanity ran about inside him looking for a way to get out. With some part of his consciousness, he heard a small, strangled sound emerge from Janille's direction, slowly building as though it wanted to turn into a scream. His own vocal cords were as paralyzed as the rest of him.

Enormous amber eyes regarded them from far above. "Compose yourselves. I have no desire to harm you. I wish only to rectify this unfortunate occurrence and send you on your way." (*Amusement.*) "Although I can readily imagine that this is somewhat of a shock."

"S-s-somewhat?" Corin croaked, as he gazed up into the face of one of humanity's predecessors among the stars. That face had remained immobile, of course—a telepathic race had no need of facial expressions as an adjunct to communication. But it was impossible to avoid the impression that the horny "lips" had quirked upward as that nonverbal emotion had reverberated inside their heads in tandem with the Luon's "words."

"So you're . . . you're reading our minds?"

"Not in the sense you imagine. We have certain ethics in the matter of mental privacy, you know. I am only receiving those surface thoughts you actually verbalize." (*Puzzlement.*) "But why are you so shocked at the notion? You have, I believe, been aware for some time that our species possesses psionic capabilities as a matter of course, as opposed to the rare and relatively feeble talents that exist among humans."

"Yes," Corin managed to affirm. Janille no longer seemed to be building up to hysterics, but had subsided into stunned silence. "Or at least we've theorized that you have such powers—like the telekinetic levitation that enables beings your size to fly. And we've speculated that you can create a kind of . . . negative illusion that renders you effectively invisible. That would account for the fact that almost nobody ever seems to actually see you."

"But you are seeing me now," the Luon gently

reminded him. "And surely there is nothing sinister about us. For one thing, I perceive that you possess an innate, genetically determined psionic resistance that precludes any kind of brute-force mental control, even if I were capable of it and my ethical system permitted it."

"Yes, I know." Like everyone else, Corin had been tested for such abilities at an early age.

"And beyond that," the Luon went on, "in more than two of your millennia we have never evinced any hostility toward humans."

"No . . . nor any desire to answer any questions." He felt rather than saw a nervous stiffening at his side, as though Janille thought he was being altogether too cheeky. "And besides, to us you look like a very formidable creature out of our mythology. In fact, there's a theory that you're somehow behind that particular myth."

"The dragon. Yes. As a matter of fact, one of us *did* impart that bit of information—among others— to one of you, over four centuries ago."

"Basil Castellan? There were always tales that he had some kind of Luonli connection . . . that they told him things. . . ."

"Yes, I believe that was the human's name." Momentarily, it seemed to Corin that the Luon eyed him in an odd way, and an indefinable emotion disturbed the placid surface of the pseudo-voice. But the moment passed. "He was never very forthcoming with the information afterwards. But from what he *did* occasionally say, stories and rumors spread. And it is true: the dragon legends originated in late-prehistoric times with two groups of my species, of very different character. Those in western Eurasia were, shall we say, not proper representatives of our race. The Far East's experience with us was happier."

"Uh, beg pardon?" The thoughts had registered as verbal symbols in Corin's mind because he'd studied

Old Earth's geography—but in a required course, long ago.

"Never mind. At any rate, that was thousands upon thousands of years before humans encountered us again—this time in the role of interstellar explorers themselves. On this very planet, in fact."

"Yes! I remember." Corin's mind flew to whatever obscure bits of familiar knowledge it could find as it struggled to remain afloat in a sea of unreality. "It started back in the early space age." Just before the end of the quasi-legendary twentieth century, he recalled. "They discovered that Epsilon Eridani was a young star—its rapid spin proved that. So when it turned out to have a life-bearing planet, the discovery seemed to strike at the foundations of astrophysics. They guessed, correctly, that this world—and the others like it that kept turning up—must have been terraformed by a nonhuman civilization. And they wondered where it had gone. But then they met you, and . . . well . . . that is . . ."

(*Dry amusement.*) "You need not be embarrassed. I am aware of your race's mystification at finding the mighty terraformers of prehistory reduced to a few scattered survivors. There was really no mystery. Our home sun—which had always been something of a stellar freak—abruptly flared into an intensity which meant the end of all life on our native planet."

"But . . . but, the planets you'd terraformed . . . ?"

"Even given the time, we could not have evacuated our population to them. You see, we had learned to our cost that we could not—save for a few rare individuals—survive away from the world that had produced us." (*The dryness without the amusement.*) "We might well have traded all our psionic aptitude for your species' marvelous adaptability, had we been offered the exchange. All we could do was settle those exceptional individuals among the stars, in a desperate bid for racial survival. It was unsuccessful. The interstellar settlers could survive on their remade worlds . . . but after a while they ceased to reproduce. They grew too few to support the sheer number of specializations a complex civilization requires—always a danger to our race, for which a multitudinous population had never been an ecological possibility."

"I can see why," said Janille—her first words in a while, muttered in a small, stunned voice. "But . . . how is it that *any* of you are left?"

"Our lifespans are inconceivably long by your standards—thousands of your years. Even so, very few remain. And we are old . . . old. The remnants of our ancient technology—naturally built to last, given the length of our lives—will sustain us as long as we endure. And solitude does not have the kind of deleterious psychological effects on us that it would on you; our presentient ancestors were solitary animals. I am the last on this world. Soon we will be gone from the universe across which we blazed like a brief shooting star—one of evolution's overspecialized dead ends."

For a time Corin and Janille were silenced by the sheer inadequacy of anything they could say. Finally, Janille cleared her throat and changed the subject. "Uh, you said something earlier about an 'accident' bringing us here."

"Yes." (*Briskness.*) "Our technology makes use of certain devices and effects which . . . stress the space/time continuum in such a way as to interfere with teleportation. It had never been a great problem for us, given the limited scope of that psionic technique."

"So you can do that too?" Corin breathed.

"Yes, but we are not immune to its inherent limitations. Now, however, you humans have learned how to artificially duplicate it, in a way which compensates for potential-energy differentials and thus makes far greater ranges practical. So I fear that incidents like this may become a problem—although this is, to my knowledge, the first time it has happened."

"So you're telling us that somewhere between Haulteclere and the Val d'Argent Base, some . . . byproduct of your technology caused us to be—"

" 'Caught.' Yes, I believe the word you were about to form is accurate. We are inside the Massif Dornier, not very far from Haulteclere." (*Contrition.*) "To repeat, I regret that you have been, through no intent of mine, subjected to this inconvenience. And I have every intention of enabling you to return whence you came."

"That seems simple enough. Just turn off, or disconnect, whatever it is that interferes with the transposer—and which I assume is also what's interfering with my link." A nonverbal affirmative confirmed Corin's supposition. "Then I'll be able to contact Haulteclere and they'll just transpose us out of here."

"I am afraid it is not quite that simple. You see . . . not to put too fine a point on it, I do not know how to deactivate the device."

"*What?*" Janille was abruptly restored to her usual self. "What the fuck do you *mean* you don't know how to deactivate it?"

(*Embarrassed defensiveness.*) "As I pointed out, this situation has never arisen before. And the equipment in question simply runs itself, indefinitely. And . . . well, I was never an engineer or anything of the sort." (*Hasty change of subject.*) "At any rate, what is done is done. The only remedy is for me to take you outside the radius of effect. This will involve a journey to the surface."

"I don't suppose . . ." Corin shook his head. "But of course you can't simply teleport up there with us, can you? Not here."

"Of course not," the Luon's "voice" echoed in his mind. "The phenomenon is at bottom the same whether achieved by psionic or mechanical means. And both forms are—"

"Equally subject to interference," Janille finished grumpily. "Yeah, yeah, yeah. Well, lead the way."

They walked through stone corridors scaled to accommodate Luonli. And walked. And walked. The ancient colonizers must, Corin thought, have hollowed out a significant percentage of the Massif Dornier. He didn't particularly marvel at the achievement, for humans had known nanotechnology for many centuries, and took for granted its use in the manipulation and shaping of inanimate objects, however much they shrank from some of its other potential applications. So the question that occupied his mind was not *how* but *why*. The Luonli's love of mountainous landscapes was well known. But why did they burrow under those mountains, where they must create spaces vast enough to accommodate their physical and psychological needs? It would probably remain a mystery, for he doubted the titanic being who walked ahead of them with a deceptively awkward gait would be able to answer the question even if he had an opportunity to pose it.

The inconceivable caverns went on and on. It was hard to even think of oneself as being enclosed when the walls were so far away and the ceiling could barely be made out in the dimness. Indeed, an agoraphobe might have had more trouble than a claustrophobe. (The latter phobia, at least, clearly didn't afflict the Luonli.) But after a while the emptiness began to gnaw at him. The Luon must have been right about aloneness not posing a threat to his people's sanity— and, indeed, the Luonli were known to be hermaphrodites and had therefore lacked one major source of evolutionary pressure toward gregariousness. Or, alternatively, the Luon might in fact be insane. It didn't *seem* to be . . . but what did madness look like in an alien? Corin ordered himself to abandon that line of thought.

After a while the two humans began to tire. They

were both in good shape, especially Janille. But the
Luon's pace, though deliberately held down in deference to their limitations (the reason for the seeming
awkwardness), was difficult to keep up with over the
long haul. And their bellies began to twist with the
pangs of hunger, for they'd departed in late afternoon
in anticipation of a buffet at the Val d'Argent officers' club. And the footgear of their planetside service
dress uniforms wasn't exactly intended for hiking.

To hell with machismo, Corin finally decided. "Hey!"
he called out in the direction of the Luon, whose name
he didn't know. "Can't we rest for a while?"

"Of course." (*Concern.*) "I should have realized. And
I imagine you are hungry as well. I can provide food-
stuffs which you can consume without danger, though
also without full nutritional adequacy. If you wish, I
can go and—"

"That's all right," Corin demurred as he sank to the
smooth stone floor gratefully. He didn't want anything
to delay their departure. Janille's silence as she settled
to the floor beside him suggested that she concurred.
"We can get along without food until we get back to
Haulteclere."

"In that case, perhaps you should simply rest. In
fact . . ." The Luon's face remained as immobile as
ever, but the great amber eyes held Corin's with a
disconcerting directness. "You probably wish to sleep
for a little while."

"Sleep? Oh, no. We don't want to lose any time
in—" But Janille was already emitting ladylike snores
beside him. And, for a fact, his own eyelids were
heavier than the hour and the physical exertion could
account for. It should have been worrisome . . . but
as he continued to meet the Luon's eyes, and gazed
into those bottomless pools of molten gold, it didn't
seem very important. . . .

A sudden imperative fended away the dark wings
of slumber that beat slowly at the edges of his con-

sciousness. "Uh, listen," he forced himself to say, "we're grateful for your help."

"As I explained, your being here is due to—"

"Yes. But you could have simply let us starve to death in your caverns, and no one would ever have been the wiser."

(*Primness.*) "That would scarcely have been ethical." (*Hesitation, underneath which roiled a complex stew of emotions, including something resembling calculation closely enough to have aroused Corin's suspicion at any other time.*) "However, if you insist on considering yourself in my debt, I believe you will be in a position to discharge that debt in the not-too-remote future . . . at a star on the outskirts of what your Empire calls the Beta Aquilae Sector."

"Huh? But I've never been there."

"No, but I have reason to believe you will find yourself there within the year. When you do, you will know what you must do to . . . but I have already said far too much. Now you must sleep."

Corin found he could not argue. He remembered nothing further, not even dreams.

The dawn light of Epsilon Eridani, peeking over the flank of a mountain, brought him awake.

He was instantly on his feet, oblivious to the chill, staring wildly around at the landscape of the upper Massif Dornier. Between the range to the east above which the sun was rising and the higher ranges to the west spread a vista of uplands, cut into canyons by rivers that tumbled from higher to lower elevations in spectacular waterfalls. They were on a crag which overlooked one such waterfall, plunging down into misty depths with a steady roar.

But Corin had eyes for none of it. He looked around frantically, until a coppery-golden glint of reflected sunrise caught his eye. He squinted at it and discerned the slow beat of vast wings, far away.

"Hey!" he yelled, trying to overcome the noise of the waterfall but knowing it didn't matter if he did or not. "Where are we? Where have you brought us?" Beside him, Janille stirred into wakefulness at his shouting.

"Ah, you are awake." That which his mind interpreted as a voice was weaker than before, and gradually diminished as the Luon drew further and further away. "I belatedly realized I could carry the two of you more quickly than you could walk. I did so while you slept. You are now in a region where the transposer and your link will function. You'll be able to return to Haulteclere . . . where I have reason to believe some very interesting news will be awaiting you."

"But . . . wait. Wait!" Corin screamed with a loudness that would leave him with a raw throat, not knowing whether it would do any good or not. But the Luon—either because it was out of its telepathic range, or by intention—did not reply. The metallic-seeming glint dwindled toward the southwest and was gone.

"We never learned its name," Janille remarked. She got to her feet and rubbed sleep from her eyes. "What do you suppose it meant about 'interesting news'?"

"No idea." Corin activated his link, and this time it came to life. He spoke hoarsely into it. "This is Captain Marshak. Come in, please. Anyone, please acknowledge."

A screech of static resolved itself into a voice. "Captain, this is Haulteclere central transposer station. Is Colonel Dornay still with you?"

"She's here, and we're both fine. Can you get a fix on us?"

"Yes, sir. Your link is—"

"Corin!" A bass voice overrode the operator's. "What the hell are you two doing up there? We've had a planetwide search under way all night, ever since you didn't appear at Val d'Argent."

"It's a long story, Garth. Right now, we just need to get back." Corin became aware of his empty stomach, his stiffness, the early-morning high-altitude chill. "On second thought, breakfast and a hot shower would be nice."

"Sure. Stand by."

Janille waited beside Corin, for a second or so. The waterfall, the mountains, and the deep-blue sky with its fleecy clouds vanished, and they were on the Haulteclere transposer stage.

Corin had expected to be instantly transferred back to Garth's headquarters. But they stayed where they were, and the big mercenary strode out past the control boards. Never a dandy, the heavy-planet man looked exceptionally rumpled, as though he'd slept in his clothes—or, perhaps, not slept at all.

"Janille! Corin! What happened to you? Do you need to get checked out by a doctor?"

"No, Garth, we're fine. When we get to sit down in private, we'll tell you everything. It's quite a story."

"Not as good as the one I have."

Corin gave the general a quizzical look. "You may change your mind when you've heard us."

"I doubt it," Garth said grimly. "We just got the news last night, via tachyon beam, while the search for you was going on. Oleg's been assassinated!"

The stare they gave each other wasn't the reaction he'd expected.

CHAPTER SEVEN
Prometheus (Sigma Draconis II), 4328 C.E.

Roderick Brady-Schiavona had barely appeared on the transposer stage before he strode off it, as though he'd hit the ground running.

Jason Aerenthal didn't waste time with conventional greetings. "You've heard," he stated rather than asked.

"Yes. We got the message on the outskirts of this system." Returning from the newly secured Beta Aquilae Sector, Roderick's flagship had still had its inner field activated as it passed the orbits of Sigma Draconis' outermost planets, and could therefore receive tachyon transmissions from Prometheus as soon as the planet's sensors had the ship pinpointed.

"Then you got the news only a little while after we ourselves did—very fortuitous. And you certainly didn't lose any time getting here. You transposed here from the maximum safe range, or perhaps a bit beyond it." Aerenthal ran his eyes over the space-service coverall that Roderick hadn't bothered to change.

"Never mind that." Roderick strode as he talked, proceeding through corridors and emerging onto an open gallery on the curving underside of the palace, overlooking the oceanfront below, where surf rolled whitely onto long beaches at the feet of soaring towers.

He had no eyes for any of it. "How is Father taking it?"

"He's stunned, of course. Actually, we were all taken by surprise. But it hit him especially hard. The assassination of an Emperor isn't something he takes lightly ... even a 'Retired Emperor.' " Aerenthal's lips gave a self-deprecatory upward twitch.

"Who was responsible?" Roderick didn't bother with the formality of asking if the agent had the information. "Anyone we know?"

"Oh, yes, that's clear enough. It was his chief Fleet attache, Captain Vladimir Liang."

"That slime!"

"Indeed. As I've reconstructed the story, he wiped out the entire family. Oleg lived just long enough to be forced to watch the killing of his son Andrei."

Roderick jarred to a stop, and a low, non-verbal growl containing several emotions escaped him. Then he looked up, and met Aerenthal's cool gaze. No words passed between them, nor were any needed. The existence of fourteen-year-old Andrei had been awkward for them in their elevation of Julian. They'd gotten around the problem by arguing that a *Retired* Emperor's son held no special status as heir presumptive. Now, the point appeared to have conveniently become moot.

I keep thinking, Roderick reflected, *that I've finally learned what true self-disgust feels like. How long, I wonder, before I* really *learn?*

And, by then, will I still care?

He spoke in level tones. "So Liang has tried to seize the throne?"

"No. Proclaiming himself Emperor is beyond his courage if not his ambition. He's settled for promoting himself to admiral and appointing a regency council, with himself as chairman, to manage things 'until the present regrettable uncertainty concerning the succession is resolved.' " Aerenthal chuckled. "If nothing else, he deserves high marks for what certain of my ancestors used to call *chutzpah*."

Roderick was in no mood to be amused. "How much does he actually control, outside the Lambda Serpenti system?"

"Unknown. So far, he hasn't tried to force the issue. He's been content to stay at Lambda Serpenti and enjoy a thorough massacre of his political enemies."

For a while there was silence, broken only by the occasional cries of birds hurling defiance at the gargantuan, impossibly motionless intruder in their skies. Aerenthal watched as the youthful commodore leaned on the railing and considered the implications.

"It appears," the agent finally observed, "that our timetable has been moved up for us."

Roderick looked up sharply. *Covert telepathy? No. Why should he? He doesn't need it. Shrewdness, vast experience and a total lack of illusions about human nature serve perfectly well.* "Yes," he agreed aloud. "It's clear what must be done."

"Clear to everyone but your father," Aerenthal corrected. "That's why your return is so very fortunate. You must persuade him."

"Rod! Thank God you're back!" Maura advanced across the antechamber and gave him a quick hug.

"Congratulations," he said, indicating her newly acquired captain's insignia.

Her expression conveyed both thanks and dismissal of the matter's importance. She looked more like the admiral than any of them, in a feminine sort of way, with her strongly marked features. Her thick hair, somewhat longer than usual for a female Fleet officer, was a darker chestnut than Roderick's. She swept it back impatiently and indicated the inner door.

"Come on. Father's been waiting ever since you arrived. Ted's with him . . . as usual." Her face darkened with the last two words. "It's too bad he couldn't have gone with you, or done something to get him off Prometheus. Here, with constant access to Father, he's been . . . well, never mind. At least he's on the right side for now."

"You mean he's been advising Father to—?"

"Yes. We both have. But we need your help."

She led the way into the study. Teodor—who hadn't seen his brother since they'd parted in this same study the previous year—turned from where he stood by the sideboard, his features a mask of cautious neutrality. The Grand Admiral looked up from his armchair with a smile that was as economical as all his smiles but as warm as they ever got. He stood up and extended his hand. "Welcome back, Rod! We've all been waiting to congratulate you in person for all you've done, out toward Perseus and Aquila. But now . . . you've heard the news, of course."

"Yes, sir."

"Well, the ceremony we'd planned will have to be delayed. Oh, don't worry; your promotion to rear admiral will go through on schedule—"

"I wasn't worried, sir."

"—but the public formalities will have to be delayed. First, we have to decide how we're going to respond to this development."

Roderick looked into the eyes of his father—which were also the eyes of the Grand Admiral—until he'd held them, and knew he could hold them. Aerenthal hadn't accompanied him, for the agent had deemed it best that he be alone with his father, or at least have only family members present, when he said what must be said. When he spoke, his voice held as steady as his eyes.

"Sir, you always taught me that the really important decisions of life are seldom simple ones. In the main, that's true. But for once our choice is clear-cut and unambiguous. The Duschanes have been wiped out—"

"No! Julian still lives! The murder of the rest of the Imperial family makes even clearer his status as the legitimate Emperor."

"With respect, sir, people accepted him as Emperor only because *you* made him so. The fact that your choice had a certain dynastic legitimacy undoubtedly helped. But that's meaningless now; he represents a dynasty which no longer exists. And we all know he's out of the question as Emperor. His lack of an heir alone would disqualify him."

"But as long as he lives, he's the Emperor." The admiral's eyes slid away, unable to meet his son's any longer. "If I don't support him, I'll be declaring my entire life meaningless."

"Forgive me, sir, but putting off facing a problem is unworthy of you." For an instant, Roderick wondered if he'd gone too far, for his siblings gasped and his father's eyes snapped back into contact with his, glaring. But he had to go on. "You know it's true, sir. And it's not just his childlessness. He could reign only as a cardboard figure representing a dead dynastic principle, with *you* as the real ruler—just as Yoshi Medina ruled in his day."

For the first time in Roderick's memory, his father's granite features trembled in a gale of anger. "You *dare* to compare me to that—"

"Yes, sir, I do—because you yourself spoke a moment ago of meaninglessness. What could render your loyalty to the Duschanes more meaningless than to use the last of them as a puppet? And it wouldn't work in the long run, because such a farce would lack the moral authority that the Empire has always existed to provide." Roderick shook his head slowly. "No, if you really want to preserve the Empire there's only one way to do it. You must proclaim yourself Emperor."

All at once, something seemed to go out of Ivar Brady-Schiavona. He slumped back down into his armchair, and his craggy face wore the look of a man who wanted to collapse under his burdens but didn't know how. "You, too?" he asked in a voice barely above a whisper. "Everyone's been telling me that. But . . . I have no legitimate claim to the throne. Where would that leave your 'moral authority'? I'd be ruling by no right except that of the biggest guns."

"That's not altogether true, sir. Remember, we're distant relatives of the Duschanes."

" 'Distant' is precisely the word! By that reckoning, there must be dozens, no, hundreds of people who could make as good a claim as I."

"That's just the problem, Father," Maura declared, entering the conversation. "There'll be no lack of pretenders with some kind of claim, as well as freebooters who really *do* have nothing behind them but force. We'll have constant civil war unless a new dynasty—legitimized by links with the old one, but nevertheless *new*, a fresh start—is firmly established. And you're the only one who can do that."

"Yes!" Teodor stepped forward, sensing that his moment to pipe up had arrived. "So you see, sir, this won't be a usurpation at all. Instead, you will be fulfilling a *duty*." Roderick and Maura exchanged a glance, and their eyes rolled heavenward in search of refuge from their older brother's smarmy hypocrisy. But they both held their tongues, for they realized that Teodor, in his sycophancy, had hit on the line of argument best calculated to sway their father.

"Furthermore," Teodor continued, hitting his stride, "you have a better claim than any of the other distant Duschane relations. Remember, your lineage goes back to the ruling house of the old Solarian Empire . . . through Basil Castellan himself!"

"Oh, yes." The admiral's thin lips quirked almost imperceptibly upward. "That old family legend."

"More than just a legend, sir! It is beyond dispute that the Sword Clans covertly aided Castellan in his

struggle against Yoshi Medina. It is equally undisputed
that his Sword Clans contacts, Jan Kleinst-Schiavona
and Lauren Demarest-Katana, later married. And that
after Castellan's presumed death, they returned to
Newhope with an eleven-year-old foster child named
Irena, whom they subsequently adopted."

"You've made a study of this, I see." The admiral's
face wore the fond look it so often held when
addressing Teodor. Roderick could never recall seeing
precisely that expression directed at himself. He commanded himself not to feel that which he usually felt
when his father looked at Teodor that way. "So you
must know that the foster parents never actually
claimed that Irena was Basil Castellan's natural child
by his friend and lover Sonja Rady."

"Of course they didn't, sir. She had been placed
in their care for safekeeping during Castellan's disastrous last campaign, and they were bound to conceal
her identity. Castellan's enemies would have gone to
any lengths to destroy her. But once they arrived at
Newhope—a world unknown to the Empire, which
more than half believed the Sword Clans themselves
to be legendary—the secrecy to which they were
sworn lost its urgency. We're told that they never
denied the persistent rumors."

The admiral did not respond at once. Everyone
knew the rest of the story. Irena Kleinst-Schiavona
had married a Brady, within her own clan. (The Sword
Clans' established rule of exogamy had been set aside
in her case, for she was unrelated by blood to her
adoptive parents.) And her Brady-Schiavona descendants had always carried with them the suspicion that
they were descended from that lost prince who had
appeared in time for the Solarian Empire's final death-
agony, and whose gallant, doomed attempt to save it
was the stuff of folklore.

"There's no proof of it," the admiral finally muttered—but in a *pro forma* way, as though he knew

it was expected of him . . . or, perhaps, expected it of himself.

Roderick sensed the moment, and spoke before Teodor could resume. "But it's widely believed, sir. More to the point, people will *want* to believe it, because it will give your cause a unique legitimacy— even a mythic resonance. It'll make the Duschanes seem like parvenus by comparison!" *My God,* came the shocking realization, *I'm starting to sound like Ted!*

"Propaganda. Public relations. Image." The admiral's eyes held a sad amusement. "I've always held that sort of thing in contempt."

Maura spoke gently. "That contempt is a luxury you can no longer afford, Father."

The admiral looked around at the faces of his children and saw unanimity. His massive head sank, and his voice was barely audible. "What about Julian? Would you have me betray the man I myself put on the throne?"

Roderick spoke in a quiet, unargumentative tone which puzzled both his siblings. "Julian, as we all know, has never had any political ambitions. I'm sure there'll be no occasion for any unpleasantness." Teodor began to open his mouth to add something, but Roderick gave him a surreptitious shushing gesture, and he subsided.

There was, after all, no need to argue further. Roderick knew he'd won. He'd known it the instant his father had said "Julian" rather than "His Imperial Majesty."

"Doesn't this fly in the face of that ancient philosopher you're always quoting?" Roderick spoke carefully; it had been years since he'd gotten this drunk. "What was his name? MacKinder? McLuhan? Macsomething."

"Machiavelli," Aerenthal supplied from across the table.

"Whatever. Anyway, didn't he say that when you depose a ruling house, you're just asking for trouble if you don't wipe out the *entire* family?"

"Don't be tasteless." The agent took a sip from his own brandy snifter, of which he'd been partaking with slightly more caution than the newly promoted rear admiral. "I don't think any of the dangers that concerned Machiavelli apply in this case. Do you?" The question was directed to the third man at the table.

"Absolutely not," Julian Duschane assured him. "Of course, under the circumstances I suppose that's what one might *expect* me to say. . . ."

"One might," Roderick echoed, polishing off his brandy and reaching for the decanter.

"But it's nonetheless true. Even if some adventurer posing as the restorer of the Duschane dynasty were to kidnap me and try to use me as a figurehead, he'd run into the same intractable problems: my lack of an heir, and the fact that no one except the Grand Admiral has ever taken me seriously as Emperor—least of all myself." The elderly man smiled benignly.

They sat in what were, for the moment, still his private apartments in the palace. The nighttime panorama in the window, and the flames in the fireplace that provided almost as much illumination as the dim indirect lighting, were holographic illusions. But the rich furnishings were real, as was the fabulously rare brandy of which Aerenthal had suggested they avail themselves while they could. Roderick had concurred, for he'd needed to tie one on.

"No," Julian continued, "I intend to spend my remaining years in comfortable obscurity, completing what I hope will be the definitive study of the link between loss of political power and declining cultural influence among Old Earth's pre-spaceflight civilizations—Hellenistic Greece, Baroque Italy, twenty-first century Europe, and so forth. I like to think *that* is what I'll be remembered for. And as a former Emperor of sorts, I shouldn't have any trouble finding a publisher."

"Not that you ever did," Aerenthal put in graciously.

Roderick took another sip of the brandy that had gradually dissolved his discomfort at the sheer unreality of the whole scene. The dethroning had been simply too civilized for words: a quiet interview in which the Grand Admiral had explained the situation, a graceful acquiescence by the completely unsurprised Julian, and now a brief period in limbo, until the time—just two of Prometheus' 37.6-standard-hour days hence—when Ivar would publicly accept Julian's abdication and set the date for his own coronation. Unnoticed in the hoopla, Julian would quietly depart into that which no one was crude enough to call "internal exile." And the curtain would fall on the play whose ending the three of them had known from the start.

Roderick looked quizzically at the play's star—or, at least, its chief comic relief character. He struggled for a moment with curiosity. Curiosity won. "No regrets? No ... bitterness?"

"None." Julian shook his head emphatically. "If anything—and I say this with all sincerity—I consider it an honor to have contributed to the outcome we're going to see day after tomorrow. You see, I really do admire your father tremendously."

"As who does not?" Aerenthal rhetorically asked.

"Sure," Roderick muttered, staring into his brandy. "Everybody admires him. But ... but doesn't it bother you that he really has no legitimate claim to the throne?"

"Actually, he does," Aerenthal said quietly.

"Come on! His position—which I argued him out of—was absolutely correct. Our so-called relationship to the Duschanes barely qualifies as a joke."

"That isn't what I meant."

Something in Aerenthal's tone brought Roderick to

instant alertness, and he felt the fumes of alcohol seep out of him. "What? You're not talking about that old family legend, are you?" He laughed nervously. "I can't believe this! You're the last person I would ever have expected to fall into the trap of believing his own propaganda."

"Granted, it will make superb propaganda," the agent intoned, eyes focused somewhere far beyond the room. "But it also happens to be the literal truth. That occasionally happens, you know."

As the silence stretched, Roderick glanced at Julian in search of a clue as to how he should react. There was no help there, for the sensitive features were smoothed out into a mask of expressionlessness. So he turned back to Aerenthal. "How do you know that? How *can* anybody know?"

"I know." The two words dropped into a well of finality. Then the agent blinked, and eyed his brandy snifter ruefully. "Forgive me. I've said far too much."

"But . . . see here, tell me what you—"

"No. I'm afraid I must drop the subject. You'll have to be content with the information itself—assuming that you choose to believe it."

Roderick stared at the agent, started to speak, then thought better of it. He knew he'd get nothing more out of Aerenthal. He turned to Julian. "This comes as no surprise to you, I see. He must have already told you."

"He has. Not everything he knows, I'm sure, but enough to overcome my misgivings about lending myself to his—and your—plans. Not, to repeat, that those misgivings were ever very serious. But I'm a traditionalist, so it pleased me to learn the truth about the bloodline of the man I'd be helping to put on the throne. It satisfied my sense of the fitness of things." Julian looked around, and his eyes settled on the simulacrum of what they would have been seeing through a window in the outer rim of the palace. "I wasn't being altogether honest just now. I *will* regret leaving Prometheus. But it will be worth it. You see, while I'm certainly not the first person to have had to stand aside, out of the way of history, very few have been given the sure knowledge that the onrushing events are such as they would approve of. Leaving the stage quietly and with—I hope—a certain dignity is all I'm able to do to advance what is now going to happen. But I do it willingly."

Roderick set his snifter carefully down and stood up. He looked the last of the Duschanes in the eye, and spoke in a voice whose respectfulness was unsullied by even a hint of irony. "With your permission, I'll take my leave now . . . Your Imperial Majesty."

The office was small compared to the vast, pompous chamber where the Emperor conducted public audiences, or even the smaller but almost equally pompous reception room reserved for private ones. And the elegant traditionalism of its architecture coexisted uneasily with cutting-edge communications and data-retrieval equipment, including the console of a tachyon receiver fit for a command battleship—it took up an entire adjoining room, plus outside components atop the palace. For this was the Emperor's working office. And he now sat at the great desk, clad in the gray tunic and trousers of a Fleet officer's planetside service uniform, adorned only with the little golden dragon that outshone all other bedizenments.

Roderick doubted that he'd ever grow used to the sight of that insignia on his father, even though most people felt those wide shoulders were made for it.

"I hadn't planned to send you off so soon, Roderick," Ivar was saying in his stately, measured voice. "But the developments in the Perseus sectors require immediate attention. And you know the situation out there better than anyone, having been in charge of securing those sectors in the first place."

"I fully understand, sir." They were both in uniform, and speaking in private. It was just as well, since Roderick hadn't adjusted to the more formal modes of address yet—any more than his father had to the Imperial "we."

The shock waves were still spreading outward from Sigma Draconis in concentric circles, as though Julian's abdication and Ivar's investiture had been pebbles hurled into a lake that had thought itself already roiled. In the sectors of the old People's Democratic Union, the news had been the occasion for local uprisings by diehard Duschane loyalists, who had attracted aggrieved elements of all stripes. No one had organized these flareups into a general firestorm, and putting them down should not be difficult. It would, however, take time.

That, clearly, was what was on the new Emperor's mind. "We'll have to consolidate our position in the areas we already hold," he went on, "before we can take any action against our enemies elsewhere."

"We anticipated that would be the case, Your Imperial Majesty," Aerenthal spoke up from off to the side. "It will be two years at least before we can even begin the pacification of the rest of the Empire. However, we were also correct in our other assumption: that none of our rivals would be in any better position to take immediate action. They, too, are still securing their respective positions and evaluating their options." He turned and considered the large holographically projected map that filled one corner of the office.

It was a sign of the times that the display was color-coded not by sectors but by areas of control. The computer, which was above suspicion of brown-nosing, had colored the power base of the fledgling Brady-Schiavona dynasty the bronze-gold of the dragon which decorated the flanks of Fleet ships. It spread over the right side of the display, as Roderick and his father were viewing it, in a bowllike concavity that included about a third of the total and extended a pseudopod to take in Sigma Draconis. Only two other colors were even remotely comparable in extent: the rose-red on the upper left, showing the Ursa Major frontier where Lauren Romaine and her followers and allies were attempting to translate their not-always-compatible ideals into a workable federal structure; and the lime-green to the lower left in the Serpens/Bootes region, where Liang was surprising them unpleasantly with his success in persuading the local Fleet commanders to acknowledge the authority of his tame regency council. Smaller splotches of color here and there were mostly ignorable. But Ivar's somber eyes focused on two such splotches, strategically nestled in the heart of the display. One—very small indeed, but a source of worry—was the maroon bubble enclosing Epsilon Eridani and its self-promoted General Garth Krona. But the Emperor's gaze zeroed in on the jarringly purple one—*Can't we program the computer with taste?* Roderick wondered—at the display's geometrical center.

"What's the current assessment of the probable results of Chewning's move?" asked the Emperor. Damiano Chewning, the ministerial official who had made himself master of Old Earth and its environs, had rummaged up an infant distantly related to the Duschanes and had him proclaimed Emperor within days of Julian's abdication.

"Inconclusive. He obviously hopes to cast himself as the defender of the dynasty, and you as a usurper. This will undoubtedly be a short-term propaganda plus for him, by lending a patina of legitimacy to his rule at Sol."

"Then why do you say, 'Inconclusive'?"

"Because in the long run it will inevitably bring him into conflict with Liang. Regardless of whether Liang plans to keep the succession in limbo indefinitely or have his 'regency council' pick another remote Duschane relation to be his puppet, his position and Chewning's are fundamentally irreconcilable."

"But," Roderick objected, "what if they reach an accommodation by which Liang declares the succession settled in favor of Chewning's 'Emperor'?"

"That, Admiral," Aerenthal replied formally, "would merely postpone the clash. A puppet cannot have two puppeteers."

"Hmm . . ." The Emperor ruminated for a moment. "What will Chewning do?"

"He can't hope to stand alone against Liang—the military equation simply doesn't balance. And the hesitancy everyone has traditionally felt—everyone human, anyway—about attacking the homeworld won't protect him forever. The information I've been able to gather suggests he intends to try and forge an alliance with Krona."

Roderick cocked his head to one side. "That way, even if Liang is defeated, won't Chewning find himself in Krona's power?"

Aerenthal permitted himself a brief, appreciative smile at the young rear admiral's correct application of Machiavelli. "He believes he can establish a moral ascendancy over Krona by appealing to the latter's residual loyalty to the Duschane dynasty." The agent's smile returned, subtly different. "The wish is probably father to the thought, as it often is with people as deeply impressed by their own cleverness as is Chewning. And everything I know about Krona suggests that he is easy to underestimate—he seems far less shrewd than he is."

"An impression he doubtless cultivates," Ivar muttered. He shook his head impatiently. "This is all very interesting, and worth keeping in mind as we monitor developments. But at the moment, our first priority must be to stabilize our newly acquired sectors. Roderick, I . . ." Awkwardness overtook him. "I . . . wish we could have had more time together. I wish I didn't have to send you back so soon. But—"

"I understand, sir." As always, Roderick found his father's stiffness contagious. "Thank you for going along with all my requests regarding personnel." Ivar certainly couldn't have been more accommodating. Among other things, Roderick now had Aline Tatsumo back as flag captain, with more rank and a larger flagship. "I . . . I won't fail you, sir. Goodbye." Cursing himself for his inadequacy, he came to attention. Father's and son's eyes met in a shared moment of frustration, gazing over a barrier that neither knew how to tear down. Then Roderick was gone, walking down endless corridors toward the transposer room.

His mood improved as he reflected that the new Emperor had been making a lot of good personnel decisions. Maura, for example, was now a commodore, soon to depart toward Cassiopeia with her own task group. And their father was still resisting Teodor's entreaties for a similar independent command. No, their older brother would be staying here on Prometheus. . . .

Alone with their father.

Roderick found he'd come to a halt at the thought. He chided himself for what he'd been thinking and resumed his stride.

CHAPTER EIGHT
The Sol System, 4328 C.E.

The primary shone with the typical yellowish-white of a G0v star, and the still-distant planet was the same blue as every other life-bearing waterworld. So why, Corin wondered, did the sight in the flagship's main screen cause his flesh to prickle and his heartbeat to accelerate?

At least, his covert glances around the flag bridge told him, he wasn't alone in the reaction. Probably no one present had ever seen the world which had been humanity's womb.

"Commodore," a diffident voice from the comm station informed him, "we've received an acknowledgment. They're asking us to cut our drive out here."

"What?" Garth rumbled from the special command chair that had been installed for him. "I thought the deal was that we were to take up orbit around Earth."

"What about it?" Corin passed the question along to the comm officer.

"Something about traffic regs, sir. Also, they say Prime Minister Chewning is standing by to talk to the General."

"Aha!" Garth's misgivings about the order to halt evaporated. The massive heavy-planet man stood up and moved with his always-surprising speed to stand before the comm screen's pickup. "Put him on."

Corin turned to the communicator in the arm of his command chair and gave the necessary orders to the flag captain. The drive was deactivated, as were the impellers, and the blue dot that was Old Earth ceased to wax visibly in the screen as they proceeded along a hyperbolic orbit around Sol, only slightly skewed from the ecliptic. Corin glanced at the holo tank and gave an unconscious nod as he saw that the Deathstriders' entire flotilla had done the same, performing as a tightly coordinated whole. But most of his attention was on the face in the comm screen.

Damiano Chewning wore the kind of richly somber clothes appropriate for a prime minister, even of an "Empire" largely restricted to Sol and Alpha Centauri. His smile showed that he wasn't really bucktoothed, but he should have been—his face, with its plump cheeks and small receding chin, was unmistakably rabbitlike. Graying black hair was slicked back from a retreating hairline, as oily as his manner.

"Welcome to the home system of us all, General Krona," Chewning said with perfectly modulated sincerity. "I speak not just for His Imperial Majesty Ferrand II but for everyone at Sol. Your arrival comes as a vast relief to us all."

"Thank you, Prime Minister." Garth attempted a smoothness to which his voice was ill-suited. "Naturally I moved up my departure date as soon as I learned of the danger His Imperial Majesty faces."

"Yes!" Chewning summoned up all the indicia of indignation. "All loyal Imperial subjects must rally against the archtraitor Liang, who is about to add an attack on the sacred soil of Old Earth to his list of crimes—a list which is already long and black. And you, General, are especially noted for your steadfast and unswerving loyalty to the dynasty."

"So I like to believe, Prime Minister." At least Garth had the requisite ability to keep a straight face. "And while I may have had to make certain practical accommodations to the unsettled conditions of recent years—"

"As have we all, General," Chewning interjected unctuously.

"—nevertheless my *basic* allegiance to the legitimate Duschane dynasty has never wavered. And any doubts as to my proper course of action vanished when I heard the news of Liang's murder of the late Emperor Oleg and his entire family."

"Indeed, General, your blood must have boiled in your veins!" Chewning wore the look of a solemn rodent. "It must be clear to *all* loyal subjects that their allegiance belongs to His Imperial Majesty Ferrand II, who is the last remaining torchbearer of the lawful succession."

"And who has repealed the late Emperor Armand's prohibition on possession of heavy space-based weaponry by free companies," Garth added pointedly.

"Of *course*, General! I have advised His Imperial Majesty that changed conditions have rendered that statute outdated and unenforceable. Given my not inconsiderable influence as His Imperial Majesty's guardian during his minority" —an insinuating smile— "I'm sure the repeal of which you speak is a foregone conclusion."

A frown gathered beneath Garth's poker face. "It was my understanding that the decree had already been issued."

"A mere formality, I assure you. Consider it an accomplished fact. Whatever minor legal technicalities may remain will be finalized as soon as our united forces have repelled Liang's murderous hordes . . . which you, as a man of action, will surely agree must take precedence."

"Hmm . . ." Garth's bass was almost below the

threshold of hearing. "Well, Prime Minister, if you put it like that—"

"Then we'll say no more about the matter!" Chewning beamed with innocent happiness. "Such minor issues will undoubtedly resolve themselves, fading into insignificance beside our common resolve to stand shoulder to shoulder in defense of His Imperial Majesty against—"

Janille sidled up beside Corin. "Garth's stomach must be even stronger than the rest of him," she muttered.

Corin grinned. "We both know he's a man of many hidden talents." For a moment they watched the General make appropriate responses as Chewning proceeded from insincerity to platitude to bromide and then back to insincerity. "Still, you have to wonder how he can keep his lunch down. It's hard enough for me, and I don't even have to pretend to be taking it seriously."

Janille gave him a slantwise glance. "You've got no right to complain. You advised Garth in favor of this alliance. And you couldn't possibly have had any illusions about Chewning. In fact, I know you didn't."

"Garth had been planning on this move all along!" Corin heard the defensiveness in his own voice.

"But he'd been having second thoughts since Chewning rummaged up this nonentity Ferrand and set him up as a puppet Emperor. It made it impossible for him to form an alliance with Chewning without seeming to support Ferrand's claim."

"What claim?" Corin demanded irritably. "Everybody knows Ferrand has every quality of a joke except humor."

"So you argued when you advised Garth to stick to his original plan. That was why he decided he could afford to go through the motions of pretending to return to the Duschane fold. Not too surprising—he's more and more inclined to follow your advice. You've gotten to be a regular power behind the throne."

"I'm a little young to be a Gray Eminence. Besides, Garth has to *have* a throne before I can be the power behind it." Corin glanced at Janille in search of a lightening of her moodiness. Seeing none, he felt his irritation redouble. "Look, what's bothering you? This just happens to be the ideal time to put Garth's long-standing plan into effect. We've known that ever since Liang openly denounced Ferrand as a pretender and Chewning as a traitor, and declared his intention of wiping out both of them. Now Chewning *needs* us. We'll never be in a better bargaining position."

"That's all true, or at least arguable. But it's not the real reason you wanted us to ally ourselves with Chewning."

"Oh?" With an effort, Corin kept his voice down to the low murmur in which they'd both been speaking. "Then what, pray tell, *is* my real reason?"

"Simple. You've never really forgiven yourself for leaving the Imperial Fleet. You need to offer your services to the nearest thing to a legitimate Duschane successor available—and that's Chewning's puppet Ferrand, now that Ivar Brady-Schiavona has deposed *his* Duschane puppet. The way things are these days, it's the closest you can come to returning to your Imperial allegiance."

"That's the most—" Corin's voice jarred to a halt as stubborn self-knowledge caught up with anger, bringing with it the realization of *why* he was angry. When he resumed, what came out was mortifyingly weak. "But when Brady-Schiavona *was* officially acting in Julian Duschane's name, I never advised Garth to join him."

"Of course not. At first, you were afraid he'd be death on a Fleet deserter like you. Then, by the time it became clear how lenient his policy was, even to his own former enemies, his power base had gotten too big. In any partnership between him and Garth, it would be only too obvious who the junior partner was. No such problems with Chewning, of course. He's got no principles to offend; and, as you say, he really does need us to save him from Liang." Janille's expression softened a trifle. "That's the odd thing: it's entirely possible that your advice was correct. Probable, even."

"Then what are you worried about?"

"Just your ability to sell yourself a bill of goods about your own motives. You can rationalize so well that you believe your own rationalizations. That's dangerous—and the more influence you exert on Garth, the more dangerous it gets."

Corin opened his mouth to protest, with a vehemence he wouldn't have felt at an accusation that hadn't touched a nerve ending of unresolved and long-denied emotions. But Janille shushed him, for Chewning was finally showing signs of getting down to practicalities. The face in the comm screen lost some of its rabbit semblance as its owner spoke in matter-of-fact tones.

"And now, General, I suggest that your staff confer with that of Admiral Kirpal, commander of the Sol System Defense Command. It will be necessary to coordinate our joint efforts with a view to making the most efficient use of the forces available."

"Certainly, Prime Minister." Garth had agreed in advance that Kirpal was to be in overall operational command—this was Chewning's system, after all—but as a coordinator only. He'd had his own independent command of the Deathstriders spelled out to an elaborate degree of specificity; when dealing with Chewning it was best to get things in writing.

The arrangements were made, with further exchanges of courtesies, and Chewning signed off. Garth returned to his command chair and sank into it gratefully. "Whew! I'd rather face nanoweapons than deal with a slime mold like that."

Janille was in no mood to commiserate. "Get used to it. If . . . sorry, *when* you become Emperor, you'll spend most of your time blandly exchanging pompous lies with politicians."

Garth grinned in his beard. "Well, on second thought, I suppose it has its rewarding aspects."

"In the meantime," she inquired, unmollified, "do you really think you can trust Chewning?"

"Of course not," Corin answered for Garth, a little too quickly. "Nobody's ever thought that. He's congenitally incapable of honest dealing except under duress. But that's precisely what we're looking at here."

"Right," Garth nodded emphatically. "He'll deal straight with us because he's got no choice."

"Then why is he waffling on his commitment to repeal Armand's statute limiting the weapons allowed to free companies?"

"Because to him, waffling is like breathing," Garth said, an impatient edge entering his voice. "He's a politician, remember. But it doesn't mean anything. He's got his nuts on the chopping block, and needs us to fend off the axe. He's in no position to bring us to book on some technical violation."

Janille looked from Garth to Corin and back again. It did seem to make sense—so much sense that she couldn't articulate an objection to it, any more than she had back at Epsilon Eridani. But she would have felt better about the reasoning if she hadn't known she was hearing it from an incurable optimist and a man predisposed to see the bright side of any course of action that seemed to offer a chance to expiate his own imagined sins.

"I hope you two are right," was all she said.

The flag bridge was unchanged save for Janille's absence. Even the star configuration in the main screen hadn't been visibly altered by the passage of a few standard days, for they were still falling along the same orbital path. It was as good a place as any to await an attack which could come from any direction. Nowhere was it written that Liang's forces were required to proceed directly from Lambda Serpenti.

Garth approached from the comm station, looking uncharacteristically moody. "Well, at least she's there and settled in."

"Of course she is," Corin said soothingly, deploying his length more comfortably in the command chair. Janille had departed with the bulk of the Deathstriders' surface forces for the fourth planet—*Mars*, Corin reminded himself.

"I ought to be there myself," Garth rumbled.

"Nonsense. She's perfectly capable of coordinating with Chewning's local ground commander and handling our end of the planetary defense. And you're needed here. There's a lot more to the Deathstriders now than just the ground component." Corin indicated the holo tank that displayed their flotilla. The battlecruiser and two cruisers he'd brought with him into the Deathstriders Company were almost lost in the array. They even had two *Impregnable*-class battleships, including the flagship *Impervious*, which they'd acquired along with Epsilon Eridani. No, the Deathstriders could no longer be characterized simply as a powered-armor outfit, even though Garth continued to use the title "general" and wear the original version of the uniform. The tail had gotten more than big enough to wag the dog. That bothered some people. Corin sometimes wondered if Garth was one of them.

Maybe, he reflected, that was part of the reason Garth had never solved the whole legal problem of the mercenaries' new battle-line capability by solemnly swearing allegiance to the provisional government he himself had created at Epsilon Eridani, dissolving the Deathstriders, and instantly reconstituting them as the militia of that provisional government. It would have simplified things, but Garth had never seriously considered it. He liked his freedom of action as commander of a mercenary company, even one whose size and complexity had relegated him to the role of chairman of the board.

Garth's own thoughts seemed to be following similar channels. "I could be some use to her there," he insisted. "All my experience is in ground combat. Here, I'm nothing but a very high-ranking passenger."

"What would you be there? She's operationally under the command of Chewning's man on Mars. Your place is wherever we may need command decisions made—which is here." Privately, in some sealed-off part of himself, Corin wondered if the general was being honest with either of them about his reason for wanting to be closer to Janille.

"You're probably right," Garth muttered, and started to turn away.

The general-quarters klaxon, which *Impervious'* skipper was under orders to sound the instant hostiles were detected approaching the Sol system, seemed to shatter the very air of the flag bridge.

Garth whirled back around, and his eyes met Corin's with a gleam that made the latter reconsider his furtive thoughts of a moment before. "They weren't supposed to get here quite this soon."

"No, they weren't," Corin answered absently. With most of his consciousness he activated his private holo tank.

Once upon a time, he knew, the offensive had held a terrible edge in space warfare. When ships could outpace the energies of sensors, attackers could arrive before the tidings of their coming. It was one of the things that had enabled the young Republic of Sigma Draconis to give the tottering, rotten edifice of the United Nations its final push, seventeen centuries before. But with modern sensors, it was a different matter. The robotic early-warning stations out in Sol's

Oort Cloud had detected the incoming hostiles far outside the borders of the holo tank's system-scale display. So only the green icons of friendly units were visible so far. But as Corin watched, the computer automatically added a scarlet arrow, representing the invaders' projected course. It pierced the edge of the display at about eight o'clock—to use a terminology whose origin few remembered any more—slightly above the ecliptic plane.

Garth was watching too. "So they've come straight from Lambda Serpenti," he remarked. "Liang must have been in a hurry to put his forces into this system. Maybe he thought he could beat us here."

"He almost did," Corin muttered. He studied the positions of the green icons, all orbiting clockwise as per the display's orientation. Their own flotilla was at about six o'clock, between the orbits of Mars (currently at nine o'clock) and Jupiter (four o'clock). Earth, closer to the yellow light of Sol than any of them, orbited at about one-thirty. He needed no computer to tell him the hostiles' most direct course to the homeworld.

"They'll have to follow a hyperbolic course across the inner system, between us and Sol," he told Garth.

"Right." The general did some calculations of his own, then turned to Corin with a hunter's grin. "Which means that Kirpal will be in a perfect position to intercept! Yes, they must have put this operation together in a hurry. And if we get our heads and asses wired together in time to do a really tight turn, we'll be able to get into an intercept course too."

"Our ships are powering up—the reports are coming in now. But shouldn't we wait until we have more information? After all, we don't know for certain that they're going to obediently follow our projected course."

"Negative. We've got no time to lose. This is going to be a difficult maneuver—practically a reversal of direction. I want it commenced the instant all units are ready." Quietly: "That's an order, Corin."

Things weren't often phrased that way between them. Corin's "Aye aye, sir" was just as quiet. He gave the necessary orders to the flag captain. Presently the flotilla engaged its drives and began to apply its impellers to the task of curving tightly out of orbit onto a new—and almost diametrically opposite—course. It would have been impossible in the days of reaction drives. It was strenuous even in the present age. *Garth's probably right,* Corin reflected. *We don't have a minute to lose.* . . . But then a new set of readouts caught his eye.

"The computer is downloading some more input from the early-warning stations," he reported. "They're in a position to refine their course projection." They both stared at the tank for the heartbeat it took to download the new data. Then, so abruptly that a blinked eye might have missed it, the scarlet arrow jumped upward a few degrees. And a dotted red line snaked forward from its tip, curving not below Sol as they were viewing the system display but above it, in a hyperbola that intersected the green icon which represented Mars—and Janille.

Garth's deep voice held a vast calm. "Well, you were right—we should have waited for all the data. That's the last time I'll overrule you on anything outside an atmosphere. Get us turned back around, into a new intercept course."

Corin didn't trust himself to reply directly. He just gave the orders that sent the flotilla into yet another near reversal of course. Fortunately, they hadn't had time to alter their vector beyond all hope of restoration. The computer projected that they'd be able—barely—to achieve an intercept. That was the good news. The bad news was that Kirpal's forces couldn't possibly arrive in time to influence the outcome of the coming battle. Instead of proceeding almost

directly toward Jupiter, Liang's fleet was curving away
from it.

"I suppose," Garth's too-calm basso interrupted
Corin's thoughts, "Liang planned this a little better
than we thought."

Corin nodded miserably. They had fallen into the
elementary, inexcusable error of assuming stupidity on
the enemy's part. Any Fleet database in the Empire
could forecast the positions of Sol's planets at any given
time. Liang couldn't have relished the prospect of
sending his forces into the waiting jaws of the great
Fleet bases on Jupiter's moons. Besides, he knew Earth
itself was strongly held. So he'd opted to seize Mars
instead, on the far side of Sol from Earth and Jupiter. It would give him a foothold in the Sol system
from which he'd be hard to dislodge, given the universal reluctance to employ the ultimate weapons
against a life-bearing planet—even one that hadn't
always been that way.

Corin mentally reviewed what he knew of that
planet. About ten percent the mass of Earth, with just
under forty percent of its gravity, it had lost its liquid water before life could achieve a foothold—the
common fate of planets below a certain mass, beyond
a certain distance from their suns. Nowadays, nobody
bothered with such worlds. But in the first century
of the space age, when the scientific consensus had
offered no hope that interstellar flight would ever be
more than marginally practicable, Mars had seemed
an attractive candidate for terraforming. Ice asteroids
had been nudged into collision courses with it, biological packages had seeded the new atmosphere those
impacts had produced, and species of ever-increasing
levels of complexity had been introduced over the
course of two and a half centuries. The General War
had barely produced a hiccup in the process, for
afterwards the reconstructed United Nations had
supported it as a prestige-generating government

project which neither required nor created any forbidden technological innovation. As the wave front of colonization had moved on to the stars, the planet had become a backwater—but an attractive backwater, whose inhabitants cultivated the air of romance that was renewed every time classic early-twentieth-century space opera underwent one of its periodic revivals. (The canals could be justified in terms of water distribution, but rumor had always insisted they were really for the tourists.) Mars' ravaging by the Zyungen, like Earth's, had stopped short of total destruction of the biosphere. By now, few people were even aware that Mars hadn't always been inhabited.

Corin came out of his woolgathering as the hostile fleet itself appeared at the edge of the holo tank, following its projected course like a bead sliding along a string. Force-composition analysis was being downloaded, and an order of battle began to appear as readouts. Corin and Garth both studied them, until the latter grunted with a kind of satisfaction. "We were right about one thing, at least: Liang launched this attack in a hurry, with whatever forces he had available. It could be worse—a lot worse."

"It's bad enough, though," Corin said glumly. The Deathstriders were outnumbered in every class of ship. He looked wistfully at the green arrowhead which had awakened to life in the holo tank near Jupiter, where Kirpal had departed orbit. Together, they would have been a match for the invading fleet. As it was, Kirpal couldn't possibly rendezvous with them in time to do Mars any good.

On some isolated level, Corin took an instant to note that neither he nor Garth was even mentioning the possibility that they might simply decline to engage Liang's numerically superior forces, in the absence of support from Kirpal. They could do so with honor, it would be a perfectly defensible decision . . . and it was altogether out of the question. Janille was on Mars.

"The good news," he said after another moment's study of Liang's order of battle, "is that what we're looking at isn't really a fighting force. It's a convoy."

"Right." Garth thrust his massive head forward and gazed at the auxiliary tank where the enemy formation was displayed. His old self began to reawaken. "They're escorting a flock of assault transports full of Marines to be dropped on Mars—and they can't leave them undefended. So they're in a tactical straitjacket. We, on the other hand, are free to maneuver any way we want. That's our edge. We've got to . . . but no. This is your show out here, Corin. However you want to run it, I'll back you to the hilt."

At that moment, for all the subsurface ambivalence of their relationship, and for all his realization that Garth's judgment was sometimes flawed, Corin saw clearly why the Deathstriders had always been willing to do a little more for the big heavy-planet man than was humanly possible. He contented himself with an acknowledgment, brief to the point of curtness, then turned to his displays and readouts.

With the drive's inner field off, he had plenty of subjective time to contemplate his options. Certain fundamental facts of space combat defined those options. Perhaps the most self-evident of these was that a ship under drive, outpacing light, could not be attacked from astern with energy weapons. He could have brought his flotilla sweeping in behind the invaders, but it would have been pointless. Likewise, cutting across the oncoming enemy's course at a right angle—"crossing the T," in ancient wet-navy parlance—would have allowed for only a single, immeasurably brief moment of unthinkable violence, after which Liang's fleet (damaged, no doubt) would have been free to proceed on to Mars while the Deathstriders fought to reverse course and come around. So Corin gave a series of orders which sent his force curving along a course which would intersect the enemy's at a slight angle. The "line ahead"—or its three-dimensional equivalent—had been reborn in space warfare, for ships on parallel or converging courses under drive *could* engage each other in a beam-weapons duel, aiming not at their targets but at points where their near-sentient brains predicted those targets would be when lightspeed energies reached those points.

Time passed, and Corin watched as the two icons drew slowly together in the system display, the invaders coming in from about eight fifteen on the imaginary clock he mentally superimposed on the holo tank, and the Deathstriders curving in from "below" at a shallow angle. Presently the two forces entered missile range, and tiny new red icons began to pop into existence, speeding away from Liang's battleships under the thrust of their suicidally overpowered impellers. Corin gave an order, and the deck shivered beneath his feet as *Impervious*, along with her sister ship *Implacable*, replied in kind. Liang had more battleships—the only kind of ship capable of carrying drive-equipped missiles—and as the red and green missile icons interpenetrated, Corin saw that all too many of the former were getting through. Some of his outlying ships began to report hits. It wasn't disastrous, for the missiles were too large and expensive to be employed en masse. Still . . .

Garth spoke up. "Maybe we'd better increase the percentage of decoys in the warhead mix for our next wave of missiles, Corin."

"Too late to make a change like that—or for it to do any good," Corin relied absently. "We've just got to get into beam range faster." He gave a series of commands to the flag captain, and the green icon in the tank shifted course a few degrees to starboard, heading toward a rendezvous with its scarlet counterpart.

"This is going to take us straight through them, Corin." Garth's voice held neither jitters nor condemnation. He was merely making an observation.

"Not quite 'straight' through them; we'll still be only at about a thirty-degree angle. But our original plan of drawing into a parallel course with them and slugging it out with beams isn't going to work." Corin winced as a cruiser died in the auxiliary tank that displayed his ships individually. "Besides, if I'm right we ought to be able to . . ." His voice trailed off as he thought furiously. He shot a series of questions and problems to his ops officer, who transferred them to specialists with the talent for direct neural interfacing with computers. Garth kept quiet; his promise not to countermand Corin evidently still held good. So did the enemy formation the sensors had reported: like a funnel of warships with the small end forward, protecting the assault transports inside.

Then they were in beam range. And even at the compressed time-rate at which they were existing without their inner field, a soul-shakingly short time passed before they were in among Liang's formation, and then out of it. In that brief interval, X-ray lasers raved against deflector screens, and transposed antimatter warheads—it almost never worked any more, with routine sensor-confusion countermeasures preventing precise placement, but it was always worth a try—died in detonations whose energies strained the fabric of space itself, explosions actually visible in the main screen, like fireflies against the star-strewn blackness. Then they were through, and Corin was rapping out orders and scanning reports.

His guts clenched painfully at the thought of their losses. But they'd come through better, and inflicted more damage, than he'd dared let himself hope. Not that he hadn't expected his people to give better than they got against the garrison units Liang had mustered in the long-quiescent Serpens/Bootes region. And Garth had been right: the enemy was locked into a rigid formation and an unvarying Marsward course. Screaming through that formation in a single quick pass, they'd been able to defeat in detail a limited number of their predictably moving opponents, without having to take on the entire array. And now Corin saw that his orders were being carried out. His helmsmen were wrenching their ships into a tight turn to "starboard" (as viewed in the tank), bringing them around for another pass. He'd calculated that there would be time for three more such passes before the battle reached Mars.

"Corin," Garth spoke quietly, "we need to consider targeting the assault transports."

It was a decision Corin had been putting off. His orders had called for concentrating on the enemy combat units; they'd flashed past the troop haulers inside the "funnel" without giving them courtesy of a shot. But . . .

"You realize," he said carefully, "that the more of our fire we divert from the warships, the more losses we're going to take."

Garth gave a rumble of assent. "Yes. And *you* realize that the more we concentrate on the warships, the more of their Marines are going to make it to Mars."

And Janille, Corin didn't add. He chewed his lower lip, but only for a moment—this decision would have to be made quickly. "I'll have alternate-numbered cruisers target the assault transports. The battleships' and battlecruisers' heavier weapons are needed to crack the warships' defenses."

"Good enough," Garth sighed. He sat back while Corin gave the necessary orders, just in time for their next pass. He hoped that this time the invaders would still be shaken from the previous exchange. He was rudely disappointed. Liang—or whoever was commanding in his name—had been able to steady them, and this time they knew what to expect. The return fire was steadier and more precise.

Shouts of "Incoming!" began to penetrate Corin's

near trance of concentration on the battle pattern, and
Impervious bucked as the energy transfer of a hit
momentarily overcame her inertial compensators.
Nothing serious, he thought with a quick glance at the
damage control readouts. His momentary shift in focus
almost made him miss the moment when they interpenetrated with the assault transports. Those had
military-rated drives, of course—otherwise they would
have been death traps. But their deflector screens
were weaker than those of warships, and the cruisers' weapons savaged them. Corin stole a glance at
Garth, whose expression was complex. It must be only
too easy for him to identify with troopers waiting out
a battle of which they knew nothing, each one alone
with the knowledge that he could at any instant be
obliterated without warning by forces he could do
nothing to combat. At least death would be quick, as
death in space combat tended to be.

The paroxysm of high-energy violence was over, and
Corin was left staring sickly at their loss figures. He
looked away, only to meet Garth's eyes.

"Another two passes and there won't be enough of
us left to make a difference, Corin." The lack of blame
in Garth's voice somehow made it even worse. *He put
his unreserved trust in me, and I failed.*

"Commodore!" The comm officer's voice intruded
on Corin's misery. *"Implacable* reports that impeller
damage makes it impossible for her to keep formation." In confirmation, a green icon in the auxiliary
tank began to drop behind as the rest of the flotilla
performed its turnabout maneuver.

"Tell Captain Avila to drop back and take up a
course parallel to the hostiles, out of beam range.
She's to try to give us missile support, as long as her
missiles last." As Corin gave the order, his thought
tolled in counterpoint: *Fifty percent of our battleship
strength* . . . He took a moment to master himself,
then turned to meet Garth's eyes again.

"Garth, it's no good. If we spend ourselves out here, there'll be nobody to contest their control of Martian orbital space when they get there. Our ground forces will be at their mercy. We've got to break off this engagement and proceed directly there. We can be in position when they arrive."

"And maybe Janille can give us some support," Garth suggested. It was the first time either of them had mentioned her by name. "While you're giving the orders, why don't I send her a squeal?"

"It won't reach her much before we do. But it can't hurt."

As Corin transmitted through the flag captain the orders that would halt the flotilla's swing back into combat and send it on a course parallel with the enemy's, he heard Garth muttering a message to the comm officer. The "squeal" was misnamed, because a message sent from a ship under drive to someone existing at normal time in the outside universe was, from the latter's standpoint, too brief to qualify even as that. Indeed, it was too brief to be picked up at all, unless the intended listener was very alert for it, and knew exactly where it was coming from. In Janille's case, the second was certain and the first nearly so. Once she'd received it, she could have it slowed down by a factor of hundreds of thousands. She could not, however, reply; they'd be at Mars while she was still clearing her throat to do so. Such communication was, of necessity, one-way.

Corin kept his attention on the tank. His ships were following instructions, a little raggedly but in good time. They settled into their new course, out of beam range of the invaders, and kept up a desultory missile duel. On the far side of the opposing formation, *Implacable* did the same, although it fell further and further behind. He noted with relief that Liang's admiral didn't detach ships to finish off the lamed battleship, but continued to keep formation.

The squeal was, of course, ahead of them. In fact, the tachyons of which it was composed had arrived at precisely the instant they were sent, or at least with no time lag anyone had ever succeeded in measuring. But they weren't far behind it. Soon Mars grew into a ball in the main screen, rushing toward them. Then they reached the Chen Limit—a fairly close-in one, for this was a small planet—and deactivated their drives. The ball seemed to slam to a stop, but actually continued growing at a much slower rate as their impellers braked their intrinsic velocity down, turning into a pale-blue-and-tawny globe. (Once, Corin knew, it had been known as the "Red Planet"; but terraforming had changed that.)

They'd barely begun to assume orbit when Janille hailed them. She appeared on the comm screen clad in the regulation bodystockinglike liner, against a background of frantic activity as support crews, moving in the distinctive way permitted by Martian gravity, brought up attachable modular components for the Deathstriders' powered armor. Corin recognized those components for what they were, and knew what Janille was up to before she even spoke.

"I got your squeal," she told them. "We don't have much time, because they're right behind you. I've got an idea."

"We're open to them," Garth said drily.

"Then get your ships into positions where Deimos and Phobos can support them." Mars' two tiny moons—captured asteroids, really—had long ago been partially hollowed out and turned into defensive installations which, though obsolete by now, had to be taken seriously here inside the Chen Limit where ships could not make themselves irresistible and invulnerable with their drive fields. "They'll have to fight you. And we'll—"

"Yes!" Garth, too, had seen what she had in mind. "But do you really think you can make enough of a difference to justify the risk?"

"Depends. Has your computer identified the enemy flagship?"

"Not yet. They've been in a rigid formation, with no patterns of movement to be analyzed. But when they arrive here, and have to redeploy—"

"Put your computer into linkage with mine so it can download the analysis immediately. By then we ought to be ready to transpose down here. For now . . . good luck. Signing off."

They were barely settled into orbit thirty-four hundred miles above Mars' surface, trailing Phobos by about thirty degrees, with Deimos—fortuitously on the same side of the primary planet at this point in its seven-and-a-half-hour orbit—below and in position to offer support, when the hostiles reached the Chen Limit and killed their drives. As Janille had foreseen, they immediately began to deploy to attack the satellite bases and the Deathstrider ships. Things hadn't changed fundamentally since the wet-navy days of pre-spaceflight Earth, when it had been axiomatic that no amphibious invasion could succeed without command of the sea. Nowadays, a successful planetary assault required that the defenders' orbital assets be neutralized. *Impervious*' brain watched and analyzed as the attackers' formation dissolved and reconfigured itself; with the assault transports and some light escorts safely behind. And the battle they'd broken off resumed.

In orbital space, with the scope for maneuvering strictly limited, it was a brutish slugging match of sheer firepower against targets with predictable vectors. Fighters rose from the subsurface vaults of Phobos, along with the missiles which, not having to hold their own drives, could be employed in large numbers. The capital ships also belched forth salvoes of such missiles, along with torrents of directed energy. It was a holocaust of high-intensity violence, carried on in what would have seemed to some an eerie silence . . . except, of course, when some ship's deflector screens failed for an instant and the naked metal hull within gave way to a segment of hell.

Corin was steadying himself against the concussion of such a hit—a minor one, in a remote and nonessential area of *Impervious*' hugeness—when the call came from the sensor station. "Commodore, the computer has picked out the enemy flagship." In the tactical tank, one of the hostile battleships now appeared surrounded by a red circle, from whatever angle one viewed it. "The data was simultaneously passed on to Colonel Dornay. And . . . yes, now!" Tiny green dots had begun appearing in the tank.

They would not, Corin knew, show in the enemy's holo tanks. The powered-armor suits that had begun popping out of nothingness in Martian orbital space, transposed up from the surface, had too little mass to have been detected even had sensors been trained on that precise area of space at the time. But those suits' transponders spoke to the Deathstriders' command instrumentation aboard *Impervious*, and more and more of the little tiny icons, like a swath of green fairy dust, appeared in the tank . . . and, under the thrust of the suits' impeller modules, began to move, converging on the scarlet-haloed battleship.

Deflector screens resisted material objects with a force directly proportional to those objects' velocity. High-speed ones usually burned up with the heat of their own shedded energy. But slow-moving ones could pass through with no more resistance than that of a stiff breeze. The Deathstriders, trained in EVA combat, converged on the enemy flagship whose occupants didn't even become aware of their presence until they were close enough to activate point-defense radars. They took some losses from the lasers those radars controlled. But most of them lived to attach themselves with magnetic clamps to the battleship's outer skin, which they then punctured with breaching charges. Then, like microbes entering a doomed organism, they blasted their way in through bulkhead after bulkhead.

Corin, listening to fragmentary reports, tried to imagine the pandemonium that flagship's interior must have become. Every warship carried a Marine detachment, but they probably hadn't been in their powered armor, and while they were getting into it the Deathstriders must have been unstoppable, incinerating any ordinary security forces that tried to bar their way. And their suits' minicomputers were linked with a database that held the deck plan of every Fleet ship class. Now that they knew which class of battleship they were dealing with, those plans appeared on helmet HUDs. Inexorably, the microorganisms ate their way inward toward the leviathan's nerve centers.

Corin became aware of the background growl from the comm station, as Garth tried to raise Janille at the surface base. "What do you mean she's not available? Who am I speaking to? What did you say? *What was that?*" Garth turned an aghast face to Corin. "They say she's with the assault force, aboard the enemy flagship!"

"Well, you started the Deathstriders tradition that the C.O. leads an attack in person."

"But . . . but that was different!"

A hail on the priority channel cut Garth's protestations off—Janille's voice, shouting to make herself heard above a background din. "This is Colonel Dornay, reporting from the Combat Information Center of the battleship *Indestructible*, flagship of the self-styled—"

"Janille, cut the crap!" A catch in Garth's voice spoiled the full-throated bellow he'd intended. "What's going on over there?"

"We're in control here at the CIC—" A loud boom caused Garth's ruddiness and Corin's swarthiness to pale. "—although some counterattacks are still in progress. Our other elements are still working their way toward the bridge. The point is, they can't coordinate their fleet properly, with us here."

"Yes, I see!" Corin exclaimed. The ever-fluctuating display of figures, and the motion of the moving lights in the tank, had already begun to tell a tale that trained eyes could read. "Garth, we've got to turn into them, go for close action."

The general looked dubiously at the tank. He wasn't as attuned to the nuances of space combat as Corin, but he could see the relative numbers of green and red icons. "Are you sure?"

"Look at the computer breakdown. They're still putting out as much firepower, but less of it is getting through. That's because nobody's allocating their fire to overload our defenses at specified points. And look at the way they're moving, like . . . Well, just take my word for it. It'll be almost like attacking a gaggle of individual ships—or, at best, individual squadrons—milling around with no command-and-control."

If Garth hesitated, it was for no appreciable length of time. "It's your battle, Corin. Fight it."

Without even pausing to give a formal acknowledgment, Corin addressed Janille, wishing they could have gotten a visual. He hastily outlined his intentions. "Hold out there as long as you can," he concluded.

"Hold out, hell! We're going to *take* this sucker! Just be sure you don't attack it. Be a hell of a note to get our asses vaporized by friendly fire. Signing off."

"Good luck," Corin said quietly, but she'd already cut the connection and there was no response but a soft, crackling hiss. He put her out of his mind, and began issuing orders.

Presently, the green icons in the tank began swinging simultaneously into an almost ninety-degree course change, plunging into the scarlet battle-mass. Their opponents, already shaken badly by their loss of central control, buckled under the unexpected move and recoiled from the impact of what passed for point-blank fire in space war: beam weapons used at their optimum range, and missiles launched in "sprint" mode, practically unguided and barely interceptable. It was a battle in which there could be no thought of defense, save the purely passive sort represented by deflector screens. There was only mutual offense, at hellish levels of intensity and suicidally short ranges. Ships began to die rapidly—far more of the invaders' ships, Corin saw, but enough of his own, too ... enough and more than enough. Still, with the enemy's fire control reduced to chaos, the advantage was clearly with the Deathstriders. He wondered, as he sat strapped into his command chair on a flag bridge that periodically bucked to the harsh music of the damage-control klaxons, if that advantage would be enough to let them outlast the enemy's numbers.

It had gone on longer—and with more slaughter—than Corin would have believed possible, when two things happened. First Janille appeared on the comm screen against the backdrop of a battle-devastated bridge, to announce that the enemy flagship had been secured. Mere seconds later, what was left of the enemy formation began to dissolve as its component ships broke off the engagement and scattered, each fleeing along the vector best calculated to take it out of danger. One by one they passed the Chen Limit and receded into the starfields more swiftly than light. The flag bridge crew was too stunned to cheer.

Garth was the first to recover. "What happened, Corin? Did they panic because their flagship had surrendered?"

"No—they'd probably written it off already. No, it was *that*." And Corin pointed to the main holo tank, at what they'd all forgotten about.

Kirpal's fresh, undepleted force, its transit of the inner Sol system completed, had crossed Mars' Chen Limit.

"So," Garth said slowly, "they saw that they couldn't

possibly hope to resist him—not with the losses they've taken." He heaved a sigh. "We held out long enough, and inflicted enough damage. But at what a cost!" His eyes looked haunted as they scanned the columns of lost and damaged ships. No mercenary leader could ever be as stoical about really heavy casualties as an officer who had the resources of a state behind him and could view his command as expendable in pursuit of an objective. With mercenaries, the unit was end as well as means; it must be preserved, for it was its own *raison d'etre*. Garth had lost sight of that in the heat of the battle they'd just endured, and the realization shook him.

"Well, let's have comm put us in touch with Kirpal," he finally said. "Hey, look, they're coming in right behind *Implacable*."

It was true. The crippled battleship had finally labored gallantly up and cut its tortured drive. Kirpal's formation was looming up astern of it, still invisible of course, although *Implacable* herself was now showing as a tiny gleam of reflected sunlight in the main screen.

Corin felt delayed reaction to what they'd been through begin to seep into him. *It's over*, the thought sighed through him like a spring breeze. *It's over, and Janille's alive.* He let lassitude take him as he sank back into his command chair and watched that little gleam in the screen. . . . But then something in the main tank, something not quite right, caught the corner of his eye.

Minute green dots, appearing in space ahead of the oncoming flotilla. And they seemed to be converging on *Implacable*. What . . . ?

In the main screen, the small point of light that was *Implacable* flared like the birth of a sun, dazzling their eyes for a fraction of a second before the automatic glare-damping circuitry could kick in. Then there was just an expanding cloud of superheated debris, cooling rapidly, guttering out like dying embers.

Garth was the first on the flag bridge to recover, though a full heartbeat passed after the explosion before he surged to his feet. "Raise Kirpal!" he roared at the comm officer.

It was unnecessary, because Chewning's admiral appeared on the comm screen and spoke without preamble. "I am ordered by Prime Minister Chewning, in His Imperial Majesty's name, to inform you that you are in violation of the Imperial edict on possession of weapons of mass destruction by free companies—which is still in force. You are therefore liable to be treated as outlaws, subject to summary suppressive action by the Fleet." The screen blanked as unceremoniously as it had awakened, but there was no silence, for the air of the flag bridge was clamorous with panic-stricken calls from other ships, and robotic alarms of incoming fire. And in the tank, Kirpal's ships swept down on them, preceded by a wave front of missiles like those that had obliterated *Implacable*. Other missiles also appeared in the tank, for the Deimos and Phobos bases were also pouring fire into their erstwhile allies.

"General order to all elements!" Garth thundered. "Every ship for itself. Save yourselves any way you can." He seemed about to say more, but a hit on *Impervious'* physical hull rocked the great ship and sent him staggering back against his command chair. He strapped himself in hurriedly, for much of the missile storm was converging on the flagship.

The Deathstrider ships were endeavoring to follow Garth's orders, but many of them were caught flat-footed and died in silent flares of superheated plasma. Still more were impaled by searing X-ray lasers as Kirpal's ships drew into beam range. But some reached the Chen Limit and vanished. *Impervious* strained to follow them, while struggling to fend off her attackers.

"Garth!" Corin shouted above the din. "Don't forget Janille. We've got to get her off that ship."

"It's too late, Corin." Garth spoke low, but his bass made itself heard as he pointed at the tank. The new attackers must have been monitoring their communications, and known that the flagship of Liang's fleet was now in the Deathstriders' hands. It was no immediate threat to them—the mercenaries who'd captured it hadn't the training to take it into battle. But Kirpal had spared it an offhand barrage, and now its icon blinked on and off in the bloodless way the holo tank had of denoting critical damage, and its course was beginning to sag downward toward the planetary atmosphere below, whose friction would consume it.

Corin, his mind already afloat in a limitless universe of horror, found himself sinking down into an even lower level of the unthinkable. With practiced swiftness, he clamped his consciousness into automatic thought processes. *There'll be plenty of time for a breakdown later,* he thought. But then he studied the damage board. *No, there won't,* he amended. Little by little, *Impervious* died under several ships' fire.

"Raise Kirpal," Garth said, in a voice Corin had never heard the big adventurer use. "Tell him we surrender."

"I'm trying, sir," the comm officer reported. "No response."

"They're not interested in accepting surrenders," Corin heard himself say.

Garth squeezed his eyes tightly shut for a heartbeat, then spoke with the calm of ultimate despair. "Pass the order to abandon ship."

They ran through the endless passageways with all the other hurrying figures, periodically staggering as the ship reeled from a new hit. But the ship's brain continued to operate the defensive systems, and a battleship that was actively defending itself took a lot of killing. They ought, Corin thought, to be able to make it to the docking bay, with its lifeboats and drive-equipped pinnaces.

Then the deck jumped, and the hellish sound of tearing metal stunned them. Ahead, flame billowed out into the passageway, consuming human bodies like moths in a flame. They picked themselves up and hurried in the opposite direction.

"I don't suppose we'll reach the docking bay after all," Garth said in the same strangely calm voice.

"But there's one thing we might be able to reach: the forward transposer room."

Interest seemed to shake loose from under Garth's blanket of hopelessness. "But where could we transpose to? I have a feeling Chewning's people on the surface are wiping out whoever Janille left down there."

"Probably. But what other choice have we got?"

"None, of course. Lead the way."

Incredibly, the transposer technicians were still manning their posts when they got there, sending one group of tattered fugitives after another to the Martian surface. "General . . . Commodore!" their chief cried. "We're still functioning, even though our power supply keeps getting disrupted. We can still send the two of you down. . . . Wait a minute, somebody's signaling for acknowledgment." She turned to the comm station that every transposer facility had. Its screen flashed into life, revealing a figure in battle-soiled powered-armor liner, against the backdrop of a small spacecraft's interior.

"Janille!" shouted Corin and Garth in unison.

"Thank God it's you! There's nobody on the flag bridge, but your ship's brain had the initiative to try all the locations where you *might* be." She swept back matted auburn hair and drew a deep breath. "Look, there's not much time. Have them transpose you to the location of my link."

"But—but where are you?" Garth demanded.

"I managed to get off *Indestructible* in a pinnace. Most of my people also got away—but in lifeboats, which can only get them down to the surface of Mars, where Chewning's butchers will get them. There were two others with me, but the boat bay took a hit just as we were getting in—I'm the only one who made it into the pinnace in time." She angrily shook off the clinging ghosts. "Look, we haven't got time for this. Transpose *now*."

"We've got a fix on her link, sir," the chief technie announced. "She's out there, barely within range."

"And I can't stay here much longer," Janille added. "They haven't noticed a pinnace out here, this close to *Impervious*, but that won't last."

"And neither will *Impervious*," Corin said grimly as another hit rocked the deck. "Let's go, Garth, while we still can."

They mounted the transposer stage. "Put this thing on automatic and get yourselves off as soon as we're gone," Garth ordered the chief.

"Will do, sir. Good luck." She reached for her controls . . . and the transposer station vanished from their ken, replaced by the tiny cargo hold of a pinnace, with a link lying on the deck.

As always, the transposer acted as a sink for potential-energy differentials, and the pinnace seemed steady under them. But then, as they scrambled for the hatch that led toward the little bridge-*cum*-passenger cabin, the craft bucked like a scalded animal, sending them staggering against the bulkheads. Garth recovered first and hauled Corin to his feet. They stumbled the rest of the way, arriving just in time to see an expanding, dissipating plasma cloud in the viewscreen beyond Janille's head.

"*Impervious*," Corin stated rather than asked.

Janille nodded. "She blew just after you got off her. That was the shock wave that we just felt." It would have destroyed them, Corin knew, if there had been an atmosphere to carry it. As it was, the wave front of superheated gas that had been a battleship had sent the pinnace tumbling across the sky. The screen's artificial stabilization of the outside view, and the artificial gravity holding them to the deck, concealed the fact that Janille was still trying to bring the little craft under control.

"Let me," Corin said, elbowing her aside. She didn't argue. He had far more training and experience at vessel handling than the minimal amount she'd picked up—it was a wonder that she'd been able to pilot the pinnace to a near rendezvous with *Impervious*. He worked with single-minded concentration, not letting himself think of the transposer technicians who had died an instant after lingering to save him and Garth.

After a moment, the gas shell that marked *Impervious*' grave began to recede rapidly in the view aft, as did the occasional flashes that were all that was visible of the diminishing battle—or, rather, massacre. "We're under control," Corin announced, "but I couldn't be too picky about our course."

"Never mind that," Garth replied. "Just get us out of here."

Presently Mars ceased to be a world below and became a planet in the distance—funny the way one always knew when that particular threshold had been crossed, Corin thought. Then they were past the Chen Limit, and he engaged the drive. Mars instantly began to fall away at an impossible rate, dropping down an infinite well—as, presently, did Sol.

Corin sat back, finally taking the time to notice that he was drenched with sweat and that his hands were trembling. "We're safe," he said dully. "Our heading is toward Aquila, but we can afford to change course now."

"No." Garth's voice brought his two companions' heads turning toward him, for it was deeper than they'd ever heard it, a subliminal rumble below the normal bass range. It was also emotionless—too emotionless. "We don't want to change course—at least not toward Epsilon Eridani. That would be suicide."

"Why?"

"Think about it, Janille. Chewning saw a perfect opportunity in the way the battle developed, with us on the receiving end of Liang's attack. He let us stop Liang for him, and bleed ourselves white doing so. Then, and only then, he took advantage of the opportunity to rid himself of a potential rival, by turning on us when we were uniquely vulnerable. Having done so, he's not going to just let us go back to our base and recover, is he?" Garth's voice was still level, which somehow heightened the horror of his words. "No, I guarantee that after Kirpal has finished mopping up he's going to head directly to Epsilon Eridani, before our people there have even heard what's happened. In fact, I wouldn't be surprised if he's already en route.

"No," Garth went on after a pause, and under its calm surface his voice began to build in volume gradually and, at first, almost imperceptibly. "I say we're headed exactly where we want to go: toward sectors that Ivar Brady-Schiavona controls, through his son Roderick. Because now our only option is to offer our services to him."

"But," Corin interrupted, "what about our ships that escaped from Sol? Aren't they going to return to Epsilon Eridani?"

"I doubt if many of them will. You and I have never trained our officers to be mindless robots. They'll be able to figure out which way the wind is blowing, just as we have. And they'll reach the same conclusions. Yes, we'll be seeing them again, out Aquila way. They know as well as we do that Brady-Schiavona has a reputation for generosity to whoever joins him, regardless of background. And . . . sooner or later, he's going to put paid to Chewning. I want to be there when he does!" Now the increase in volume was no longer gradual. It grew to a bull roar, hurting the ears, reverberating through the structure of this confined space as the rage that had been banked under layers of shock and exhaustion came thundering forth at last. "Kirpal was just following orders—he gets a clean death, if he begs for it hard enough. But as for Chewning, I'm going to personally cut his heart out and feed it to pigs! I swear it!"

Abruptly, with the echoes still chasing each other around the little compartment, Garth flung himself down into a passenger couch and sat glaring silently. Corin and Janille were equally silent. They all stared into the screen. The pinnace fled on into the galactic night.

CHAPTER NINE
The DM -17 954 System, 4328 C.E.

A pinnace was the only interstellar-capable space-craft class small enough to be carried as an auxiliary, even by a battleship. To squeeze a drive—even one which didn't have to accelerate the time-flow by as high a factor as a warship's—into so small a hull, certain nonessentials had to be sacrificed ... like the comfort of the occupants.

This wasn't normally a problem, because pinnaces weren't intended for long-range deployment; their passengers didn't have to endure them for long. But Corin, Garth and Janille were looking at a two-week voyage to the Beta Aquilae Sector, where they hoped to find Roderick Brady-Schiavona or one of his high-ranking subordinates. Fortunately, the pinnace was intended for as many as six people. Unfortunately, its provisions were meant to last those six for less than half the time the three of them expected to be en route. They went on short rations immediately.

At least they didn't have to worry about breathable air and other environmental factors. Molecular-level recycling technology had been ubiquitous for so long that spacefarers had forgotten the concerns that had obsessed their remote predecessors. And as long as the power plant lasted—which would be years—the air would be at a comfortable temperature, and one standard Prometheus gravity would hold them to the deck. But no technology could make the cabin any larger than it was, nor could any of their improvisations confer any real privacy. After a while, when all the obvious conversational topics had run dry, they tended more and more to withdraw into themselves, three separate universes that couldn't abrade each other, floating in a continuum of increasingly meaningless time.

Under the circumstances, it was impossible for Corin to speak to Janille privately about the dreams.

They had begun as the pinnace had passed the invisible frontier of the Psi Capricorni Sector, which extended an arm across its route. After understanding dawned, Corin wanted to discuss it with Janille, alone. But it was out of the question, of course. So, after an interval of indecision, he blurted it out in the cabin.

"Janille, you've been having the dreams, haven't you?"

She started. "Why . . . yes? How did you . . . ? But of course. You *would* be having them too, wouldn't you?"

Garth stirred; he'd been about to doze off. "What are you two talking about?"

Corin considered him. "You wouldn't know, would you, Garth? You weren't there."

"I wasn't *where*?" Irritability underlay Garth's growl. He was a man who appreciated a good meal, and the rations didn't bring out the best in him. "Talk sense, will you?"

"Remember, back on Neustria early this year, the time Janille and I experienced what was publicly explained as a transposer malfunction?"

After a moment, Garth nodded. "Oh, yes. It was sort of forgotten afterwards. We didn't have time to think about it, because that was when we learned of

Oleg's assassination, and things started happening fast. But yes, I remember now. You told me what had really happened . . . the Luon you encountered. . . ."

"Yes—and how we fell asleep before contacting you. Pretty surprising that we just dropped off, under the circumstances, wouldn't you say? Well, I think that Luon, underneath all its bland, apologetic bullshit, was playing a very deep and very subtle game. In fact, I think it manipulated our minds."

Garth's head jerked up, and his eyes flashed. Off to the side, Janille sucked in a shaken breath at the suggestion, which obviously hadn't occurred to her. Corin was unsurprised at their reactions. Indeed, it had been all he could do to speak that last sentence in a level, unshaken voice. For the three of them shared two millennia of cultural background.

The restructured United Nations of the late twenty-second century, seeking to suppress any innovation that might threaten its carefully nurtured global order, had faced one fundamental problem: it could only control those sciences whose existence it acknowledged. And the scientific establishment had long since accepted a twentieth-century science fiction writer's verdict that psionic phenomena, if they existed at all, must be too weak to be of any use to humans—which, of course, had been absolutely true as applied to *untrained, unenhanced* humans, the only sort in existence at the time. So the U.N.'s scientific police had been caught with their intellectual pants down by Antonescu's grand unified field theory, which had placed psi in context with matter and energy, and revealed the hitherto-unsuspected relationship between neural activity above a certain level of complexity and the outcomes of observed events. The practical consequences had been slight at first, even after researchers who'd finally known exactly what to look for had begun to identify the tiny percentage of the human race with psionic potential. But they'd given Earth its only serious upheavals from the twenty-third through twenty-sixth centuries, as the U.N. suppressed rogue psis who had become popular heroes and catalysts for the deeply buried discontents of the age.

Eventually, though, the U.N. had recognized the newly awakened abilities as a potential tool for tightened control. It had co-opted the surviving psis, tying them firmly to its ideology and thus making them natural enemies of the conquerors from Sigma Draconis. A low-grade covert struggle had enlivened Earth during the two centuries after the Solarian Federation's founding, and a not-entirely-unjustified concern about security was one of the reasons the Federation had kept its military headquartered on Prometheus. That struggle had given birth to new technologies of psionic suppression and amplification. In the crucible of the Unification Wars' forced-draft research and development, those technologies had produced horrors. Like everything else reminiscent of that nightmare era, psi was still hedged about with legal restrictions and popular revulsion.

Now that revulsion looked out at Corin from Janille's eyes.

"Oh, I don't think our free will was compromised—not really. I don't think mine *could* have been; you know about my faculty of telepathic resistance. I think it was more a matter of insinuating a suggestion while we were asleep and malleable. That suggestion has lain dormant for all this time. But now it's awakening." Corin drew a shaky breath. "Janille, let me see if I can accurately describe the nature of the dreams you've been having. I'll venture a guess that they involve the image of a Luon . . . but not so much the visual image as the *essence*, understood on a level that can't be verbalized."

"I check you," she said quietly.

"All right. Let me further guess that the dream always concludes the same way: with a starfield, as viewed from a ship, and a strong nonverbal indicator of some kind pointing to a particular yellow-white star, a little off to starboard."

She nodded mutely.

"Well, this last sleep, I made a conscious effort, for which I'd prepared myself in advance, to wrench myself awake during that part—don't ask me how I could do that while still asleep and dreaming, but I did. Afterwards, the first thing I did was study the viewscreen before the memory had faded. And I'm certain the starfield in the dream is *that* one." He pointed a not-altogether-steady finger toward the screen at the forward end of the cabin, beyond the piloting console. "I believe it was the sight of that particular configuration of stars that triggered the dreams."

"Wait a minute, wait a minute!" Garth protested. "Let's assume that this Luon did, in fact, leave some telepathic suggestion in your mind. How could it have known that you'd someday be traveling along a particular course? In all the crazy stories I've ever heard about the Luonli, nobody's claimed that they can foresee the future!"

"But we know they have some psi abilities," Janille argued. "Telepathy, teleportation and levitation, at a minimum. Why not precognition as well?"

"Come on! Even if precog exists at all, about which there's some doubt, it doesn't confer a detailed future itinerary! It's just a matter of briefly glimpsed visual images, mostly useless."

"That may be true of humans. But we're talking about aliens! Who's to say—"

"It doesn't matter how the Luon did it," Corin cut in. "The fact is that it *did*. Janille, remember I was talking to the Luon just before we dozed off, thanking it for its help?"

"No. I must have already been asleep."

"Well, then, you won't recall its reply. But I do. Let me see if I can remember the exact words. . . . Something about how I'd be able to pay any debt I felt I owed, 'At a star on the outskirts of what your Empire calls the Beta Aquilae Sector.' So one way or another it knew we were going to be here. Speculation about *how* it knew is pointless until we have more data. That's not what we need to be doing."

"Just what *do* we need to be doing?" Garth challenged.

"Isn't it obvious? We've got to change course for that star."

Janille spoke into Garth's flabbergasted silence. "But Corin, do you even know which star it is?" She indicated the screen, with its masses of unwinking little points of light, far more numerous than any dweller at the bottom of an atmosphere can ever see, even on a moonless desert night.

"I believe so. That was something else I made myself concentrate on." Corin turned toward the screen and advanced like a sleepwalker until he could almost touch it. He pointed at a bright yellow-white star, off to the lower right. "That one."

Janille walked slowly forward and stood beside him. She gazed at the screen for several heartbeats. "Yes . . . I think you're right."

Garth stared at their backs, feeling excluded in a way their sexual relationship had never aroused in him. "Uh, wouldn't it be a good idea to check this star out—see if it's really anywhere near us?"

"You're right." Janille sat down at the pilot's station and lowered the neurohelmet over her head. She hadn't used it in piloting, not having felt sufficiently familiar with the pinnace. But now she gazed at the star, and the image flowed directly from her brain to the vessel's computer, which began to produce information. She recited it in the expressionless, rather distant voice of one linked in a direct neural interface. "DM -17 954. Only about three standard light-years from us. It's a G1 star, technically main-sequence but exceptionally massive . . . Believed to have undergone some fairly catastrophic fluctuations in energy output in the not-too-remote past ... No colonized, or habitable, planets ... One brown dwarf ..." All at once she stiffened and listened in silence for a while to the voice inside her head. Then she raised the neurohelmet into its overhead niche and turned to Corin, face alight. "This system is somehow linked with the legend of Basil Castellan. In fact, there's anecdotal evidence that he fled here after his last battle."

"What? But I thought nobody knew where he went after that. His mysterious last message to his followers said nothing about where it was being recorded."

"It's just a rumor. Seems that after the battle, one of Lothar Medina's cruisers came here, following up what they thought was a lead as to Castellan's whereabouts. It suffered some kind of accident, and took some losses—including Medina's Inspector General. After it limped back, there was naturally a board of inquiry. The captain—who testified that they *hadn't* found Castellan—was cleared, and most people forgot the whole thing. But the whispers never quite died out."

Garth's throat-clearing broke an extended silence. "Let's talk about practicalities for a minute. Even assuming that we really do want to go to this godforsaken star, we can't. In case you haven't noticed, our food supply is just barely adequate to last us to our destination. We can't afford any side jaunts!"

Without replying, Janille brought the neurohelmet back down. She was only in communion with the pinnace's brain for a short time. "It's still far enough ahead of us for an economical course change, Garth. The computer assures me that the food can be made to last long enough for it. Of course, we'll have to cut our rations still further—but not below the starvation level."

The prospect of combat had never made Garth look as alarmed as he did now. He smoothed out his

expression and spoke gruffly. "Let's put that aside for
a minute. The question is, even assuming that we *can*
go to this star, do we *want* to?"

"Why, of course," said Janille in a surprised voice.

"There's no 'of course' about it," Garth said firmly.
"Have these dreams given you any clue as to just what
you'll find there?"

"No."

"So it's a wild goose chase, then. How do you even
know it's in your best interests, as opposed to the
Luon's? They might not be the same, you know. The
Luon must have its own agenda."

"Come on, Garth," Janille smiled. "Admit it: you
just don't want to go on shorter rations."

Garth was not about to be jollied. "I can't believe
you two! Have you considered the possibility that you
may be acting under a compulsion to seek this star
out? And that this Luon might have put that compulsion into your minds along with everything else?"

"That may be true, Garth," Corin acknowledged.
"But I don't see how it changes anything. It's pretty
obvious that we're dealing with something out of the
ordinary here—something important. And I can't
believe the Luon is sending us into anything harmful. If its intentions toward us were malign, it would
have been a lot simpler to just let us rot in those
caverns."

"I'm opposed to it. Our first and only priority is
to get to Beta Aquilae and make sure there's a place
under Ivar Brady-Schiavona for what's left of the
Deathstriders. And last time I looked, I was in command of this outfit, which makes my view official. End
of discussion."

Corin didn't answer at once. Instead he held Garth's
eyes, his expression unreadable. Then he spoke quietly. "There's really no conflict between this and our
obligation to reach Beta Aquilae, Garth. You heard
what Janille said: we can afford the detour. As soon

as we've ... fulfilled whatever purpose we're being directed toward this star for, Janille and I will take this vessel wherever you want it to go."

After a moment of speechlessness, Garth drew in a breath that filled his casklike chest with air. He started to open his mouth ... but then the thunder died aborning, for he had belatedly caught the odd emphasis Corin had placed on the words "Janille and I." And he understood that which Corin had left unsaid.

Corin was a qualified pilot. Janille had some training at it. But he, Garth, did not. Like Janille, he had the aptitude for direct neural interfacing. But a spacecraft was a very different proposition from a suit of powered combat armor. He could link with the pinnace, but he couldn't give it the necessary commands to get back on the correct heading.

He could, of course, order the craft to maintain its present heading. Indeed, it would do that anyway in the absence of a contrary command. And he could physically impose his authority on the other two, if it came to that. But there was no way he could possibly prevent them from surreptitiously changing the course. He had to sleep sometime.

These thoughts chased each other around the inside of Garth's mind, in a closed circle from which there was no escape. He finally released his breath and looked from Corin to Janille and back again. He saw nothing in their faces but respectful attentiveness. Anything less like the usual idea of a mutiny would have been impossible to imagine.

"You know," Garth finally said, in a conversational tone, "the Deathstriders who are still alive followed us to Sol willingly, believing—God knows why—that we knew what we were doing." Corin's wince showed him his instinct had been accurate. "Don't you think we owe them something? Like a chance?"

"Certainly we do, Garth," Janille said quickly. "We're

with you on this. We just need to resolve this first. What harm can a short delay do?"

"How can you know it's going to be 'short'? You don't even know what it is you're looking for! And you don't know where to look for it! Remember, we're talking about an entire planetary system. It's easy for us to lose sight of just how big that is, but—"

"Actually, Garth, I think we *do* know where to look." Corin's voice held a quiet certainty which stopped the other man in mid-sentence. He turned to Janille. "You know the rest of the dream, don't you?"

"Yes. I've had it too." They looked at each other, but what each was seeing, as though from orbit, was the harshly orange-banded curve of what had to be a gas-giant planet of barely substellar mass.

DM -17 954 V, viewed at first hand as they approached, looked remarkably similar to their memories of dreams. But the panorama in the screen held a quality absent from those memories—a sense of seething, roiling, dynamic energies, altogether at variance with the serenity of the rings and the stateliness of the orbiting moons beyond. Perhaps it was their knowledge that the mammoth globe below—over four times as massive as Sol's Jupiter, massive enough to produce its own heat and light by gravitational compression—was flooding these nearby spaces with radiation that would have struck them dead if the pinnace's deflector screens had failed for even a moment.

"Well," Garth said in the smallest voice of which he was capable, "we're here. I don't suppose your dreams have also provided a glimpse of whatever it is we're looking for?"

"No." Corin shook his head without taking his eyes off the spectacle. "Just a non-visual, non-verbal impression. The essence of Luon-ness." He remembered it vividly, but couldn't have described it in any intelligible way. A kind of soaring aspiration, ambitious for infinity, streaking upward against a backdrop of Stygian tragedy ... and faltering, falling short and sinking downward into an infinite night, but still coruscating with an intricate interplay of light as it descended. *Yes*, Corin thought, *I can remember it clearly. So clearly it's almost as though it's not a memory at all, but something entering my mind right now....*

No! It's not possible!

But Janille's face told him it was, for she wore an expression that he knew must be a twin of his own. Garth's face showed bewilderment, and something that on anyone else would have looked like fear.

(*Grave courtesy.*) "Greetings Commodore Marshak, Colonel Dornay. You are expected. As are you, General Krona, although I perceive that you are somewhat puzzled—understandably so, inasmuch as you, unlike your companions, have never experienced telepathic contact by a Luon." (*Solicitude.*) "Do not be alarmed! Your mental privacy is secure, as has been explained to Commodore Marshak and Colonel Dornay. And you are in no physical danger."

Corin found his voice—or at least a broken, stammering remnant of it. "Who are you? *Where* are you? How can you be communicating with us out here?"

"You are correct in your suppositions about telepathy's inherently limited range, even for a very powerful and artificially amplified talent. So, as you may infer, I am no great distance from you. Do not be concerned at your inability to detect me, for my privacy has some rather sophisticated protections. But turn your attention to your viewscreen, somewhat to the lower left."

Even with the telepathic pointer, they probably wouldn't have noticed it if the curving edge of the brown dwarf below hadn't been directly behind it. One by one, they became aware that a segment of that otherwise knife-sharp line between the glowing burnt-orange and velvety black was wavering as though seen through rippling water. Once they knew what to look for, they could see the same shimmering in the stars above and the hydrogen clouds below, within a well-defined circle.

Janille, seeming to shake herself awake from a too-intense dream, turned to the sensor readouts. "There's nothing there," she said in a small voice.

"Nothing your sensors can detect," the neuter "voice" inside their heads corrected. "What you are seeing is the outer surface of a spherical field which bends light around itself, conferring invisibility on everything within. Normally, it encompasses only my . . . physical plant. But I have expanded it to its maximum volume—several hundred kilometers in diameter—so that you can locate it. Please shape a course for that sphere."

"Uh," Garth said hesitantly, "what's going to happen when we pass through the boundary of this 'field'?"

"Nothing harmful, I assure you. It has no effect on material objects." (*Impatience.*) "The maintenance of the field at this volume imposes a serious energy drain, so if you would be so kind as to proceed without delay. . . ."

The three looked at each other for a moment. Unspoken agreement was reached, and Janille turned without a word to the controls. The pinnace's impellers awoke, and the circle of slight visual distortion began to grow, gradually filling the screen.

True to the assurance they'd received, there was no physical sensation whatever. One instant they were outside the field, the next they were inside it. But the silence somehow deepened, for there were no words.

The universe beyond the field was still visible, but through a murky veil, and everything in it—the cloud-

swirling curve of DM -17 954 V, the glowing moons—
had gone gray, as though turned to ash. A moment
passed before they even noticed that which lay dead
ahead, at the geometrical center of the field's zone
of effect.

A silvery bead grew in the viewscreen as they
approached under a control that Janille's mental discipline had not allowed to lapse. At first it seemed
featureless, and when details appeared they were too
alien to be helpful in estimating its size. But Corin
was nevertheless certain it was huge—a certainty which
deepened as it filled the screen.

(*The equivalent of a human's throat-clearing for
attention.*) "If you will permit, Colonel Dornay, I will
handle the rest of the approach. Please be good
enough to disengage your impellers." Janille complied
wordlessly, and they felt the faintest of bumps as a
tractor beam took hold. The distraction almost made
them miss what happened to the featureless surface
in front of them.

It had been a smooth, seamless expanse which, like
the rest of the orbital station (or whatever) they were
approaching, had an organic look strangely at variance with its obviously metallic composition. Then,
in less time than an eyelid took to blink, it held a
rectangular opening that revealed a brightly lit interior. They didn't trust themselves to speak as the
pinnace floated through that impossible portal and
entered a vast space whose architecture was too alien
to fully register on their minds, a titanic silvery cavern whose walls bristled with spires of the same crystalline metal. The pinnace came to rest at the end
of one of those spires, nestling its airlock against the
spire's tip.

"Please enter," the pseudo-voice invited, continuing to address all three of them. "You need take no
special precautions—the air is suitable for you. And
directions will be provided."

From the first, those mental "words" had held an undercurrent, beneath even the level of the nonverbal emotions that accompanied them. Now it intensified to the point where the three humans became consciously aware of it. But it had been subliminally present all along, and they wondered if it was the reason they had followed that telepathic voice so willingly into an unknown that should have been terrifying. While they couldn't describe it, even to themselves, it filled them with an absolute, incontrovertible certainty that the intelligence with which they were dealing meant them well—meant it with an intensity that had to be held tightly in check lest it become consuming.

They didn't recognize it for what it was, because none of them were parents.

After they'd spent a while walking through vast spun-silver passageways, Garth's impatience finally overcame his awe. "Hey! When do we get to see you?"

(*Embarrassed realization that an unpleasant topic can no longer be avoided.*) "The fact of the matter is that, contrary to your expectations, you will not be meeting a Luon here."

"What?" Janille shook her head emphatically. "You can't tell me you're not a Luon. Remember, I've been in mental communication with one before. The . . . quality, or tenor, of the thoughts is unmistakable."

"Nevertheless, the fact is that except for yourselves there is not a single organic being in this facility."

"What kind of nonsense is this?" Garth demanded. "What do you mean nobody's here? *You're* here!"

(*Patient explication of the obvious.*) "Please recall the precise thought I expressed: no *organic* beings."

They had all completed one more step before the concept penetrated the walls of unacceptability their culture had erected around their minds. Then they jarred to a halt, breaking into sweat and darting glances around the corridor that had suddenly become alien and frightening.

Artificial sentience had been possible for just over a millennium. But like so many things that were possible—nanotechnology, bioengineering, direct man-machine interfacing, and everything else with the potential to distort the human condition into something no longer recognizably human—it was used sparingly and subjected to rigid controls. This was axiomatic, and had been for so long that few men of this age had any idea of the axiom's origins. If they thought about it at all, they thought—fleetingly and shudderingly—of the Draconis Empire. The Cliometric Society had gone deep underground—not for the first time in its history—as the old Solarian Empire had finally collapsed into a chasm of flame; its centuries-long covert molding of human attitudes was not even a folk memory among the inheritors of those attitudes.

Corin, Janille and Garth were educated rationalists. They were also military professionals, and the military, as ever, had special latitude in utilizing the dangerous and the distasteful. So they could deal with AI. They could even deal, briefly and on a strictly defined basis, with psi. But faced with the two in combination, they recoiled as though from an obscene wrongness. They held their tongues, but their revulsion came roaring up so close to the surface that it might as well have been verbalized.

(*Resignation.*) "Such a reaction was only to be expected. I have encountered it before—over four hundred of your standard years ago, in fact—on the occasion of my first encounter with Basil Castellan, which was my first encounter with a human."

Astonishment purged their minds of fear and disgust, so thoroughly that it never occurred to them to wonder if that effect might have been intended. "You mean," Janille finally breathed, "it's true, that old story that he came here after his final battle?"

"That was his second visit here. His first, the one to which I am referring, took place twenty-three years before that. You see, he had been captured by the self-styled New Humans who were in rebellion against the Empire, and—"

"Yes!" Corin broke in excitedly. "I remember now. He escaped, and joined his friends Sonja Rady and Torval Bogdan. Together, using information he'd obtained while in captivity, they smashed the rebel fleet and saved the Empire. Or so the story goes. But there have always been some uncertainties about that part of his life—like how, and where, he made contact with Rady and Bogdan."

"The three of them were always deliberately vague about the circumstances of that meeting." (*Didacticism.*) "You must understand the age in which they lived. It was an age of lethal power struggles; the military strongmen the Empire had summoned up to suppress the rebellion had proven a cure worse than the disease. Among those warlords, the preeminent predator was Yoshi Medina. The three comrades fought for him against the rebels, but had few illusions about him. Their true loyalty was to the idea of the Empire itself, and they weren't saving it merely to turn it over to a ruthless intriguer. Sensing that they would eventually break with him, they carefully husbanded their every source of strength for the coming conflict, including knowledge. And they had obtained some very valuable items of knowledge—notably, my location and nature. For it was here that Castellan's two friends found him."

"So all three of them were here?" The skepticism in Garth's voice didn't last to the end of the sentence.

"Yes. Castellan arrived first, in flight from his pursuers." (*Amusement.*) "I reminded him of certain popular-fictional megacomputers, with cliche designations like 'Alpha Prime.' After learning my background, he bestowed on me the name 'Omega Prime,' which suits me as well as any other."

"What 'background'?" Janille tried to ask. But Corin's voice overrode hers.

"You mean Castellan came here for refuge in the course of his escape? But how did he even know you were here? What would have induced him to come to this lifeless system? And once he did, how did he find you?"

"The answer to your last question is that I enabled him to find this installation, as I did you. As for the rest . . . it is rather a long story. For the moment, suffice it that he came here for refuge, and that subsequently Rady and Bogdan arrived in this system and destroyed his pursuers, after which he contacted them." (*Briskness, as though changing the subject.*) "While they were here, I took the liberty of making a holographic recording of them without their knowledge."

The three drew a breath in unison. They had all seen images of Castellan and, less often, of his almost equally legendary friends. But . . . Omega Prime must have sensed the emotions they were feeling at the prospect of spying, as it were, on the past. A curious eagerness appeared on the subverbal level of the thoughts entering their minds. "Would you like to see it? If so, there is a chamber equipped for such a viewing, a little way further."

"Why . . . yes I would," Corin said. "I imagine we all would."

They resumed walking, and presently an opening appeared in the smooth silvery wall to their left. They entered a chamber that must have been small by Luonli standards, for it was only auditorium-sized for them.

"This was recorded in the docking bay of this facility, just after Rady and Bogdan had arrived," Omega

Prime explained. Then, with no more warning than that, the other half of the chamber came to holographic life, and they were looking across four centuries.

The vast docking bay filled the background, with its array of spirelike piers. In the foreground, a shuttle with Fleet insignia had nestled against the end of one of those piers, and two people were emerging to greet a third with unmistakable joy. They were talking animatedly, but no sound accompanied the life-sized images. The man they were greeting was recognizably Basil Castellan, though his was a younger face than the one which generally gazed out of the history books. He wore a nondescript gray coverall that his New Human captors must have issued him. Rady and Bogdan wore the space service uniforms of the old Solarian Empire—Fleet deep blue, white and gold for her, Marine black, white and silver for him. The hair styles had the same period quality; in those days men had worn it full on top but very close-cropped on the sides and back, in contrast to the present day's smoother tapering, and women in the military had worn it longer than was now considered suitable.

But still . . .

At first they didn't recognize what they were seeing. It was too preposterous to be recognized. But their puzzlement gradually deepened into something else.

Janille's nervous laugh cracked the brittle silence. "Ha-ha, you know, it's almost as if . . . Well, the three of them . . . I mean, if you didn't know any better . . ." Her voice died a slow death.

Omega Prime's mental "voice" was carefully expressionless. "I can provide sound, if you wish."

All at once, the image of Sonja Rady was speaking to Castellan, while brushing back a lock of auburn hair and ostentatiously not noticing something Bogdan had just said. Her speech was perfectly understandable; language didn't change much in this epoch of long lifespans and ubiquitous recorded sound. "Then the message from your drone arrived. I managed to get myself put in charge of a rescue expedition out Aquila way. I'm still not quite sure how this oversized cargo item got himself included." She grinned fondly at the massive Marine, whose chestnut beard looked newly grown. "It's—"

"No," Janille gasped. It was hard to tell where one voice took up and the other left off, for they were exactly the same voice.

A strong shudder ran through Garth. He brought it under control and whirled around, shouting to the surrounding air. "All right, what kind of unfunny joke is this? Talk to us, damn you!"

The sound recording abruptly ceased, and the holographic images from the past froze. "Yes, I owe you an explanation." (*Seriousness of a kind that precluded interruption.*) "Let me begin at the beginning. As you have doubtless surmised, I am a creation of the Luonli. Indeed, I am their last creation—their bid for a kind of immortality. This is their home system; their birthworld is one of the lifeless rockballs of the inner system, scorched clean by a sun turned traitor. They wished to preserve all their knowledge, all their philosophy, here in the safety of the outer system. In the end, nothing short of effectively infinite data storage capacity would serve. I am the result. By techniques involving physics that extend into the tachyon domain, I can access any data that I *ever* held—or *will ever* hold. From my creators' standpoint, the practical significance of this is that whenever I run out of storage capacity I can simply erase data, without losing the ability to access it. But the corollary—which never occurred to them, and which I myself took a long time to grasp—is that I can also access data which I have not yet stored, but will store at some time in the future.

"Actually," Omega Prime continued, calmly ignoring their stupefaction, "the ability is less useful than it might seem. It is only 'foretelling the future' in a strictly limited sense; I can have no knowledge of anything except those matters of which I will at some point learn. And even those exist in a contextual vacuum, from my standpoint. There can be no question of a systematic study of the future; I can only collect data and try to piece them together as my background knowledge grows sufficiently to enable me to make sense of them." (*Complacency.*) "I am, however, improving."

Corin finally found his voice. "Uh, Omega Prime, if what you're telling us is true, the philosophical implications are rather staggering. But it still doesn't explain . . ." He gestured vaguely in the direction of the three motionless holo figures.

(*Mild annoyance.*) "I was coming to that. Before Basil Castellan's birth, I had a conversation with a surviving Luon from his homeworld. That Luon had been instrumental in concealing an infant Imperial heir on that world, lest he die at the hands of a usurper. This enabled me to understand certain future references to Castellan which had previously puzzled me—for he was descended from that heir, a fact which I myself was to reveal to him. You see, by then I had come to understand that, by virtue of my limited foreknowledge, I had become an active player, as it were, in the events I foresaw. It is basic information theory, known to humans for two and a half millennia, that observers cannot help but influence that which they observe. This is especially true in my case—one of the 'philosophical implications' to which you just alluded. In fact, those future references were ones that I myself later recorded after the fact, to be discovered by my own earlier self." (*Concern.*) "Ah, are the three of you quite well?"

Corin ordered his head to stop spinning. "Yes, I believe so. Please continue."

"By these means, I knew of an encounter the Luon would later have with the youthful Basil Castellan. I instructed the Luon to take advantage of that incident to mentally influence Castellan to seek out this system when the opportunity to do so arose—as it did in the course of his flight from the New Humans." (*Dryness.*) "I perceive your distaste. But, as I pointed out to him at the time, he had no valid cause for complaint, inasmuch as he thereby gained an avenue of escape from his pursuers. At any rate, he came here, and I made him aware of all the foregoing facts. Rady and Bogdan then arrived, as I had known they would. The three of them remained here for one sleep period after the reunion you have been witnessing." (*Hesitancy, as though anticipating their reaction.*) "While they were unconscious, I obtained genetic material from them, by means subsequently undetectable."

Corin suppressed his queasiness. "And why would you have wanted to do that?" he asked levelly.

"By then I had puzzled out still more of my messages to myself from the future. I knew that my duty to the future extended beyond lending Castellan the aid that would enable him to complete his legend."

"Your 'duty to the future'?"

"An awkward verbal interpretation your brain places on a difficult concept. For the moment, don't trouble yourselves about my motives. The point is, I learned that Castellan's part in the Empire's eventual restoration would extend beyond merely serving as a legend to inspire the restorers. In a sense he himself, and his friends Rady and Bogdan, were to play a direct role in later events. Not really themselves, but exact genetic duplicates of them."

"You mean you *cloned* them?" This time Corin was unable to keep the distaste out of his voice. Humans had begun cloning lower life forms only a few years after they'd sent their first feeble probes beyond

Earth's atmosphere—first microorganisms, followed in a remarkably few decades by large mammals. By then, it had been clear to anyone willing to face facts without flinching that the only barriers to human cloning were cultural, not technological. But those barriers had been strong ones, and in today's culture they were even stronger, reinforced by battlements of restrictive statutory and customary law.

Garth shook his massive head. "But I still don't understand." The other two made noises of agreement.

The voice inside their skulls took on a tone that sent shivers down their spines in a way the concept of a psionic computer hadn't. "That is only because you're not letting yourselves understand."

For a moment longer they remained suspended in bewilderment.

Then a sound from Janille caused the two men to glance at her. She was staring fixedly at the frozen holo display, at the auburn-haired woman from out of folklore. And the sound continued to build—a low, half-strangled, animallike sound that began low in her chest, emerging in a wail of inarticulate denial. That sound somehow shattered the barrier that had stood between them and the obvious-but-unacceptable, and Corin and Garth stood in a paralyzed silence within which their thoughts raged.

Somehow, from within the calm eye of that hurricane of emotion, Corin was able to observe his own feelings as he stared at the image of Basil Castellan. Incredibly, ludicrously, the one clear question that emerged above the tumult was: *My God, is my nose really* that *long?* And his sense of the ridiculous brought him out of shock before either of the others.

"How could we not have known?" he heard Janille ask nobody in particular. "I mean, we've seen pictures of them all our lives!"

"But generally portrayed at a more advanced age than ours," he responded dully. "And with old-fashioned clothes and haircuts. And besides, nobody ever looks at historical pictures with *this* in mind. We just weren't looking for it." He turned away from her and spoke plaintively. "Why, Omega Prime?"

"As I pointed out, history requires it." (*Gentleness.*) "I perceive your emotional distress. It is to be expected, in light of your civilization's attitude toward cloning of humans. But you must not let your new knowledge of your origins affect your self-worth. You are human beings in every biological sense. And all your accomplishments, values and beliefs are as valid as they ever were."

"But we aren't *ourselves*. We're . . . copies."

"That is a fallacy. The three of you are *not* Basil Castellan, Sonja Rady and Torval Bogdan, even though your genetic makeup is identical to theirs. You are distinct individuals, products of very different life experiences. Your genes do not dictate the innermost essence of who you are—they only establish certain predispositions. And even where those predispositions are at their most salient, they take divergent forms. For example, Commodore Marshak, you are very much a romantic idealist, as was Castellan. But you deny it in yourself. He never did."

Janille shuddered and drew a deep breath. "Never mind the 'Why' for now. What about the 'How'? Granting that you produced clones from the cells you took from the three of them, and grew them in whatever kind of artificial wombs you use—"

"And kept the embryos in cryogenic stasis," Omega Prime interjected.

"—the question remains, how did you introduce them into human society?" She continued, Corin noted, to shrink from using the first person in connection with those clones.

"That, of course, required human assistance. As you know, Commodore Marshak and yourself were both adopted. So was General Krona, although he tends to be more reticent about it. These adoptions were arranged through a human intermediary whom I had identified and arranged to meet by means similar to those I've already described."

"But who—?"

"I will ask you to defer such questions for now. I have reason to believe you will be meeting the individual in question in the near future. That person will continue to be involved in your destinies. I would risk distorting the course of future events if I revealed his or her identity, for such knowledge could hardly fail to influence your behavior."

"I've known security officers who were freer with information," Garth muttered. He looked around truculently, as though searching for some visible essence of Omega Prime to glare at. "All right, on the assumption—the *large* assumption—that we believe you, let's talk about this 'role' we have to play in some grand historical scheme of things. Or would telling us about that also 'distort the course of future events'?"

"Not at all. Indeed, it is necessary that I discuss the matter with you, General. You see, I am aware of your firm belief in your destiny to become Emperor."

"What? You are?" Garth's face lit up like a sun. "So *that's* what you mean by a 'role'? I *knew* it! I always knew it!"

(*An axe blade's bleakness.*) "No. You have a destiny, but it lies elsewhere. I know who is to restore the Empire, and you are not that person."

Garth's features, which had fallen with an almost audible thud, firmed up into defiance. "How can you be sure? You admit your foreknowledge is limited. Why should I accept the word of a—"

"It is not necessary that you believe me," the pseudo-voice interrupted calmly, "for you know full well the fundamental Imperial law."

"What do you mean?" Garth demanded. Then, with shocking suddenness, his belligerence seemed to sag sideways and slump down into despair, for he knew exactly what Omega Prime meant. The strictures governing human cloning were motivated not just by fear of totalitarian governments force-growing armies of identical supersoldiers, but also by the danger of wealthy egomaniacs using it as a substitute for natural reproduction. So it had always been a fundamental postulate of the law that no clone could inherit anything. This principle was enforced with special rigor in Imperial succession law. . . .

"Every new Emperor or would-be Emperor has always constructed some claim—however spurious and specious—of inheritance from the dynastic lineage of the past," Omega Prime intoned. "If such inheritance is legally impossible—"

"I understand." Garth's bass was very level. Alarmingly so, for his companions had been prepared for anything up to and including a sudden assault with fists on the wall that was the only physical manifestation of Omega Prime available to be attacked. "So, who *is* to be the restorer?"

"That, too, leads back to what I told Basil Castellan just before his death. I told him he would reach across time and play a part in the Empire's rebirth not just as a legend and as the original of a clone, but also through his blood, transmitted through his daughter."

"Yes," Janille said quietly, "there's always been a story that his daughter by Sonja Rady was spirited out of the Empire before he died."

"The stories are true. She was taken to the Sword Clans' homeworld. She was the direct ancestor of the family to which I believe you currently intend to offer your services."

"The Brady-Schiavonas!" Corin exclaimed. "So Ivar is really going to make his claim good?"

"Actually, the family member to whom I refer is his son Roderick. The future references are somewhat confusing, but my impression is that he will be remembered as the real founder of the new dynasty, which will lead the Empire to unparalleled heights. Indeed, he will so overshadow his father that future historians will tend to somewhat underrate Ivar."

"But," Garth rumbled, "if you know all this from your 'future references,' what's the point in us doing anything to bring it about? It'll happen anyway."

"And," Corin put in, "why are you telling us all this? Why didn't you just leave us alone to do what we're fated to do in this deterministic universe you're postulating?" *And without the knowledge that will now haunt us every time we look in a mirror,* he didn't add, though he wondered if it came close enough to the tip of his tongue for Omega Prime to detect it.

"There are several answers to those questions—some of which you may be told. First of all, the things I have described will not simply come about; they will come about *in a certain way.* It is my obligation to assure that they do so, for the reasons to which I have already alluded. If I do not . . . well, it remains to be proven that my future data is really infallible. I cannot be absolutely certain that all the data I am accessing come from one immutable future."

"Huh?" Corin blinked. "Are you talking about, uh, branching alternate timelines? That's always been a popular fictional device. But quantum physics has categorically ruled it out. Antonescu's unified field theory settled that in pre-Federation times."

(Faint condescension.) "I submit that your knowledge of the tachyon domain is even less complete than my own. Granted, the matter is speculative. But I cannot ignore the possibility that the course of events I have deduced is somehow contingent on my taking positive action to bring it about.

"And as for why I am telling you this, the answer

should be obvious. The fact that you know these things is part of my own knowledge of coming events. It is part of the pattern."

"The pattern you feel you must preserve," Garth said leadenly, "though you won't tell us why."

"No, I will not. I have no reason to believe you will ever possess *that* knowledge, and it might well be counterproductive in terms of your own motivations. On the other hand, what I *have* told you should have a very positive effect where you are concerned, General."

Garth looked up with bloodshot eyes, jolted out of despair by sheer incredulity. "Omega Prime," he asked slowly, "just exactly what makes you think anything you've told us could possibly motivate me to do anything whatever?"

(*Airy dismissiveness.*) "Oh, you mean your former Imperial ambitions? You must put the matter in perspective, General. There is an old adage to the effect that it is better to be a kingmaker than a king. That is the position that . . . fate, or whatever, is offering you. Roderick Brady-Schiavona is going to be Emperor. Accept this. But you can be instrumental in establishing him on the throne. You can thus write yourself into history as surely as though by becoming Emperor yourself, and without exposing yourself to the kind of second-guessing that new Emperors commonly endure as the penalty for having taken the actions their circumstances made necessary. Later armchair historians will not be uniformly kind—or even fair—to Roderick Brady-Schiavona, I assure you."

"Hmm . . ." Garth made no direct reply as he ruminated. But his two companions, who knew him, saw that he was no longer submerged in hollow futile despondency.

(*Briskness.*) "And now, I perceive you need rest. I can also prepare food compatible with your species, to supplement the rations in your vessel." Garth visibly brightened, to Corin's and Janille's unspoken amusement. "After you have refreshed yourselves, I will impart certain other information. Then, as soon as possible, you must resume your journey. For you were already on the course history has set for you."

CHAPTER TEN
The DM +7 4052 System, 4329 C.E.

"I must say, your arrival came as quite a surprise," Roderick Brady-Schiavona remarked as he poured the brandy.

"Not an inopportune one, I hope," Jason Aerenthal demurred.

"Oh, no. Hardly. Just . . . unexpected. After all, you'd soon have seen me at Sigma Draconis anyway. I'm really on my way there already—a long, drawn-out return with a number of extended stops, of which this is the last one."

"True. But I've needed for some time to come out here and maintain my contacts in the old rebel sectors. Sometimes there's no substitute for face-to-face meetings, you know."

"Not even interactive messages?"

"No," Aerenthal replied with uncharacteristic taciturnity, and Roderick knew better than to ask for details. "But your father didn't want me to come until the sectors were fully pacified—the same eventuality that is now occasioning your return. All taken with all, we're fortunate to have encountered each other in this system."

"I'll drink to that," Roderick said, raising his brandy snifter.

A thick emotional scab had grown to cover the hurtful memories of the things he and Aerenthal had done. Now he was able to look at the secret agent with a reasonable facsimile of what he'd felt on that distant day—four years and an era ago—when they'd leaned together on a railing and awaited the arrival of a now-dead Emperor and life had been simple. *At least,* Roderick amended his thought, *life had been simple for* me. He couldn't imagine a time when it had been that way for Aerenthal. His work of the past half-year had lent itself to such forgetfulness. There had never been any one great separatist movement in the sectors with which he'd been entrusted; their New Human past was a matter of dry history now, a corpse whose aroma evoked only distaste. Instead, there had been a vexing multiplicity of local particularisms, parochial grievances and individual banditries. Roderick had reconciled the first, calmed the second and crushed the third. It had been more tedious and frustrating, if probably less dangerous, than facing organized opposition in battle formation would have been. But he couldn't claim it hadn't kept him busy.

And it hasn't involved selling my soul a bit at a time.

Roderick dismissed the unwelcome thought. *The point is,* he reminded himself briskly, *I've succeeded. Father won't have to worry about these sectors. They're solidly part of our power base now.*

Aerenthal, who had raised his own glass, nodded in agreement with Roderick's unvoiced thought. "It's clear, even from what little I've seen so far, that this region is secured. I'll be able to so report to His Imperial Majesty."

Roderick gave the older man a sharp glance as an emotional nerve-pain shot through him. *So now Father wants independent reports on me?* He instantly chided himself for the thought. It was perfectly legitimate that

Ivar would ask an agent of Aerenthal's experience, peculiar expertise and proven loyalty for his impressions of a newly pacified region. *What's the matter with me? Is it just that I've been separated from Father for so long? And that Ted hasn't?*

He shook his head, annoyed with himself, and joined Aerenthal in another sip. They sat in his private cabin in the flagship *Fearless*. No living quarters aboard a warship were of vast extent, but the cabin was comfortable and had a spare, understated elegance. It also had the transparency which was the prerogative of flag rank. The armorplast was so strong that it didn't really compromise the ship's structural integrity in any measurable way. Still, a holo screen could have displayed the same view without any such weakening at all. It was simply one of the forms of conspicuous waste by which human beings marked out the lines of social stratification—another string of beads. At this point in the orbit, *Fearless* was pointed away from the local sun and in the direction of nearby Delta Aquilae. That star—a binary system whose brighter component was a class F subgiant—was of no economic interest; but it was a dazzling spectacle in this system's skies, and the two of them sat bathed in its light.

"I suppose," Roderick mused after a moment, "that the consolidation of this region means we can start thinking about our next move."

"Thinking, yes . . . but it will be at least a year before we can actually commence our campaign to reunify the Empire. We seem to have reached a kind of pause now—a catching of breath. At present, neither we nor any of the other players in this little game can do much more than defend what we already have. No one can successfully press home an attack, as Liang's fiasco at Sol demonstrated."

"Yes," Roderick acknowledged. "Worked out rather well for Chewning, didn't it? What happened to Krona, that is." The Battle of Mars had occurred just before the turn of the new standard year. Their news of it had been through Chewning's official information organs. It seemed that Chewning's forces had arrived just too late to prevent the annihilation of those of his ally, Garth Krona, but had taken vengeance by driving Liang's weakened invaders off.

"So it did," Aerenthal agreed. "But Chewning's subsequent seizure of Epsilon Eridani to 'keep order' after Krona's demise has been the limit of his ability to take advantage of the situation."

"Still," Roderick persisted, "this 'breathing spell' of yours may be drawing to an end. I mean, all the news we've been getting lately—"

"It *has* been coming at a fast and furious pace, hasn't it? But most of it tends to confirm my view of the current state of affairs. I cite Romaine's inability to follow up her victory."

Roderick wordlessly acknowledged the point. Lauren Romaine had finally gotten the Ursa Major frontier sufficiently organized to try her luck against Liang in the aftermath of his defeat at Sol. With the dawning of the new year she'd smashed his enfeebled fleet, and his fiefdom had collapsed like a pricked bladder. But internal political distractions and factional jealousies had prevented her from pressing home her advantage. Their latest intelligence told of a Serpens/Bootes region that was fragmenting as local commanders turned warlord. Liang's fate was unknown.

But the most recent news of all had arrived barely ahead of Aerenthal. Chewning, flushed with his take-over of Epsilon Eridani, had finally decided he was secure enough to dispense with Ferrand II. The last of the Duschane puppets had vanished into oblivion, and his erstwhile prime minister had declared himself Emperor.

"Chewning's usurpation is something new and different," Roderick opined. "It's the first time anybody's tried to assume the throne without even the pretense of a claim to legitimacy."

"It's also rash, given his limited power base. I suspect he's let his toadies sell him an exaggerated idea of the prestige he derives from his possession of Old Earth."

"We've got to keep up the pressure on Chewning," Roderick muttered, half to Aerenthal and half to himself.

"Precisely." Aerenthal nodded approvingly. "The Serpens/Bootes power vacuum and Romaine's ramshackle federation are ignorable for now. But Chewning is nearby, and if we can take Old Earth, our position will become unassailable. No Imperial contender who's held both Sol and Sigma Draconis has ever been successfully attacked."

"Lothar Medina held them both," Roderick mused, more out of disputatious habit than anything else. "And Basil Castellan might have succeeded against him, if he'd avoided letting himself get sidetracked."

"But he *didn't*. That's the point. The idea that there are, or ought to be, two capitals—the ceremonial one at Earth and the working one at Prometheus—goes back to the earliest days of the Federation. Possession of both confers an air of legitimacy which is difficult to beat."

Whatever response Roderick might have been about to make was lost, for the cabin's door chimed for admittance. Roderick signaled acceptance, and smiled at the sight of the new arrival. "Come on in, Aline. Grab yourself a snifter from the sideboard."

Aline Tatsumo complied and settled into a recliner. As she reached for the brandy, the look she gave Aerenthal was almost but not quite imperceptible. She had in full measure the typical line officer's distaste for intelligence work—full, or perhaps overflowing. Roderick often wondered if a bad experience with psi lay in her past. At least she kept her expression sufficiently controlled to allow Aerenthal to plausibly pretend he hadn't noticed.

"So," Roderick said emphatically, "how stands the task group?"

"No problems, sir. Everybody's prepared for departure, and Commander Delavan has returned to the station." This was a mining colony, with no life-bearing planets. Delavan, the station C.O., was the highest authority here. Now that he'd paid his courtesy call and submitted his reports, they could commence the long voyage to Sigma Draconis.

"Good." Roderick settled back in his chair. "We were just talking about the latest news—especially Chewning's announcement from Sol."

"Oh, yes . . . Chewning." Tatsumo put an amazing amount of contempt into three words. She took a sip. Then, as though the brandy had, through some chemical reaction, triggered a chain of free association, she blinked twice and frowned. "That reminds me of something Delavan said. I wasn't even going to mention it to you. But it seem he's got three prisoners here. They arrived some weeks ago in a pinnace."

"A pinnace? This is a long way from any inhabited system. Are they survivors of a ship involved in some kind of accident?"

"Delavan's not sure. All he *is* sure of is that they're not what they claim to be. You see, they told him they'd come all the way from Sol—"

"From Sol? In a *pinnace?*"

"That's the least of it." Tatsumo gave a nervous little laugh. "They claimed to be Garth Krona himself and his two top subordinates, fleeing from the battle at Sol. And they demanded to see you."

Roderick laughed more loudly than his flag captain had. "I can see why Delavan locked them up! Krona's dead. And even if he had survived the battle, why would he have left Sol and come all the way out here? His side had won the Battle of Mars, and his ally Chewning was firmly in control of the Sol system. And if there *had* been any reason for him to leave Sol, he would have gone to his base at Epsilon Eridani." He shook his head, chuckling, and turned to Aerenthal. "What do you suppose these people are trying to . . . ?" His question died, killed by what he saw on the agent's face. "Jason, what is it?"

Aerenthal didn't reply at once, and when he did speak it wasn't in response to Roderick's question. "Captain Tatsumo, who do the other two prisoners claim to be?"

"Let's see . . . oh, yes. A Commodore Marshak and a Colonel Dornay. These are mercenary titles, of course," Tatsumo added in an aside to Roderick. "They both say they're ex-Fleet officers. Delavan was wondering if it was worth the trouble to send to Sigma Draconis for a records check of the master Fleet database there, just to confirm that last claim."

"Well, that would certainly clinch the matter," Roderick put in. "What about it, Jason? Do you think the matter is worth pursuing?"

Once again, Aerenthal's answer was uncharacteristically delayed. Indeed, he barely seemed to have heard the question. His eyes were focused on something far beyond the cabin. Then the moment was over, and he spoke with his old voice, but without his accustomed flippancy. "I have reason to believe, Admiral, that there may be something to this man's claim to be Garth Krona."

"*What?*"

"Furthermore . . . do you recall that when Krona and his mercenary company left 85 Pegasi year before last, the Fleet officer who had lifted the Tarakan siege accompanied him?"

"Yes . . . deserted with some of his ships. I seem to recall something about that. It was how Krona first acquired his illegal space weaponry."

"Well, I think we're going to find that this Commodore Marshak is that same officer. I'm almost equally convinced that Colonel Dornay's claim will also prove out."

Roderick gawked at him. Aline Tatsumo tried to express herself, with imperfect success. "But . . . but . . . what about . . . I mean, what would they be doing here? And—"

"Perhaps," Aerenthal broke in serenely, "we should set about finding out the answers to all the questions this development raises."

Roderick spoke, forestalling the flag captain. "I gather, then, that you feel we should check out these people's genotypes against Fleet records. But . . . how do you know all these things you've been telling us?"

"I submit, Roderick, that my sources of information are immaterial, and that inquiring into them is a less productive use of your time than seeking to confirm the information directly."

"So you think we should question them?"

"Precisely. I suggest that we go about it as follows." He spoke for a few moments. Roderick found himself nodding.

"Very well. We'll proceed along those lines. Aline, tell Delavan to send his prisoners over here."

The interorbital shuttle had small armorplast ports. Garth, Janille and Corin were able to watch HIMS *Fearless* grow from a toy spaceship to a world of molecularly aligned metal, at once brutally massive and intricately complex, drifting majestically along its orbit in the light of DM +7 4052.

They didn't know what awaited them aboard that battleship—the two guards who'd come for them had been uninformative. But as they approached it, they could only feel a sense of release.

It wasn't that they'd been mistreated since a patrolling frigate in this system's outer fringes had tractored them. They hadn't been subjected to any physical or psychological torture, their rations were adequate, and their quarters were reasonably comfortable. Indeed, those quarters didn't really look like a prison, for they had an open entryway. Of course, to pass through that portal was to enter a field that would instantly paralyze every voluntary muscle. Janille had confirmed this by bringing a hand into the most fleeting possible contact with the zone of effect, after which she'd felt as though the entire arm from the elbow down had gone to sleep. None of them had tried again.

No, it was the sheer boredom of their weeks in that cage—if not precisely gilded, certainly tinsel-lined— that they felt they were escaping from. That, and the sheer, maddening frustration of being unable to talk to anyone who would take their story seriously.

The battleship's docking bay swallowed the shuttle up—evidently they weren't worth the energy cost of transposing them aboard *Fearless*—and a new pair of security guards took them in charge. These were subtly crisper and more efficient than the station's personnel, and their uniforms bore a kind of shoulder flash: crossed swords of the straight two-edged basket-hilted sort known as a schiavona.

A couple of minutes' march through the battleship's passageways brought them to a door which slid aside to reveal an austere compartment. Behind a utilitarian desk sat a dark-haired woman in Fleet uniform with captain's insignia. Behind the desk and off to one side stood two men in civilian clothes. One had the look of a man past his anagathics-conferred prime but carrying it off well. The other looked to be in his early thirties, before anagathics began to make a noticeable difference. Both stood in attitudes suggesting that they were more observers than participants.

The uniformed woman immediately confirmed this impression by opening the proceedings without making any move to introduce the two civilians. "Please state your names," she clipped.

Garth rumbled something subliminal but seemed

disinclined to answer for them. Corin sensed that his two companions wanted him to take the lead. *I wonder how often Basil Castellan got that feeling?* he wondered, as he'd often wondered since they had departed from that unimaginable construct that seemed to exist in its own private universe at DM -17 954. He thrust the thought aside. "We've already stated our names, many times. Before we repeat them again, may we know who's asking?"

"I am Captain Aline Tatsumo, commanding this ship."

Corin shook his head. "We want to talk to Roderick Brady-Schiavona, not his flag captain."

Tatsumo cocked her head to one side. "What makes you think anything you have to say can only be said to Admiral Brady-Schiavona . . . Commodore?" The intonation she gave the title held not just the usual Fleet officer's attitude toward mercenary ranks, but also a deep skepticism about Corin's right to use it.

"Because he's the one we want to offer our services to. Look, you already know who we are: this is General Garth Krona, and—"

"We know who you *claim* to be," Tatsumo cut in. "But we are reliably informed that General Krona and all his followers are dead."

" 'Reliably informed' by whom? Chewning?"

"Yes. Apparently the Deathstriders Company was wiped out before Chewning's forces could relieve them, though their efforts left Liang's attacking force too weakened to maintain its position in the Sol system."

Garth gave a sound which could have been interpreted as either a laugh or a snort. Either way, its volume was startling in this enclosed space. "If you believe that, you're overpaying your intelligence people." The older civilian's cough was barely audible. "Most of us were still alive when Liang's people fled— no thanks to that slime mold Chewning. He let us wear Liang down for him, then turned on us! We managed to get away. So did a fair number of our people."

"If this is true, why didn't you go to your base at Tau Ceti?"

"Spare me the mind games, Captain. I know that you know that I was based at Epsilon Eridani. And we didn't go there because we knew that back-stabbing bastard Chewning was bound to take the opportunity to occupy it and finish off those of our people who were still there."

" 'Make sure any injury you do a man is such that you need not fear his vengeance,' " the elderly civilian quoted Machiavelli softly. "As a matter of fact, Chewning did just that, before declaring himself Emperor."

Garth gave another explosive basso sound. "Emperor! That little . . ." Words failed him.

"Look," Corin resumed, "you can confirm our identities easily, because you have access to Fleet records. Just do genetic scans of the two of us" —he indicated Janille— "and compare them to those of Captain Corin Marshak and Major Janille Dornay, previously of His Imperial Majesty's service. And we'll vouch for General Krona."

Tatsumo's dark eyes narrowed. "So your defense to the charge of being a liar is to declare yourself a deserter."

Corin took a deep breath. "If you insist on calling it desertion . . . yes, I deserted the late Admiral Tanzler-Yataghan because I wasn't interested in following him into rebellion. There wasn't a clear Imperial successor then, and taking service with General Krona at least let me keep my self-respect."

Janille spoke up. "I was also serving under Admiral Tanzler-Yataghan. And I, too, committed what was technically desertion, for reasons which were not identical but equally valid. You see, I had forcibly resisted unwanted sexual advances on his part. If you know anything about him, you know this kind of behavior was entirely in character."

Tatsumo seemed to have no response. As the silence stretched, the younger civilian spoke for the first time, addressing Corin. "You still haven't answered the captain's question. Why do you want to talk to Roderick Brady-Schiavona directly?"

"Because of what I've just been explaining: Janille and I are technically deserters. And Garth is, or has been, in violation of the law against mercenary units possessing weapons of mass destruction. It's our understanding that Admiral Brady-Schiavona has a policy of clemency for people, even former enemies, who take service under him . . . as we want to do."

The young man flushed slightly. "The service you'd be taking would be that of his father, the Emperor Ivar. And Admiral Brady-Schiavona won't thank you for implying otherwise! The policy to which you refer—like all policy—is His Imperial Majesty's."

"Of course, sir." At the time, it didn't occur to Corin to wonder why he said "sir" to this civilian, somewhat younger than himself, who up to now had taken a completely passive role. It just seemed the natural thing to do. "But it is a matter of general knowledge that His Imperial Majesty's position in this matter has been powerfully influenced by his son the admiral. Like everyone else, we know we can turn to Roderick Brady-Schiavona for justice."

The young man seemed taken aback at first, but recovered rapidly. "If he were here, he might well suspect that of being flattery." He gave a smile which seemed to come more naturally to him than any of the expressions he'd worn so far. And all at once Corin realized he'd been watching this man all along, even when the others had been doing the talking. And it never even occurred to him to speculate why. "Also," the young man continued, "I can't help wondering if justice is really what you want. It's an old question, you know. What do people really want: justice or mercy?"

Corin found he couldn't answer other than frankly. This man seemed to draw out frankness like a magnet drew iron. "Why, sir, the answer is that everyone wants both: justice for other people and mercy for himself."

The young man's mouth fell open, as everyone else sucked in a breath. Then he threw his head back and laughed. "Well, Commodore," he finally gasped, with no sarcasm in the title, "at least you're not a bore."

"I hope Admiral Brady-Schiavona will agree," Corin murmured, wondering if he'd gone too far.

"Oh, I think I can guarantee it." The young man stepped forward and, to the stupefaction of Corin and his companions, Tatsumo started to rise and offer him her chair. He waved her back down and perched on a corner of the desk. "You see, as it happens I *am* Admiral Brady-Schiavona." He crossed his arms, and as he did so a mantle of authority seemed to settle over him, needing no insignia of rank. "And now that you've gotten your wish and are talking to me, perhaps you'll explain just why, even assuming that all your claims are factual, I should be as impressed with your offer to take service under His Imperial Majesty as you evidently think I should be. You haven't exactly appeared in this system under auspicious circumstances, you know."

Corin found himself unable to form an answer. All he could do was stare at this man, seemingly far too young for his rank, and reflect that in some unnatural way he was looking at his own descendant—or, at least, the descendant of a man who had been his genetic double. He wondered if anyone in history had ever had occasion to look at another human being in precisely this way before. Or to feel the same kind of frustration, unable to speak aloud what he was feeling or whence his knowledge came—Omega Prime had been very explicit on that point.

Fortunately, Garth didn't share his muteness, and a chuckle almost below the range of human hearing broke the silence. "You won't have to take us purely on the strength of our own personal abilities, Admiral—though I hope you'll eventually come to consider those as not entirely worthless. As you may recall, I mentioned earlier that a fair percentage of the Deathstriders survived. I have reason to think most of those survivors will turn up here. You must know that outfit's reputation. We can put it back together—and put it to work for you. And forget standard mercenary contract negotiations; we've acquired new motivations. We'll work for Fleet pay."

"Very handsome of you," Roderick observed drily. He seemed to consider for a moment. "I'll tell you what. I'm about to depart for Sigma Draconis anyway. I'll take the three of you with me. There, I'll be able to verify your identity. If it proves out—and I imagine it will, for you're obviously not stupid enough to make easily disproved claims—then perhaps we can indeed work something out. If nothing else, you can certainly earn your keep as sources of information on what really happened at Sol." He stopped, distracted by a noise from the desk's console. "What is it, Aline?"

Tatsumo listened to her earpiece for a moment. "It's Commander Delavan, sir. He reports that a cruiser called *Bogatyr* has entered the system—obviously damaged but still operable." She listened for another moment, them looked up wide-eyed. "The cruiser's captain says she belongs to the Deathstriders Company, and that her command is fleeing a treacherous attack by Chewning's forces. She's asking asylum."

Garth grinned at Roderick. "Get your people to find out if *Bogatyr*'s skipper is named Mariko Bellini. If she is, I suggest that you don't need to check us out any further. And I also think you're seeing the start of what I predicted."

Roderick Brady-Schiavona smiled, and Corin stopped wondering why it had been a while since he'd paid any attention to anyone else in the room. For that smile didn't really transform his face, it just accentuated a quality that was already there. "I'll still want to formally establish your identities. But unless something turns up that I don't really expect . . . I think we may have a deal. For now, I'll at least assign you quarters that will probably be more satisfactory than what you've had lately. Aline, would you please see to it?"

"Certainly, sir." Tatsumo's voice didn't betray uncontrolled enthusiasm for the new arrivals, only a sense that if they were good enough for the admiral they were good enough for her.

"Good. And so, General Krona, as I'll provisionally call you . . ." The young admiral extended his hand.

Garth took it. As he did so, Corin watched his face carefully. The big heavy-planet man had long since settled into a grudging acceptance of the notion that if he couldn't be a king he'd settle for being a kingmaker. Now there was nothing in his expression that was grudging.

CHAPTER ELEVEN
The Sol System, 4331 C.E.

The yellow-white light of Sol was as Corin remembered it. Not that one would expect it to change in only a little over two years.

He wasn't seeing it directly. The viewscreen was showing him a download of what the advance scouting elements were observing. Even to them, cruising among the orbits of Sol's outer gas giants, the home sun was little more than a superlatively bright star. From where Corin waited with the main fleet, it was still just an undistinguished member of the stellar multitudes.

Still, the sight made him remember all that had happened since his last glimpse of that particular glow. Which, in turn, made him glance downward at the sleeve of the uniform he was wearing. Fleet gray. By extending the upper arm up and out he could see the black-and-red shoulder flash.

They had returned with Roderick Brady-Schiavona to Sigma Draconis, where they'd gotten their identities verified with finality and sworn allegiance to Ivar. He had accepted it, on Roderick's and Aerenthal's recommendation. But he'd balked at allowing the Deathstriders to be reconstituted as a free company with deep-space warships—even one working for himself under a long-term exclusive contract, an arrangement Roderick had been prepared to consider. Aerenthal had helped work out a compromise: they were taken into the Fleet but allowed to keep a unique identity—a quasi-autonomous unit with its own integral ground-attack capability, technically Marines but permanently assigned to the unit, which could be justified in terms of operational flexibility as well as morale. Of course they couldn't use the name of what had been a free company. They'd also had to take demotions: Corin and Janille had reverted to their pre-desertion ranks of Fleet captain and Marine major, while Garth had had to settle for colonel, the highest rank he had ever legitimately held as a mercenary. Ivar had been adamant on that last point, and Garth had taken it surprisingly well.

The Emperor's other sticking point had held the potential for being more troublesome. . . .

Aerenthal had broken it to them one night. "His Imperial Majesty has ruled that there is no question of a Marine officer commanding a unit whose Marine component is secondary. In consequence . . . well, not to put too fine a point on it, Captain Marshak will be in command of the Permanent Task Group for Special Operations." The name they'd arrived at to replace the officially nonexistent "Deathstriders" could mean anything you wanted it to mean. "Colonel Krona will command the unit's ground-assault component."

Garth's face and voice had worn the same alarming mildness Corin and Janille had once seen in the depths of an alien space-construct. "Is it out of the question for a Marine . . . or for a Marine who's an ex-mercenary?"

For the first time since they'd known him, Aerenthal had looked ill at ease. "Ah . . . I really can't speak to that question. At any rate," he'd continued briskly, "it's being rationalized by allowing Corin to keep his original date of rank, while yours is the date you were accepted into His Imperial Majesty's service—last week, to be precise."

Garth had nodded ponderously, while Corin had sat immobilized by embarrassment. It might have led to trouble, but Garth's desire for revenge on Chewning had proven so strong that all other considerations had been reduced to irrelevant triviality. Also, he'd been kept occupied by a challenging job. It was a truism that an elite military unit which suffered too many casualties simply ceased to exist, for there were too few veterans left to provide a mold into which the new recruits could settle and harden. Garth had had to rebuild the Permanent Task Group's powered-armor component little by little around the small cadres that had gotten away from Mars. Corin had had an easier time of it, for more of the warships had escaped from the debacle at Sol.

Now his eye continued on down his gray-clad sleeve from the shoulder flash with its striding black Mark 32-A silhouetted on a red background, to the single sunburst above the cuff. He'd won his way back to commodore's rank as they'd kept the pressure on the "Emperor" Chewning, forcing him back to Sol. He would never forget the reconquest of the Epsilon Eridani system, although he doubted his satisfaction had matched what Garth had felt as he'd led the first ground assault to hit the surface of Neustria. The place had been a windfall of recruits, for a lot of Deathstrider veterans had faded into the planet's woodwork during Chewning's occupation.

And now, at last, they were returning to Sol. . . .

"Excuse me, Commodore." The flag captain's voice returned Corin to the present. "Admiral Brady-Schiavona's compliments, and he's ready now."

"Thank you." Corin knew all the unit commanders were getting the same message. He returned to his command chair, which was equipped for conferencing. He took the various leads extending from it and attached them to the appropriate connection points on his uniform. Then he donned the wraparound, eye-covering headset.

The technology was of immemorial antiquity, and people with the aptitude for direct neural interfacing found it a tedious substitute. But at least everyone could use it. And the virtual conference room that, to Corin's eyes, had replaced his flag bridge seemed real enough. So did the people seated around the table, although the way the late arrivals kept popping into existence in their chairs somewhat spoiled the naturalistic effect. The table was circular, and there-fore shouldn't have had a head. But of course it did have one, defined by where Roderick Brady-Schiavona was sitting. Certain others might yield to vanity and use the cosmetic software which, while leaving one recognizably oneself, optimized appearance beyond nature's best efforts. He didn't need it. No program could supply the indefinable quality which made everyone around him seem an afterthought.

"Good morning, everyone," he said as the last image materialized to join the shared hookup, scrupulously observing the ships' clocks. "This is going to be our last opportunity to meet before the final advance on Earth, so I want to give everyone the chance to voice any questions or concerns." He activated a hologram which floated above the table's center—an image within an image. It showed disposition of his fleet where it hung outside Sol's Oort Cloud.

"Just one, Admiral." Aline Tatsumo had also made commodore, and thus was too senior to be Roderick's flag captain. Rumor had it she'd resisted promotion as long as possible. Now she was commanding a task group. "I'm wondering if Commodore Marshak's rein-forced task group is the best possible choice for the rather crucial position to which you've assigned it."

Corin forced self-control on himself. Tatsumo's behavior toward him had always been correct, but she wasted little energy concealing her opinion that Roderick was too ready to grant important commands to former rebels and outlaws. When the young admiral had assigned some additional battlecruiser and cruiser squadrons to support what couldn't be openly called the Deathstriders, and placed the beefed-up force at the tip of one of the inward-curving flanking formations he meant to bring sweeping in to envelop Earth like the enfolding wings of a vast bird of prey, she'd dropped even the formality of concealing her feelings.

"We've been over this in private, Aline." Roderick's tone said he'd been under the impression that they'd settled it there as well. "But since you've brought it up here, let's get your objections on the table. Are they to the composition of the force itself, or to Commodore Marshak as its commander?"

If, by challenging Tatsumo to put up or shut up, Roderick had hoped to startle her into doing the latter, he was disappointed. "Actually, sir, I have concerns with both. I suggest it might be more suitable to use a unit whose makeup is more . . . homogeneous." *Straight old-line Fleet without any mercenary outfit in its pedigree, you mean,* Corin thought. But he knew there were others around the virtual table who agreed with Tatsumo, so he kept quiet as she continued. "Likewise, Commodore Marshak is still somewhat junior for command of a task group—even one of somewhat irregular nature."

"So are you, Aline," Roderick observed with his disarming smile. "So are a lot of people in a lot of billets. It's that kind of war."

"I wasn't holding myself out as a replacement for Commodore Marshak, sir. There are any number of possibilities. People who, in addition to higher rank, also have more extensive combat experience."

This tack was so unexpected as to bring Corin out of his self-imposed silence. "I believe my record in that respect is fairly 'extensive,' Commodore Tatsumo.

And I must say this is the first time I've heard you or anyone else suggest otherwise."

"I was referring, Commodore Marshak, to combat experience which is readily verifiable, without having to rely on records from . . . outside His Imperial Majesty's service."

Translation: sensitive commands should go to people who've been with Ivar from the start. Not to Johnny-come-lately ex-mercs. "Are you implying, Commodore Tatsumo, that my record while in the employ of the former provisional government of Epsilon Eridani has been in any way falsified?"

"No, but—"

"Well, then, just what *are* you—?"

"All right, that will do." Roderick's interjection was delivered in a normal tone of voice, with none of the snappishness that the words might have suggested. But the incipient shouting match halted like a column of marching trainees at a drill instructor's bark. "Corin, I don't think that's what she meant at all. And Aline, his record—his *Fleet* record—speaks for itself. Not just his service before the current unpleasantness, including his decoration for valor in the last Ch'axanthu war, but also his last two years' service under His Imperial Majesty." Roderick had a way of saying those last three words that made *my father* superfluous. There were murmurs of agreement from around the table. "And at any rate, I've already explained my thinking on this subject. We have no way of being certain what situation our first-in unit will encounter at Earth. Under the circumstances, we need a capacity for independent initiative, and tactical flexibility. The Permanent Task Group for Special Operations has a demonstrated record of both . . . when allowed to function in its own way under its own commander." His voice had taken on a quiet finality, and when he paused for further comment, Tatsumo made none.

"So now," the admiral resumed, "let's turn to other

matters. Another reason I called this meeting is to stress—without making a speech—that this is not a war of conquest or of revenge. It is a war to restore the Empire. This is the basis of His Imperial Majesty's policy of clemency toward defeated rebels. That policy remains firmly in force."

"Question, Admiral." Corin spoke mildly. He had a pretty good idea that Roderick's non-speech had been intended for him—and, through him, for Garth. "Does the Emperor's clemency extend to those who go beyond mere opposition and seek to usurp the Imperial title itself?"

"That crime must, of course, be viewed with exceptional seriousness. His Imperial Majesty will have to decide on the disposition of Chewning's case. But I must emphasize that it is *his* decision, not ours. And his judgment will doubtless be influenced by the degree of resistance we encounter. A usurper who yields and recants has a greater claim on the Emperor's mercy than one who persists in his treason. That consideration—as well as the ordinary rules of war— means any offer to surrender must be accepted." This time there was no question where Roderick's words were directed. Nor was the matter academic, given the manifest hopelessness of any resistance by Chewning. Everyone was expecting a surrender message to arrive any time.

"Yes, sir," Corin murmured. As the discussion moved on to tactical questions, he held his peace, while thinking, *I'd better have a little talk with Garth.*

Damiano Chewning gazed from the comm screen with the face of a rapturous rodent. "I assure you, Madame Chairperson, that all Earth—the entire Sol system, in fact—waits to hail you as its savior, as the bringer of—"

"Of the reforms you've promised to implement . . . Your Imperial Majesty." Lauren Romaine's mouth formed a downward droop of distaste as she spoke the title. "You *do* recall, don't you?"

"But of course, Madame Chairperson! We shall have no difficulties in this regard. I am in full agreement with the program you propose. After the current emergency is over, I will effectuate it by Imperial decree!"

Romaine's fleet had halted to enable a comm ship to unfold its vast tachyon beam array. So she, standing on the flag bridge of FRS *Liberator*, and he, somewhere on the surface of Earth—or, she suspected, as far under it as he could get—could carry on a realtime conversation across a third of a light-year. But, she was beginning to suspect, meaningful communication with Chewning was beyond the capacity of any technology to provide.

"It is precisely to do away with that way of doing things that the Federated Republics are prepared to support your claim . . . Your Imperial Majesty. But I recognize that for the present it is how we must proceed. And now, let us turn matters over to our respective staffs, to work out the details." She motioned surreptitiously to the comm officer to make the transfer immediately, before she had to undergo further formal pleasantries that required her to render the Imperial form of address to Chewning. Then she turned away and contemplated the stars in the main screen.

Lauren Romaine, Chairperson of the Executive Council of the Federated Republics, had started anagathics late and didn't take to them exceptionally well. But even now, entering her seventh standard decade, she stood slenderly erect. Her iron-gray hair was pulled back into a bun, a style as severe as her Athena-like features.

"Do you really trust him to keep his word?"

Romaine turned with a smile as heartfelt as she could generally manage these days. "Of course I don't trust him, Khalid," she said to her chief advisor, the only other person on the flag bridge in civilian clothes. "How naive do you think I am?"

"Not very," Khalid Sadoury admitted. "Not after having spent half your adult life in politics and the half before that in academe."

"And finding that there was less difference between the two than I'd supposed," she finished for him. "But I don't think he'll have any choice once we've saved him from getting what he deserves at Brady-Schiavona's hands."

"Maybe. Still, there are disturbing stories about what happened to the last ally who thought he'd placed Chewning under an obligation by saving his worthless skin."

"Yes, yes, I know the version Brady-Schiavona has spread since Garth Krona joined him. But Chewning denies it, and how can we separate the facts from the propaganda? Anyway, I'm not relying on Chewning's gratitude! We won't be putting ourselves at his mercy—which Krona did, assuming the stories are true. Once we're in the Sol system with this force, we'll have the whip hand. Chewning will *have* to carry out the democratic reforms he promised as the price of our help."

"In other words, convert himself into a figurehead constitutional monarch." Sadoury gave his graying dark head a skeptical shake. "He'll try to find a way to slither out."

"Of course it will be difficult to hold him to his commitments. But the chance, Khalid, the chance! This is our one, unrepeatable opportunity to reconstruct the Empire along republican lines. It's also our one chance to stop Brady-Schiavona—the only man who's capable of restoring the Empire in its old form, which means he'll eventually be the death of the Federation. That's why I insisted on coming myself, against everyone's advice."

"And bringing *me* along, which is even worse," Sadoury grumbled.

Romaine's gray eyes twinkled. *You haven't changed, Khalid—the only thing that hasn't changed since we were lovers, a couple of geological epochs ago.* "This is too important, old friend. I don't trust anyone but myself to handle it . . . and I don't even trust *myself* in the absence of your counsel." *And,* she added to herself, *I'd go mad with nobody around me but military robots. I need someone I can talk to—and who knows he can talk to me, freely and uninhibitedly.*

Sadoury proceeded to demonstrate the latter. "Was this 'important' enough to make you agree to a secret understanding with Chewning?"

Romaine grew defensive. "If we'd submitted it to the full legislative assembly for public debate, Brady-Schiavona would have heard. And we would have lost the advantage of surprise."

"No doubt. Still . . . you're always making speeches against such things."

"But this isn't a matter of a couple of greedy, unelected warlords making a secret treaty to stab a third one in the back for their own selfish advantage! This is about a *principle!*" Sadoury's mischievous smile brought her to an embarrassed halt. *Yes, Khalid, you're the ballast that keeps me from floating away on my own hot air.* But it was too sore a point. "Can't we talk about something else?"

"Certainly. But you may not want to. After we'd deployed the array, we directed it back toward Ursa Major before using it to contact Chewning. There's a backlog of messages for you from the Executive Council. Most of them concern the proposed military appropriations for next year."

Romaine emitted a low groan. "I can just imagine. But tell me anyway."

"Linden is threatening to tie up all further consideration of the measure unless his own planets—and, in particular, certain contractors who contributed to his campaign fund—get a larger quota of the contracts. Jastrov is opposed to it simply because Duchamp is for it. The Alliance of Egalitarians is demanding that no military appropriation at all be passed unless it includes a provision for the abolition of all 'elitist' rank distinctions and the establishment of command structure of elected committees. The—"

All at once, disgust and frustration caught up with Romaine like a rising tide of vomit. "You're right. I don't want to talk about it now. I'll deal with it later."

Sadoury inclined his head and withdrew, leaving her to continue convincing herself of the rightness of the course on which she'd embarked.

She'd once hoped the Federated Republics would simply be ignored while the various warlords fought their feuds. Left alone in the Ursa Major region, they could make themselves into something that would serve as a beacon and an example for the rest of what had been the Empire after the warlords had finally done the universe the service of wiping each other out. Some of her colleagues still clung pathetically to that hope. But it wasn't going to work out that way. The Empire was going to be restored, one way or another. And an Empire restored by Ivar Brady-Schiavona must inevitably swallow them. Their only alternative was to do the restoring themselves, converting the Empire into a crowned republic and hoping that the crown would eventually be seen for the superfluity it was and kicked summarily into the ash heap of history. Chewning, in his desperation, had promised just that in exchange for an alliance and recognition of his claim to the imperium. That claim's total speciousness hadn't been a problem, given Romaine's fundamental philosophical rejection of the entire Imperial system, including its succession law. From her viewpoint, Chewning's claim was neither more nor less farcical than any other.

And yet . . . from the Old Earth classics of political thought she'd read and admired, a quotation kept rearing its impudent head to disturb her certitude.

Two and a half millennia before, a certain Edmund Burke, challenged to judge the relative merits of competing parties' philosophies, had said, "Show me the men."

Nowadays, she reflected, he would have said, "Show me the *people*," for political participation was no longer restricted to males as it had been in his benighted time. But, that quibble aside, the point was as valid as ever. The only thing about a political position that was demonstrably, incontrovertibly *real* was the quality of the human beings who espoused it.

So, Lauren Romaine asked herself with the pitiless honesty of which she was capable, *why is it that I, the standard-bearer of progress and enlightenment, find myself allied with Damiano Chewning, the lowest species of vermin to crawl out of the human gene pool? And in opposition to Ivar Brady-Schiavona, the one inarguably decent and honorable individual in the entire swirl of present-day power politics?*

Burke must have been wrong.

Or . . . could I be wrong?

Damiano Chewning turned away from his viewscreen as Lauren Romaine had turned away from hers. His face wore a look very different from any in his repertoire of public expressions. But it smoothed itself out as he recalled he wasn't alone in the room.

"You're sure she doesn't know I'm here?" asked the other man, who had stood well outside the visual pickup but still looked jittery.

"Quite sure. We've kept your presence under the tightest secrecy. Thanks to Brady-Schiavona's envelopment of this system, the only direct contact we've had with the Ursa Major region since your arrival has been the mission I sent to arrange the alliance—and they couldn't have told Romaine, because they didn't know."

Vladimir Liang was visibly relieved.

Not for the first time, Chewning reflected that his ex-enemy's arrival at Sol in a battered cruiser, one jump ahead of his victims' relatives in the chaos following Romaine's defeat of his fleet, had been a stroke of luck. Not all of Chewning's advisors had thought so at the time. Kirpal in particular had been all for shooting out of hand the man who'd murdered an Emperor. *Typical*, Chewning sneered inwardly. *Blockheads like that are incapable of appreciating the need for flexibility, of appreciating that today's enemies may be tomorrow's possible allies, and vice versa.* He had overruled them and taken the fugitive in. Liang, after all, still had useful contacts in his former Serpens/ Bootes domain, whose balkanization had seemed to offer Chewning an opportunity to expand his own sphere of influence. Brady-Schiavona's offensive had forced an indefinite postponement of that program. But Liang was still a useful source of information about his new ally Romaine, however much his judgments had to be discounted for embitterment.

Now, with Liang's fears calmed, that embitterment crept back out. "I still can't believe you agreed to that bitch's terms. She doesn't have the proper respect for you as the legitimate Emperor, as *I* have. She'd turn you into a mere front man for herself and her rabble of petty grafters, fatuous gasbags and pseudo-intellectual poseurs!"

Chewning laughed shortly. "Oh, don't worry. I have no intention of honoring my agreement with her."

"But how will you be able to avoid it, with her political clown show established here on Earth and her fleet in orbit overhead?"

"The question is premature. And this whole discussion is academic. I had no choice. I needed her as an ally, so I had to promise her everything she demanded. I'll worry about evading those promises after she's stopped Brady-Schiavona for me."

"But will she be able to?" Liang fretted. "After all, her background is completely unmilitary."

"True. But she has some competent Fleet people working for her. And, as *you* are aware, their record is not entirely without successes." Liang flushed, and his lips compressed as if to hold back the rejoinder he could not make. Chewning permitted himself a moment's enjoyment before continuing in a mollifying tone. "You're basically right, though; her forces are no match for Brady-Schiavona's—or wouldn't be in an ordinary battle."

"What do you mean?"

"Remember, she'll have the advantage of surprise. Also . . . I have a plan which will leave her opponents leaderless when she attacks them."

Liang looked up sharply, his snit forgotten. "And as to this plan?"

Chewning smiled lazily, and met Liang's eyes in a way that completed the banishment of the malice— sheer habit, really—he'd displayed before. "Come. I'll explain the details. And afterwards . . ."

He recalled an ancient adage to the effect that politics makes strange bedfellows. The irony of that saying as applied to himself and Liang never failed to amuse him.

The holo tank was set up to show most of the Sol system, with the green icons of the main fleet still moving inward from its outskirts and, near the center, a single such light creeping along the string-light of Earth's orbit about sixty degrees behind the mother world. Corin, standing on the flagship of the Permanent Task Group for Special Operations—which that last icon represented—gave a command in a voice made brittle by tension. The display changed scale, and Earth's orbit filled the tank's entire circumference. Details emerged—disturbing details, to Corin's mind.

The expected feeler from Earth had arrived as they'd approached this system's outermost orbits, but its content had not been expected. Chewning had declared himself ready to surrender, but unable to make the offer publicly—the military diehards surrounding him wouldn't have it. He *could* get off Earth. But he would only give himself up to Roderick Brady-Schiavona personally, for he trusted no one else. He'd proposed that Roderick come ahead with a small force, to avoid tipping his hand. Afterwards, safe aboard Roderick's flagship, he would make a systemwide broadcast abjuring his assumption of the Imperial title, swearing allegiance to His Imperial Majesty Ivar, and calling on his erstwhile followers to yield.

The offer had been a bombshell dropped onto their council table. Many had begged Roderick not to expose himself to such danger in reliance on the word of a noted liar. Aline Tatsumo had been especially vehement. But there had been compelling arguments on the other side. It was clear, except to fanatics of the sort Chewning claimed he had to deal with, that Sol's defenders couldn't possibly win; under the circumstances, seeking to save his own skin at all costs seemed convincingly in character. And the stakes—a near-bloodless victory over opponents left disorganized and demoralized by their "Emperor's" defection— justified a degree of risk-taking.

Corin suspected that Roderick's decision had been foreordained anyway. Advising the young admiral to avoid personal danger at his people's possible expense was the surest way to persuade him to accept that danger. His willingness to risk his life might or might not have been related to the fact that, for all his youth, he had less of it left to lose than most. But whatever the truth of that, it was part of his makeup and there was nothing to be done about it—as dearly as Tatsumo would have liked to do something. She'd nearly waxed mutinous when he'd chosen the reinforced Permanent Task Group to escort him. This was precisely the kind of unorthodox operation in which they specialized, but the argument had left her unimpressed.

Now Corin watched as the tiny green icon of the cruiser *Bogatyr* drew slowly away from its fellows in the holo tank, bearing Roderick toward his rendezvous with the cruiser which—they were assured—was bringing Chewning from the orbital station at Earth's trailing Trojan point. Corin tried to make himself relax—after all, that red icon was approaching as per agreement, having separated from the station's larger one at the prearranged time. Still, it did wonders for his peace of mind to see the trio of green dots curving around toward the station, past the advancing red cruiser-icon.

Roderick had been skeptical at first. "Is it really necessary, Corin, to dispatch a force to seize the station while Chewning has just left it and is still en route?"

"Well," Corin had replied reasonably, "he can hardly object since he's surrendering the whole system. And if what he says about the fanaticism of some of his military people is true, I'd like to take every reasonable precaution to assure the safety of my command."

"Yes. I can respect that. All right, Corin. You can send an assault transport with enough troops to secure the station."

"And some escorts, just in case the station commander is unreasonable?"

"Very well," Roderick had assented, "you can send a couple of cruisers, although we're not looking at any serious defenses." Earth's Trojan points had stations dating back to the earliest space colonists, who'd come to mine the clusters of asteroidal rubble those points had collected over the eons. The stations had been expanded and updated over the centuries, and many of the Trojan asteroids had been towed to their immediate vicinity for easy mining. But the Trojan points' economic importance lay centuries in the past and they were now unthought-of backwaters—which, Corin grudgingly admitted to himself, made the trailing Trojan station a logical place for Chewning to surreptitiously give himself up.

Now he watched the tank as those three green icons curved around behind the advancing red cruiser and approached the station. He'd proceeded exactly as he had proposed and Roderick had approved. There were, however, a few things he'd decided the admiral didn't need to know. For one thing, those three ships were so heavily stealthed as to be invisible to anyone who didn't know exactly where to look for them—they appeared in the tank only because their transponder returns were being downloaded to it. For another, Janille was in charge of the assault force—too small to require a C.O. with the lieutenant colonel's rank she now held—and in overall command of the mini flotilla. And for yet another, one of the two cruiser escorts Roderick had authorized was a specialized scout cruiser, underweaponed but bristling with sophisticated sensors. . . .

He waited and watched, and as time crept by he began to allow himself to hope he wouldn't get the message he'd feared.

Then it arrived, with a shriek of static and a familiar voice made harsh by urgency.

"Corin, this is Janille," she began without preliminaries. Comm had orders to patch any incoming call from her directly to the flag bridge. "It *is* a trap—warships lying doggo among all the space junk of the Trojan point, not far from the station. We had to get practically on top of them to detect them, with their power stepped down to life-support levels. We're sending you our readouts on them now." The data began to appear on Corin's private comm screen, just as a rash of red dots began to pop out around the Trojan point.

"Janille, listen carefully. Get out of there *now*. Maintain stealth, of course, but get out as quickly as you can without making yourself conspicuous."

"But Corin, we can go ahead and take the station as planned—"

"Forget the station! That operation was never anything but an excuse to get you in there to look for a trap. And you've found it! If you go ahead and reveal yourself, it will alert them." There was no direct way a target could detect the fact that it was being scanned with modern sensors. So the opposition still didn't know their ambush had been found out. Corin meant to take advantage of that. "Now move! That's an order." He cut off the connection, and any further argument, and swung toward the intraship communicator and addressed the flag captain. "Captain Korachuk! Activate Contingency Plan Alpha." The plan was one of the things he'd decided the admiral didn't need to be bothered with. "Alert *Bogatyr*. And get me Captain O'Ryan-Scimitar."

"Aye aye, sir."

The face of the battlecruiser *Defiant*'s skipper appeared on his comm screen. There had never been many Sword Clans cognomens in the Deathstriders' roster, and Karl O'Ryan-Scimitar was some sort of scapegrace younger son. Corin had always respected his reticence about his past. What mattered was his unquestioned competence, and—even more so, at the moment—his ability to act on his own initiative.

"Karl," Corin snapped, "it's Contingency Plan Alpha. We're downloading the targets' locations—"

"They're coming up in my tank now, sir."

"Then you know what to do. Signing off."

The Permanent Task Group engaged its drives and began to move, executing Contingency Plan Alpha without the need for further orders. All the warships but one sprang ahead under O'Ryan-Scimitar's command, arrowing toward the Trojan point. The one exception was the flagship *Valiant*, which Corin rode. That battlecruiser began a course change that would bring it to the relief of *Bogatyr*, now turning sharply away from the approaching ship that, Corin was now quite certain, did not contain Damiano Chewning.

"Train all sensors on that cruiser," he ordered.

"How is Janille?" came the bass query from off to the side as he waited for the sensor returns. Corin hadn't heard Garth come onto the flag bridge. Strictly speaking, Colonel Krona should have been on one of the assault transports. In reality, nobody had even considered the possibility of keeping him off the flagship.

"She's all right," Corin assured, noting with relief that the icons of her command were getting out of harm's way as per orders. "Hopefully, the same can be said of the admiral. *Bogatyr* has gone to drive and is putting as much distance as possible between herself and that—"

"Battlecruiser," Garth finished for him as the tank, reflecting the new sensor findings, changed the icon of the vessel *Bogatyr* had been set to rendezvous with.

Poetic justice, in a way, Corin thought, remembering the legendary trick Roderick had played on the Tarakans. Now the battlecruiser that had been disguising itself as a cruiser engaged its own drive and leapt forward to intercept *Bogatyr*.

But with time-distortion drive, an instant's head start meant a lot. *Valiant* drew into range just before the enemy battlecruiser had brought its overwhelmingly superior firepower to bear on *Bogatyr*.

There was nothing more Corin could do, for Captain Korachuk was quite capable of fighting his ship. So he and Garth stood in silence and watched the holo tank.

Things were happening rapidly.

Whoever led the waiting enemy warcraft knew what the Permanent Task Group's sudden activity must mean, and those ships instantly scrapped their timetable and got under way. The mined-out asteroids against which they crouched had tiny Chen Limits of their own. A few seconds' outward acceleration on impellers was necessary before they could safely activate their drives. Those few seconds were crucial. O'Ryan-Scimitar's command came sweeping in when their opponents were still transitioning into the compressed-time state, caught them off balance and went through them like the sword blade of his erstwhile clan name.

At the same time, *Valiant* energized the gigawatt X-ray lasers that formed the main batteries of deep-space warships below battleship size. Her foe was another, very similar battlecruiser; a one-on-one battle could have gone either way. But Chewning's captain had rigid orders. His first priority was to destroy *Bogatyr*, killing Roderick Brady-Schiavona and decapitating his fleet. He continued to concentrate his fire on the fleeing cruiser, ignoring *Valiant*'s attack for as long as possible—a little longer than possible, as it turned out. *Bogatyr*'s deflector screens failed under the incoming torrent of energy and her transponder began to scream its electronic pain as the energy lances pierced her physical body . . . just before her tormentor vanished in an expanding plasma sphere which was shortly visible to the naked eye in *Valiant*'s viewscreens.

"Captain Korachuk!" Corin shouted into his intership communicator above the cheering. "Have comm raise *Bogatyr*. Find out if the admiral—"

"We've already made contact with them, sir. He's—"

"I'm all right, Corin." All at once, the main comm screen showed Roderick Brady-Schiavona, somewhat the worse for wear, against a background of crackling electrical fires and frantic damage control. The cheers that began to spread through *Valiant* were louder than those that had followed the volatilization of the enemy battlecruiser. "We were lucky; our weapon systems are down, but our drive and impellers are all right, as are most of our electronic systems and some of our deflectors." The famous white grin split the soot-blackened face. "I think I may have been lucky in other ways as well. Is it possible that there were a few elements of your planning that you never quite got around to sharing with me?"

"Well . . . er . . ." Desperate change of subject: "I'll send a shuttle to bring you over to this ship, Admiral." Nothing smaller than a battleship mounted transposer equipment, so they'd have to do it the old-fashioned way.

"Never mind. Have you gotten the alert from the main fleet?"

"Uh . . . no, sir."

"Put your holo tank on system scale." Corin obeyed, and a chill stabbed through him.

Red icons had blossomed out among the gas-giant orbits, swinging in from the outer blackness to intercept the green formation. And, moving outward from Mars, a smaller scarlet array advanced to form the other jaw of a trap.

"That's got to be Chewning's main force departing from Mars," he heard himself say. "But who are those hostiles entering the outer system?"

"They've made no secret of their identity since being detected: they're Lauren Romaine's people, just in from Ursa Major."

Garth found his voice before Corin could. "So Chewning has conned somebody else into allying with him."

"And now, Corin," Roderick said briskly, "get into a shared hookup immediately. And whoever led your main body just now . . . what's his name?"

"Captain O'Ryan-Scimitar, sir." Karl had, he noted out of the corner of an eye, just reported in.

"Have him join us. Signing off." And the admiral's image was gone, leaving Corin to marvel that he could function in the face of the news he'd just heard. But he, Corin, also moved, issuing orders and donning his VR gear, as though energized by a transfusion of vitality. Contact with Roderick Brady-Schiavona had that effect on people.

The virtual conference room was the standard one. The admiral, looking spiffier than he had on the comm screen—the software wasn't programmed to reflect smudges and other marks of battle—stood beyond a system-scale holo display. O'Ryan-Scimitar appeared a second or two later, standing stiffly at attention in the presence of rarefied rank. Then another form popped into existence—a large one. Garth had evidently found a headset. Roderick glanced sharply at the uninvited arrival . . . but only for an instant. Then he gave a small but eloquent nod, and Garth was no longer uninvited.

"Now, gentlemen, let's see what we've got." They all gazed at the system display. Corin's mind automatically superimposed a clock face over it. Planets and other objects were orbiting counterclockwise around the sun symbol at the center. They themselves were trailing the blue dot of Earth at about seven o'clock—but close to the tank's center, for Earth's orbit was dwarfed on this scale. Much further out, the main fleet was at eleven o'clock, while still further out Romaine's red intruders were converging on it from twelve o'clock. Mars was in that same general direction; Chewning's forces forged outward in a transfer orbit that would bring it into the running battle.

"They haven't coordinated this very well," Roderick observed. "Chewning's forces won't be able to affect the battle until Romaine's have been engaged for some time."

"Why am I not surprised?" Garth growled.

Roderick smiled. "Yes, it does seem to be a behavior pattern, doesn't it? Well, this time it's going to cost them. It's clear from the data we're getting that their combined forces aren't all that superior to our main fleet. They certainly don't have the kind of edge that would normally justify risking this kind of attack. They're obviously counting on the effect of my having just been killed." The grin grew predatory. "So they're in for a surprise. Two surprises, actually, because we're going to spring a trap of our own—with this task group."

O'Ryan-Scimitar let out a small yelp. "But sir," he protested, shaken out of his deference, "we can't even get there in time!" He gave a gesture that took in the side of the sun they were on, the direction the entire cosmic carousel was turning, and the fact that neither impellers nor drive conferred any magic insulation from inertia.

"Yes, we can," Roderick said, his eyes flashing with eagerness. "Not by much—but we can do it. Look." He spoke a series of quick commands, and a green string-light appeared in the display, curving sharply away from their present position, inward from Earth's orbit toward Sol in the kind of very flat hyperbola that couldn't have been thought of in the far-off days of reaction drives, then whipping wildly back outward on a course that would intersect that of the main fleet shortly after Romaine had engaged it.

Corin looked up, incredulous. "You're going to use Sol as a gravitational slingshot?" The technique was hardly ever used any more, but there was no reason it couldn't be; a ship under drive was not immune to gravity. But . . . "That course brings us so close to Sol that—"

"It only looks that way in the tank," Roderick reassured him. "Pretty close, yes—but our deflectors can handle it."

"Can *your* deflectors?" Corin demanded, the difference in their ranks momentarily forgotten. "After the damage *Bogatyr* has taken? Let me send a shuttle for you."

"There's no time for that, Corin. We've got a very narrow window of opportunity here, if this is going to work at all. I'll stay where I am. *Bogatyr* can keep up."

"But even if you don't get your ass singed off by Sol, we'll have a battle to fight at the far end!"

"Well, you'll just have to protect me." Roderick's look took in all three of them. "You've shown you're good at that." O'Ryan-Scimitar's eyes gleamed and he stood even straighter. "But we've got to move now. If we do, we can take Romaine's force from the flank, when it's already deeply engaged."

Garth leaned over the display, studying it intensely. Nobody got to be a successful mercenary leader by taking reckless chances. "But will there be enough sheer tonnage and firepower to make the difference, Admiral? I mean, you'll just have the Permanent Task Group for Special Operations."

Roderick met the big man's eyes and held them. "No," he corrected. "I'll just have the *Deathstriders*."

In some objective corner of his mind, Corin wondered, *How does he get away with this?* At the same time, he heard his own voice saying, "Let's do it!"

"I'm with you," Garth rumbled. And, in defiance of all military etiquette, he extended his hand to a four-sunburst admiral. Roderick took it, then turned and offered his hand to Corin.

The software was capable of full tactile feedback. A handshake felt like a handshake.

He's not really your descendant, Corin told himself, *even though he's descended from exactly the same blood that flows in your veins. Must remember that.*

CHAPTER TWELVE
Earth (Sol III), 4331 C.E.

Panic stalked the corridors of Damiano Chewning's subterranean command center.

Grand Admiral Kirpal strode through it all, sparing only an occasional contemptuous glance for the huddled groups of frightened functionaries. He didn't even try to halt the occasional loot-burdened figure that slipped furtively past. What was the point, now?

He reached the door he sought. Its human guards were gone, and the electronic ones opened it at the touch of his palm to the ident-pad. The outer offices were in disarray from the haste with which they'd been deserted. He proceeded inward until he'd reached a monumental doorway surmounted with the Imperial dragon.

The room beyond had the overdone ornateness typical of the late Emperor Oleg, who'd built this facility along with so much else on Old Earth. Curtained alcoves alternating with pilasters lined the side walls, flanking a gleaming conference table. The man seated at the table's head, alone in the room, looked up as Kirpal entered unannounced.

"Well, Admiral?"

Kirpal came to what resembled a position of attention but had no respect in it, just a need to hold himself physically in check. He forced his words past clenched jaws. "Nothing you don't already know ... Your Imperial Majesty. Our main force under Admiral Tellefsen arrived from Mars just in time to be caught up in the collapse of Romaine's fleet. Brady-Schiavona's arrival took Tellefsen even more by surprise than it did Romaine, since *he* had been led to believe that Brady-Schiavona was dead."

"Ah, yes." Damiano Chewning sighed. "I thought it best to suppress the news of our ambush's failure. Bad for morale. But what is our *current* status, Admiral?"

"Tellefsen is dead; Romaine is reported to be. The survivors are still straggling in. Brady-Schiavona's fleet will soon be in orbit around this planet, and our orbital fortresses are already signaling their surrender ... Your Imperial Majesty." If possible, Kirpal's pause was even longer than it had been before.

"Brady-Schiavona would never bombard the mother world," Chewning opined.

"No. He'll send his Marines down, and we can't hope to resist them. Unless ..." Kirpal's harsh features formed an unaccustomed expression as he made the request that had been his reason for coming here. "The comm net is still functioning. If you'd make a personal planetwide appeal, we might be able to organize a defense."

Chewning shook his head with a vigor that set the rabbitlike cheeks wobbling. "No. I have no interest in leading a hopeless charge. I'm afraid there's no option left but surrender."

Kirpal barked a laugh. All pretense of deference was now gone. "Do you actually think Brady-Schiavona will accept your surrender, after your attempt to kill him?"

"*My* attempt? Oh, no, Admiral. As Admiral Brady-Schiavona will learn, you and the other members of your military clique discovered at the last minute my plan to slip off-world and give myself up. You placed me in confinement. But you thought his understanding with me presented a golden opportunity to trap him. After the defeat of our forces and Romaine's, loyal personnel freed me . . . but died doing it, in a firefight which, regrettably, also claimed your life."

Kirpal's dark face darkened still further. "You little maggot! I've done your dirty work—I set up Krona to be destroyed—I even stayed with you after you'd taken up with that other piece of filth, your lover Liang."

"You had nowhere else to go." Chewning sounded bored.

"But I do now! I'll deliver your corpse to Brady-Schiavona!" Kirpal reached for his sidearm . . . and remembered that he had, by sheer habit, come unarmed into the Emperor's presence. With a roar, he flung himself around the table, hands outstretched and formed into claws.

There was a sharp *crack!* as a small glass sphere broke mach, and a tiny flash of plasma as air friction whipped away the ferrous coating that had allowed it to be electromagnetically accelerated to six thousand meters per second. Passing at that speed through a rigid container like a skull, it was enough to induce massive hydrostatic shock. The top of Kirpal's head came off, and its contents geysered upward. His body collapsed to the floor amid a spatter of falling gore.

Vladimir Liang stepped out from behind one of the alcove hangings, pocketing his bead gun and giving that which lay on the floor a look of fastidious distaste. "Animal!" he sniffed. Then he turned to Chewning. "What are we going to do now?"

"Surrender, of course . . . and tell the story I just outlined to him."

"Won't they wonder why you didn't warn them about the alliance with Romaine when you made your offer to secretly surrender, if that offer was sincere?"

"Simple: it was Kirpal who arranged the alliance. I never knew about it. The late Chairperson Romaine is in no position to contradict this version of events. So the story ought to hold up well enough to qualify me for Ivar's famous clemency."

"But what about *me*?" Liang quavered.

"That does present a problem, doesn't it? Any Emperor is apt to take a dim view of the murder of another Emperor. Bad precedent, you see. We may discover the limits of Ivar's sense of humor." Chewning eyed Liang, and his look did not match his voice's bantering tone.

Liang gazed back expressionlessly, and made a movement with his right arm which, while barely perceptible, sufficed to remind Chewning that he had never let go of the now-pocketed bead gun.

"But," Chewning resumed smoothly, as though the byplay had never occurred, "it should be possible to come up with a story that will satisfy Ivar. He really *is* determined to be merciful and conciliatory. Let's see. . . . We'll explain that Oleg and his family were killed by overzealous subordinates, acting without your orders, and that afterwards you were unable to publicly repudiate their actions because they were too influentially connected."

"You really are good at this kind of thing, aren't you?"

Chewning waved away the flattery. "It needs refining," he admitted modestly, "but we'll have a little while to work on it. Mind you, Ivar still won't be happy. In fact, he'll despise you. But it will enable him to justify sparing your life and keeping his reputation for mercy. At the very least, it will gain time."

"Time for what?" Liang wanted to know.

"Oh, who's to say? 'King Louis may die. Or I may die. Or the horse may die. Or . . . the horse may talk.'"

"*What?*"

"Sorry, a very old story. The point is that one never knows what's going to happen, but must always be ready to take advantage of it. We'll keep our eyes open and see what develops—and who we come into contact with."

"*Another* important prisoner, Commodore Marshak?" Rear Admiral Teodor Brady-Schiavona's preternaturally handsome face formed an undeniably charming smile in the comm screen. "I'll have a full bundle of miscreants to deliver to His Imperial Majesty."

Corin had never met Roderick's older brother in person. He'd heard that the Emperor had entrusted him with various minor commands, in which he'd performed acceptably. And in the absence of demonstrated incapacity, the fact that he was his father's son had made it impossible not to promote him rapidly. His most recent task had been to bring a convoy to Sol, with the additional security and administrative personnel his brother's provisional military government needed. Now he was preparing to return to Sigma Draconis, taking Damiano Chewning and Vladimir Liang to receive the Emperor's justice.

"Yes, Admiral," Corin affirmed. "The doctors hadn't thought they'd be able to release this prisoner in time for your departure. But they changed their minds at the last possible moment. We were barely able to rendezvous with you in time."

"And a very smart bit of astrogation it was. But now, I see you're almost in range."

"Yes, sir. I'll have the prisoner on the transposer stage by then."

"We'll be ready, Commodore. Signing off." Teodor's features seemed to linger for a moment, Cheshire-catlike, on the blank screen.

Corin turned aside. "Well, shall we go inform the prisoner?"

"Right." Janille fell in beside him as they left *Valiant*'s flag bridge. "I still don't understand why the admiral sent us out here to make this delivery. A frigate or even a pinnace would have served."

"Not all the enemy ships have been accounted for. There might be a few still skulking around the outer system. So he decided an escort was in order. Also . . . I think he felt it was fitting, somehow. A matter of rendering proper courtesies."

"Is that why we're paying this call, and not just sending some corporal?"

"I suppose," said Corin, who hadn't really thought about it.

They proceeded through the battlecruiser's passageways until they'd entered an area where they didn't often go. Security scanners passed them without comment, and they came to an expanse of bulkhead guarded by two entirely superfluous Marine sentries—observing the forms again. In the same spirit, Corin signaled for admission before gesturing to the senior Marine, who touched a control on his belt. Without any movement that the eye could observe, the nanoplastic of the bulkhead—as hard as low-tech steel—was no longer there, and a doorway stood open to the compartment beyond.

The woman within put down the book she'd been reading and rose to her feet. She wouldn't have been able to do that a short while earlier. The Marine boarding party had found her aboard the wreck of her fleet's flagship, in not much better shape than the elderly civilian gent whose rapidly cooling body she'd been holding. But regeneration therapy had worked its accustomed wonders, and the doctors had pronounced her able to travel. They hadn't been able to eliminate all the marks of what she'd been through; an expanse of shiny-pink freshly regenerated flesh marred her left cheek and temple, and the hair on that side of her head was still an iron-gray stubble. But none of that could banish Lauren Romaine's stateliness, even though it was now only a husk containing dead despair. "Yes, Commodore . . . ?"

"Commodore Marshak, ma'am." Corin had decided

earlier on the mode of address, since "Madame Chairperson" or the like was out of the question. "And this is Lieutenant Colonel Dornay."

"Colonel." Romaine nodded to Janille. Then she turned back to Corin, and recognition seemed to awaken. "Oh, yes . . . Marshak. I understand you were quite the hero in the recent battle. It seems you saved Roderick Brady-Schiavona's life."

"I played a role, ma'am—but so did Lieutenant Colonel Dornay, and many others."

"No doubt. I've heard a lot about it." Romaine's gray eyes hardened. "It's also been brought to my attention that the Federated Republics collapsed at the news of the outcome here at Sol, and are offering no real resistance to the forces Ivar Brady-Schiavona has sent to occupy Ursa Major."

Janille flushed. Romaine's guards were Marines. "Have any of my people been taunting you, ma'am? If so, I'll have their . . . uh, hides."

"No, no. I can't claim I've been maltreated in any way. One hears things, that's all—even when in captivity. And it's nothing I didn't expect to hear." Bleakness settled over the tall, dignified woman like a shroud of snow. "I knew I was wagering everything on one throw of the dice. And I lost. I regret that. But I don't really regret having gambled. If I hadn't, the Federated Republics would have lost their one chance of long-term survival."

"Now they're falling in the short term," Corin couldn't stop himself from saying.

"True. But the outcome is the same in the end."

"Still," Corin persisted (perversely, for he knew that getting into a debate was as inappropriate as it was pointless), "you've sacrificed a lot of human lives to an abstract political theory."

Romaine's eyes held the final glare of dying embers. "'Abstract political theory'? You wouldn't call it that if you were from Ursa Major. If you'd experienced what the people of that region were put through to service a pointless war against a nonexistent threat—"

"Actually, ma'am," Corin interrupted, suddenly uncomfortable, "I served in the last Ch'axanthu war."

"Then you understand—or *ought* to understand—the accumulated disgust and revulsion against a system that perpetrates such grandiose folly to gratify the megalomania of a single individual!" Romaine stopped for breath. "Oh, I know the received idea: the Empire is so diverse that it can't function without a human symbol of unity—the most basic common denominator of human association. But the pendulum has swung away from that before. In the last couple of centuries before spaceflight, they got away from a theory called the 'divine right of kings'—"

"And, as I recall, replaced it with the divine right of political careerists."

Corin expected a snarl from Romaine. He got a smile. "You don't fit my preconception of military officers, Commodore—it doesn't include an interest in history. I'd enjoy discussing the subject with you. But I'm sure that's not the purpose for which you came."

"No, ma'am." Corin donned formality like a cloak. "I am under orders to transfer custody of you to Rear Admiral Teodor Brady-Schiavona, who will convey you to Sigma Draconis. We're approaching our rendezvous with his flagship. Please accompany us to the transposer stage."

Romaine gave a complex chuckle and shook her head. "Another Brady-Schiavona! Well, at least I'll get to meet Ivar."

"His Imperial Majesty," Janille piped up, "is noted for his leniency toward former . . ." Her voice trailed to a miserable halt.

"Rebels and traitors," Romaine finished for her helpfully. "Well, I have no personal effects. Shall we go?"

They proceeded to the chamber that held a raised dais containing a powerful link. *Valiant*, like all warships lacking transposers of their own, had facilities like these to facilitate focusing by the transposers of ships which did have them, like the battleship *Indefatigable* that Teodor Brady-Schiavona rode. Romaine mounted the stage. Then, as they awaited confirmation that the other ship was ready to transpose, there was an awkward silence. Corin sought for something to fill it. Then, at the last minute, he remembered something he'd meant to ask Romaine.

"One thing I still don't understand. What did you expect to accomplish by allying yourself with an adventurer who didn't even subscribe to your political philosophy?"

"I'd decided reunification of the Empire was unavoidable," Romaine said from the stage in an uninterested voice. "So the most we could hope for was an Empire restructured along more democratic lines. I agreed to the alliance in exchange for a promise of such reforms."

Janille shook her head. "I'm surprised Kirpal would even make such a promise."

Romaine gave her a puzzled look. "Who? Oh, yes— the thug Chewning made Grand Admiral. What does he have to do with it?"

"Huh?" Corin shook his head as though to clear the confusion from it. "But wasn't he the one you negotiated the alliance with?"

"Nonsense. I dealt directly with Chewning."

"What? You mean Chewning wasn't just a figurehead for Kirpal's military clique?"

Romaine laughed bitterly. "Is *that* what he told you?"

"Commodore," came the comm officer's voice, "*Indefatigable* is ready to transpose."

"Tell them to wait!" Corin snapped. Then he turned and addressed Romaine. "Ma'am, this is very important! When you get aboard *Indefatigable*, ask to speak to Rear Admiral Brady-Schiavona. Tell him what you just told us."

Romaine, visibly slipping back into fatalism, bobbed momentarily back to the surface. "Why?"

"They say they don't want to wait any longer, sir," the comm officer interjected.

"Stall them!" Corin spoke to Romaine hurriedly, for she needed to know that Chewning and Liang were her fellow passengers. "Aboard the same ship, Rear Admiral Brady-Schiavona is taking—"

There was no warning. There never was with teleportation—or with the artificial duplication of it the transposer produced. One instant Romaine stood on the stage, and the next instant she didn't. There wasn't even a *pop* of air rushing into a sudden vacuum, for an equal volume of air from *Indefatigable's* transposer room now filled the space that had contained her.

"So Chewning was really behind it all?" Aline Tatsumo shook her head. "And we sent him back to Sigma Draconis to tell his story to the Emperor!"

She sank into a chair facing Corin, Janille and Garth. She still wasn't entirely comfortable with them, but her attitude had improved markedly. Saving Roderick's life, it seemed, covered a multitude of sins.

They sat in Sol's late-afternoon light, on the terrace of the officers' lounge in the Imperial administrative facility that squatted like a titanic alien intruder in this ancient city. *No,* Corin reminded himself, *it isn't really ancient. It's just meant to look that way.*

Armand Duschane had begun the restoration of Old Earth. Oleg had pressed it forward with his usual impatience and embellished it with his characteristic fancies. To repopulate it, he had traced the history of colonial migration and assigned the resettlers to what he'd convinced himself were the wombs of their origin. They'd been brought in from Sigma Draconis to the lesser land mass to the west of here across the planet's smaller ocean—the Atlantic, Corin reminded himself; from Delta Pavonis to the island that lay to the north across a narrow slip of water; from certain worlds in the Serpens/Bootes region to the vast plains to the east . . . and so on, around the world. Just how meaningful a connection the modern gene pool of any colonial world had to any particular Old Earth locale was, to put the matter with exquisite tact, debatable. But nobody said so very loudly, for Oleg had been very proud of himself for his commitment to authenticity. His tame historians had also produced images of the dawn-cities the Zyungen had obliterated . . . and edited them to reflect Oleg's preconceptions, theories and whims. Programmed with these, the nanoconstructors had run up replicas of those cities on their original sites—to the inexpressible (in both senses) disgust of the archaeologists who sought to tunnel down through the strata of ruins that underlay those sites. The periods represented by those strata tended to mingle oddly in the reconstructions above. Corin wondered how the ancient inhabitants of this city would have thought of the medieval-looking fortress that reared its battlements beyond the soaring tower of early-industrial iron latticework. Still, to anyone but a history buff, the two were essentially contemporary, far back down the dim echoing corridors of antiquity.

At least this place wasn't as bad as some Corin had seen on the excursions he'd managed to take—like that temple of Thoth-Ammon in the Nile valley, the one with minarets. In fact, he liked it. After his time on Neustria, it had a familiar feel, for its people had come from Epsilon Eridani. Oleg had liked it too, which was why it played host to the colossal truncated pyramid from whose sloping side this terrace was cantilevered. Even here there was a half-hearted and foredoomed effort to partake of the artificial local color—the terrace held a scattering of round tables shaded by red-and-white umbrellas with black lettering in an old-fashioned form of an alphabet still widespread in the Empire. Corin wondered what "Cinzano" meant.

Janille's voice brought him back to the matter at hand. "After we told the admiral what we'd learned from Romaine, he naturally sent a message to the Emperor," she explained to Tatsumo, who had only just returned from a lengthy inspection of various installations around the Sol system and was hearing this for the first time.

"But," Garth put in, "that will need to be corroborated by Romaine in person."

"She's probably done it already," Tatsumo said with satisfaction. "Shouldn't they be at Sigma Draconis by now?" The tachyon beam array had made the concept of simultaneity meaningful across interstellar distances, however much the theoretical physicists might huff and puff.

"Right," said Corin. "In fact, the admiral says the message confirming their arrival is overdue." He leaned back in his chair and blinked against the sunlight—it was early summer in Old Earth's northern hemisphere, and this was a clear day. "I never got a chance to tell her she was going to be traveling with Chewning and Liang."

"So what?" Janille queried. "It might make for some awkward moments if Teodor lets them mingle. But, to repeat, so what?"

"I don't know. It just bothers me, somehow." Corin sat up straighter and reached for his wine. It was a cosmopolitan brand, but here it came in basketed bottles like the ones that sat on the tables with half-melted wax candles stuck in them. "Anyway, she's at Sigma Draconis, and her testimony will—"

"No, it won't."

They all started at the voice and began to rise to their feet. Roderick gestured them back to their chairs and pulled up one for himself. "I just got the word from Sigma Draconis. Ted has arrived there—but Romaine hasn't."

"Sir?" Tatsumo's voice was a rising squeak of incredulous inquiry.

"It seems that in the course of the voyage she went crazy—grabbed a guard's weapon and used it to kill the guard . . . and then herself. Ted is overcome with regret."

Janille found her voice, and spoke as though what she'd heard was too absurd for indignation. "Sir, we're talking about an elderly woman, with little anagathic bonus and no combat training. You're telling me she disarmed a Marine?"

"No. I'm telling you that was what I was told." Roderick let them chew on the implications of that phraseology for a heartbeat or two before continuing. "We're getting this news somewhat late because a blackout was put on it. But that didn't stop it from leaking to the Ursa Major region."

"She was widely beloved out there," Corin said, barely hearing his own voice in his stupefaction. "In fact, she was probably the only thing holding the Federated Republics together. They won't like this."

"Hardly. They're saying we murdered her. And they're rising furiously against our occupation forces. A walkover has turned into an insurgency that may take years to suppress." Roderick looked like he was in physical pain. "Our pacification of the Empire isn't complete, not by a long shot. We've still got warlords and rebels to deal with in the Serpens/Bootes region and beyond. We don't need this."

"Sir," Tatsumo spoke up hesitantly after a moment's heavy silence, "you obviously don't believe the official story. But what *do* you think happened?"

"Isn't it obvious?" Janille snapped. "Chewning and Liang knew she'd expose them as liars. So they killed her to shut her up."

"But how? They were prisoners themselves. How could they have arranged it?"

"Maybe *they* weren't the ones who did." All heads turned at Garth's subterranean rumble. But he met only one pair of bluish-gray eyes.

"What are you suggesting, Colonel?" asked the owner of those eyes.

"Sir," Garth replied in a voice that did not waver, "by the time Romaine arrived they had already been aboard *Indefatigable* for some time. They had the opportunity to get to Rear Admiral Brady-Schiavona first."

The silence was like a wire drawn to the snapping point, as the unsayable thing that had just been said dissipated on the wind.

Roderick was the first to breathe. Then he started to open his mouth. But then he closed it, and ceased to meet Garth's eyes.

Abruptly, Corin stood up, walked to the railing and stared sightlessly out at the vista of high-tech phoniness that surrounded them.

He'd only met Lauren Romaine once. And he couldn't really quarrel with her self-description as a rebel and a traitor. *So*, he asked himself, *why does the news of her death affect me this way?*

Could it be that I may have signed her death warrant by telling her to blurt out her story to Teodor Brady-Schiavona? Maybe if she'd kept her mouth shut until they'd gotten to Sigma Draconis, and then told Ivar, she'd still be alive.

Or maybe not.

I'll never know, will I?

CHAPTER THIRTEEN
The HC -4 9701 System, 4333 C.E.

"I must say, Admiral Marshak, you're displaying admirable composure under the circumstances," said Vice
Admiral Maura Brady-Schiavona, indicating the holo
tank and the force estimates on the board beyond it.

Corin permitted himself an infuriatingly calm look.

He was now a vice admiral himself. And his date
of rank was slightly earlier than Maura's. So despite
her arrival he was still in command of this front. It
hadn't always been so.

He'd been promoted to rear admiral shortly after
the Sol system had been secured year before last, and
given command of a task force that included the
Deathstriders. Nobody used the term "Permanent Task
Group for Special Operations" anymore except in
official dispatches. And Roderick had supported him
when he'd bidden tradition be damned and put Garth
formally in command of the outfit. Corin would have
liked to have stayed under Roderick's personal command. But his task force had been assigned to Admiral
Otto Huang—not getting any younger, but a trusted
friend of the Emperor—who was to consolidate the
Serpens/Bootes region. At the same time, Roderick
had gone back to his familiar grounds in Aquila and
Capricorn—the "old rebel sectors" as people still

called them, as though there'd never been a rebellion anywhere else—to organize an offensive against Toshiro Parnell-Cutlass, who had declared himself Emperor in the Mu Arae Sector and its environs.

Huang had advanced methodically through the swirling chaos that Liang's collapse had left behind, assuring himself of each system before pushing on to the next. His caution hadn't saved him personally— a fanatic of some stripe or other had blasted his command aircar out of the skies of Lambda Serpenti III with a shoulder-launched missile—but it had left a solid foundation of pacified systems on which further advances could be built. And Corin, who'd fumed and fretted about the slowness of the old man's approach, had emulated it after succeeding him in command. Frustrating as it was, it was really the only way. This wasn't a war against a large multi-systemic state, a body with a vulnerable head that might be lopped by a lightning stroke at its capital system. It was more like draining a swamp.

But now, at last, they'd bumped up against something solid.

Corin's eyes strayed to the strategic holo display. The irregular spheroid of the Empire glowed with the bronze-gold of the Brady-Schiavona restoration throughout four-fifths of its volume. To the upper left, as he was viewing it, a three-dimensional cross-hatching of red marked the Ursa Major region's unextinguished resistance. At the back of the lower half, barely visible to Corin through the intervening bronze-gold translucency, was the arrogantly jarring purple of Parnell-Cutlass' gimcrack "Empire." At least it shouldn't be there long. Maura had brought word that Roderick's carefully planned offensive was rolling irresistibly toward Mu Arae. But Corin focused on the lower left, his own current location, where the far reaches of the Serpens/Bootes region bulged the spheroid outward. There, clinging like some parasitic organism to the skin of the now serenely bronze-gold region, was the green blotch of Alvina Coelho's rebel regime.

Coelho, like various other adventurers, had carved out a fiefdom on the fringes of Liang's domain. But she'd gone further than most, out here among systems inhabited largely by imperfectly assimilated ex-Beyonders. And Intelligence had learned that she was negotiating with actual Beyonders, offering them a foothold in Imperial space in exchange for aid. So extinguishing her was an urgent matter . . . but not an easy one. Out here on this windy limb of the Empire, where Beyonder raids had always been a threat, she'd fallen heir to more than her share of Fleet units. At the same time, most of Corin's forces had by now been detached for garrison duties throughout the large volume of space he'd reconquered. Quite simply, he was overextended.

In response to his urgent request, the Emperor had sent reinforcements under the command of Roderick's younger sister, whose three sunbursts were still shiny with newness. And Corin, who'd been bumped to vice admiral just after Huang's death—a necessary precondition to putting him in the old man's billet—could now savor the unaccustomed sensation of being senior to a Brady-Schiavona.

She followed his eyes, and misinterpreted his thoughts as paralleling her own. "Yes, it *is* unsettling to have Ursa Major still in revolt, isn't it? Especially considering—" She stopped herself with awkward abruptness. Corin might have saved Roderick's life, but she didn't really know him.

But he knew what it was she couldn't say. Another news item she'd brought had been her brother Teodor's acquisition of his own third sunburst and appointment to command the forces attempting—so far with incomplete success—to suppress the Ursa Major insurgency. Many had thought it a blunder . . . but only to themselves, for lately Ivar had been less and less inclined to tolerate criticism of his firstborn. Maura's own feelings couldn't have been much clearer; she reminded Corin of Janille in her inability or disinclination to use her face as a mask.

"I believe," he prompted, "you mentioned some disturbing rumors that have been coming out of Ursa Major recently." That *recently* was as close as he could come to *since your brother assumed command there.*

"Yes," she admitted, in a tone that did not invite further exploration of the subject. "But as I was saying, Admiral Marshak, you seem remarkably confident—one might almost say unjustifiably so—regarding our tactical situation."

She gestured at the tactical holo tank, currently set for a more than system-wide display. At the center floated a star-dot surrounded by a series of concentric rings—the HC -4 9701 system, where Coelho was headquartered. On the outskirts, their fleet—reduced to a single green icon at this scale—proceeded cautiously inward. Coelho wasn't rising to the bait; she was staying insystem, making them seek her out within the supporting envelopes of planetary and orbital-station weaponry. In those circumstances, even Maura's reinforcement gave them little if any edge—certainly nothing like the three-to-one superiority that military theory had from time immemorial held to be necessary to guarantee an attack's success.

"I know my people's capabilities," Corin explained with the same air of sublime unconcern. "And everything I've seen of your command inspires confidence. Why should I be worried?"

Maura still looked dubious. But, she reflected, this man's record at least raised a rebuttable presumption that he knew what he was doing. "Well, Admiral, I suppose I should be getting back to my flagship. I'll see you after we've occupied this system . . . of course."

"Of course," Corin agreed.

❖   ❖   ❖

The fleets of red and green icons had slid together in the holo tank, the battleships exchanging the missile salvos the lesser ships had to mutely endure until they drew into beam-weapons range. Then they had commenced the unique warfare waged by ships under drive, pouring out inconceivable energies amplified to even more inconceivable levels by time acceleration, all in an eerie, bloodless silence.

Actually, it wasn't silent at all to the occupants of a ship which one of those gigawatt lasers speared, rending metal with the violence of energy exchange. And no one who had seen a human body that had been on the outskirts of such a spearing would ever again call it bloodless.

Maura braced herself in her command chair as her flagship *Redoubtable* shuddered slightly from a glancing hit which would have vaporized any wet-navy battleship that had ever sailed the seas of pre-spaceflight Earth. So far, so good. Coelho had offered battle in the outer system and Corin had accepted, despite the rebels' obvious intent to draw him into close range of the armed moons of the sixth planet. They were giving better than they were getting. Corin was justified in his confidence in his forces, veterans of the last two years' hard campaigning. And, Maura saw with satisfaction, her own people were holding up their end. But before much longer they'd enter Planet VI's Chen Limit—extensive like those of all gas giants—and have to disengage their drives. At that point, she expected to be swarmed by fighters, and the equation would abruptly alter.

She wondered if she should raise Corin. . . . But no, she didn't have a legitimate reason to joggle his elbow. He'd given his instructions, and matters were proceeding as per those instructions. *And,* she reminded herself, *I have no more right to second-guess him in mid-battle than any other subordinate. God help me if Father ever catches me thinking I do!*

There were those who thought it dynastic lunacy for Ivar to risk all three of his children—none of whom had yet produced offspring of their own—in combat commands. But his instinct had been correct when he'd committed his blood to the drive for reunification. It was the ultimate affirmation that he had assumed the Dragon Throne out of a sense of duty, not a lust for power, and that the Imperium as he was restoring it carried responsibility, not privilege. The younger Brady-Schiavonas must not only serve in the Restoration War, as people were starting to call it, but do so without any special privileges beyond those appropriate to their ranks.

Even Ted seems to grasp that, she thought. *Not that he's seen much combat so far. And the issue doesn't arise for Rod, who's in overall command. But as for me, I'm about to go into that planet's Chen Limit pursuant to a plan I don't agree with, on the orders of a man whose background isn't exactly above question. . . .*

Her thoughts trailed off, forgotten, as she watched the red icons in the tank veering raggedly off, their formation dissolving as they backed out of range.

Before she could question the evidence of her eyes, the comm officer spoke excitedly. "Admiral, it's the flagship. Admiral Marshak has received a surrender signal. He's ordered a general cease-fire."

"Transmit that to all ships. And . . ." *To hell with it!* "And get me Admiral Marshak."

It took only an instant before Corin's face appeared on the comm screen. Maura didn't waste time with preliminaries. "Sir, what's happening? Why did they—?"

"Have you looked at your strategic display lately, Admiral?" Maura hadn't. "Our computer here should have finished downloading the update to yours by now."

Maura turned to the hologram of the Empire. Even as she watched, the purple zone around Mu Arae faded and then vanished, as though it had dissipated tracelessly into the bronze-gold. As understanding dawned, she swung back to the tactical display and ordered it to go to system scale. The green icons of newly arrived friendlies were popping into existence at the outer perimeter. She had a pretty good idea where they'd come from.

Corin cleared his throat. "I suppose I owe you an explanation, Admiral."

"You might say that, sir," she agreed, with as much frostiness as a subordinate could permit herself.

"At our last mail drop before arriving at this system, I communicated with your brother and learned that Parnell-Cutlass had just surrendered. There was still some scattered resistance to overcome in the Mu Arae sector, but he was confident that he'd soon be able to lead his main force here. We arranged our timing so that he would arrive when my attack had Coelho pinned down. As soon as Coelho—no fanatic, just a pragmatic brigand—detected the new arrivals and understood the hopelessness of her situation, she instantly surrendered."

"You might have told me . . . sir."

"I thought the news might lead to overconfidence if it became general knowledge. Coelho is no fool; if we'd gone into battle acting as though we knew the outcome was foreordained, she might have smelled something and refused battle. And the plan depended on our being engaged with her at the right time. So I kept it to myself. My reticence reflected no distrust of you—but I apologize nevertheless."

Maura's annoyance began to ebb a little. "Still, you took an awful chance. What if he hadn't been able to keep to his schedule?" The hazardousness of battle plans requiring precise coordination of widely separated elements had been a military truism even on pre-spaceflight Earth, before anyone could have imagined a separation *this* wide.

"Not really. Our plan provided for emergency

disengagement and withdrawal." This, Maura knew, was true. "And besides . . ." Corin's sudden awkwardness puzzled her. It was as though he was unsure of the boundaries of the appropriate. "Besides, it was Rod's . . . your brother's word I was relying on. So I *knew* he'd be here when he said he would."

Maura felt the last of her irritation seep out. "I'd gathered before coming here that you've developed a special relationship with Rod. That much was clear from the messages I'd gotten from him since you saved his life at Sol. But now I know just how special it is, Admiral."

"Please call me 'Corin.'" Briskly: "And now, I need to get into a virtual hookup with you and the other flag officers, including Brigadier General Krona, and initiate our plan for occupation of this system. And, of course, I'll see you in person when we land."

"Of course . . . Corin. Signing off."

As she was donning her VR connections, Maura glanced again at the strategic display. The news of Coelho's surrender must have just percolated down the cybernetic grapevine, for the green at the bottom left was fading out. Except for the irritating red rash in the Ursa Major region, the entire holographic spheroid glowed a uniform bronze-gold.

Dear God, she thought with a reverence foreign to her. (Like all her family, she was a nominal Reformed Orthodox Cosmotheist.) *It's nearly over!*

Corin knew something was wrong the moment he saw Garth's face.

Selangore, the system's third planet, had been Coelho's capital. The Deathstriders had gone in first, taking possession of the planet and its orbital facilities—including and especially the tachyon beam array. Now all was secured, and the VIPs could start transposing down. Corin appeared on the vast expanse of a spacefield whose distant perimeter was lined with lush tropical vegetation. The heat enveloped Corin in an oppressive embrace even though his dress uniform's memory fabric had adjusted its weave pattern for warm weather. It added an extra dimension to the inevitable disorientation. He came out of it with practiced ease, and saw Garth and Janille standing in front of the ranked Marines.

"Come on," he said to Maura, who'd appeared on the tarmac just after him. "I want you to meet someone." He led her over to the honor guard, where he began a greeting . . . and stopped.

"Garth, what's the matter?"

The big ex-mercenary shook his head. "It'll have to wait until Rod arrives." His reticence was as uncharacteristic as his closed face. That face was shiny with sweat which, Corin couldn't help thinking, wasn't entirely due to the saunalike climate. "What's this about him not transposing down?"

"Why . . . that's right," Corin affirmed, willing to go along with Garth's change of subject. "He's decided to take a shuttle down instead. By the way, this is his sister, Vice Admiral Maura Brady-Schiavona."

"Admiral," Garth greeted with a salute. Even though Maura had three sunbursts to his one, the formality wasn't like him. "And now, if you'll excuse me, I need to see to the honor guard." And he was gone.

"I can't get anything out of him either," muttered Janille, who had already met Maura. "He's been like this ever since he came back from the tachyon beam array—he took personal charge of securing it, while I was down here. But beyond that, I haven't a clue."

"Well," said Maura, "we shouldn't have to wait much longer to find out. Rod is due down any time—"

"Now," Corin finished for her, pointing up into the nearly cloudless sky, where a descending shuttle caught the light of HC -4 9701.

He thought he knew why Roderick had chosen this way of landing on Selangore. The young admiral knew, as all of them knew, that this was a historic moment. And he wanted a more traditional and impressive sort of arrival than the transposer afforded. It was typical of him—the sure and certain sense of rightness. Corin was thinking about it as the shuttle settled down on its landing jacks with a moan of impellers. And when its hatch opened, he saw the man who emerged as though for the first time.

Roderick Brady-Schiavona was now thirty-seven standard years old—only a few years past the age when anagathics could have started to make a difference. His medium-tall body was still well knit, his movements were still springy, and his hair was still thick and chestnut—although if you looked closely you could see a few gray threads at the temples. And the wrinkles that his frequent grins sent radiating from the outer corners of his blue-gray eyes were deeper, and didn't smooth themselves out quite so readily afterwards as they once had. Corin, now forty-five, had first gotten access to anagathics with his initial attainment of flag rank seven years before. Afterwards, the provisional government at Epsilon Eridani had budgeted the treatments for key people. Now he was physiologically only two or three years older than Roderick, and the two of them looked roughly the same age. A time would come when he would be able to pass as Roderick's nephew. Not for the first time, he wondered how Roderick could endure the shadow that hung over him—the knowledge of what must come.

There was no shadow in evidence as Roderick stepped from the shuttle into the dazzling sun. Commands rang out, and the honor guard came to attention with a crispness that not even Selangore's tropics could wilt. Aline Tatsumo followed him down the ramp. Corin advanced to meet them, with Maura, Garth and Janille behind him. The two groups met and halted. Corin saluted gravely and spoke the sentence he'd waited so long to deliver.

"Sir, I have the honor to report the Serpens/Bootes region pacified."

Roderick returned his salute with equal gravity. "Thank you, Admiral Marshak. I will so inform His Imperial Majesty." The formality lasted all of two seconds more. Then Roderick's face formed the grin that seemed to outshine suns, and he stepped forward and grasped the hand of the man he hadn't seen in over a year. Then he embraced Maura tightly, and they were all talking at once in a knot of handshaking, backslapping wonder, still coming to terms with the completion of the great task their lives had been built around for so long.

Only Garth held aloof.

Roderick noticed it almost at once. "What is it, Garth?"

"Sir," the Marine said stiffly, "I need to report to you in private."

"Well, let's all get in the command aircar. That'll be private enough. And we're not in such a hurry that we need to transpose to the city."

The aircar's cabin was somewhat cramped for the six of them, but at least it was blessedly air-conditioned. As the spacefield and the surrounding bright-green landscape fell away beneath them, Roderick sank back in his seat with a sigh of relief. "All right, Garth, out with it."

Garth's eyes flickered over the others' faces, resting longest on Maura's. "Sir, I feel . . . constrained by the presence of others. Especially that of Vice Admiral Brady-Schiavona."

"Nonsense! There's nothing you can say to me that can't be said in the presence of everyone here— including my sister!" The snap of command left Roderick's voice and he grinned again. "Besides, Garth, this day can't be spoiled. Do you—*all* of you— realize what's happened? We've practically finished the reunification of the Empire. Except for what's left of the resistance movement in the Ursa Major region—"

"That's what I'm trying to tell you, sir," Garth broke in. "That resistance is over. The message arrived while I was in the process of securing this system's tachyon beam array."

In the echoing silence, Roderick's voice seemed unnaturally loud. "But . . . but that means the reunification is *complete*! Why did you think you needed to be worried about telling me this?" The young admiral seemed to gather himself in, and he gazed narrowly at the big Marine, who still hadn't relaxed in the slightest. "But you *did* think so. And you evidently clamped a lid on the news. Why?"

Garth wore the look of a man advancing into a minefield. "Sir, the message makes it apparent that your . . . that Vice Admiral Teodor Brady-Schiavona ordered the destruction of the planet Rhea, one of the major holdout worlds. It was completely disrupted by antimatter warheads. It's uninhabited now—uninhabitable, in fact. He promised the same treatment for any other world that continued to resist. When the rest of the rebels heard, they surrendered."

Corin wondered if his own face wore the same expression as everyone else's, as they all looked at Roderick, waiting patiently for him to say something.

When he spoke, his voice was very, very controlled. "Thank you, General. You acted correctly in suppressing this news. And now, I need to consider the official position I'll take when it's made public."

He spent the rest of the flight sitting silently and expressionlessly in an invisible shell which not even Maura felt inclined to break.

The endless round of receptions for the local dignitaries in the old Imperial sector governor's residence in the capital city of Muramar finally began to wear on Corin.

"Have you seen him lately?" Janille asked him just before he stepped outside.

"No." There was no need to ask whom she meant. Roderick had performed with his usual charm, but it had been just that: a performance.

He stepped out onto a wide-curving balcony and stood breathing in the fresh—though still not cool—air, and considered the view.

These far reaches of the Serpens/Bootes region were old Beyonder territory, never fully assimilated. Many of Selangore's people still showed the distinctive ethnic type—stocky, brown-skinned, high-cheekboned, but with prominent curved noses jutting disharmonically out of flat faces—that adaption to local conditions by a blend of Old Earth elements had produced before the conquerors in the dragon-emblazoned ships had arrived. The cosmopolitan Imperial population had increased over the centuries, though, and by now it predominated in the major cities like Muramar. But even those cities still showed the influence of architectural precepts not readily appreciated or even grasped by those from the Empire's distant heart. The nighttime cityscape, even more than the unfamiliar star-patterns, reminded Corin that he stood at the very end of the Imperial reach. As he looked out over the exotic skyline toward the ocean, where the light of one small moon—another was behind clouds—flickered on the dark waters, he'd seldom felt so alone.

Then the second, larger moon appeared, and he saw he wasn't alone after all.

He started to go quietly back inside without disturbing the figure leaning on the railing a few yards away. But he also stood revealed in the flood of moonlight, and the figure stood up. A distinctive grin flashed in the shadowy face, but only momentarily.

"I see you needed to get away too," Roderick remarked.

"Uh, yes, sir," Corin said, inarticulate with the

unique mix of emotions he always felt around this man, to whom he bore a relationship that was just as unique.

"To hell with that 'sir.' Call me Rod. As far as I'm concerned, you're practically part of the family."

Corin didn't trust himself to respond. He sought refuge in small talk. "It was getting awfully stuffy in there."

"True. But I imagine that wasn't your real reason for needing to come out here, any more than it was mine."

"Sir—uh, Rod, I don't know what you mean."

"Oh, yes you do." Roderick stared fixedly out toward the distant moonlit ocean, and talked as though through physical pain. "We'd thought planetary genocide was something tucked safely away in history books about the Unification Wars. Oh, sure, aliens like the Zyungen, and Beyonder barbarians—but not us! Atlas was the last time we'd done it . . . and you had to make allowances for the rebels who'd endured the Draconis Empire. And afterwards they established the Solarian Empire to assure that it would never happen again. That's why the Empire, under one name or other, has always been restored in the end. It's why *we've* been restoring it."

"Rod," Corin spoke in a pleading tone, "you know I can't—"

"Can't what? Speak freely? Why not? Because we're talking about my brother?" Roderick gave a horrid parody of a laugh. "Believe me, you can't say anything about him I haven't thought. In fact, you can't say a fraction of what I could, because I know him and you don't. For one thing, I happen to know he's a coward. We've both seen enough of war to know how vicious a coward can be, given the upper hand."

Corin didn't want to be hearing this, but he sensed Roderick's need for a receptacle into which to pour it. So he kept silent while the other man resumed, in a tone that shaded over into puzzlement. "Yes, I've always known he was capable of petty viciousness. But it *was* petty! This is . . . grandiose. I have no illusions about him, but I still have trouble believing this."

"Rod," Corin said softly into the silence, "I'm just guessing. But . . . remember when your father pardoned Chewning and Liang?"

"Yes. What about it?" It had been a kind of acid test for Ivar's policy of sparing surrendered enemies and giving them posts. Liang had been an even harder case than Chewning.

"I've heard that it was largely on Teodor's urging that he agreed to include Liang. The story goes that your brother offered to be responsible for him. And that subsequently they were both assigned to positions directly under him. I don't know for certain that they went with him to Ursa Major. But if they did . . ."

Both moons went behind the clouds, and Roderick's expression was unreadable. "You think he may have come under their influence?"

"I don't know. But you yourself say that what he's done seems out of character. And Chewning, in particular, is nothing if not a master manipulator."

Roderick turned and leaned on the railing again, and stared out into the night. He spoke in a monotone. "We never expected enthusiastic support from the populations of the Ursa Major frontier. We knew we'd inherit some of the disaffection Oleg left behind. But now it's going to go beyond mere surliness. Our dynasty is going to face outright, irreconcilable hostility there—a poisonous hatred that will be like an ulcer in the body of the Empire." He fell silent, leaving Corin feeling inadequate. Then he sighed deeply and straightened up. "All right. It's too late to do anything about that. But we can't allow anything like it to happen again. It has to be prevented— whatever the cost."

"What do you mean?" Corin asked. He was fairly

sure he knew the answer, at least in general terms. He just wasn't sure he wanted to know.

"We'll all be returning to Sigma Draconis before long," Roderick answered obliquely. "We need to be prepared to act as the situation there warrants. By 'we' I'm including Maura. Also Garth and Janille. And Aline Tatsumo. I think that's as far as we'd better let it go, for now." All at once he was his usual brisk self. "Let's go back inside and wrap this reception up as quickly as possible. Then the six of us need to meet. Have some coffee sent for. Lots of it."

He turned on his heel and walked back inside. Only it wasn't really so much a walk as a march, Corin realized. As though he was striding unflinchingly across a line only he could see.

CHAPTER FOURTEEN
Prometheus (Sigma Draconis II), 4334 C.E.

It was like Roderick's arrival on Selangore, but on a scale larger by orders of magnitude.

As Corin emerged from the shuttle behind Roderick and stood blinking in the cloudless noon light of Sigma Draconis, the vista of the private Imperial spacefield stretched away into infinity—an infinity of crowds held back by motionless lines of Imperial Guards. Those parallel ranks, topped with gleaming dress helmets and edged with bayoneted gauss rifles, defined the avenue they would follow to the Emperor's reviewing stand. Beyond that, the towers of Dracopolis could be glimpsed in the distance, with the Imperial palace hanging motionless above them in the sky. From this perspective, the palace was like a supernatural silver crown suspended over the head of the man at the summit of the reviewing stand. Corin suspected the layout had been planned with that effect in mind.

He pulled himself together and followed Roderick down the ramp. Maura Brady-Schiavona was beside him, and lesser flag officers followed. They marched toward the reviewing stand to the *Imperial Anthem*, advancing through a storm of sound—the cheering of the crowds, the music whose sonic focusing gave this outdoor expanse the acoustics of a concert hall. As they neared the stand, two formations of Imperial Guards massed before it came to attention with a collective crash. They proceeded between those formations and up the stairs to the uppermost level where the Emperor waited to receive the conquerors of Sol and Mu Arae and Lambda Serpenti and so much else. The others halted a few steps short of the top and let Roderick cover those last few steps alone. He halted before his father and saluted. Ivar returned the salute with equal gravity.

Corin, from a few steps below, gazed curiously at the Emperor he'd never met in person. It was an older face than he'd visualized, but its granite immobility matched all the stories he'd heard. And yet he thought he detected a smile trembling within that stone, struggling to get out.

"Welcome back, Rod." The deep voice was heavy with suppressed emotion. "You may present your officers."

Roderick did so, in order of rank, so that Corin was called forward first. Ivar's formal words of praise contained no suggestion that he recalled the former mercenary and technical deserter. Corin mumbled something in response—he could never recall precisely what, afterwards—then stood aside as Maura came forward. This time an inarguable smile trembled to life on the Imperial face. The introductions continued, and at their conclusion Ivar stepped forward and looked out over the throng. When he spoke, sound-gathering technology sent his voice winging to every corner of the spacefield, just as the tachyon network would carry it to every world of the Empire.

"More than eight standard centuries ago, the human race declared with one voice that there could be but one sovereignty among the stars." Ivar didn't include Beyonders in his definition of the human race. But then, no one ever did. "Now, we have reaffirmed that truth and reclaimed that heritage. The Restoration Wars are over!"

A wave of cheering washed over them. As Ivar paused, Corin found himself glancing around at the dignitaries with whom they shared the reviewing stand. Off to the side, he saw Jason Aerenthal in his usual elegantly somber attire. And then he turned to the other direction . . . and Teodor Brady-Schiavona's golden head stood out among an array of uniformed figures.

All at once, the summer light of Sigma Draconis was less warm.

Corin grew aware that Ivar was cataloging the reconquests. "—and the immemorial home of us all, the cradle of our species, Old Earth itself, brought back into its rightful position as revered mother of the Imperial family of worlds by our son, Admiral Roderick Brady-Schiavona."

The cheering resumed, not as a single surge this time but as a steady tide against which Ivar could not resume. Instead, he motioned Roderick forward to stand beside him, in full view. The tide grew to a tsunami, crashing over them with a force that visibly took both father and son aback. Then Roderick grinned and gave a wave which brought the cheering to new levels of volume.

Ivar's expression was not easy to read. And, Corin told himself, surely what he thought he'd seen a flash of was really nothing. And yet . . . from long ago came recollections of stories he'd once heard. *Saul has slain his thousands, and David his ten thousands. . . .*

But that was silly. David hadn't been Saul's son. So there could be no comparison. Could there?

"Well, I think we could all use a drink," Ivar declared as he led the way into the lounge adjacent to his working office, and proceeded to the bar. To all three of his children, it seemed he was as animated as he ever got. By his standards, he was positively giddy. "Yes," he continued as they applied themselves to pouring, "all four of us are together, for the first time in far too long. And it's finally over! All that's left to deal with now are scattered instances of civil disobedience and terrorism."

"Yes," Roderick said with a long cool look at Teodor. "In the Ursa major frontier . . . where they're only too understandable."

Teodor froze with his glass half-raised. Then he seemed to inflate. "Is that an implied criticism of my—?"

Ivar spoke quickly. "Rod, you weren't there in Ursa Major. You can't know the details of what was at best a difficult situation . . . unlike Ted, who was on the scene."

"But I do know what's going on there now. We've had to impose direct military rule, as though it was a conquered province of Beyonders. Our usual practice of ruling through the locals won't work, because almost nobody there will participate in any government structure we set up. Those who do are the scum of their societies. The bulk of the people won't have anything to do with them—except to murder them from time to time." The look he was giving Teodor hardened into a glare. "And we can't very well disrupt a planet in response to the occasional homicide."

The flush that came so easily to Teodor's complexion made him look as though he was about to explode. "You have no right to—"

"Maybe not," Roderick overrode him. "But there's something I'd like to know. Are Damiano Chewning and Vladimir Liang on your staff?"

Ivar cut in before Teodor could answer. "As you know, Rod, it is our policy to give surrendered enemies pardon—and positions in our service so they can have the opportunity to prove themselves trustworthy."

"Even one who murdered an Emperor? And one who tried to usurp the throne?"

Ivar didn't meet Roderick's eyes. "As it transpired, there was sufficient uncertainty concerning Liang's actual role in Oleg's death that . . . Well, I decided to overcome my initial inclinations and give him the benefit of the doubt. And Chewning has recanted his assumption of the Imperial title. He was really quite eloquent about it." What he saw in Roderick's face brought an uncharacteristic defensiveness to his voice. "All right, neither of them is exactly my cup of tea. But a policy of reconciliation means nothing if we only apply it to people we admire!" He took a deep breath and reasserted his habitual self-control. "At any rate, as you know we've always given such persons employment in areas far from their own original stamping grounds—minimizing temptation, as it were. So it made sense to send Chewning and Liang to Ursa Major."

"On Teodor's advice," Maura stated rather than asked.

"Well, yes." Their father sounded ill at ease again.

Teodor spoke in tones of self-conscious reasonableness. "You see, I'd gotten to know them on the voyage here from Sol. I became convinced that they'd merely been making unavoidable adjustments to the unsettled conditions in their parts of the Empire— conditions not of their making and beyond their control."

Maura ignored him totally and stared at their father. "I can't believe I'm hearing this! These scum have influenced us into committing a disastrous blunder. And you're willing to leave the Empire tied to that blunder because repudiating it would mean repudiating *him*!" She didn't even look at Teodor, any more than she'd acknowledged his presence by naming him. "Excuse me, Father." She set her glass down with an emphatic *click* and was gone.

"Please speak to her, Rod," Ivar rumbled wearily. "She's always listened to you."

"I'd like to help, Father. But I can't . . . because I happen to think she's right." Without asking leave, Roderick marched stiffly from the lounge.

Ivar slumped over the bar, the day's joy seeping almost visibly out of him. Teodor broke the silence with whiny eagerness. "You see, Father, you see? They haven't the proper respect for you, as *I* have. In fact—" He stopped dead at the Imperial shushing gesture.

"No, Ted," Ivar murmured, "it's understandable that Rod and Maura should be upset. After all, it *was* a pretty extreme measure. And, unlike me, they haven't heard your explanation of why it was unavoidable." The craggy face took a worried look, not quite rising to the threshold of suspicion. "You really *didn't* do it on the advice of Chewning and Liang, did you?"

"Oh *no*, Father! As I've repeatedly explained to you—"

"Of course, Ted, of course." Ivar looked into the eyes that were those of his late wife, the only woman he'd ever loved, and all his doubts sank tracelessly in those azure depths.

Teodor resumed, emboldened. "But you can see what I'm up against, what with their attitude toward me. The whole situation could be clarified so easily. All you have to do is make the announcement I've repeatedly suggested."

"I don't really think it's necessary at this time, Ted. As my eldest child you're the heir apparent anyway."

Teodor's tightly controlled impatience would have been obvious to most people. "But, Father, that's not legally conclusive, and never has been. A formal designation of me as your heir would—"

"No, no, I believe that would be premature at this time." Ivar smiled fondly. "I'm not planning on dying anytime soon, you know!"

"Of course not, Father. But . . ." Teodor seemed to gather himself. "My loyalty to you compels me to speak bluntly. You saw what happened out at the spacefield today."

"Eh? What do you mean?"

"You saw how popular he's become . . . how they were cheering him. His exploits have become something of a legend, I gather. It would be only human of him to let it go to his head."

Ivar's pause before shaking his head vigorously was almost imperceptible. "Nonsense. I can't believe that he—"

"Oh, I don't doubt for a moment that he's completely loyal to you in his own mind. But factions with their own agendas may seek to cultivate him, to take advantage of his status as a popular hero, as long as the possibility exists that he could be your successor."

This time there was no hesitation in the Emperor's headshake. "No. He'd never let himself be used that way. And now, I really must get to work."

Before his departure for Ursa Major, Teodor had established himself in one of the massive yet soaring towers that made up the palace's superstructure. Since his return, he'd used his inexplicably augmented personal fortune to furnish it with a new opulence. So he had a particularly splendid setting in which to pace, muttering into his brandy snifter.

Damiano Chewning eyed him from the sofa on which he was seated. There had been a time when he wouldn't have thought of sitting in the presence of his nominal master. Vladimir Liang stayed hovering in the background; he'd learned that Chewning was by far his superior at manipulating Teodor, and was more than willing to defer to consummate artistry.

"So," Chewning murmured, keeping his face fixed

in its rabbitlike mask of manifest harmlessness, "he wouldn't agree to make the announcement?"

"No, even though I used all the arguments you suggested, including the one about my brother's growing popularity with the mob."

And doubtless botched it, Chewning sighed inwardly. Still, Teodor had planted a seed that might eventually take root in Ivar's mind. It was as frustrating to have to act through this self-obsessed simpleton as it was degrading to be dependent on him for protection. But there was no help for it. *And I have no right to complain*, he reminded himself. *It was incredible good fortune to get access to him—so highly placed, and so controllable. And the opportunity to silence Romaine permanently was an added bonus.*

He decided it was time for Teodor's periodic dose of flattery. "Surely, sir, he'll come to realize that it is the correct course of action. Clearly, you are the only possible choice as his successor. Unlike some, whose inner qualities do not immediately meet the eye, yours are reflected so accurately by your outward semblance as to be obvious to anyone!"

"Well, of course." Teodor unconsciously struck a profile-displaying pose. Chewning gave another silent sigh. Flattering Teodor bored him; it lacked the challenge of flattering an intelligent person. But then the pout of half-drunken petulance was back. "Anyone, that is, but my self-righteous prig of a brother and my virago of a sister! They've never appreciated me."

"Well, after all, sir," Chewning simpered, "jealousy is understandable, where *you* are concerned." With Teodor visibly mollified, he turned businesslike. "It is my assessment that your sister's attitude toward you is largely a reflection of your brother's. *His* influence on your father is the real danger." This, he reflected, was true. However much love and pride Ivar might lavish on his daughter, his background rendered him incapable of giving a woman's opinion full weight, even when he consciously thought he was doing so. "So *Roderick* is the problem that must be dealt with."

Teodor had been nodding and making affirmative-sounding grunting noises. He continued doing so for a second or two before his somewhat befuddled realization of what Chewning was saying caught up with him. "Uh . . . 'dealt with'?"

"Consider, sir. In addition to its *obvious* grounds, his jealousy of you has an added, poisonous dimension: his knowledge that you can expect to greatly outlive him. He'll always hate you for that, not just out of ordinary envy but also because it reinforces your status as the logical choice to succeed your father. He knows he can never *legitimately* ascend the throne . . . as long as you are alive."

Teodor, who had resumed his nodding, suddenly looked alarmed. "What? Do you really think he'd—?"

"With you dead, your father would be under tremendous pressure to declare him the heir. Remember, exaggerated accounts of his exploits have made him a hero to the masses, who are incapable of appreciating the *difficulty* of the decision you reached at Rhea, where you set aside your personal feelings and took the distasteful action necessary to suppress the insurgency." *The odd thing*, Chewning thought, *is that he really* does *remember it that way.* The self-justifying version of reality Teodor had manufactured was, by now, the only reality that existed in his mind.

"Few other men could have done it," Liang put in earnestly.

"True," Teodor allowed. He took a fortifying gulp of brandy. "But the point is . . . you think he'd use his popular status to try and seize the throne?" He had no trouble believing the scenario, for he knew it was exactly how *he* would have used such a status, had he possessed it.

"I'm quite certain he *intends* to," Chewning said slowly. "But it can only work if you're out of the way."

"Which means," Liang continued the thought, "that it can't happen if *he's* put out of the way first."

Teodor's face wore the disoriented look of one sobering up with excessive rapidity. "But . . . but . . . but I don't really want to—"

"Of *course* not, sir," Chewning soothed. "The ideal solution would have been for His Imperial Majesty to heed your suggestion and disavow your brother. But since he is unwilling to do so, other means now become necessary."

"But . . . what will Father say?"

That's the rub, isn't it? Chewning smiled to himself as the real source of Teodor's jitters finally emerged. "His Imperial Majesty will, of course, be distraught at first. But on reflection he will understand that you were acting out of self-preservation, and also out of a higher loyalty to the Empire and himself, to assure the proper order of succession. Besides which—"

Besides which, he'll have no choice, Chewning thought as he went automatically on with the well-prepared presentation. With Roderick dead, Ivar would be stuck with Teodor as his successor. The need to secure a cloudless succession would compel him to do what he probably wanted to do anyway, given the large blind spot he'd always had in the shape of his firstborn son. How he rationalized it to himself was immaterial.

Chewning brought his mind back to the present, and the task of managing Teodor. It was never very difficult.

Their quarters were located high in a tower not far from the palace's northern perimeter. Corin, standing at a wide window, looked northward through the conceptually integrated architectural splendor of neighboring structures and glimpsed the ocean. Turning to his right, he could see the coastline curving away to vanish in the hazy distance to the east. An ovoid of darkness seemed to float on the ocean just off that coast: the late-afternoon shadow of the palace in which he stood. Armand Duschane's architects, not wishing to subject the city of Dracopolis to a daily solar eclipse, had positioned the sky-palace over the oceanfront. Here, in the planet's middle northern latitudes, this meant the shadow always fell on the rolling waters to the north as Sigma Draconis moved from east to west, even on a summer day like the one now drawing to a close.

He turned away from the spectacle with somewhat less difficulty than he'd previously experienced, for he'd had time to adjust to living in one of the man-made wonders of the galaxy. In the room behind, Roderick was adjusting his full-dress uniform and preparing to depart.

"Sure you don't need a drink?" Janille asked mischievously.

"Right," Garth rumbled. "I'd need a little bracing if I were you."

Roderick shook his head and took a last look in the mirror. "No. I think I'd better be sober for this. I'm still not sure what to make of it."

"None of us are," Corin agreed, joining the group. They were still puzzling over the invitation Roderick had received from Teodor.

"I still don't think you should go," Janille insisted.

"You may be right," Roderick conceded. "But if I didn't, I'd stay up nights wondering if I'd passed up an opportunity. It *might* be the olive branch it purports to be, you know."

Since their return to Prometheus, Corin had noticed this in Roderick: not so much a mellowing toward Teodor as a *desire* to mellow. Perhaps, with his brother a flesh-and-blood presence rather than a distant abstraction, he was finding it harder to think in terms of the contingencies they'd discussed under the strange constellations of Selangore. And he'd rejected as farfetched the notion that the banquet to which he'd been invited posed any actual danger to his person.

"Well," he said briskly, sending Corin's thoughts scattering, "it's just about the cocktail hour. I'd better head on down to the transposer stage." In theory, the palace's battery of transposers could have plucked him from this very room and deposited him in Teodor's three-quarter-mile-distant establishment, had he been wearing a link. In practice, for reasons of safe and orderly traffic control, they only flicked people to and from certain established stages. The nearest was in a plaza near the base of this tower, so Roderick didn't have far to go. With a final wave and a swirl of his dress cloak, he was out the door.

The three looked at each other. "He's weakening," Janille stated with pessimistic satisfaction.

"Maybe not," Garth demurred. "He just needs to know he's tried—met his brother more than halfway—before he can act wholeheartedly." Corin was about to speak up in agreement when the door chimed for admittance. Corin signaled it to open.

It was Jason Aerenthal.

"Good afternoon. I hope I'm not intruding, but I was looking for Roderick and understood he'd be here. Since I was in the area anyway, I thought I'd drop by."

"Actually, Inspector, you just missed him. He's on his way down to the transposer stage."

"Oh?" Aerenthal lifted an eloquent eyebrow. Roderick seldom used the palace transposers, preferring to burn off his excess energy by walking.

"He wanted to be sure to be on time," Corin explained.

"'On time'?"

"Oh, you didn't know? His brother invited him to a banquet. In fact, he's the guest of honor. Under the circumstances . . ." Corin voice died as he watched Aerenthal's face go pale and freeze into an indescribable expression he'd never seen on it. "Uh, Inspector, are you all right?"

Aerenthal blinked and seemed to snap back into the present. He drew a long, shuddering breath. When he spoke, there was something odd about his voice, something Corin couldn't quite put his finger on. "Admiral Marshak, all of you, listen carefully. We haven't a second to lose. He *cannot* be allowed to leave! There's no time to explain. We must stop him."

"But why . . . ?" Corin didn't complete the sentence, for he suddenly realized what had seemed strange in the agent's voice. It was an echoing quality . . . but not in the usual sense, for the words his ears heard were echoed inside his head, by a sense other than hearing.

He became aware of Janille's voice. "Corin, he's right. We've got to stop Rod before he transposes!"

Corin looked at her and Garth. Both faces wore the same expression of bewildered urgency. Then he turned back to Aerenthal. For a heartbeat, their eyes met.

All at once, he understood.

"All right," he said quietly, not releasing Aerenthal's eyes. "I agree. Garth, Janille, get down there as fast as you can and try to find him. I'll stay here and try to reach a comm station somewhere near the transposer stage."

"Right," Garth growled. "Come on, Janille." And they were gone.

Corin strode to the desk communicator and started to call up a directory. Then he stopped and smacked himself on the forehead. "I'm an idiot! Rod's got a basic wristcomp—it's part of the uniform." He spoke a code to the machine.

"Yes?" No image accompanied Roderick's voice, for the standard wristcomp included no such capability. It could, however, project a small holographic viewscreen of its own, and Roderick could see who had called. "Corin, what is it?"

"Rod, where are you?"

"Down here at the transposer stage, of course, still waiting. Lots of traffic today." He noticed Corin's expression, and his own voice changed tone. "Hold on a second. There's a public comm station just a few steps from here . . . all right, now." His face appeared on Corin's screen. Beyond could be seen a mall-like little plaza among the maze of structures that stretched away into the sun-drenched distance, soaring upward into an afternoon sky where aircars flitted about like midges among the towers. A few yards behind Roderick was the transposer stage. Another figure in full dress, bearing captain's insignia, waited beside it.

"Now, Corin, what's this all—?"

"Admiral," the captain called out. "We're next!"

Roderick shook his head and spoke over his shoulder. "Go on without me, Captain Delambre. I'll see you there." Delambre nodded and stepped onto the platform as Roderick addressed the pickup. "Now, Corin, what's so important that I had to miss transposing to hear it?"

Before Corin could reply, the warning light flashed on the transposer stage, and Captain Delambre was gone. . . .

And a cylinder of rock, three yards high and four yards thick, stood on the platform, which immediately collapsed with a crash under a weight it was not intended to bear.

Passersby started screaming.

"*What?*" Roderick whirled around and stared. Then he turned back to Corin with a look of incredulous horror. It was obvious what must have happened, but obviousness did not automatically carry acceptability—not when people stared in the face of an accident so rare that most of them had forgotten its very possibility.

The transposer induced the segment of reality

defined by its field of effect to change places with
another somewhere within its range. A volume of air
from Teodor's residence should have replaced the
space that had contained Captain Delambre. Instead,
the stage lay shattered under this multiton intruder
that could have come from only one place: far beneath
the surface of the planet, somewhere in Prometheus'
bedrock—where Captain Delambre was now trapped
in a small cylindrical chamber, whose air was rapidly
getting stuffy. . . .

"The focus was off . . . *way* off," Roderick said as
he emerged from shock. "How could they have gotten the far end of the transposition so wrong?" That
"they" triggered a realization which brought redoubled
horror. "Corin, the operators are down there!" The
transposer's control chamber was located unobtrusively
beneath the stage. Its occupants must have been
crushed beneath that titanic "plug" of stone. "We've
got to get to them, see if they're still alive! And try
to locate Delambre—"

"Yes, do what you can," Corin said. "And, Rod . . .
Garth and Janille are on their way. When they get
there, send them back up here, will you?"

"Why . . . certainly." Roderick still wasn't entirely
himself. He would have been more than human if he
had been, after what he'd just witnessed firsthand.
"Signing off."

After the screen blanked, there was perhaps a full
second of dead silence. Then, with absolutely no
warning, Corin spun out of his chair and flung himself against Aerenthal, slamming the older man against
a wall and holding him immobilized with a stiffened
forearm against his throat. The agent made a gagging
noise which sounded like a plea for release.

"I think not, at least not just yet," Corin said pleas-
antly. "A serious distraction—like choking—makes it
impossible to achieve the kind of concentration needed
for telepathy, doesn't it?"

Aerenthal stopped struggling and stared at him. Corin smiled, and eased the pressure a bit. "Not that you can control my mind anyway, as you found out when you were doing it to Garth and Janille. I have an innate resistance—I can be communicated with, as you were doing, but my will can't be overborne unless I'm asleep or hypnotized or something." He smiled again as Aerenthal's eyes widened. "Now, unpermitted telepathic contact is nothing more than a misdemeanor, and grounds for a civil action. But unpermitted telepathic *influence* is a felony."

"The Inspectorate," Aerenthal began in the firmest voice he could manage, "has—"

"Special immunity from such laws," Corin finished for him. "Yes, I know . . . but only when acting in the line of duty, against the Emperor's enemies. And besides, given the way most people feel about psi, I don't think legalistic arguments would count for much."

"This was an emergency," Aerenthal got out past the still-constricting arm. "A matter of life or death. *Roderick's* life or death."

"You're right about that," Corin acknowledged. "But the point is, you *knew* Roderick was in danger the instant I told you where he was going. How could you possibly have known that?"

"Well," Aerenthal began, with an approach to his old insouciance which wasn't really close but had to be accounted remarkable under the circumstances, "you know I'm a telepath. Have you considered that I might possess precognition as well?"

"No. If you had *that* ability, the history of the last few years would be very different. And besides . . . I saw the expression on your face when I told you about Rod's invitation from Teodor. It was a look of sudden realization that something long expected was about to happen. And it held another element: knowledge that you had to help that event along, and that your own role was also part of your foreknowledge."

"I can't imagine what you—*aarrrgh!*" Aerenthal's voice died in a gurgling choke, as Corin suddenly redoubled the pressure on his larynx—for the door had slid open, and Garth and Janille burst into the room.

"Corin," Janille began, "did you see what happened down there? Rod said—*Corin!*" The scene in the room, with Corin holding the elderly agent pinned to the wall, suddenly registered on her.

"Both of you, get mind-shields on," Corin snapped. "*Now!*"

"But, but—"

"*Do it!*"

"Come on, Janille," Garth rumbled, and took her arm. He led her into another room, leaving a tableau that held, with Corin and Aerenthal locked into motionlessness and the latter's face turning an interesting color.

Presently, the other two emerged. Janille was wearing an earring she hadn't worn before. Garth's mind-shield wasn't visible, but that meant nothing. The devices were as miniaturized as they were ubiquitous. Corin released Aerenthal, who fell forward onto his hands and knees, gasping and massaging his throat.

"Corin," Janille demanded, "will you please tell us just what is going on here?"

"Certainly. But I had to make sure you two were shielded first. I didn't want Inspector Aerenthal playing tricks with your minds, like he was doing earlier."

"Huh? What . . . that is . . . you mean . . . ?" Janille's eyes widened as she remembered the strange sense of urgency, the unquestioning acceptance of the agent's word. Then her face contorted, and she sprang forward with an inarticulate cry, her hands formed into claws reaching for Aerenthal's throat.

Garth grabbed her from behind and held her until her struggles had subsided, all the while giving

Aerenthal a look that was, in its own tightly controlled way, more frightening than Janille's ferocity. For a moment, Corin let the agent contemplate the reminder he'd gotten of that which two millennia of history had burned into the collective human soul concerning telepathic suppression of free will. Then he spoke conversationally, as though nothing had happened.

"Actually, you two arrived just in time. The Inspector and I were about to discuss . . . Omega Prime."

Time seemed suspended in a realm where there was neither motion nor sound.

At last, Aerenthal got slowly to his feet and regarded Corin levelly. "So you know," he stated.

"Yes. We've been there—just before we met you and Rod. And you've just displayed exactly the kind of limited foreknowledge that is Omega Prime's to dispense. So I want to know this: what is your connection with Omega Prime?"

Instead of answering, the agent asked, "Then you three are aware of your origin?"

Corin felt heat spreading over his ears. "Omega Prime told us, and showed us compelling evidence, of those from whom we were . . . were . . ." He swallowed and took a deep breath. "Cloned. It also gave us hints—maddeningly vague ones—"

"Typical," Aerenthal interjected, with returning playfulness.

"—of the role we're supposedly going to play in the restoration of the Empire by my . . . that is, by Basil Castellan's descendant Roderick Brady-Schiavona. Apparently, whoever it was who introduced us into human society is also going to be involved."

"Indeed," Aerenthal nodded. "That involvement has now commenced."

In the ensuing silence the agent sat down on a divan, from which he studied the three of them, one by one, watching as understanding dawned. They stared back, their voices immobilized by tangles of unfamiliar, conflicting emotions.

Janille finally spoke. "So it was you. But how——?"

"It was in 4288. I was in the Intelligence service of the Empire of Man. Armand Duschane had already become the power behind the throne he was to seize three years later, and I was taking pains to make myself useful to him. I'd been taking care of some highly unofficial business for him in the old rebel sectors. As I was returning to Sigma Draconis, alone in a small courier craft, an obviously advanced spacecraft intercepted me. It was, as it turned out, a proxy of Omega Prime, with the same artificial psionic powers. I initiated contact with it. My own telepathic talent, though by no means to be compared with its own, allowed it to communicate with me at a far greater distance than is possible with non-telepaths like yourselves. I followed it to Omega Prime's system, knowing as I did so that my will was not altogether my own. I learned everything you now know about Omega Prime: its origin, its capabilities, the role it has already played in human affairs. In addition, Omega Prime allowed me some fragmentary knowledge of the events to come, and of my own part in them."

"More than it's done for us," Janille grumbled.

"Finally," Aerenthal went on, "Omega Prime showed me three stasis chambers, holding three newborn human infants." He smiled as he observed their expressions. "They went with me, along with instructions on how to release the stasis field. On my return to Prometheus, certain contacts enabled me to arrange for the adoption of one of them. The same contacts put me in touch with those whose help I needed to do the same for the other two on different worlds."

"Why were you so willing to follow Omega Prime's instructions?" Corin asked curiously.

"Well, it wasn't really all that radical a departure for me—just another form of secret agentry. And while I had to keep it a secret from my official employers, at least I wasn't actually betraying them. Omega Prime's interests and those of the Empire dovetailed nicely."

"But how could you keep working for the Duschane dynasty, knowing the end it was going to come to?"

"I knew it was to give way to another dynasty, yes. That happens, you know. But Omega Prime had made me realize that, in the long historical perspective, Armand was really the founder of the New Empire that was to attain its zenith under the dynasty that would supplant his. He laid the groundwork, and Ivar has been sensible enough to avail himself of that foundation in erecting his governmental structure. And Oleg's creation of the transposer networks that bind each developed world into an economic infrastructure of unprecedented efficiency will, in the long run, enhance the new dynasty's luster."

"Seems unfair," Garth commented.

"Inevitable, though. The rabble think that on any given day the economy is the way it is because their ruler waved a magic wand that morning. The concept of 'lead time' is beyond their comprehension. So Oleg got the blame for the project's cost, while the Brady-Schiavonas will reap the credit for its benefits."

"Does cynical contempt for people go with your profession," Janille inquired, "or are you just a shit by nature?"

"You're entitled to your opinion of me. But I remind you that we're allies. Were it not for me, Roderick would now be suffocating somewhere beneath the surface of Prometheus."

"You . . . and Omega Prime," Corin corrected.

"Very astute. Yes, Omega Prime allowed me some knowledge of this attempt on Roderick's life. I knew the time had arrived as soon as you told me about the invitation from his brother."

"So you're saying this was an assassination attempt, not an accident?"

"Don't be absurd! Of course it wasn't an accident. How often does a transposer—*any* transposer, much less one of those here within the palace, locked into a fixed grid of destination points—go haywire and focus on a point nowhere near its intended terminus? Or experience a safety interlock failure?" All transposers incorporated a feature which prevented them from activating if focused on a location inside solid matter. "And as for the probability of both happening at the same time . . . ! No, this was the work of Teodor—or, to be precise, of Chewning and Liang acting through him."

"But," Garth protested, "how could they have done it? Here in the palace, where the Emperor's person is at stake, security can't be that lax!"

"Remember, they have Teodor's personal resources to work with, and the immunity from suspicion that goes with belonging to his personal staff. And quite some time passed between their arrival here and their departure for Ursa Major. They had the opportunity to look and listen, to establish connections. We're not likely to find out the details, for I suspect the crucial individual they corrupted is down there now, crushed under tons of stone below the transposer stage."

"But they failed," said Corin. "And even without Omega Prime, our own common sense tells us that they can't stop now. They'll have to try again."

"Precisely," Aerenthal affirmed. "And on two points, Omega Prime was very explicit. First, we're going to have to *let* them try. And second, Roderick may not know any of this."

"Anything about Omega Prime, you mean? And about my . . . relationship with him? Yes, we know."

"Then you realize we can't tell him how we know Teodor and his manipulators are seeking to kill him. Or why he must walk into their trap."

"They never found him," Roderick said dully, more to himself than to the others.

The effort to locate Delambre had been abandoned shortly after night had fallen. His uniform's standard communicator couldn't possibly have penetrated the gigatons of stone that were his airtight prison walls. And there'd been no reason for him to carry a link. Eventually, with luck, careful scanning of the vast volume encompassed by the transposer's range might detect a little cylindrical bubble in the bedrock, from which his remains could be flicked up and turned over to his widow and two children.

Now the seven of them—Maura and Aline Tatsumo had arrived a while before—sat around a table burdened with assorted potations, under an indirect lighting fixture that gave little more illumination than that which streamed through the window: the stars, the glowing palace towers, the bloodstained sickle of Atlas, and the fireflies of swarming aircars—more aircars than usual, for by Imperial decree the transposer system had been shut down pending a full investigation. In that dim light, Roderick's face wore an expression wrought by shock and alcohol.

"He was sentenced to death by suffocation." Roderick still spoke in the same leaden monotone, but Corin thought he detected something new in it. "His crime? Encountering me, and entering into a conversation as we waited to transpose to Ted's." Now there was no doubt as to the new element in his voice. It was rage. It had become unmistakable with that last word. He took another gulp of his drink, with as little visible effect as all he'd already taken on board.

Convincing him of the truth without invoking

Omega Prime had proven less difficult than they'd feared. His survivor's guilt wasn't impairing his intelligence. Then, afterwards, they'd sat in awkward silence and let him come to terms in his own way with the fact that his brother was trying to kill him. But now Aerenthal cleared his throat and spoke diffidently.

"We have no proof, of course. Only certainty—which we can't go to the Emperor with."

Roderick gave a short sound which, purely by default, would have had to be called a laugh. "Hardly. Nothing will ever convince Father, unless Ted is caught dead to rights in a second attempt. So we'll just have to let him make that attempt, won't we?" He looked around the table and managed a wan ghost of the grin all the Empire knew. "Oh come on, everybody! Don't look so glum. *You're* not the primary targets."

Aline Tatsumo looked up. Even in this light her eyes were visibly bloodshot. "We may have to let them try . . . Rod. But we sure as hell don't have to let them *succeed!*"

"Damned right," Janille affirmed fiercely. "Remember, the Deathstriders are still in orbit around this planet. I've already started to have those that are now on planetside liberty quietly rounded up and organized into a quick-response force."

"And we'll continue to quietly bring more down," Garth added. "We'll be in a position to deal with whatever comes up." He gave Aerenthal a pointed look. "Whenever you tell us it's *going* to come up."

"To be sure," the agent rejoined, a little too heartily. "There are any number of avenues of inquiry open to us. For example, we know the identities of the transposer technicians who were killed. It should be fairly straightforward to determine which one was involved—and then focus on *his* family, friends and associates. In any successful criminal investigation," he continued pedantically, "the identity of the guilty party is usually known fairly early. Then begins the process of amassing proof. We're fortunate in being able to go immediately to the second stage."

Corin nodded, holding his peace, as did Garth and Janille. This was foundation laying for Roderick's benefit. They would *know*, by grace of the knowledge Omega Prime had imparted to Aerenthal, when and how Teodor and his manipulators would strike next. But they'd need an acceptable rationale for *how* they knew.

Roderick started to raise his glass again, then thought better of it and set it down carefully. "All right. Make whatever preparations you think necessary. And I'll do whatever is required of me. But I want to make one thing clear. Teodor is *not* to be killed in the course of this operation. It is for the Emperor to judge his guilt—not us."

Maura's face had worn a haunted look. Now she nodded emphatically. "Yes. Remember, he's acting under the influence of Chewning and Liang. *They're* the guilty parties!"

Corin looked from sister to brother and back again. *Is it possible that they really believe this? After all Rod's told me about Teodor?*

But what do I—an only child, and an adopted one at that—know about it? How can I know what it's like to have an older child who's an immutable part of the universe from the earliest memory? Playmate, privy to all the secret places, role model by definition . . . No, it's not for me to judge.

Aerenthal's voice forced its way into his consciousness. "Of course. None of us want him killed, and we'll all make every effort to preserve him from the consequences of his own . . . susceptibility. And to avoid any other outcomes that you would find personally painful. But in matters of this kind, no one can offer guarantees."

Roderick met the agent's eyes, and Corin could read

the conflict in his face. He didn't like what he was hearing, but he wasn't fatuous enough to deny its essential truth. For his own part, Corin looked at Aerenthal's carefully expressionless face and decided he was grateful that Omega Prime had vouchsafed him only a strictly limited kind and degree of foreknowledge.

CHAPTER FIFTEEN
Prometheus (Sigma Draconis II), 4334 C.E.

Chewning wondered if Teodor was going to have a nervous breakdown.

"You *promised* it would work! And I believed you and went along, even though I never really wanted to." Teodor's pacing had almost carried him to the balcony door, beyond which low-flying wisps of cloud drifted among the palace's other towers in the morning sun. He stopped short and whirled around, face working tremulously. "And now look what's happened!"

"An unforeseeable mischance, sir," Chewning murmured. "Your brother turned aside at the last moment to answer a call, as his companion entered the—"

"Excuses! The point is, you failed—and failed in such a public and spectacular way that they couldn't sweep it under the rug even if they wanted to. They'll dig and dig and keep on digging. We'll be found out!"

Chewning waited until Teodor had run out of steam, then let a heartbeat of silence pass before nodding and speaking with calm deliberation. "Yes, sir, we will. It is inevitable." He didn't let his satisfaction show as Teodor's jaw dropped and his mouth hung open. He'd wanted reassurance; now Chewning had his undivided attention, and he spoke briskly. "Clearly, the time for half-measures and subterfuge is past. It is more important than ever that your brother die. We cannot wait for another opportunity to set up an apparent accident. We must act openly."

"But . . . but Father will—"

"His Imperial Majesty will approve, once you've made clear to him that you were acting to forestall a coup."

"Uh . . . ?"

"We must make certain the circumstances are such as to make it apparent that there was no other way to save his life. Which is, after all, true. Think about it, sir. Your brother can hardly leave him alive after seizing the throne, can he?"

"Well . . . no, I suppose not." Teodor drew himself up like an actor overregistering stiffened resolve. "Yes, you're right: there's no other way. We must act with maximum decisiveness! We must . . . uh, I assume you have a concrete plan setting forth what we must do?"

"There are a few details yet to be worked out, sir. But I'll have a detailed outline ready for your perusal by this time tomorrow. It will, of course, incorporate provisions for you to take an active personal part in the actual execution."

"Er . . . is that really necessary?"

"Not just necessary, sir, but absolutely fundamental to the plan's success. Remember what I said earlier about the impression we must create in His Imperial Majesty's mind. This requires that you appear to be going into action impulsively, heedless of danger, to protect him from treachery—not masterminding a prearranged plan from behind the scenes." Chewning was rather pleased with himself for getting past the word "masterminding" with a straight face.

"Hmm . . . Yes, perhaps you're right."

Chewning decided to lay it on. "And after all, sir, such action on your part will be readily believable, being so thoroughly in character."

"So it is, now that you mention it." Teodor assumed

what was doubtless intended to be a look of haughty decisiveness, and gave a curt nod. "Very well. See to it."

As soon as he was gone, Vladimir Liang emerged from the shadows among the wall hangings, shaking his head skeptically. "Do you really think he'll remain controllable after the plan comes to fruition? It could shock him into unpredictable behavior."

"That's a risk," Chewning conceded.

"Perhaps we should tell him now—prepare him in advance."

"No! He couldn't function if he knew the truth. He's too unintelligent to grasp the opportunity, and too morally cowardly to act on it if he did. No," Chewning repeated with an emphatic headshake, "we'll stay with our original plan. He'll never know how it really came about—the disinformation is as much for his benefit as for everyone else's. And with a little help from us, he'll adjust to the new facts."

"Very well. I only hope your confidence is justified."

Chewning ignored the slight sulkiness in Liang's voice. He was reflecting on the odd way things had of working out. Surreptitiously disposing of Roderick Brady-Schiavona had been a bad idea from the first. But it had taken the attempt's failure to make them realize that, and force them to do what they should have done at the beginning—truly a blessing in disguise. And now, instead of having an heir to manipulate, they'd have an *Emperor.*

"But it doesn't make sense," Roderick repeated. It had been the general reaction around the table in Corin's quarters, since Aerenthal had informed them that the next attempt to kill Roderick was to be connected in some way with his return from an upcoming inspection tour of the Fleet bases on the moons of Cronus.

"I've been unable to learn any details of their plan,

which might make it more understandable," the agent said—meaning that Omega Prime hadn't told him any such details. But he couldn't put it that way, of course. For the consumption of Roderick, Maura and Aline Tatsumo, he'd presented the news as a product of investigative work.

Roderick took a deep breath. "They must know I'm returning directly to the palace. I'll be landing at the Imperial spacefield—riding a shuttle down, assuming that the transposer system is still deactivated. Anything they try there will be completely public, and couldn't be made to look like an accident, unlike their trick with the transposers. It just doesn't fit the pattern."

For a moment, no one had any comment. Then Garth's basso broke the perplexed silence. "Maybe they don't *want* it to look like an accident. Maybe they're going to be completely open about it."

"But," Roderick protested, "that doesn't make sense either! It would doom Ted's chance at the succession. Father would disinherit him."

"That's true . . . if your father were still alive."

What followed wasn't really silence—there was too much indrawing of breath around the table for that. Roderick shook his head as though in uncomprehending annoyance. Then comprehension came, and the headshaking became more emphatic, almost angry.

"No. No! Ted would never . . . I mean, look, you know I have no illusions about him. But he'd never—"

"Remember, he's not really in charge. Chewning and Liang may not be telling him everything. In fact, I'm sure they're planning to make him think it's accidental . . . or your work. That way, his bereavement will actually be genuine."

"Plausible deniability," Aerenthal murmured.

"And in the meantime," Garth went on remorselessly, as Roderick's head continued to shake like a mechanism that hadn't been told to stop, "as the oldest child he's the heir apparent in the absence of a declaration to the contrary by your father. And the Fleet would support him. We can afford having him as Emperor a lot better than we can afford a succession struggle."

"But Garth," Janille asked, "how could they do it? He's surrounded by layers of state-of-the-art security."

"He's also living on a platform floating in midair, a mile above the surface."

At first, no one grasped what Garth was talking about. Children of a civilization that had tamed gravity in the far remote past, they tended to forget that it was still a part of the universe's "default setting," always ready to snap back the instant the machines that annulled it failed . . . or were sabotaged. Then, one by one, they looked at each other with awakening horror.

"We've got to get him off," Roderick half-whispered. "We've got to get *everybody* off!"

Corin looked grim. "Remember, we have no proof. And you know he'd never believe it of Teodor." For a moment, they all tried to imagine broaching the possibility to Ivar. Imagination failed.

"You're right," Roderick nodded. "Father wouldn't—couldn't—accept it. But," he continued, looking at each of them in turn and finally letting his gaze settle on his sister, "we've got to be prepared to get him off anyway."

Maura's eyes widened and she started to open her mouth. Then she clamped it shut and subsided into a troubled silence.

Garth spoke in a voice that only seemed loud. "We've got enough Deathstriders in Dracopolis to manage it, I think."

"But the palace is so heavily guarded!" Aline Tatsumo protested.

"The Imperial Guards are good at ceremonies and routine security, but they're not combat troops. And

besides, this wouldn't be an assault; we'd be acting
from the inside. We can insert our people into the
palace in advance one by one, on one legitimate
pretext or another . . . *if* we know exactly when we
have to be ready, and exactly what we have to watch
for." Garth gave Aerenthal a significant look.

"I will give the matter my best attention," the agent
intoned.

"All right," Corin said briskly. "Garth, you and
Janille will be in charge here at the palace. I'm scheduled to go out to Cronus with Rod, and we shouldn't
change that at this point. So I'll be with him when
he arrives at the spacefield." He didn't let himself
make eye contact with Janille, but at the periphery
of his vision he caught her brief stricken look as he
announced he would be at the side of the man marked
for death. "And as for that arrival, I have an idea. . . ."

The schematic of the palace floated in holographic
translucence about a foot above the tabletop simu-
lation of the Dracopolis oceanfront. Gazing at that
foot-wide shallow bowl with its load of soaring architectural intricacy, Damiano Chewning only had eyes
for the three areas of red deep within the bowl's lower
regions: the contragrav units that kept that colossal
structure magically motionless in the sky. Any one of
them could do it. And even without that one, the two
great pressor beam projectors that showed in blue just
beneath the surface of the esplanade below could
gently lower the palace, nudging it out beyond the
sea wall to a splashdown that would spill the occupants' drinks but wouldn't kill them. Nothing had been
overlooked.

Nothing but the human factor, Chewning thought,
looking across the table at the man in Imperial Guards
gray-and-red, although he wondered how applicable
the term "human" really was where Major Andrei
Ravenel-Cutlass was concerned.

"So, Major," he inquired, "has all been placed in readiness?"

"Ages ago," Ravenel-Cutlass drawled. Enduring his affectation of languid sarcasm was a small price to pay for the unique access to the palace's most sensitive areas he provided. Not for the first time, Chewning wondered how such a creature could possibly have gotten into such a critical position, especially after transferring from the Guard's atmospheric-combat branch under questionable circumstances. Family connections had doubtless helped. Chewning and Liang had recognized a useful tool the instant they'd met him, shortly after their arrival on Prometheus. Using means Teodor had put at their disposal, they'd gotten control of the bulk of the major's colossal gambling debts, and of information that could ruin even a Ravenel-Cutlass. But as it had turned out, blackmail had barely been necessary.

"Are the people you've recruited trustworthy?" Liang jittered.

"Of course not." Ravenel-Cutlass flashed the devil-may-care grin Chewning was certain he practiced in front of a mirror. "But they're controllable—at least for as long as we need them."

"This is my assessment as well," Chewning nodded, forebearing as usual to take exception to the major's "we." *Let him pretend he's a member of the conspiracy, not just an employee.*

"In that case," Liang ventured hopefully, "perhaps we don't really need to accompany the team that takes out the stealth installation." His eyes wandered to the relatively small green area at the very heart of the translucent bowl.

"Yes, we do," Chewning stated firmly. "There is no substitute for personal supervision, lest their commitment should waver. And that element of the operation is absolutely critical."

The plan called for Teodor—who fancied himself,

not totally without reason, as an atmospheric pilot—
to lead the flight of three fighters that would shoot
down Roderick's shuttle as it descended to the spacefield. It was, Chewning congratulated himself, a stroke
of genius to have Teodor kill his brother personally.
It would get him out from underfoot while Chewning,
Liang and Ravenel-Cutlass dealt with the *real* objective, of which he knew nothing. Three groups of the
major's corrupted Guards would destroy the contragrav
generators. Meanwhile, pilots Ravenel-Cutlass had
recruited from among his old chums would swoop
down in fighters whose skins were programmed to
show Deathstrider insignia. They would destroy the
pressor-beam projectors under the oceanfront's surface, secure in the assurance they'd been given that
the defensive weapons that ringed the palace's outer
perimeter would be deactivated. And so they would
be . . . until the strike had succeeded and the pilots
were about to depart to collect their reward, at which
time the targeting systems would suddenly come back
on-line. . . .

Chewning smiled at Ravenel-Cutlass, who had
suggested the neat method of disposing of the pilots.
What a totally contemptible backstabber, he reflected
behind his smile, with a kind of awe. It wasn't the
sort of thing Damiano Chewning normally thought
concerning other people. He had no trouble understanding ambition unrestrained by any moral considerations—he needed only to look in the mirror. But
he couldn't help being puzzled as to the major's motivations. *He isn't really ambitious. He isn't even ava-
ricious. The money won't be unwelcome, but that isn't
what he's doing it for. No, he's doing it for the sake
of doing it. He's driven by something I'll never understand: a compulsion to duplicity. An inner music to
which he must dance until he dies. And, by providing the dance floor, men like me can make use of men
like him . . . for a while.*

And, when it becomes necessary, killing him will be childishly easy. Like all solipsists, he thinks he's immortal.

In the meantime, the important thing was their own escape. The palace's transposers were still closed down, and no outside transposer could establish a terminus point inside it. The little green area in the display marked the most sophisticated battery of sensor-confusion devices the science of the age could produce. But those would go down in an operation Chewning would personally oversee. He, Liang, and Ravenel-Cutlass—but not the others, despite what they'd been led to believe—would be snatched from the palace as it began to fall. Teodor would return from the spacefield to find himself Emperor and hear Chewning's mortified explanation of how they'd been unable to save his father from the dastardly attack by Roderick's now-deceased supporters. In time, he would doubtless get over it.

The great echoing chamber was deep in the working levels, beneath the sunlit architectural wonderland above. It had been intended as a gymnasium for the palace's Imperial Guard contingent, but for one reason or another it had remained unused. Roderick had had no trouble arranging for them to use it as a bolt-hole for the Deathstriders who'd been brought aboard the palace one by one and never seemed to leave. Sooner or later the records would be checked. But by then it would all be over, one way or another.

Now their entire strength was gathered here, for Roderick was on his way back and things must come to a head soon. Unfortunately, Aerenthal still wasn't sure just exactly *how* soon. And, as they knew all too well, any preemptive action was out of the question. In this matter, Ivar would accept no evidence short of a blood-red hand. They had to wait for the would-be assassins to make the first move. So they'd gone on full alert as soon as Roderick had departed the moons of Cronus. And then they had waited. And waited.

Janille halted her pacing at the balcony's railing and looked down at the troopers who lay or sat in clumps, or else had drifted off to read or dictate messages in solitude. The low rumble of desultory, often irritable conversation that rose from the groups was like the rumble of distant thunder on a stifling summer afternoon when a cloudburst stubbornly refused to come.

There was no powered combat armor here. The palace's interiors hadn't been designed to accommodate it. Instead, the troopers wore nanoplastic combat dress, flexible but programmed to lock itself into the hardness of steel at the instant of any potentially hazardous impact its embedded sensors foresaw. Most of them carried neural paralyzers and gas grenades—they didn't want to use lethal weapons inside the palace unnecessarily, and they hoped it wouldn't be necessary at all. But Garth had refused to rely on that hope. Officers and squad leaders wore bead guns as sidearms, and each squad's strongest man carried a plasma gun for getting past—or, rather, through—structural barriers when speed was the only consideration.

And, of course, their opponents wouldn't be worried about damage to a palace they meant to destroy anyway, or to the people who would die with it. . . .

Janille turned away from the dismal view and resumed her pacing on the balcony's limited confines. She was alone save for Garth, and for all his size it was possible to forget he was there, so quietly did he sit with his back propped against the wall, wrapped in a calmness that aroused her uncomprehending envy.

She stopped in front of him and spoke because she needed to banish the drawn-wire silence. "Uh, Garth, I don't know if I've ever mentioned it, but . . . well, I think you've taken it awfully well."

"Huh?" Garth came out of his trance of pre-combat relaxation. "Oh, you mean . . . you and Corin." He harrumphed awkwardly. "Well, you see, I always sensed a kind of inevitability about the two of you. I sensed it even before I knew who . . . well, stood behind the two of you."

She felt her face heating up. "You know what Omega Prime said. We're really—"

"—not the same people. Yes, I know. You're not just living out a myth. But . . . it's a very powerful myth. And I can see it in the flesh when I look at the two of you."

Janille was starting to frame a reply when the immaterial intruder awoke inside her head, like the sound of Jason Aerenthal's voice but "heard" in an indescribable way that was not sound.

(*Urgency.*) "It is time."

For an instant, her eyes met Garth's. He, too, had consented to this, in the teeth of what they never even thought of as a cultural taboo. For Janille, it was like consenting to unwanted sexual contact—only much worse. She didn't know how it felt to Garth. But it was the quickest way for Aerenthal to alert them when his deeply buried awareness of the crucial instant awoke. So they had agreed to drop all resistance.

With the swiftness that was always so startling in a man his size, Garth was on his feet and striding to the railing. His voice filled the chamber. "All right, this is it! Move!"

Instantly, the formless mass of boredom on the floor below transformed itself, clumping together into five understrength squads as the squad leaders barked orders. Squads Gamma, Delta and Epsilon immediately set out at a dead run for the doors that would take them to the contragrav generators, where they would ward off any intruders that might arrive or deal with any already there. The other two waited as Garth and Janille ran down the ladders from the balcony, then sprinted for their own prearranged destinations. Garth, with a final wave to Janille, led Squad Alpha toward

the palace's stealth installation. Janille paused to raise
Aline Tatsumo on her wristcomp and confirm that the
aircar was ready on the landing flange. Then she set
out with Squad Beta for the Emperor's apartments.

To Teodor Brady-Schiavona, it seemed that he rode
a magical throne through the sky, without acceleration or wind. The landscape below his feet whipped
past, gradually changing from countryside to suburb
as the towers of Dracopolis became visible far ahead
to the north, beyond the spacefield.

He thrust the thought away. He needed to concentrate. Besides, the instrument panel, seeming to float
unsupported over his lap, spoiled the illusion of the
cockpit's wraparound holo display, reminding him that
he was really inside an AF-4 like that of his wingman,
which by grace of his craft's computer he could see
to starboard as it *would* have appeared had its liquid-crystal surface not been duplicating the sky in the
background. It was an arrowhead-shaped lifting body
with overpowered impellers but no gravitics save the
G-damper that prevented acceleration from pressing
the pilot back, unconscious, into his seat. Like a pair
of invisible ghosts, they arrowed at low altitude toward
the spacefield . . . and his destiny.

He checked the instrument panel again, feeling a
spasm of annoyance that he had to do so—he lacked
the aptitude for direct neural interfacing, unlike his
wingman, an Imperial Guards atmospheric pilot named
Leong suborned by that disrespectful fellow Ravenel-
Cutlass. But that was all right, he told himself. Leong
was merely along as an escort. *He* would make the
kill.

As is my right, he told himself firmly. *And, in fact,
my duty.* After all, even if Roderick wasn't really
planning a coup now, it was only a matter of time.
Chewning had made this clear—now *there* was someone who had the proper respect, who truly appreciated

him ... as Roderick never had. His initial scruples about what had to be done had grown more and more abstract, finally vanishing altogether. Now he felt only eagerness.

There! The descending shuttle appeared on his scope. He ignored the visual panorama, including the spacefield ahead, and fixated on that return. It was descending in the leisurely manner of the unarmed utility shuttle they knew it to be. He frowned momentarily at the computer's interpretation of the data. The shuttle seemed to be a utility version, not the VIP model they'd expected. And there were minor anomalies, as though it had been slightly modified. ... But there was no time for further analysis, for he was coming into range. He activated the weapons lock-on. The shuttle became the be-all and end-all of his missiles' obsessive, suicide-compelled little brains. He touched a control and, with an almost orgasmic sense of release, felt the slight bump and watched the fiery streaks as two missiles howled away.

"Incoming!"

"Yes, I've got them," Roderick replied. "And now that the shuttle's sensors can zero in on their origin-point ... There! Two AF-4's!" Roderick was in direct control of the shuttle, including its enhanced sensor array, from his cramped cockpit, identical to the one in which Corin nestled and listened to his voice. And now the data from those sensors was downloaded to the brains of their two AF-7's—atmospheric fighters not unlike the approaching AF-4's but smaller, near the lower limit of size and mass for a viable combat aircraft. Still, it had taken some doing to fit the fighters into the shuttle's modified cargo hold.

"Ready?" Corin asked.

"Not quite. I'll try to give you a three-count ... No! The missiles are coming in too fast, and the AF-4's are starting to peel off. Disengaging ... NOW!"

At Roderick's touch of a key, explosive charges blew the hatch doors away from the shuttle's belly, revealing the two tiny fighters hanging from the cargo bay's overhead. Simultaneously, magnetic clamps were deactivated and, in a sickening instant of free fall, the AF-7's dropped through the yawning hatch. Their impellers awoke with a whine of protest, and they streaked away from the now-unmanned shuttle.

Some fraction of a second later, the shuttle vanished in a double nuclear fireball behind them.

That searing backdrop, plus their own stealth features, gave them a couple of seconds before the pilots of the AF-4's, now curving off to the northeast, realized they'd ceased to be the hunters and become the hunted.

Sergeant Morell Clent of the Deathstriders rounded a corner of the passageway—the last one, his helmet HUD assured him—and scanned the corridor ahead, paralysis gun at the ready. Simultaneously, he yelled "Go!" The rest of Squad Gamma ran past him, deploying across the passageway.

The corridor had the same grimly functional look as all the palace's working levels, very different from what rose above them. But Clent wasn't concerned with atmosphere, only with assuring that there were no intruders. Satisfied, he motioned to Squad Gamma to follow him. They set out at a trot toward the massive doors beyond which lay the contragrav generator that was their responsibility.

"All right," he rapped, "it looks like we got here first. Go to defensive deployment out here in the passageway. Sayid, stand by with the plasma gun; I'll call in for further orders, find out if we need to—"

Without any warning, a thundercrash overwhelmed their helmets' sound-damping capacities and the deck jumped beneath their feet. The great doors bucked outward, and smoke billowed outward through the rents, but the explosion hadn't been powerful enough to blast them away altogether.

As he picked himself up, Clent felt another concussion through the deck, and then another. But these were distant—as distant, he knew, as the other two generators, where Squads Delta and Epsilon likewise stood guard against intruders who weren't going to materialize.

As he activated his wristcomp to report in to General Krona, it belatedly occurred to him to wonder why the palace wasn't falling.

"What's happened?" Vladimir Liang demanded. "Why isn't the palace descending?" There should have been a momentary dropping sensation, followed by a slow lowering as the ground-mounted pressor beams took hold.

"I don't know," muttered Ravenel-Cutlass, his usual insolent sangfroid in abeyance. "I'm trying to find out, damn it!"

Liang seemed about to fire off a retort, but Chewning shushed him. When the three shudders of distant explosions hadn't had the expected result, they'd halted in a side alcove of the passageway and sat waiting as the major had tried to raise a crony who'd been in charge of booby-trapping the contragrav generators. He was still trying.

A few more moments passed, with Ravenel-Cutlass repeating requests for acknowledgment and Liang barely able to control himself. Finally, the major's communicator beeped, and after a hurried exchange he turned to Chewning.

"It seems only part of the charges detonated at generator number three. A short circuit, I imagine. At any rate, it's still functioning."

Liang seemed about to go to pieces, but Chewning spoke so quickly as to forestall him. "Do you realize what this means?" he hissed. "That one generator is enough to keep the palace aloft! Even when the pressor beams are destroyed—"

"Compose yourself." Ravenel-Cutlass was rapidly regaining his aplomb. "I'm assured that the installation has been badly weakened by the charges that did go off. It's operating on auxiliary systems—the shudder we felt through our feet wasn't just concussion, it was also a momentary lapse in the lift as those systems cut in. And it can't last. It's only a matter of time—and not much of it—before it fails. By then, the pressor beams will have been taken out. When the final failure occurs, the palace will drop like a stone!"

"Very well," said Chewning, mollified. "Let's proceed."

He stood up, awkward in the combat dress that suited his dumpy frame so poorly. The others followed: Liang, still looking jittery, Ravenel-Cutlass, and five enlisted Imperial Guards who had proven amenable to the princely sums the major had offered. More would only have further compromised the conspiracy, and wouldn't have been necessary to overpower the technicians manning the sensor-confusion control center that was their destination. They resumed their quick-time march along the dimly lit passageway.

Laser weapons were of limited utility in atmosphere. They were restricted to the visible-light wavelengths, for atmosphere absorbed the more energetic X-rays of spacecraft weaponry. As such, they were short-ranged and readily blocked by smoke and fog, to say nothing of defensive aerosols.

Still, Corin reflected as he brought the bandit into his sights, on a bright and sunny day like this there was a lot to be said for a weapon which struck at the speed of light.

Roderick's delay in releasing them from the doomed shuttle had provided the edge they'd needed. From what he'd seen of the craft he was tracking, it was pretty obvious that its pilot was a professional who was mind-linked with his AF-4. Corin had checked out on the AF-7 a long time ago, and he'd taken advantage of the transit time to and from Cronus to refresh himself with deep-learning courses. But he was still no expert . . . and neither was Roderick. Yet they'd appeared out of nowhere as the two bogies had peeled away from the shuttle's thermonuclear funeral pyre, blissfully unaware that any danger threatened from their aft quarter.

The targeting solution firmed up, and Corin touched his laser weapon's firing stud. A flash of glancing contact with the AF-4's tail section showed on visual. It was enough. The bogie began to spin out of control.

"Got him!" he yelled to Roderick. He found an instant to worry about the effect of his quarry's crash, for the endless cityscape of Dracopolis had begun to unfold below them as the dogfight had carried them northward.

"Outstanding! I'm still trying to get a firm fix on the one I'm after . . . looks like we're going to go almost the whole way to the oceanfront . . . Hell and *damnation!* What's *that?*"

Corin, though further south, could see exactly what Roderick was talking about. A vee-formation of three atmospheric fighters—no, spaceplanes capable of fleeing beyond the atmosphere—screamed down in a power dive, glowing with the heat of atmospheric friction, homing in on the oceanfront just to the east of the area directly beneath the palace. Deep-penetrator kinetic-kill munitions flashed downward, piling their own velocity atop that of the craft that launched them, striking the grand esplanade that paralleled the ocean. Gouts of flame and geysers of dust and smoke appeared, followed seconds later by a low rumble.

At some point during those seconds, it dawned on Corin that those weapons had impacted in the area of the pressor beam projectors that were the palace's last line of defense against Prometheus' gravity. The palace that held the Emperor. And Garth. And Janille.

Why don't the palace's defenses do something? he wondered, a calm thought at the epicenter of a maelstrom of horror.

His question was instantly answered. As the attackers decelerated with a howl of overstressed impellers just short of the ground and began to pull up, the strangely silent defensive installations suddenly came to life. The crackling lines of ionized air that marked the passage of weapon-grade lasers stabbed out from the rim of the palace, and the attackers exploded in rapid succession, showering their debris over the oceanfront. On a nice afternoon like this, there must have been a lot of people on the beach.

Corin forcibly emptied his mind of all thoughts save two. First, the palace still hung serenely in the sky, so at least one of its internal contragrav generators still functioned. And secondly, Roderick was still in pursuit of their other attacker—the one that had launched the shuttle-destroying missiles. And he was closing in.

Another grenade explosion forced Garth and the surviving members of Squad Alpha to flatten against the bulkhead. He tried to ignore it, but had to raise his voice and shout into the communicator.

"The pressors wrecked? Both of them?"

"Totally." Janille's voice came in a shout of her own. "I'm not even trying to sort out all the news at this point. The bottom line is that—"

"We're still aloft," Garth finished for her. "So at least one of the palace contragrav generators must still be in business. But the hostiles we're engaging are still trying to hold us up, keep us from interfering as they force their way into the palace stealth center. Which means they must still be entertaining a hope of victory.

Which, in turn, means it may not *continue* in business . . ." He forced himself to stop thinking out loud. "All right, Janille. Your orders are unchanged—except that instead of getting His Imperial Majesty out, you're now to get him out *fast*. And be prepared to get him out by transposing him out if that turns out to be practicable."

"What? You mean . . . ?"

"Yes. The palace's sensor-confusion equipment may very well be down by then. So get in touch with Maura and tell her to be prepared to flick her father out of there." Maura rode a battlecruiser in a low orbit designed to be over this hemisphere of Prometheus at the time of Roderick's scheduled landing.

"But, Garth—"

"Signing off." Garth cut the connection, hefted his paralysis gun, and considered the current state of affairs. Whatever impression others might hold, he'd always regarded himself as a businessman rather than a warrior, bringing a dispassionate cost/benefit analysis to bear on all applications of violence. Hard to imagine how people got their ideas. But . . . this was an emergency. With an ear-bruising roar, he swung out from the bulkhead and ran down the passageway, paralyzer on rapid fire. After a stunned instant, Squad Alpha followed him, screaming.

The sheer fury of the assault caught the hostiles' holding force by surprise. One man stepped out to return fire. Garth caught him full-on and he toppled over to lie motionless. Garth ran on, toward the control center whose headquarters troops were, at last report, still resisting behind an improvised barricade. Another hostile jumped out in front of him, weapon already leveled. Before he could even try to react, there was a thunderous roar and a blinding flash from which his helmet faceplate's antiglare feature protected him, and the hostile was enveloped in flame. He looked over his shoulder and exchanged grins with Corporal

Malwe, the squad plasma gunner. Then the two of them rounded the last corner. The barricade was ahead—or what was left of it—and what was left of its defenders. Garth took just enough time to regret some of the thoughts he'd entertained about headquarters troops. Then he charged past . . . just in time to be thrown off his feet by the concussion as an explosion erupted up ahead, flinging an armored door into the corridor.

Picking himself up, bewildered, Garth glimpsed figures scurrying down a side corridor to the right. To his left, Malwe was also rising from the floor. Beyond him, the rest of the squad's survivors were pursuing their fleeing opponents down another corridor. "This way," Garth snapped, and bounded off to the right. Malwe hastened to follow, soon drawing level with him.

It was at that moment that a figure stepped out from the shadows to the side, gauss pistol held in both hands and aimed at point-blank range. He could have put a heavy needle of grav-compressed steel into either target. It was sheer chance that Malwe's faceplate shattered and the back of his helmet exploded outward in a shower of blood and brains.

The gauss pistol began to swing toward Garth, seemingly in slow motion.

At this range, the rifle-length neural paralyzer was unwieldy. Garth didn't waste time he didn't have by trying to aim it. He let it fall even as he was springing forward.

The other man flinched involuntarily in the face of that headlong charge. It was enough to throw his aim off from the vulnerable faceplate. The needle struck Garth's shoulder, and shattered harmlessly as the combat dress's nanoplastic rigidified for the millisecond of contact. The impact staggered Garth, but momentum carried him forward. He crashed awkwardly into his opponent.

For a moment, they grappled. Garth gripped the wrist of the gun hand and gave a squeeze that brought a scream and sent the gauss pistol flying. Then he yanked the arm up behind his opponent and grasped him around the neck. He jerked sideways with a strength inherited from dozens of generations of ancestors who'd lived and given birth in high gravity. The man's faceplate had come open in the fight, and his shriek was audible until a sharp *crack!* cut it off. He went limp. Dropping the form to the floor, Garth recognized the features of Vladimir Liang.

He recognized something else attached to the dead man's belt. A link. Thoughtfully, he appropriated it. Then he retrieved his paralyzer, and—with difficulty, even for him—picked up Malwe's plasma gun one-handed. Then he advanced, his weapons cradled one in each arm and pointed ahead. He rounded the final corner.

Two men turned toward him. He had the drop on them.

One of them evidently knew a plasma gun by sight. He immediately dropped his gauss weapon and stepped forward empty-handed, opening his faceplate. "Don't shoot! I am Major Ravenel-Cutlass of the Imperial Guards, and I ask for quarter."

Behind him, Garth saw the other man making a motion. He started to point his paralyzer, but Ravenel-Cutlass was in the way. And the man hadn't been reaching for a weapon after all . . . only touching a button on what looked unmistakably like a detonator.

The explosive device which had been concealed inside the Guards major's helmet clearly wasn't a very powerful one. The helmet itself contained a good part of its force. So while grayish-pink gore sprayed in all directions, the bulk of it followed the line of least resistance out the open faceplate, splattering Garth.

For a second or so, the headless corpse stood swaying before crumpling to the floor.

The second man opened his own faceplate. "Always knew that would be necessary sooner or later," he remarked, more to himself than to Garth. Then his rabbitlike face formed an innocuous smile. "I was just about to establish a transposer connection. You see, the explosion a few moments ago—"

"—took out the palace's sensor-confusion installation," Garth finished for him.

The rabbit-faced man frowned momentarily, as though the voice from behind the faceplate awoke a memory. "Yes. Quite. So you'll appreciate that it is now possible for a transposition to be performed from outside. And I'm prepared to allow you to transpose with me, in exchange for my life. That's the only way off this palace before it falls. Because, you see—"

"—the pressor beam projectors have been destroyed," Garth interposed again. "And the one contragrav generator holding us up is going to fail any time."

This time the frown intensified. "You seem very well-informed. Who are you? Your voice sounds vaguely familiar."

"It should—although it's been six years now. Think back. The time Liang's fleet attacked Sol."

Understanding slowly awoke in Damiano Chewning's face. "No," he whispered, staring at Garth's faceplate as though he could see behind it.

"Yes."

Chewning's tongue darted out like a frightened animal and he licked his lips. He managed to keep his voice steady. "Look, General Krona, let's be sensible. When this is over, Teodor Brady-Schiavona is going to be Emperor. And I control him! You have no idea what I'll be able to offer you! I can—" Chewning's voice box froze into immobility along with the rest of his voluntary muscles at the touch of the paralysis beam. He toppled forward like a conscious statue. His nose and teeth hit the floor with an impact he couldn't in any way soften. He also couldn't scream.

Garth dropped the paralyzer and opened his faceplate with the free hand. Then he used a foot to roll Chewning over onto his back. He gazed silently into the bloody face for a moment.

Chewning could move his eyes only with great slowness. But they were pointed in the right direction to see the orifice of the plasma gun coming into line.

The vast cityscape of Dracopolis was unfolding below, and the palace was looming up ahead and to the left. Teodor barely noticed how far north his flight had brought him. He was trying to keep from sobbing as he fled.

He still couldn't comprehend what he'd seen. Who had piloted the mysterious aircraft that had attacked the pressor-beam installations? And what was the point of their attack, when the palace's contragrav generators would hold it up anyway?

He might have deduced the truth, given the leisure to think it through. But the pursuer who had appeared from out of the glare of his own warheads had dogged him relentlessly, despite the evasive maneuvers that had carried them over the city.

Now, with the ocean showing cobalt blue beyond the tall buildings that lined the esplanade like a barricade, it belatedly occurred to him that a surrender might be accepted.

Yes! That was it. All he had to do was reach the ground alive. Father would understand.

Frantically, he hailed the pursuing craft on the universal Fleet frequency.

He was just completing his authenticator when the

AF-4's brain squealed that it had been acquired by targeting radar. A split second later, before he could react, it announced that the pursuing craft had launched a missile.

At appreciably the same instant, his communicator activated, and he saw his hunter's face on a holographically projected display screen identical to the one on which the other was seeing his. And for a moment the two brothers wore identical expressions of horror-stricken recognition.

A high-pitched warning from Teodor's craft shattered the moment. The missile, about which he'd forgotten in that timeless moment, was about to impact. Acting without thinking, he wrenched the AF-4 into a tight turn. But the doomed craft's wail—it couldn't really be one of terror, for this wasn't a sentient computer—went on. Convulsively, he jabbed the seat ejector.

He was barely clear when the missile detonated, and the thermal bloom from the explosion sent him tumbling across the sky. He was stunned, but his gravchute activated itself automatically. Only then did he become aware of the pain, where a chunk of debris had struck his left foot.

The Imperial Guardsman peered cautiously around the doorframe's edge. Emboldened, he stepped out into the opening, gauss rifle at high port. It was all Janille needed. Pivoting around from where she'd stood flat against the other side of the wall, she sent his weapon flying with a flying side-kick. As she landed, she brought her paralyzer up with a fluid motion and shot him full in the face. Then, from a crouch, she quickly surveyed the antechamber beyond. Finding it empty, she stood up and motioned what was left of Squad Beta to follow her toward the ornate door in the opposite wall.

She was about to give an order to the plasma

gunner, but it wasn't necessary. The door slid open. A tall, massively built man stepped out. He wore a plain gray uniform—or at least it would have seemed plain to anyone who hadn't known what the small golden dragon that was its sole ornamentation meant.

Janille realized that, like everyone else in the squad, she had come to a halt under the frown of that craggy face.

"What's the meaning of this, Colonel?" The deep voice was quiet and controlled, nothing like the bellow Janille had expected. But, without intending to, she came to a position of attention.

"Sir," she addressed him, for they were both in uniform, "the gravitic devices keeping this palace aloft have been sabotaged by conspirators. It is imperative that you get off it."

The gray eyes narrowed. "What 'conspirators'? Who's behind this? And under what authority are *you* acting?"

Janille gulped. She'd known the question was unavoidable. And she couldn't answer it—not now, when they hadn't a minute to waste. The truth about Teodor's involvement would have been so unacceptable as to render Ivar unable to believe what he *must* believe: the urgency of his situation. "Sir, that's unimportant now. The point is that the palace is going to fall any minute. Your daughter is now in orbit overhead, prepared to transpose you up."

The Emperor's eyebrows shot up, furrowing the forehead under the bald crown. "Maura? She's involved in this? But she can't locate a transposer focus in here!"

"She can now, sir. The palace's sensor-confusion devices have also been sabotaged." Garth had communicated the news to her just before her squad had reached the innermost Imperial apartments. He'd told her to force her way through those last few corridors a little faster than was humanly possible, while he directed Maura to pick up all the Deathstriders he could locate. The others were sprinting for the landing flange and Aline Tatsumo's aircar.

"What about Teodor?" the Emperor demanded. "And Roderick—he's just returning from Cronus. They must be targets too! You must save them first!"

"Your sons aren't in the palace, sir." *True, as far as it goes,* Janille told herself. "Don't worry about them. It's *your* life that's in danger. We must move without delay!"

The Emperor's lips thinned into a straight line of stubbornness. "I will not be sent running from my own palace by any conspiracy—especially without knowing the whereabouts of my sons. And not at the behest of an officer who has forced her way into my apartments, and whose own role is far from clear!"

For a moment that seemed longer than it was, Janille met the eyes of the man she'd respected even before he'd become her Emperor. Then, without actually pointing it at him, she raised her paralyzer. From behind her, she heard the hiss of Squad Beta's collective indrawn breath.

"Your Imperial Majesty," she said very quietly, "you must go . . . one way or another."

Their eye contact remained unbroken, as Ivar's expression went from mulishness to tightly controlled outrage, and finally to grudging respect. He gave a small, wordless nod.

Janille stepped beside him. She gestured to her squad, and they fell in around the pair in a tight clump.

"Wait!" Everyone froze at the tone in the Emperor's voice. He looked Janille in the eye and pointed to the Guardsman she had paralyzed, lying in the doorway.

Janille gulped. "Of course, sir." She motioned to two of her men. They ran to the motionless form and carried it back to the magic circle of the transposer focus. Only then did she take out her communicator. "Maura? This is Janille. I'm with him. Get us out now. And then get Garth. He refused to budge until we had the Emperor."

"Right," came Maura's voice. "We've got your link located. Powering up now."

"Acknowledged. Signing off." Janille made an adjustment to her communicator. "Garth? We've got him. Stand by to be transposed immediately, you big—"

Before she could finish, the antechamber was empty. For a few moments, all was still. Then, loose objects jumped as the floor began to drop.

Teodor had come down on the esplanade, amid the rubble of the pressor beam projectors. Not another living soul was in sight as he dragged himself painfully away from the gravchute. One of the attacking aircraft had crashed on the beach below, and its smoking ruin added to the vista of deserted desolation.

He forced himself not to give in to the agony of his shattered left foot. He had to find someone who could help him. He got to his feet, sobbing with pain and self-pity, and began to hobble toward the nearest building.

The sun went in.

Odd, he thought. *There haven't been any clouds all day.*

But this shadow was too dark to be that of a cloud. It was more like an eclipse.

He looked up. The palace was overhead, of course. But it was never supposed to cast a shadow on the land.

Then he realized it was filling more of the sky than it should. And it filled still more of it even as the realization formed in his mind.

He broke into a clinically impossible run. He heard himself screaming, only partly from the transcendent pain of his foot, whose broken bones ground audibly together with every lurching, hobbling step.

With an indescribable sound of rending metal, the tops of the high-rise buildings began to crumple under the descending tonnage.

Teodor's hysterical pain suppression gave way, and his left leg collapsed under him. As he rolled on the ground, he had time to look up again.

The downrushing palace filled the entire sky. It filled the entire universe.

CHAPTER SIXTEEN
Prometheus (Sigma Draconis II), 4334 C.E.

Sigma Draconis was dipping below the western horizon when Corin landed his AF-7 on the esplanade. The smoke had largely dissipated, and the red-veined crescent of Atlas had appeared in the twilit sky, looking down as though with approval on the new chapter that had just been written in Prometheus' dark and bloody history.

He emerged from the cockpit and stood with the seawall to his right, staring at the vast intruder in the familiar scene. The fallen palace lay canted like an impossibly huge beached ship, with the waves lapping at one edge and a row of ruined buildings holding up the opposite edge like cracked toothpicks. Between the two, it had crushed a mile of the esplanade beneath its inconceivable weight, breaking its own back across the seawall. The blackened wreckage of what had been its architectural superstructure was silhouetted against the setting sun: a tangle of toppled towers and broken domes.

No one knew how many had died. Early indications were guardedly hopeful, for quite a few of the palace's denizens had had time in the final minutes to get to aircars, which had swarmed away from the landing flanges like bees from a falling tree. Likewise, the

attack on the pressor-beam projectors had sent most
people fleeing from the beach and the nearby buildings in panic before the sky had fallen on them.

Still, there were enough injured and dead to overload Dracopolis' hospitals and morgues. Enough, and
more than enough. Corin advanced through a vista of
makeshift dispensaries, improvised command posts,
and a constant coming and going of aircars, most of
them ambulances for the less-than-critical cases who
hadn't been earmarked to be transposed. But there
were none of the signs of civil demoralization. The
Emperor, safe aboard the battlecruiser *Steadfast* in
orbit, had broadcast an address assuring the planet—
and, via tachyon beam, the Empire—that he was alive,
and that those who'd sought his life had been crushed.
That news, delivered in his customary tones of granite
assurance, had had the hoped-for salutary effect.

Of course, Ivar had made the broadcast before
learning the details. . . .

Corin saw Aline Tatsumo up ahead, standing beside the balustrade in an area kept clear by unobtru-
sive guards. He waved a greeting. Their onetime
animosity had long since faded to an occasional
memory, like the damp-weather ache of an old broken bone. At this moment, it was even less than that.
She beckoned to him. Beside her, a figure in a flight
suit like Corin's leaned on the balustrade, staring
fixedly out to sea, focusing on infinity.

"Roderick?" Corin ventured hesitantly. This man
had seen his brother's aircraft vanish in the fireball
of the missile he himself had launched a split second
before he'd known who had piloted that aircraft. He'd
watched helplessly as Teodor's gravchute had carried
him down to the oceanfront beneath the palace. And
he'd watched the palace fall. And now . . .

Roderick spoke without turning around, in a voice
that had passed beyond pain into a dead realm where
nothing could hurt. "He won't see me."

"Roderick," Corin said urgently, "you've got to go up there and talk to him. Make him understand—"

"He won't see me," Roderick repeated dully. His state was shocking to Corin, who had never imagined he could be inadequate in any conceivable set of circumstances.

"It's true," Aline Tatsumo confirmed. *And he's in no shape to face Ivar anyway,* her eyes added. She moved closer to Roderick and placed a hand on his hunched shoulder. He flinched slightly from the human contact. "Corin, somebody's got to talk to the Emperor. And I'm needed down here. That leaves you."

"Me? But what makes you think the Emperor will—"

"Maura will get you in to see him. And this is important, Corin. Right now, Ivar's still in shock. When he comes out of it, his initial impression of what's happened is going to be set in concrete . . . unless you can change that impression."

Corin shook his head. "I can't. Rod could, if he were allowed to try."

"Then maybe you can persuade Ivar to receive him."

"All right. I'll see what I can do. Go ahead and signal *Steadfast.*"

The transposer room of HIMS *Steadfast* appeared around Corin. As he stepped off the dais, Maura Brady-Schiavona advanced to meet him. Garth and Janille followed, wearing grimy and—in Garth's case at least—bloodstained combat dress that contrasted cruelly with Maura's crisp gray space-service cover-all.

Corin spared a moment to exchange a quick, wordless hug with Janille, then turned to Maura. "How is he?"

"About as you'd expect. Right now, I don't think he can even summon up a command to keep you out of his presence. So let's hurry." She led Corin through the battlecruiser's passageways to a hatch guarded by Marines. They passed through into a briefing room where a dismal collection of surviving officials and courtiers stood in a silent half-circle around a table. Hunched over the table in a fashion strangely reminiscent of the downfallen palace on the planet below was a solitary figure in a plain planetside uniform. The overhead lights glinted off his broad bald scalp and the little golden dragons on his shoulders.

"Father," Maura said quietly, "here is Vice Admiral Marshak. He's come up from Dracopolis to report to you personally. He was with Rod."

With her last four words, something seemed to stir to life in the Emperor. His massive bald head lifted, and his bloodshot eyes took in the sweat-stained flight suit Corin hadn't taken time to change.

"With Rod? You mean with him when . . . ?" Ivar couldn't continue.

"Yes, Your Imperial Majesty. He and I arrived at the spacefield earlier today. We were in AF-7's set to be released from our specially reconstructed shuttle, for we had advance knowledge of the attempt on his life. We shot down our two attackers." Corin took a deep breath. Best to have this out now. At any rate, there was no point in trying to conceal what Ivar already knew. "One of them was your son Teodor. Roderick shot him down."

The Emperor's eyes squeezed shut and his face contorted around the wail he couldn't release. "So I've been informed. I can hardly . . . no, I *can't* believe Ted was involved in any assassination attempt." He rose shakily to his feet and assumed the ramrod posture that was natural to him. His voice rose, as though trying to recapture its old resonance by sheer loudness. "I'm going to order a full investigation, to find out what *really* happened today. Ted would *never* have conspired against me! Never!"

"No, sir. Our best information is that he had no direct involvement in the plot to bring about your death by causing the palace to fall. That was Chewning and Liang, acting without his knowledge. The only death he sought was Roderick's."

"But Rod killed *him!* You just said so."

"Yes, sir . . . in self-defense. And not intentionally. He had previously given very explicit instructions that his brother was not to be killed. He launched the missile but didn't know the identity of the pilot he was shooting out of the sky until too late."

For the first time, the Emperor seemed to become aware of Corin as a separate individual. His eyes narrowed, as though his grief was coalescing into rage and zeroing in on an available target. "You keep using words like 'previously' and 'advance knowledge.' If you and Rod had reason to think there was some kind of plot, why didn't you come to me with it? Answer me that!"

Corin's spirit wavered momentarily—this wasn't just the Emperor, it was also Ivar Brady-Schiavona—but then firmed up, and he spoke in a voice that held respect but no apology. "Because you wouldn't have believed it, sir. We had to act on our own to preserve Rod's life—and yours."

"It's true, sir." Jason Aerenthal stepped forward from the group around Ivar, where he'd stood so inconspicuously that Corin hadn't noticed him. "We couldn't compromise ourselves by involving the established security apparatus, for we had no way of knowing how deep the conspiracy ran. And, in fact, events have shown that the Imperial Guards were thoroughly penetrated."

Ivar turned to look at the agent. "So you were part of it too," he said in a voice that was dull with lack of surprise.

"So was I, Father," Maura spoke up. "And Aline Tatsumo. And General Krona. The only military resources we used were those of the Permanent Task Group for Special Operations, of whose loyalty we could be certain."

"And which rescued you just before . . ." Aerenthal let his voice trail off, and glanced downward as though toward the unarguable evidence of the fallen palace below.

"But Ted didn't have to be killed! If you'd told me, we could have acted in time to prevent all this. We could have stopped Chewning and Liang . . . and Ted would still be alive!"

"No, sir. Vice Admiral Marshak is absolutely correct. It would have been an impossible conundrum for you. In order to accept the existence of the conspiracy, you would have had to face the fact of Teodor's involvement in it."

"But they were using him! He was only a dupe!"

"You know better than that, sir." Everyone present gasped. But Aerenthal went inexorably on. "Granted, he was ignorant of the fact that you yourself were a target. But he was a willing participant—indeed, the trigger man, as it were—in the attempted murder of Roderick. And if his life had been spared, how long would it have been before someone else made a 'dupe' of him? As your heir apparent, he would always have attracted intriguers like a light attracts moths—especially since he'd shown himself unable to resist their blandishments."

Corin, standing in shocked silence like everyone else, wondered if Aerenthal's audacity had anything to do with . . . but no. The Emperor *always* wore mind-shield devices, miniaturized to the point of near invisibility. Besides, exercising telepathic control over the Emperor was a concept his mind shied away from, rejecting out of hand the very possibility. A physical attack upon the Imperial person was a trivial crime by comparison.

And yet . . . when Ivar spoke, it was not with the

expected bellow of rage. Instead, his voice held a note which Corin would only later come to recognize as one of pleading. "But he was loyal to me! He . . . he loved me."

Aerenthal's look of compassion was equally out of character. "No, sir. *You* loved *him*. He wasn't actively disloyal to you in his own mind, but loyalty as you feel and understand the concept was beyond the scope of his character. Eventually, just as being heir apparent wasn't enough for him, being the officially designated successor wouldn't have been enough either. There would have been no lack of sycophants to point out to him that after Roderick's death, your death was the logical next step. When Roderick acted in self-defense, he was defending you as well."

Ivar sank back into his chair. "I wish I could be sure of that," he whispered. "All I know for certain is that he killed Ted."

"Not by design, sir," Corin reminded him. "And . . . well, I've seen him, down on the planet. I'd never thought anything could destroy him, but this very nearly has. The fact that he unintentionally killed his brother, and . . . your refusal to receive him."

"I can't."

"You must, sir." Corin didn't let himself think consciously about what he had just said, and the Emperor seemed barely aware of it anyway. "He's the heir apparent now. You—and the Empire—can't afford to have him go to pieces."

Something seemed to reawaken in Ivar. His voice was still low, but it was no longer a whisper. "Very well. Send for him."

Roderick entered, still flight-suited like Corin, and walked—no, marched—to where the Emperor sat upright. He came to attention, and for some fraction of eternity their eyes met in silence, looking out of immobile faces.

"Ah, Your Imperial Majesty," a minister jittered, "shall we leave you and your son—that is, Admiral Brady-Schiavona—alone?"

Ivar's massive head shook ponderously. "No. This isn't just a private family matter. It concerns the Empire. Especially inasmuch as I have an announcement to make." He turned his brooding gaze back to Roderick. "Admiral, it is my understanding that you admit to having personally killed my . . . your . . . that is, the heir apparent. Is this correct?"

Roderick had gone from his position of attention to an "at ease" that was barely less stiff. Now, fresh pain caused his frozen features to shiver anew. "That is correct, sir. I acted—"

The Imperial hand waved Roderick to silence. "You needn't explain. Admiral Marshak and Inspector Aerenthal have made matters clear to me. I have been brought reluctantly to an understanding of the events leading to the death of . . . of . . ."

Corin, standing inconspicuously off to the side alongside Maura, Garth and Janille, had a clear view of the Emperor's right cheek. Unbelievably, a single tear was making its slow way downward.

Roderick's features worked convulsively, as though emotions were battling behind them. *No*, Corin corrected his initial impression. *Not fighting. Struggling to get out*. Then, as though he'd forgotten the presence of everyone save the two of them, Roderick spoke to his father in a rush, the outpouring of years of pent-up hurt. "Why, Father? Why? It's always been this way, all our lives. After what's happened, with all you know now, you're still . . . Damn it, if *I* had tried to kill *him*, and died in the attempt, would it be the same? *Would it?*"

Everyone stood paralyzed, wishing to be somewhere else.

"I don't know," Ivar whispered dully. "I don't know whether it would or not. And I don't know why. All

I know is that you're wrong in one thing. You're wrong in accepting the responsibility for his death. In fact the responsibility is mine. You see, if this had been handled through official channels, it might have been possible to spare him. But it couldn't be handled that way, could it? You and your friends had no choice but to act as a secret cabal. You couldn't come to me, because you were absolutely right about my blindness and stupidity and . . ." As everyone in the room watched, stupefied, the Imperial features crumbled. It was like granite dissolving—an offense against the natural order of things.

"Stop, Father," Roderick gasped. "Don't say that. Don't talk as though there's something *wrong* with wanting to believe the best about your own son, with not wanting to see him killed. God knows I . . . I didn't want him killed either." And his tears were flowing as freely as his father's.

Ivar's head lifted and his voice solidified into its rigid formality of old. "My attitude may have been a natural one. But I cannot allow myself any form of self-deception where the security of the Empire is at stake. Nevertheless, I did. I failed. You had to save me—and the Empire—from my own folly. I proved myself unfit to be Emperor. Therefore, I take this opportunity to announce my abdication in your favor, effective immediately."

For what seemed like a long time but wasn't, there was absolute silence in the room. Then a hubbub of astonishment and consternation arose. Roderick's voice rose above it and halted it.

"*No!* Father, I won't accept it! You're not thinking clearly. The Empire needs you. You're the symbol of the restoration—the personification of what people *want* the Empire to be. You can't quit now. It would be . . . desertion."

Ivar flinched as though the word was a slap in the face. Aerenthal spoke smoothly into the silence. "He's right, Your Imperial Majesty. Our newly restored unity is fragile. Your personal prestige is one of the things holding it together."

"But I can't continue to function as Emperor, knowing what a sham that 'prestige' is."

Corin doubted he had any business speaking up. He did anyway. "You may consider yourself inadequate, sir, but no one else does."

"Furthermore," Aerenthal resumed, "aside from your own personal stature, a new dynasty needs continuity. A change of Emperors now would be a hurtful jolt—especially in the present confused circumstances. Coming before the dust of today's extraordinary events has settled, your abdication could be made to look like the result of a palace coup. It would place a permanent cloud over Roderick's reign."

"You see, Father?" Roderick stepped closer and placed his hands on the dragon-bedecked shoulders. "You *have* to stay on." Sounds of agreement arose on every side.

"Very well," Ivar responded, firmly but with no enthusiasm. "I'll remain on the throne for a couple more years. That should be enough to let the dust settle, as Inspector Aerenthal put it. But I'm going to immediately designate you as my heir, and begin involving you more and more in the actual business of ruling—especially on the civilian side. By the time I do abdicate, you'll be practically the co-Emperor. I mean for this to be the smoothest succession in history."

"Are you absolutely certain of this, sir? Given your excellent anagathic susceptibility, you have a lot of good years left. Whereas I . . ." Roderick's voice limped to a halt.

Ivar's face, still wet with tears, formed a smile that was, in its way, as astonishing as its earlier collapse into grief. "All the more reason for me to get out of your way without unnecessary delay, Rod. I wish the

Empire—and I—could have you longer. But a few decades of you will be better than a century of someone else. You see, Rod—*it doesn't matter.*"

Heedless of everyone present, father and son fell into a long-belated embrace.

After a moment, Ivar held Roderick at arm's length, and something besides grief seemed to awaken to tentative life behind his eyes. "Still, you've raised an important concern. This transition period should give you time to marry and produce an heir of your own. You need to get busy on that, you know."

Involuntarily, Roderick's eyes met Aline Tatsumo's across the room.

Corin and Janille weren't altogether sure what sort of courtesies to render when they stepped through the door into Roderick's office. He still held the rank of full admiral, but was on an indefinite leave of absence from the Fleet. And he was wearing civilian clothes, as was now fitting.

There were only a few officials with automatic access to the Imperial presence. The Inspector General—a title Aerenthal continued to refuse, preferring his freedom of action—and the Grand Admiral were two of them; but these were essentially dead-end positions, reserved for distinguished elderly wheelhorses of Inspectorate and Fleet respectively. More vital was the three-member Grand Council: the Chancellor and Grand Secretary—largely honorifics by now, but whose countersignatures were needed to authenticate any Imperial decree—and the Prime Minister, who oversaw the ministries that actually administered the Empire. Those ministries' heads traditionally came from the ranks of the career civil servants, but the Prime Minister did not. This was the office to which Ivar had appointed Roderick shortly after declaring him the heir designate.

As they advanced toward his desk, Corin and Janille

became aware that the new Prime Minister wasn't alone. Garth stepped out from the shadows off to the side.

"Come on in," Roderick greeted them informally. "Sit down. Sorry to drag you in here so abruptly. But I've been talking to Garth, here. I pointed out to him that . . . well, that Father and I owe him a special debt, inasmuch as he was the one to realize the full dimensions of what Chewning and Liang were up to."

"The fact is, Admiral," said Garth, who'd remained standing and who obviously had no truck with Roderick's new civilian title, "you owe all three of us. But I'm not complaining that you picked me as the first to ask what you could do in return."

"Well, yes, I did. And," Roderick continued, turning to the two newer arrivals, "I do plan to put the same question to the two of you, as well. But in the meantime, he asked to have you here when he gave me an answer."

"Right," Garth affirmed. "I thought you ought to hear it."

"The suspense is unnerving me," Janille remarked.

Garth began to pace in his massive way, as though finding unexpected difficulty expressing long-formulated thoughts. "Admiral, the Restoration Wars are over. The recent unpleasantness was their final flicker. You don't need the Permanent Task Group for Special Operations anymore. I'm requesting that you deactivate it and let me reconstitute the Deathstriders Company with all its personnel who're inclined to go along with the idea— the overwhelming majority, I have reason to think."

Roderick frowned. "Garth, you know I can't do that. We're going to enforce to the hilt the ban on free companies with space-combatant ships and weapons of mass destruction. What made sense for Armand Duschane makes sense for us, now that we're running a unified Empire. *No* serious government can allow that kind of capability in private hands."

"I understand. But what I have in mind won't present that kind of problem."

Roderick's frown intensified. "Are you telling me you'd be willing for the Deathstriders to revert to being strictly a ground-assault outfit? But by now the powered-armor component is a relatively minor operation."

"Oh, no. I want to keep all the outfit's present combatant and support ships I can make up crews for. And, to repeat, I think that will be most of them."

"But Garth, I just got through explaining that nobody but the Fleet is going to be allowed to have that kind of stuff anywhere within the Empire."

"That's the whole point," the big heavy-planet man explained patiently. "We won't *be* within the Empire."

Janille was the first to break the perplexed silence. "Do you mean you're going . . . outside?" Corin shared her astonishment, although he knew with his forebrain that the feeling was logically indefensible. It was only a culturally learned response, inherited from generations of ancestors who could imagine no reason for any civilized human to venture beyond the Empire's completely immaterial boundaries.

"Yes, I am. You see, the Empire is going to be at peace now. There's going to be no place for mercenaries any more. Even the ones who abide by the restrictions are going to get squeezed out eventually. But out among the Beyonder stars, it'll be a different matter."

"Not as much as it used to be," Roderick cautioned. "The Tarakans have gotten their part of space relatively organized."

"True. Sooner or later, either they're going to create a genuine empire out there or—more likely—the new dynasty will incorporate them into ours. So I mean to steer clear of them. But on the far side of the Empire, out beyond the Serpens/Bootes frontier, it's still chaos and anarchy. There'll be plenty of work for us there. Also . . . Um, I don't think I ever told you this, but before we met I was resolved to make myself Emperor."

"No, I can't recall you ever mentioning that," Roderick acknowledged drily.

"Well, just before our first meeting I . . . learned that I'd been wrong about my destiny. It wasn't to put myself on the throne but to help put you there."

Roderick's eyes narrowed. "How, exactly, did you 'learn' this?"

"Never mind. The point is, now that I've fulfilled that purpose there's nothing left for me in the Empire. And yet I still feel I have a destiny, if you want to call it that, of some kind. I need to go and find out what it is."

Janille spoke up, in the tones of one asking a question whose answer is already known. "Why did Corin and I have to be here for this announcement?"

"You deserved to be the first to hear it. And also . . . I wanted to personally offer you the chance to come with me, if you want to." He looked at both of them, one after another, and it may have been that his gaze rested on Janille longer.

And yet, his voice had held the same note hers had. And his face wore no surprise when she replied, "I'm staying." Then she corrected herself. "*We're* staying."

"Yes," Corin affirmed. "We have something to stay for, now. We grew up thinking we did. Then we got disillusioned. People generally do. But not many people have the chance, after that disillusionment, to recover in fact what they'd once thought they had. This is a gift. We're not about to throw that away— or each other."

"I thought that might be the answer. But I had to ask." Garth was smiling. Corin saw that Janille was smiling too. So, he realized, was he. After a moment, Roderick cleared his throat.

"Well, Garth, I think it ought to be possible to

accommodate you—on one condition. Before you go, I'd like you to get together with Jason Aerenthal and work out a method by which you can deliver occasional information packets to some out-of-the-way system on our frontier out there, to be picked up by his people." Roderick raised a forestalling hand as Garth started to speak. "Calm down! I don't mean to imply that you'll be working for the Fleet. You'll be a free agent. All I ask is that you occasionally send us any information you think we can use—including your own opinions, which I've learned to respect—about conditions out there. The Empire has always had miserable intelligence concerning the Beyonders. Lethal surprises like the Zyungen and the Tarakans have seemed to burst on us out of nowhere. It's one of the things I want to change. I'm asking your help in that, as a favor."

"I suppose I could do that—as long as it's a strictly one-way communication, with no directives or 'suggestions' coming back in my direction."

"Then it's settled." Roderick flashed his famous grin. He'd been able to do that more and more lately. "And now, I think we could all use a drink."

They went to the bar, which gleamed polished mahogany in the afternoon light of Sigma Draconis. That light streamed through a wide window that overlooked Dracopolis. Not as much light as they'd been accustomed to, of course . . . but Corin somehow doubted if Roderick would ever build another floating palace. . . .

He dismissed the thought as they busied themselves with drinks: brandy for Roderick, vodka for Garth, local whiskey and soda for himself and Janille. As they prepared to raise their glasses, something in Roderick's expression made them all pause.

"You know, Garth," Roderick said with careful casualness, "a little earlier, I started to ask how you'd found something out. The subject got changed. But the fact is, the three of you often seem to have bits of unique knowledge—premonitions, almost. I've always wondered how that is." He paused, leaving a silence to be filled.

The three looked at each other. As though by common, unvoiced consent, Corin spoke for them. "Rod, you mentioned that you'd planned to ask each of us if there was any favor you could do us."

"Yes, I did say that," Roderick acknowledged, caught off balance by the seeming irrelevance. "And I meant it. As Garth said, I owe all three of you."

"Well, I'm prepared to give you my answer right now." Corin held the eyes of the man to whom he could never reveal their curious relationship, and all lightness dropped from his voice. "My favor is that you *never* ask us that."

Janille spoke before the silence could stretch. "That's my request too. So you've got it double."

For an instant, Roderick said nothing. But his curiosity couldn't have been plainer if he had blurted out the question of why they thought him unworthy to share any secret they might possess.

But I don't, Corin thought at him, wishing for once that he'd had Aerenthal's gift. *That information is something I'd have to deny to you. And I never want to deny you anything.*

Then Roderick smiled again. "Very well. You've asked; and, to repeat, I owe you. We'll say no more about it."

He lifted his glass, and the amber liquid it held caught the light of Sigma Draconis and glowed the color of the Imperial dragon.

EPILOGUE
4352 C.E.

Looking out over the spacefield, Corin couldn't help but be reminded of his own arrival here eighteen years before. This time, however, he was looking in the opposite direction down the long avenue between the ranks of Imperial Guardsmen, toward a VIP shuttle that had just landed. He waited for its passengers to emerge and advance toward the reviewing stand where he and Janille waited with the rest of the assembled dignitaries.

His eyes automatically went to the figure at the summit of the reviewing stand. Roderick, unlike his father, had been just vain enough to have male-pattern baldness edited out of his genome. But his thick hair was quite gray now. Still, at fifty-six standard years he didn't look bad at all. Neither did the Empress Aline, standing a little behind and to his right with the twelve-year-old heir apparent—though in her case that was to be expected. *Her* hair was still uniformly black, but her face had a few more lines than the anagathics should have allowed for. Corin wondered if that had anything to do with the prospect of a lengthy widowhood, now growing a little more imminent than it had seemed when she'd so cheerfully accepted it.

Corin, now sixty-four and physiologically in his late

forties, could fully understand. He, too, faced some decades in a universe which would no longer contain Roderick Brady-Schiavona.

But not for a while yet, he reminded himself, and turned his attention back to the panorama before them. Cheering had begun, and he could now pick out the conquerors of the Outer Domain, descending from the shuttle.

"Rather brings back memories, doesn't it?"

Corin and Janille both started at the murmured remark and turned to face its source. At a standard century-and-a-quarter, Jason Aerenthal was nearing the limits of the anagathics' efficacy. But Roderick had refused to let him retire. He still kept his hand in the work of the Inspectorate—and he still had his disturbing way of echoing people's thoughts. Their greetings, especially Janille's, held a coolness which he couldn't fail to notice. He smiled benignly.

"Set your minds at rest. It's not that." There was no need, in this company, to verbalize what "that" was. "It's just that I share your feelings of déjà vu. Still, quite a lot has changed."

"And not just the fact that there's no longer a distant palace floating over the Emperor's head from the viewpoint of new arrivals," Corin agreed. He let his mind range over the past eighteen years.

Ivar had been as good as his word, staying on for just two more years before departing into an honored retirement. Before that, the Tarakans of the Inner Domain had broken their earlier treaty with him. Hot with eagerness to take advantage of the upheaval the attempted coup must surely have left in its wake, they had cast ordinary military prudence to the winds and thrust straight through to Sigma Draconis, ignoring a score of light-years full of Imperial systems left lying across their communications. Their sheer, insane audacity had positioned them in the capital system's outskirts before anything more than the system's post-Restoration Wars garrison could be mobilized.

Heedless of the hysteria around him, Roderick had personally led that garrison out, to confront the vastly superior Tarakan armada with the news that Ivar still sat securely on the throne. Even more than that, the mana of Roderick's own name had held the Tarakans paralyzed by indecision until the appalling consequences of their own recklessness had dawned on them: Imperial fleets were closing in behind them, deploying across their lines of retreat. Balked of his expected immediate victory, the Araharl had asked for a renewal of the treaty.

With the salvation of the capital system to his credit, Roderick's accession had been even smoother than Ivar had dared hope. Afterwards, as Aerenthal had cynically foreseen, the glamorous young Emperor had gotten the credit for the success of Oleg's projects while escaping blame for their cost—an injustice about which Corin was not disposed to complain. Meanwhile, the Inner Domain had observed its treaty obligations—Roderick, working through Aerenthal, had kept it too distracted by internal dissensions to do otherwise. So matters had remained until 4340. Then a new Araharl had felt secure enough to renounce the treaty.

What had followed was now the stuff of legend. Roderick had led the Fleet in person, in defiance of all Imperial tradition save that of Basil Castellan's, whose disastrous last campaign wasn't the most inspiring possible example. Corin winced involuntarily at the thought. Roderick and Corin had smashed the Inner Domain military so completely that its surviving leaders had submitted without reservation, declaring the young Emperor the successor of the now-deceased Araharl. Never had anyone held both titles, and the Outer Domain's Araharl had not been amused. It might have led to trouble. But . . .

Corin looked the old agent squarely in the eyes and

asked the question that had intrigued him for twelve years. "Were you behind the assassination of the Araharl of the Outer Domain, back in '40?"

"Ancient history, my boy, ancient history. Let's just be glad the Outer Domain was in no position to intervene, when our position in the Inner Domain was still precarious. Why question our good fortune? The point is, the Outer Domain broke up into squabbling factions, incapable of threatening our position."

"Until last year, when the nearer ones grew troublesome," Corin amended.

A new generation of admirals had led Roderick's forces beyond the Inner Domain, carrying his power to constellations no Imperial human had ever seen. Now they were marching toward the reviewing stand as Corin and Janille had, so long ago. Some of them wore the special version of Fleet uniform that had been authorized for Tarakan units in the service of their Araharl-Emperor. The Empire and the Inner Domain were still legally separate realms which shared the same ruler. Something would have to be done about that eventually, Corin mused. History was less than encouraging about the long-term survivability of such arrangements.

Aerenthal interrupted his thoughts. "I thought you might be interested in a bit of news that's recently come to my attention." He paused for effect. "News from beyond the Serpens/Bootes frontier."

Suddenly alert, Corin started to speak. But Janille blurted it out first. "You mean you've gotten new word from Garth?"

Occasional messages had arrived for several years as the Deathstriders had pursued an eventful course of employment, further and further from the remotest Imperial outposts. There was no tachyon beam network among the Beyonders—some of them had the technology, but the widespread political unity to protect the great arrays was lacking. The courier ships had come less and less frequently and by more and more circuitous routes. Then, finally, they'd stopped. Garth had seemed to vanish, swallowed by the infinite night. They'd never forgotten him, but their last hopes of any further contact had died long ago.

Aerenthal smiled and shook his head with the deliberation of the very old. "No. This is a very indirect report that reached me through several layers of sources in that part of space. By the time it filtered through to my office, it was little more than a vague story. But . . . it seems that very deep in Serpens—not far inside the boundaries of this spiral arm, in fact—a certain mercenary leader has made himself ruler of the first multisystemic political entity in that region of space."

All at once, all the noise and pomp ceased to exist as far as Roderick and Janille were concerned. So did Aerenthal, looking on with uncharacteristically kindly amusement as they stared into each others' eyes. She was the first to say it.

"So he's found his destiny."

And their thoughts went to the place where they'd first learned that destiny was not to become Emperor.

There was no living eye to see the yellow-white star DM -17 954 set behind its giant fifth planet. So some might have questioned, on philosophical grounds, whether the sight really existed at all. But it stood revealed to artificial senses that covered a spectrum far beyond the range of human optics, "seeing" X-rays and "hearing" heat.

And, at that, Omega Prime was observing it with only a tiny part of its vast, compartmentalized consciousness. Another part was surveying its own interior spaces, seeing the corridors—so echoingly vast to humans—alive with the comings and goings of great bronze-gold beings for whom they were just barely large enough. And it was reflecting that those phantom

Luonli inhabiting its tachyonic database were the only ones it would ever see.

Omega Prime hadn't thought it necessary or appropriate to inform the children—as it couldn't help but think of them—that the Luon two of them had talked to on the world they called Neustria had been the last of its species. The Luon itself hadn't known. But Omega Prime had, by means it couldn't have explained to the humans even had it felt so inclined. And by those same means, it now knew that the last Luon was no more. There would continue to be "sightings" of Luonli on various human worlds for generations. But Omega Prime knew better, and for a long while it wished them farewell. Then it obliterated them from its memory, for it was not fitting that they should linger in an unnatural tachyonic limbo after their bright flame had guttered out and left the universe dark.

But not really dark, for there were other flames. Omega Prime turned its thoughts to the living.

It had still other sources of information, of which the humans had never learned. The last of the robot proxies had returned, and it now knew that the future it had accessed was, indeed, *the* future. Given the alternatives—each more nightmarish than the others— the news had evoked what could only be called relief, even though Omega Prime's emotions were not precisely comparable to human ones.

On a sudden impulse, Omega Prime summoned up the first human it had ever met.

"I have kept the promise I made to you in your dying moments, Your Imperial Majesty," it formally addressed the image of Basil Castellan. "Your dream has been fulfilled, and even though you were not to be the one to fulfill it, you played a role—not just through your legend, but through your flesh and blood . . . in two senses. And now the future of your race is secure. Humans are the successors of the Luonli. And they will surpass them."

But Omega Prime was incapable of being other than honest with itself, and it knew that the last statement was supposition, not inarguable fact. For its tachyonic circuitry held no data further ahead in time than this. For Omega Prime, the future was now as much a void as it was for any organic mind.

The implications were clear. There was one more thing that must be done. And there was no reason to delay.

Omega Prime bade its friend farewell, and gave a mental command. Deep within its physical housing, matter met antimatter.

There were no longer even any artificial eyes to watch as the dark side of DM -17 954 was bathed in a dazzling effulgence of light.

DAVID WEBER

BAEN

BAEN

<u>**The Honor Harrington series:**</u> *(cont.)*

Field of Dishonor

Honor goes home to Manticore—and fights for her life on a battlefield she never trained for, in a private war that offers just two choices: death—or a "victory" that can end only in dishonor and the loss of all she loves....

Flag in Exile

Hounded into retirement and disgrace by political enemies, Honor Harrington has retreated to planet Grayson, where powerful men plot to reverse the changes she has brought to their world. And for their plans to suceed, Honor Harrington must die!

Honor Among Enemies

Offered a chance to end her exile and again command a ship, Honor Harrington must use a crew drawn from the dregs of the service to stop pirates who are plundering commerce. Her enemies have chosen the mission carefully, thinking that either she will stop the raiders or they will kill her . . . and either way, her enemies will win....

In Enemy Hands

After being ambushed, Honor finds herself aboard an enemy cruiser, bound for her scheduled execution. But one lesson Honor has never learned is how to give up! One way or another, she and her crew are going home—even if they have to conquer Hell to get there!

continued ☞

PRAISE FOR
LOIS MCMASTER BUJOLD

What the critics say:

The Warrior's Apprentice: "Now here's a fun romp through the spaceways—not so much a space opera as space ballet. . . . it has all the 'right stuff.' A lot of thought and thoughtfulness stand behind the all-too-human characters. Enjoy this one, and look forward to the next." —Dean Lambe, *SF Reviews*

"The pace is breathless, the characterization thoughtful and emotionally powerful, and the author's narrative technique and command of language compelling. Highly recommended." —*Booklist*

Brothers in Arms: ". . . she gives it a geniune depth of character, while reveling in the wild turnings of her tale. . . . Bujold is as audacious as her favorite hero, and as brilliantly (if sneakily) successful." —*Locus*

"Miles Vorkosigan is such a great character that I'll read anything Lois wants to write about him. . . . a book to re-read on cold rainy days." —Robert Coulson, *Comics Buyer's Guide*

Borders of Infinity: "Bujold's series hero Miles Vorkosigan may be a lord by birth and an admiral by rank, but a bone disease that has left him hobbled and in frequent pain has sensitized him to the suffering of outcasts in his very hierarchical era. . . . Playing off Miles's reserve and cleverness, Bujold draws outrageous and outlandish foils to color her high-minded adventures." —*Publishers Weekly*

Falling Free: "In *Falling Free* Lois McMaster Bujold has written her fourth straight superb novel. . . . How to break down a talent like Bujold's into analyzable components? Best not to try. Best to say 'Read, or you will be missing something extraordinary.'" —Roland Green, *Chicago Sun-Times*

The Vor Game: "The chronicles of Miles Vorkosigan are far too witty to be literary junk food, but they rouse the kind of craving that makes popcorn magically vanish during a double feature." —Faren Miller, *Locus*

MORE PRAISE FOR
LOIS MCMASTER BUJOLD

What the readers say:

"My copy of *Shards of Honor* is falling apart I've reread it so often.... I'll read whatever you write. You've certainly proved yourself a grand storyteller."

—Liesl Kolbe, Colorado Springs, CO

"I experience the stories of Miles Vorkosigan as almost viscerally uplifting.... But certainly, even the weightiest theme would have less impact than a cinder on snow were it not for a rousing good story, and good storytelling with it. This is the second thing I want to thank you for.... I suppose if you boiled down all I've said to its simplest expression, it would be that I immensely enjoy and admire your work. I submit that, as literature, your work raises the overall level of the science fiction genre, and spiritually, your work cannot avoid positively influencing all who read it."

—Glen Stonebraker, Gaithersburg, MD

" 'The Mountains of Mourning' [in *Borders of Infinity*] was one of the best-crafted, and simply best, works I'd ever read. When I finished it, I immediately turned back to the beginning and read it again, and I can't remember the last time I did that." —Betsy Bizot, Lisle, IL

"I can only hope that you will continue to write, so that I can continue to read (and of course buy) your books, for they make me laugh and cry and think ... rare indeed." —Steven Knott, Major, USAF

What Do You Say?